MAGIC TREE HOUSE®

PIRATES PAST NOON

MARY POPE OSBORNE'S

✦ MAGIC ✦ TREE HOUSE®

PIRATES PAST NOON

THE GRAPHIC NOVEL

ADAPTED BY
JENNY LAIRD

WITH ART BY
KELLY & NICHOLE MATTHEWS

A STEPPING STONE BOOK™
RANDOM HOUSE 🏠 NEW YORK

This is a work of fiction. Names, characters, places, and incidents either are the product of the author's imagination or are used fictitiously. Any resemblance to actual persons, living or dead, events, or locales is entirely coincidental.

Text adapted by Jenny Laird

 Published in the United States by Random House Children's Books, a division of Penguin Random House LLC, New York. Adapted from *Pirates Past Noon*, published by Random House Children's Books, a division of Penguin Random House LLC, New York, in 1994.

Random House and the colophon are registered trademarks and A Stepping Stone Book and the colophon are trademarks of Penguin Random House LLC. RH Graphic with the book design is a trademark of Penguin Random House LLC. Magic Tree House is a registered trademark of Mary Pope Osborne; used under license.

Visit us on the Web!
rhcbooks.com
MagicTreeHouse.com

Educators and librarians, for a variety of teaching tools, visit us at RHTeachersLibrarians.com

Library of Congress Cataloging-in-Publication Data is available upon request.
ISBN 978-0-593-17483-8 (pb) — ISBN 978-0-593-17480-7 (hc) —
ISBN 978-0-593-17481-4 (lib. bdg.) — ISBN 978-0-593-17482-1 (ebook)

The artists used Clip Studio Paint to create the illustrations for this book.
The text of this book is set in 13-point Cartoonist Hand Regular.

MANUFACTURED IN CHINA
10 9 8 7 6 5 4 3 2 1
First Graphic Novel Edition

This book has been officially leveled by using the F&P Text Level Gradient™ Leveling System.

For Teddy and Clark Lettice
—M.P.O.

For June and Willie—beautiful,
beloved creatures of the sea
—J.L.

For Bones and Whitney—
thanks for believing in us!
—K.M. & N.M.

CHAPTER ONE
Too Late

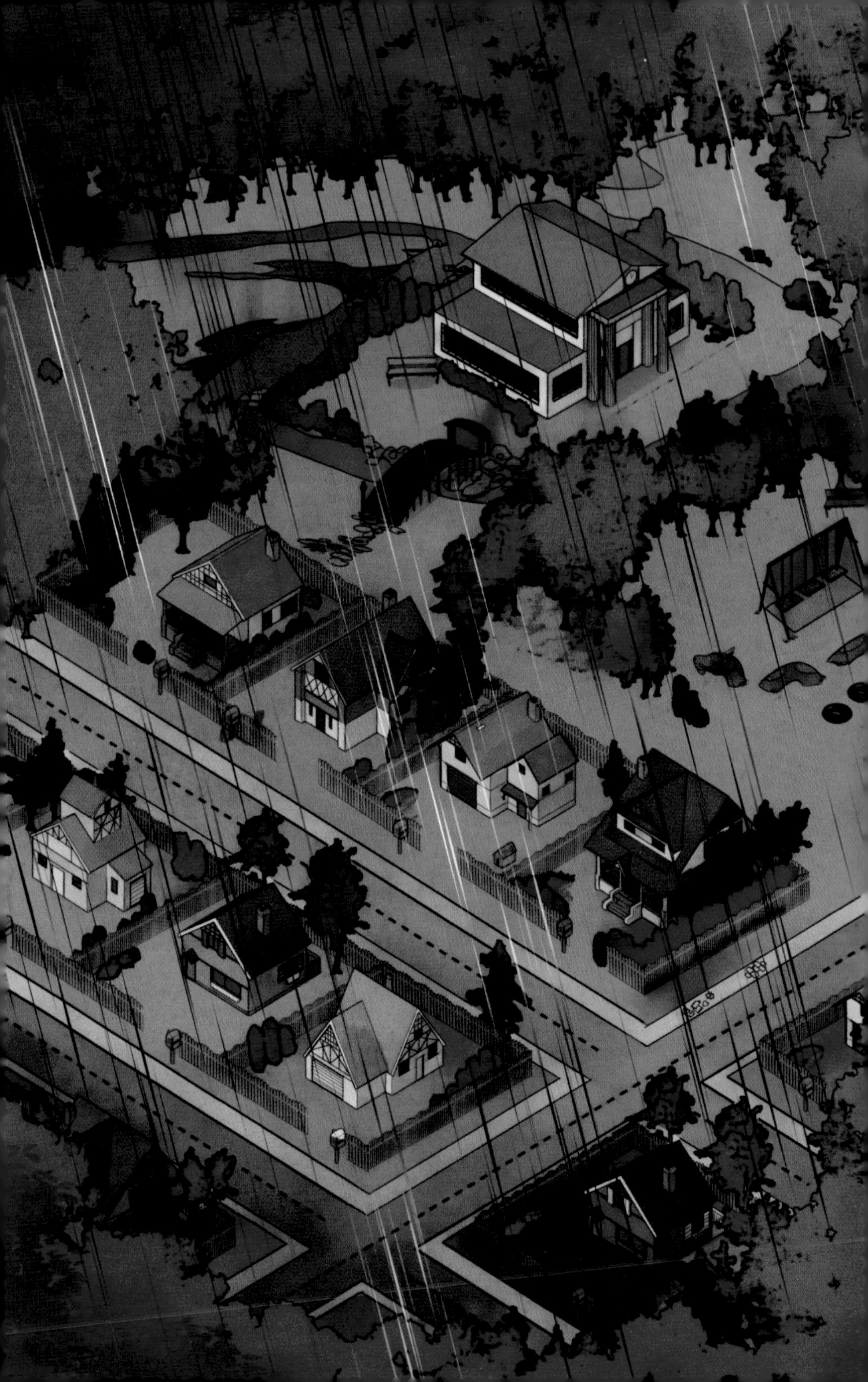

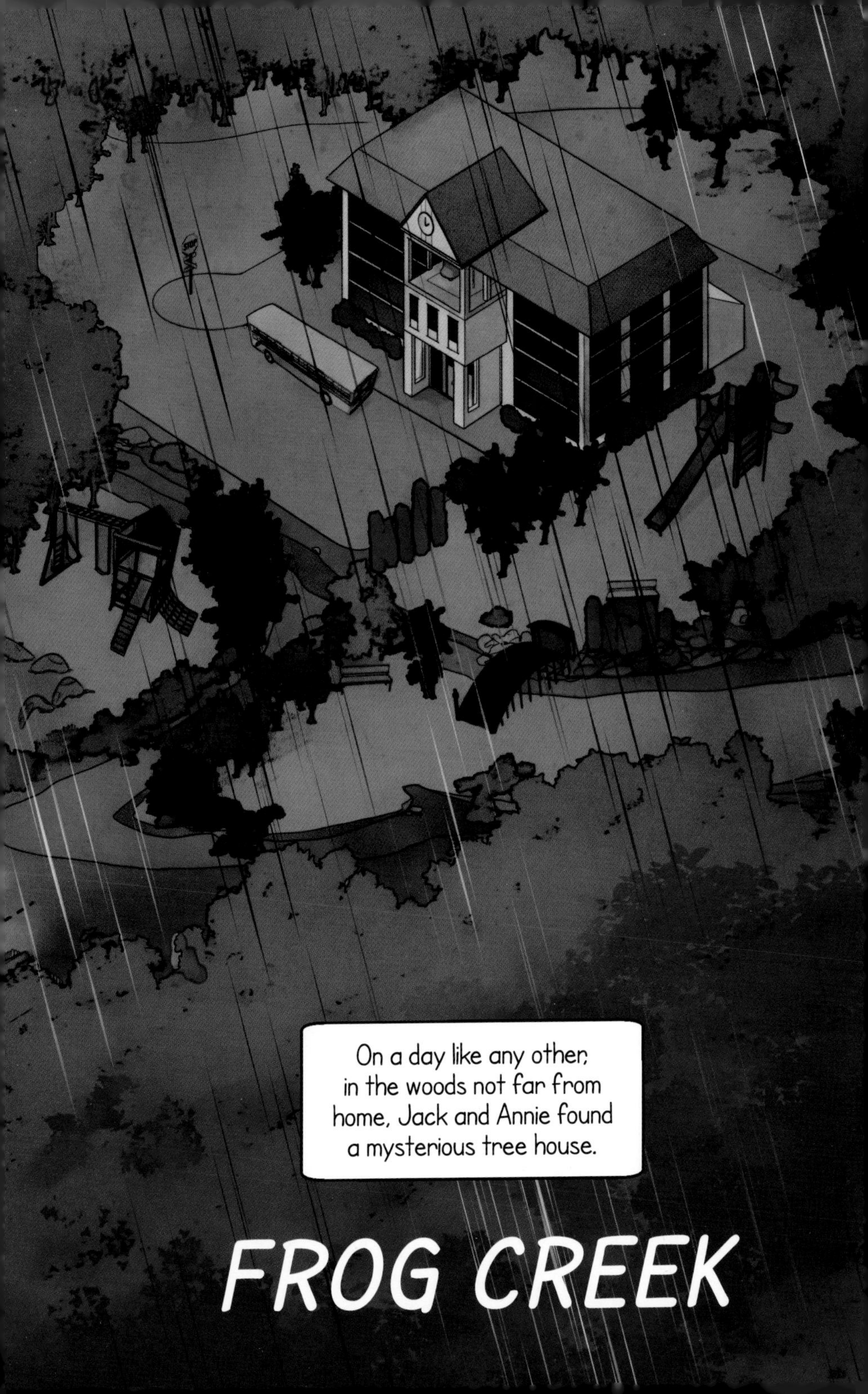
STOP
On a day like any other, in the woods not far from home, Jack and Annie found a mysterious tree house.
FROG CREEK

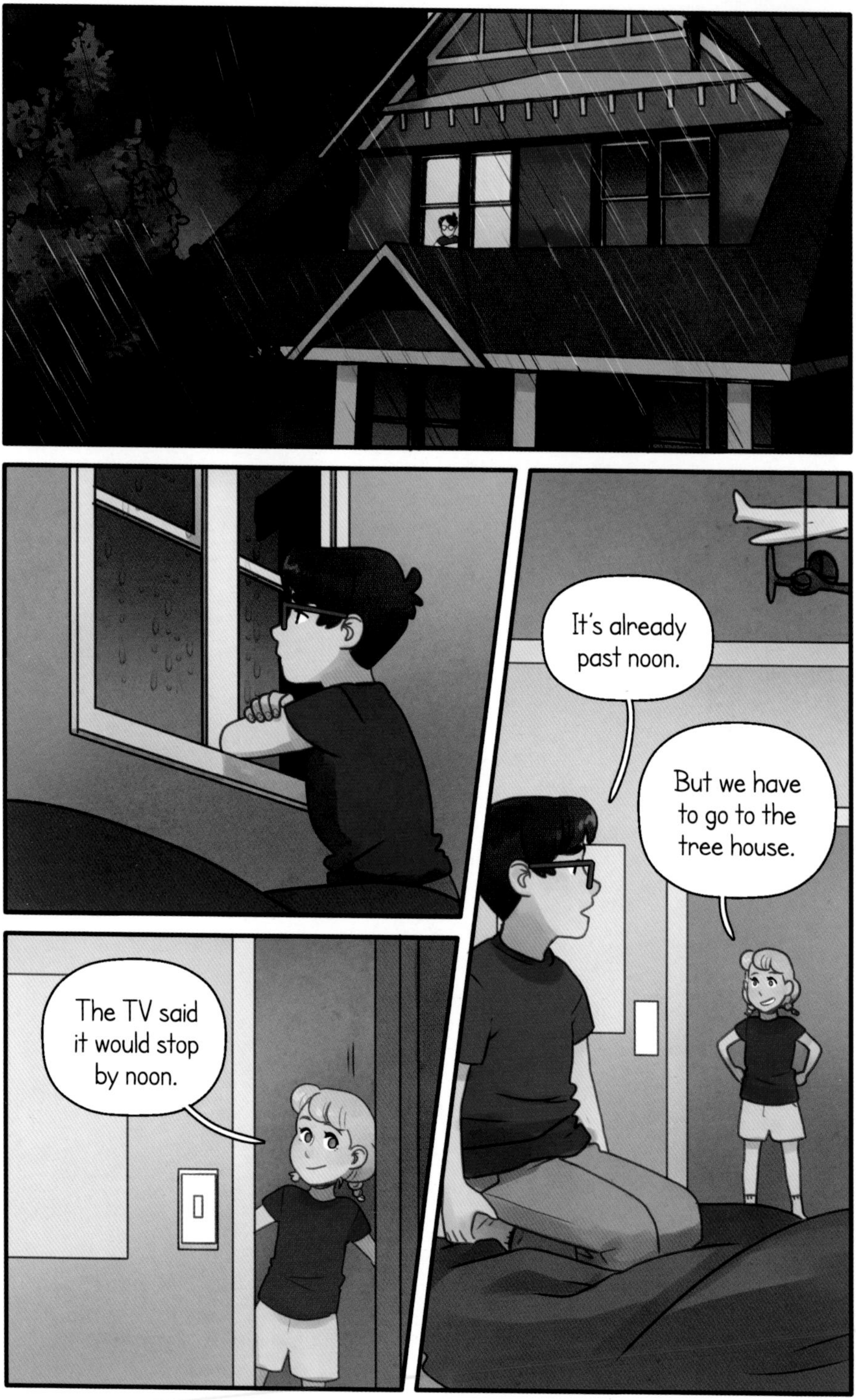
It's already past noon.
But we have to go to the tree house.
The TV said it would stop by noon.

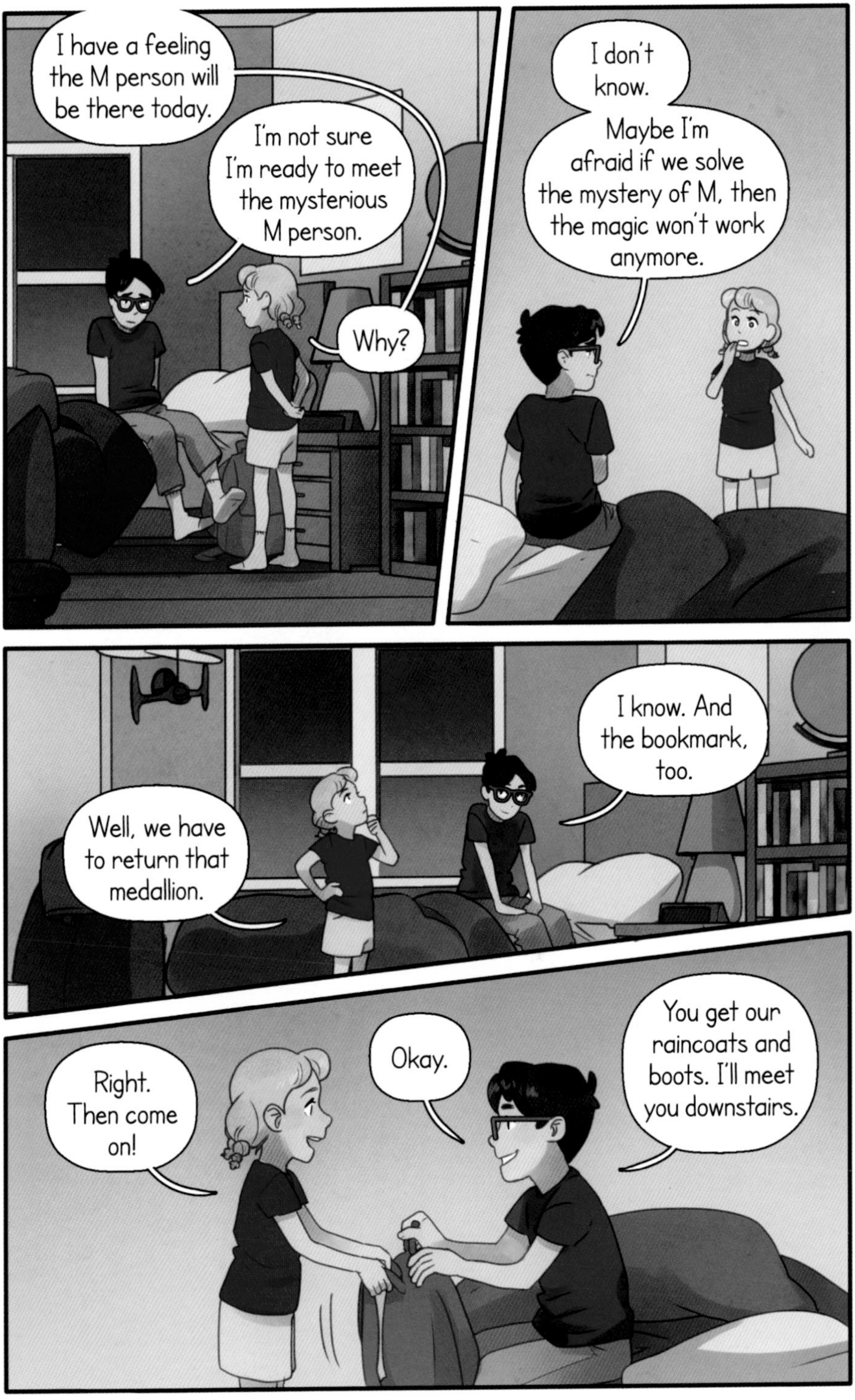
I have a feeling the M person will be there today.
I'm not sure I'm ready to meet the mysterious M person.
Why?
I don't know.
Maybe I'm afraid if we solve the mystery of M, then the magic won't work anymore.
Well, we have to return that medallion.
I know. And the bookmark, too.
Right. Then come on!
Okay.
You get our raincoats and boots. I'll meet you downstairs.

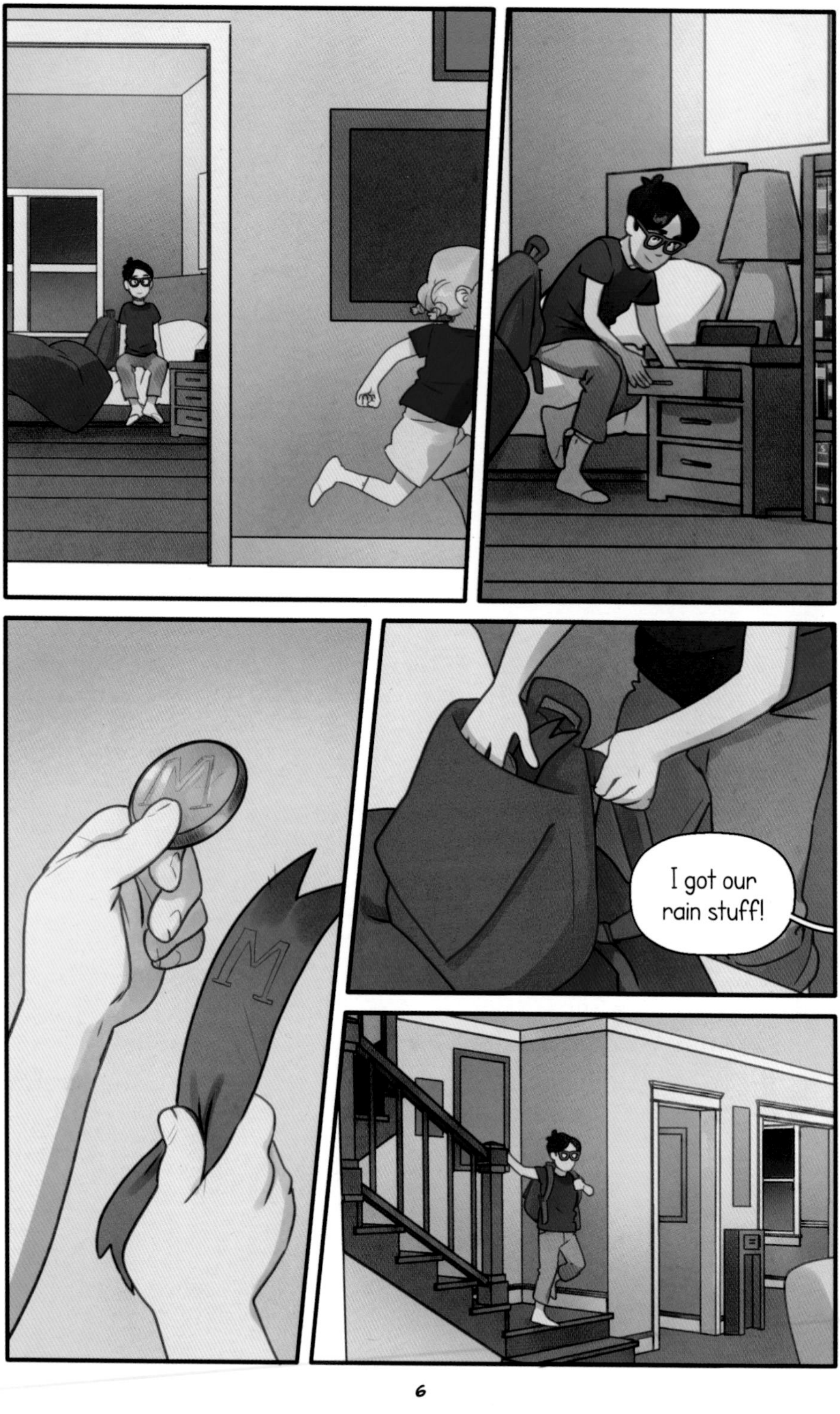
I got our rain stuff!

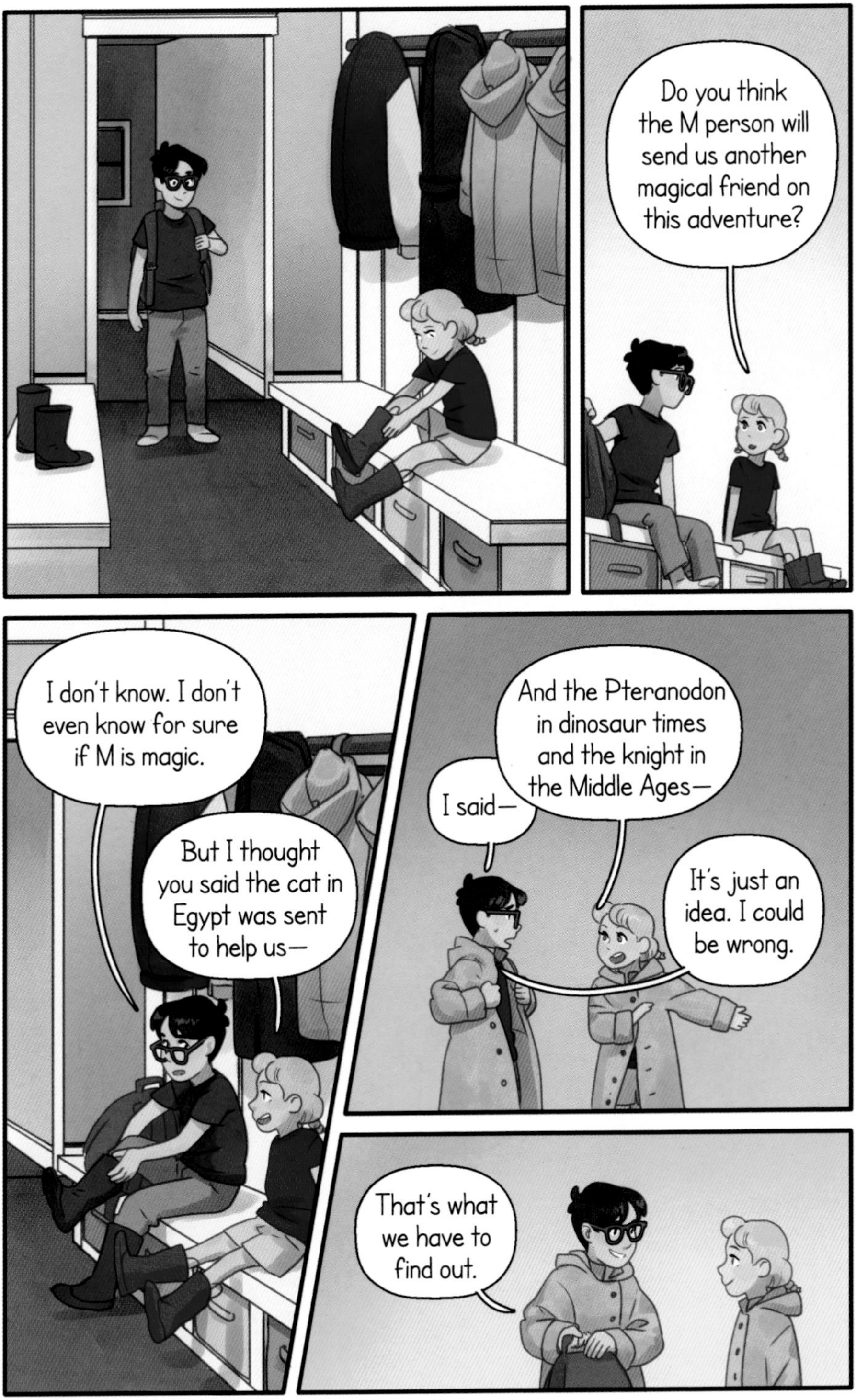
Do you think the M person will send us another magical friend on this adventure?
I don't know. I don't even know for sure if M is magic.
But I thought you said the cat in Egypt was sent to help us—
I said—
And the Pteranodon in dinosaur times and the knight in the Middle Ages—
It's just an idea. I could be wrong.
That's what we have to find out.

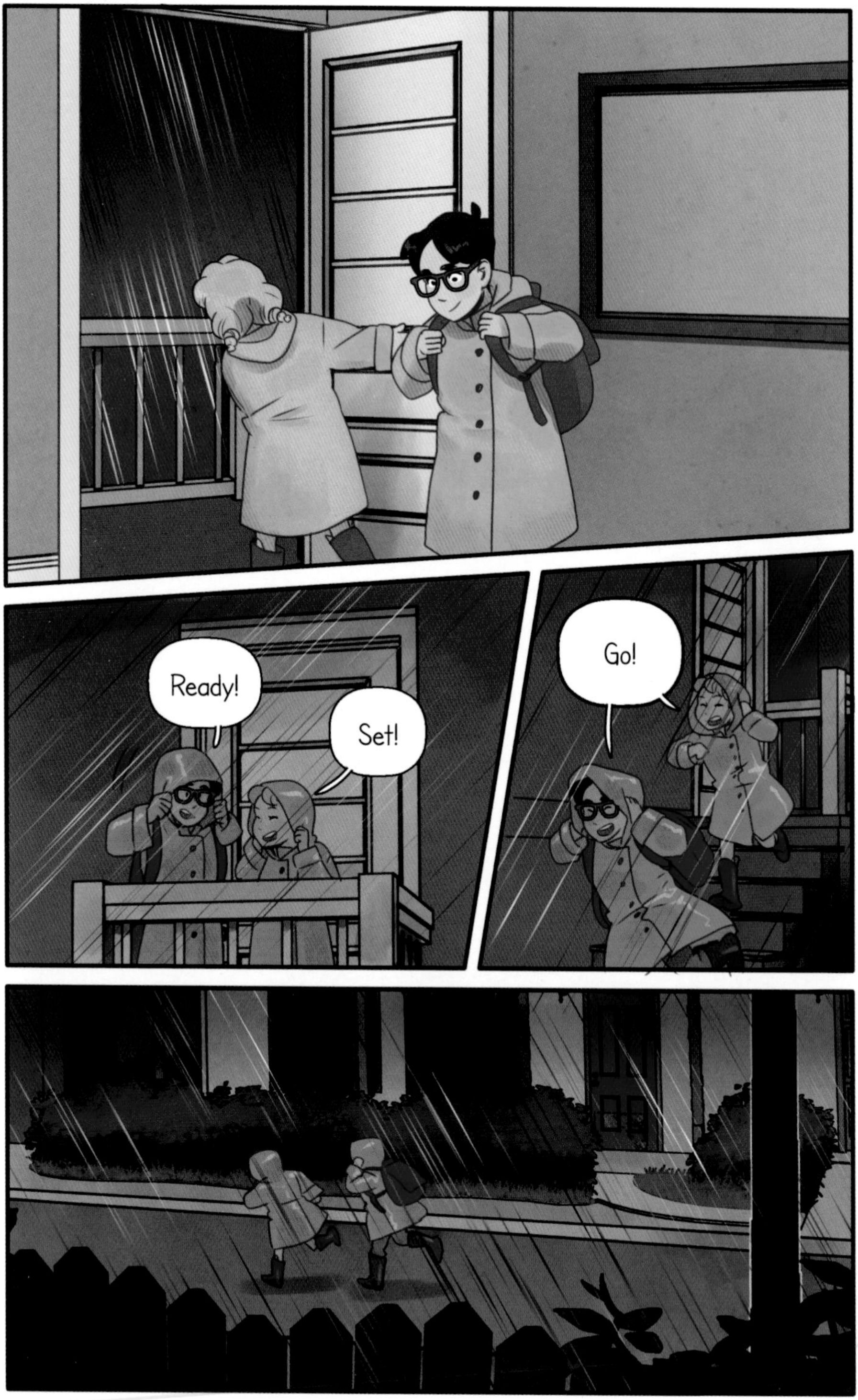
Ready!
Set!
Go!

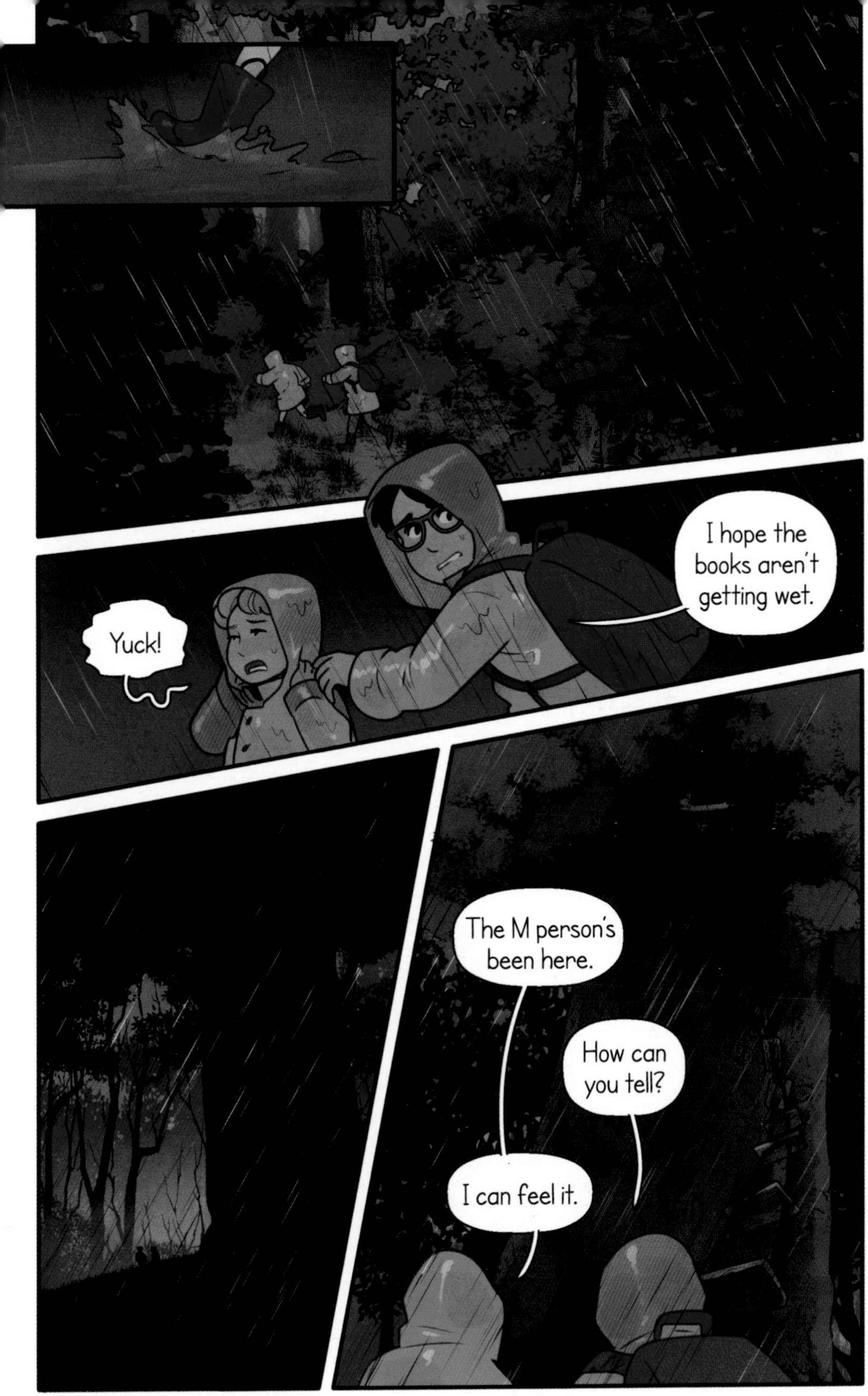
I hope the books aren't getting wet.
Yuck!
The M person's been here.
How can you tell?
I can feel it.

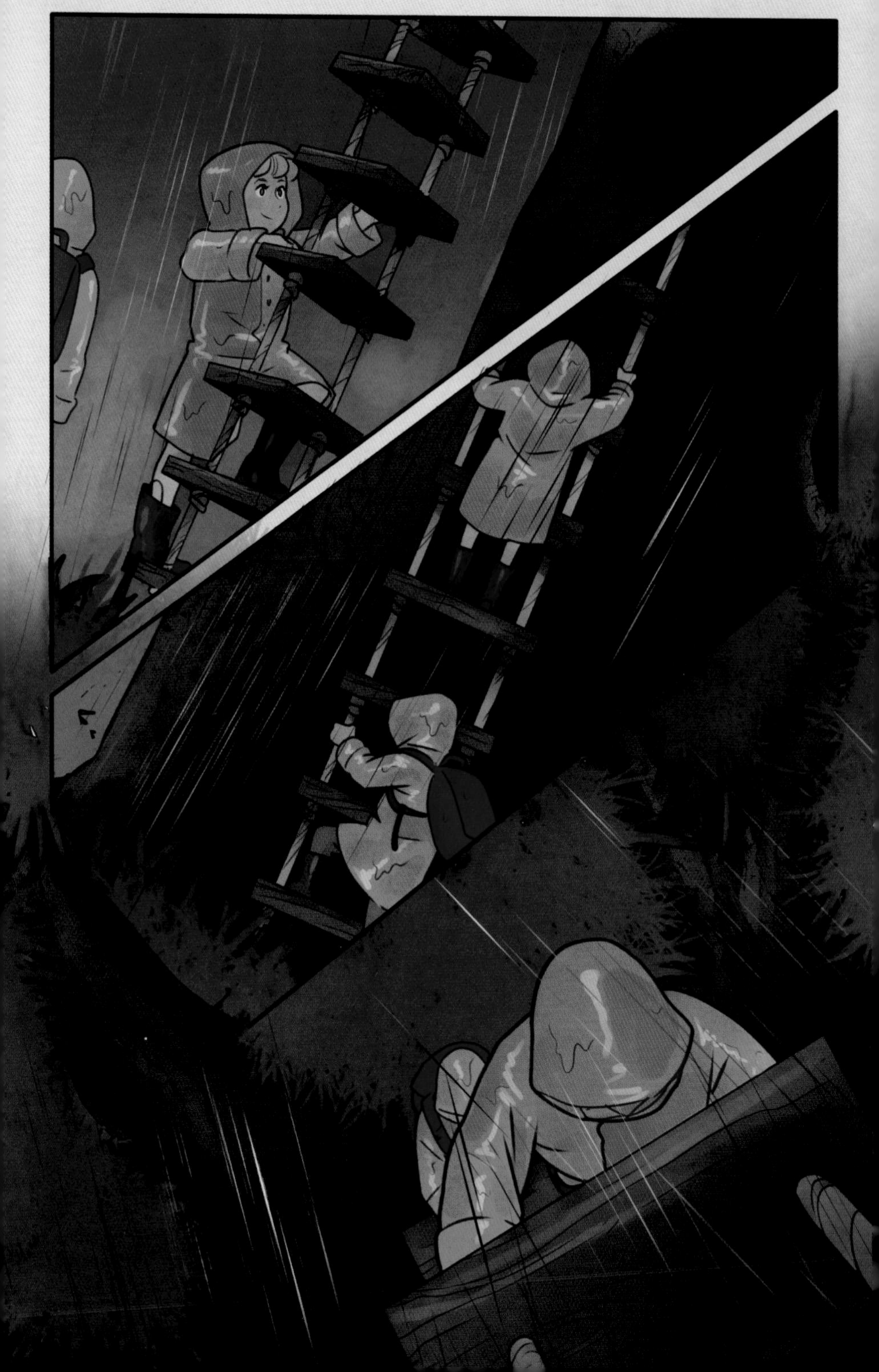

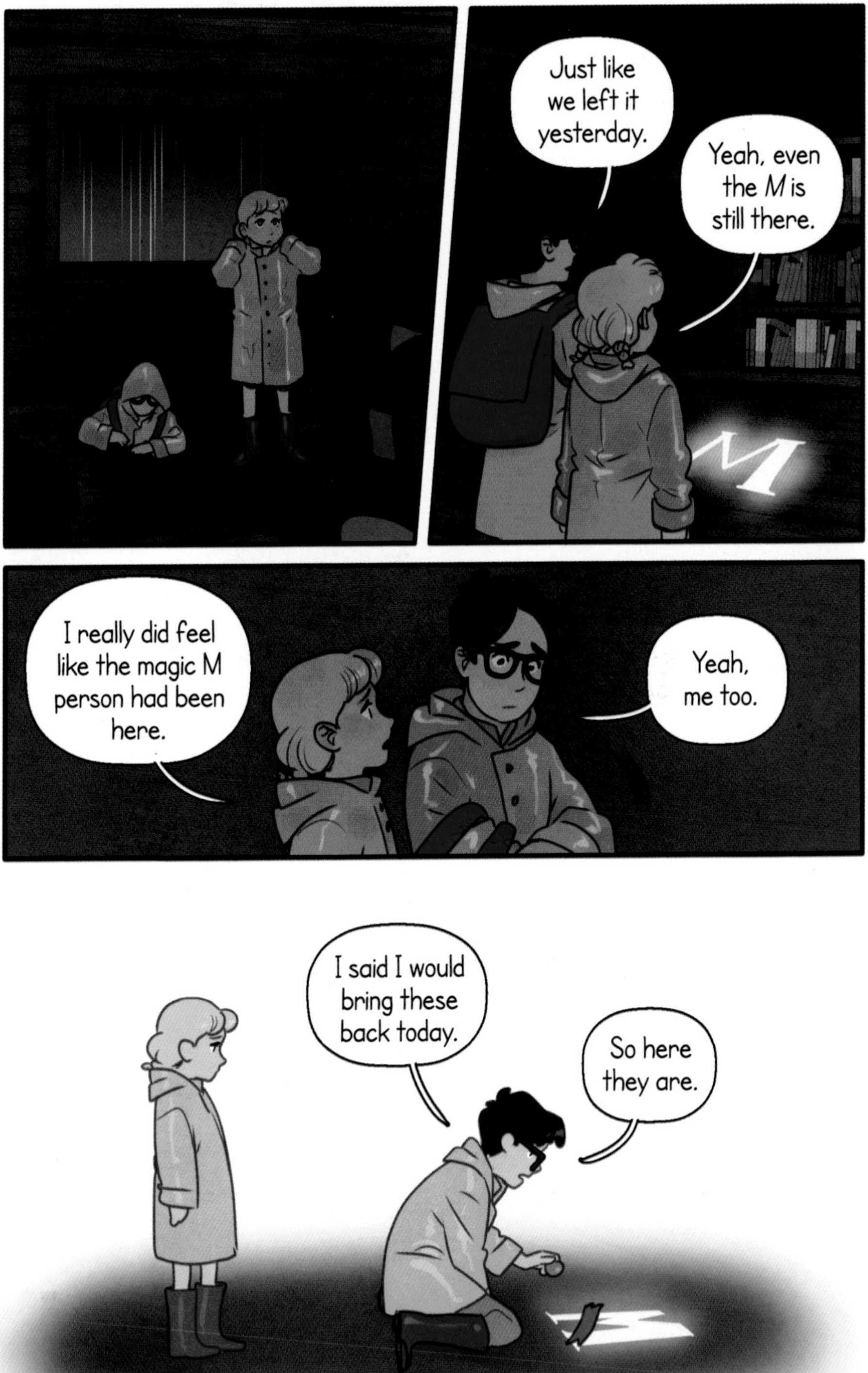
Just like we left it yesterday.
Yeah, even the *M* is still there.
I really did feel like the magic M person had been here.
Yeah, me too.
I said I would bring these back today.
So here they are.

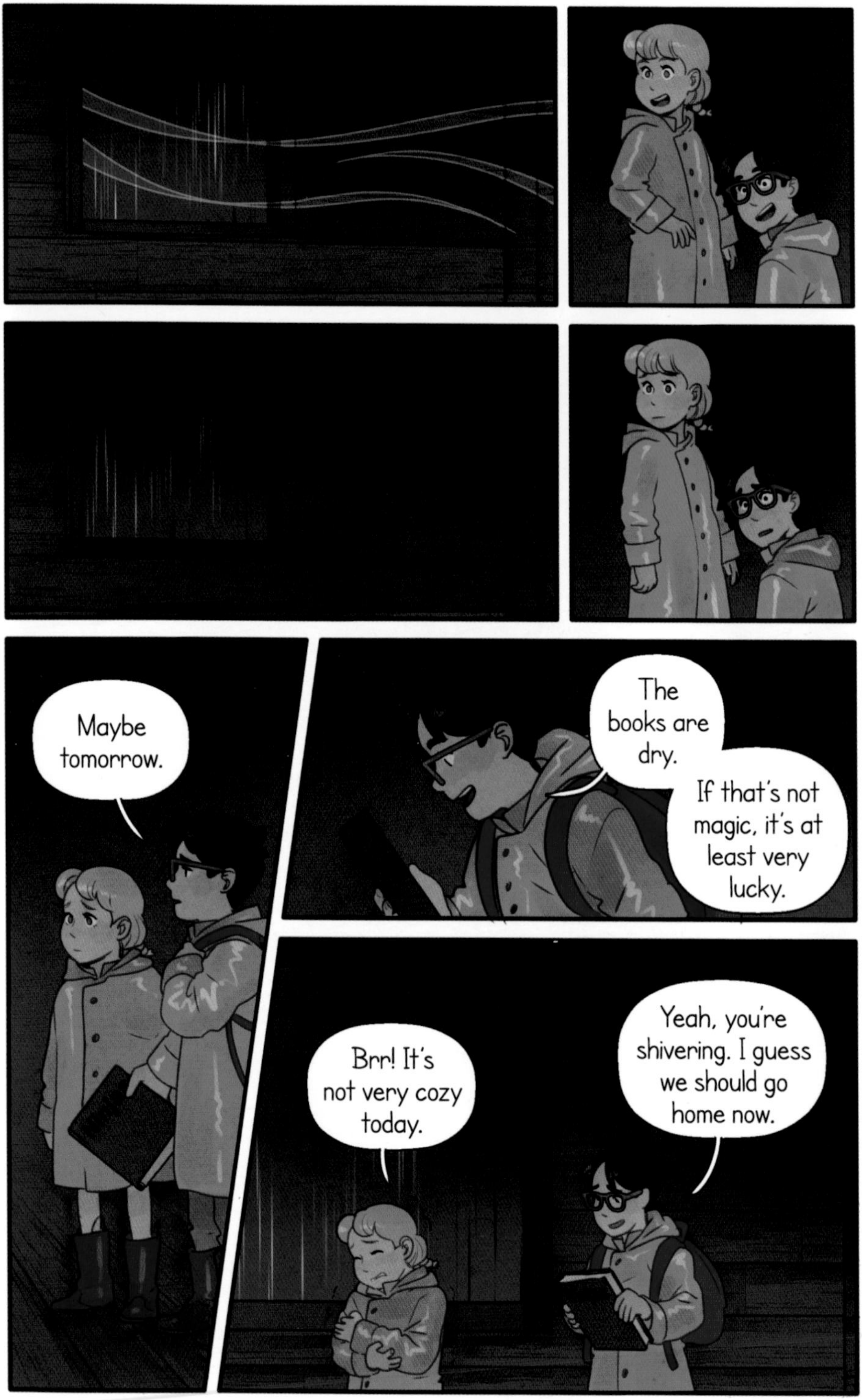

Maybe tomorrow.
The books are dry.
If that's not magic, it's at least very lucky.
Brr! It's not very cozy today.
Yeah, you're shivering. I guess we should go home now.

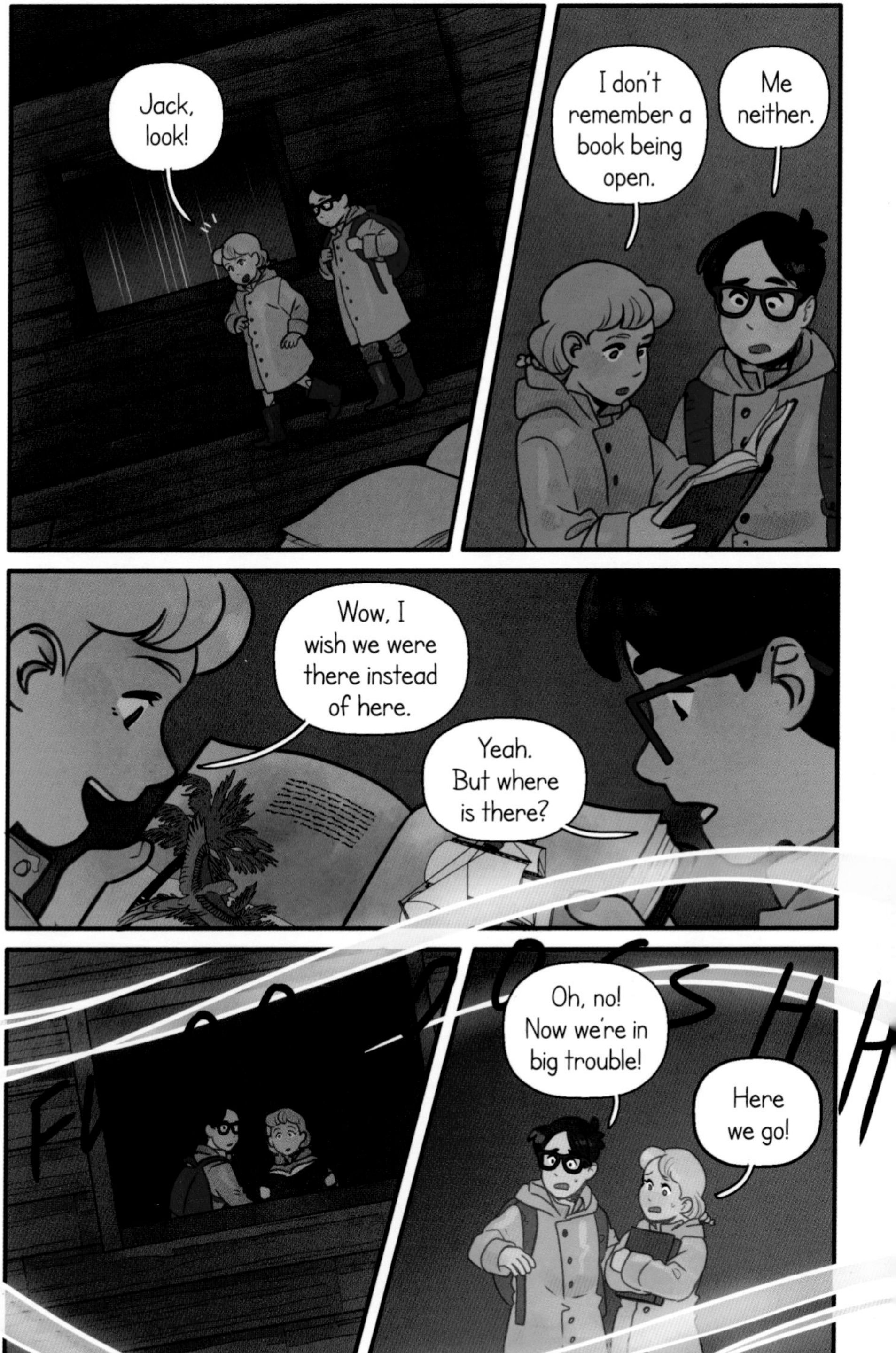
Jack, look!
I don't remember a book being open.
Me neither.
Wow, I wish we were there instead of here.
Yeah. But where is there?
Oh, no! Now we're in big trouble!
Here we go!

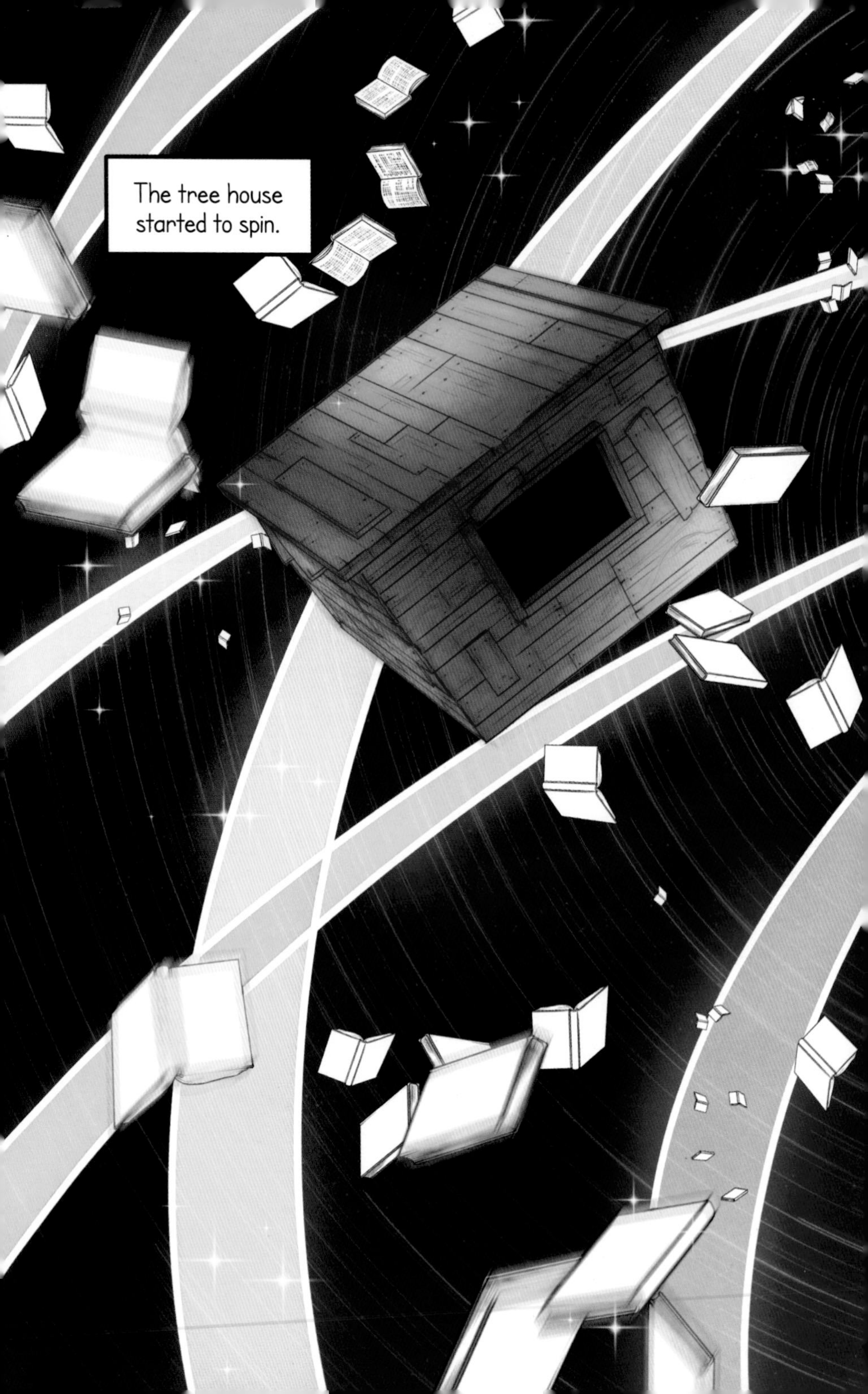
The tree house started to spin.

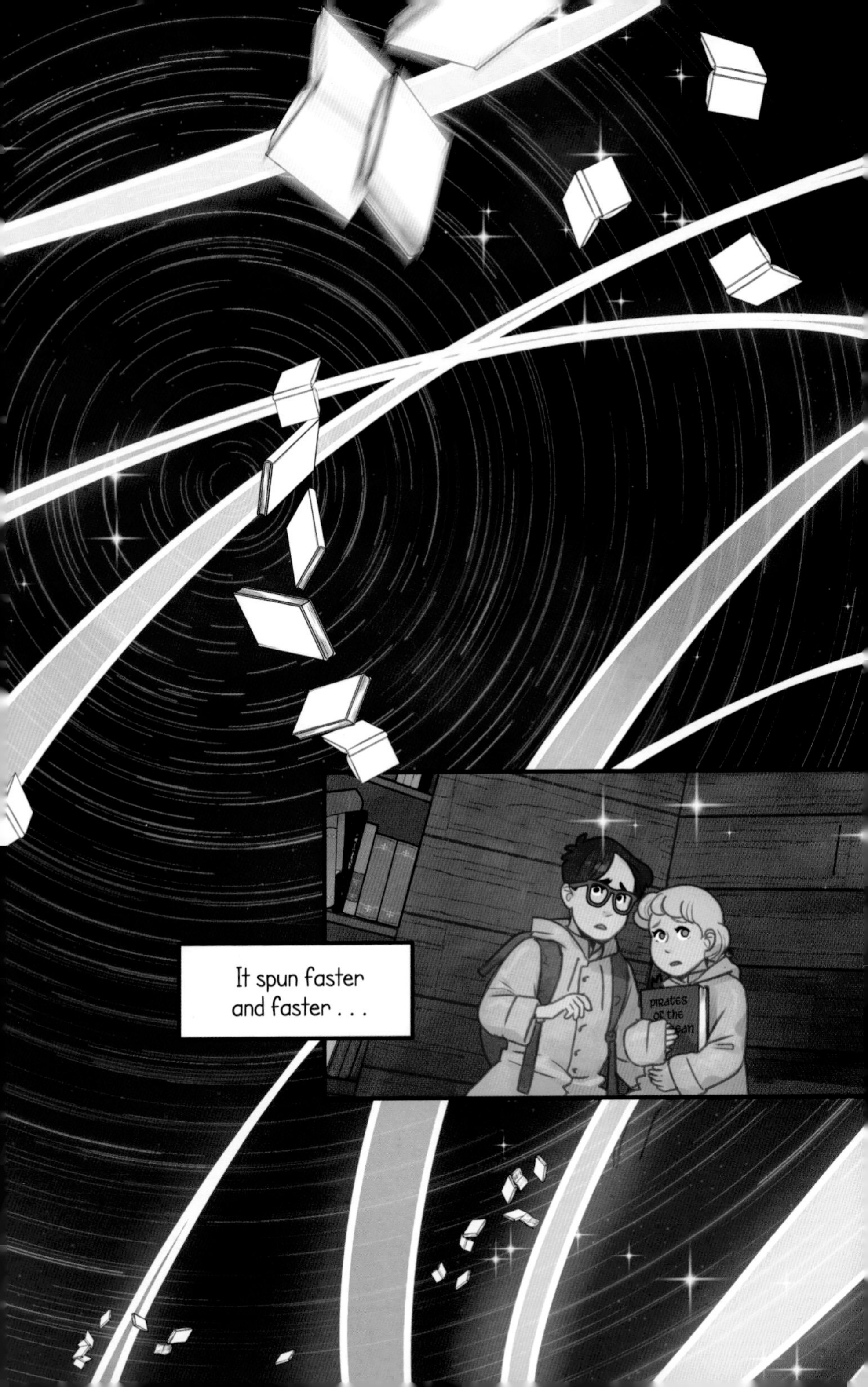
It spun faster and faster . . .
PIRATES of the

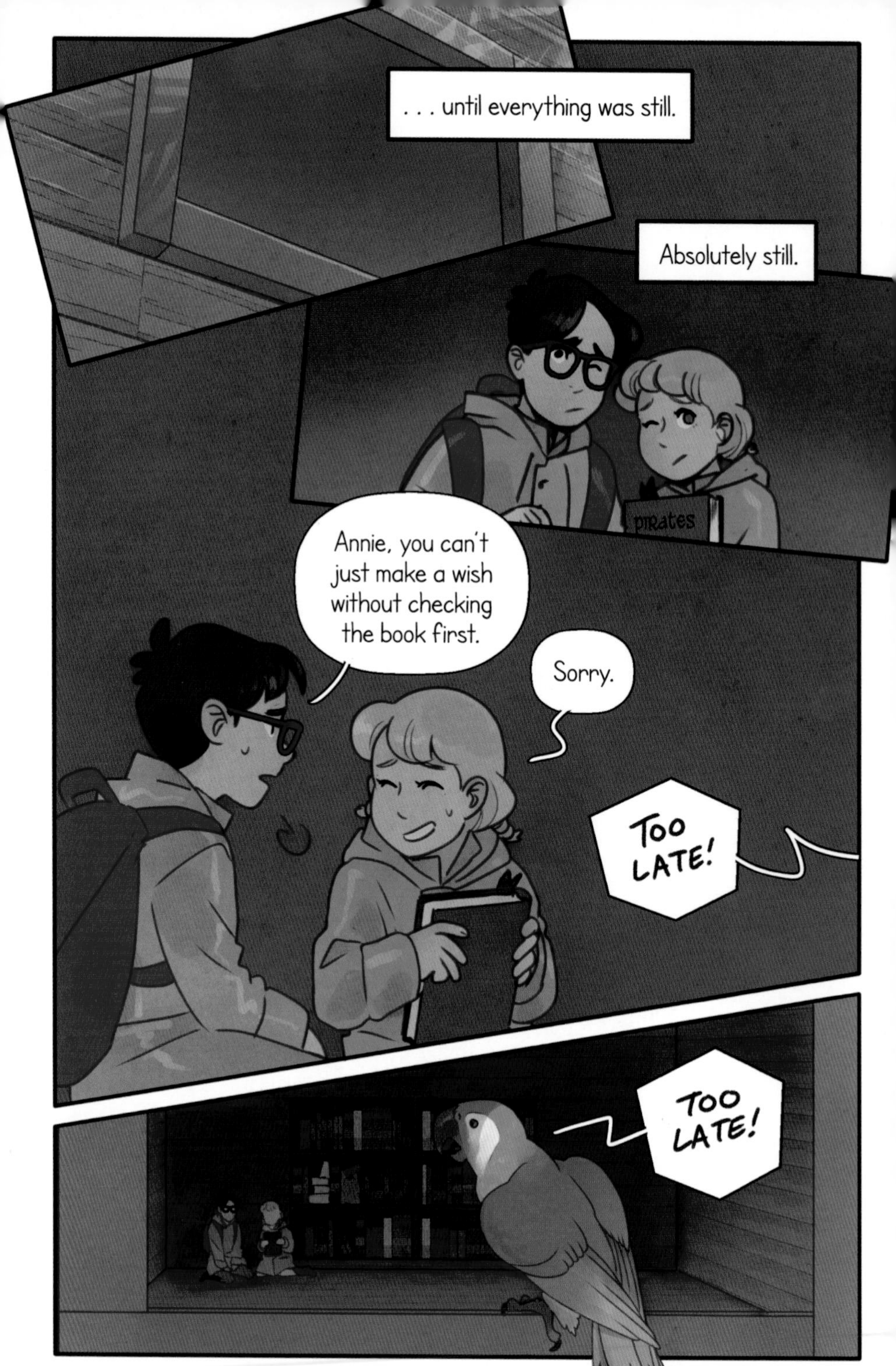
. . . until everything was still.
Absolutely still.
PIRATES
Annie, you can't just make a wish without checking the book first.
Sorry.
TOO LATE!
TOO LATE!

CHAPTER TWO
The Bright Blue Sea

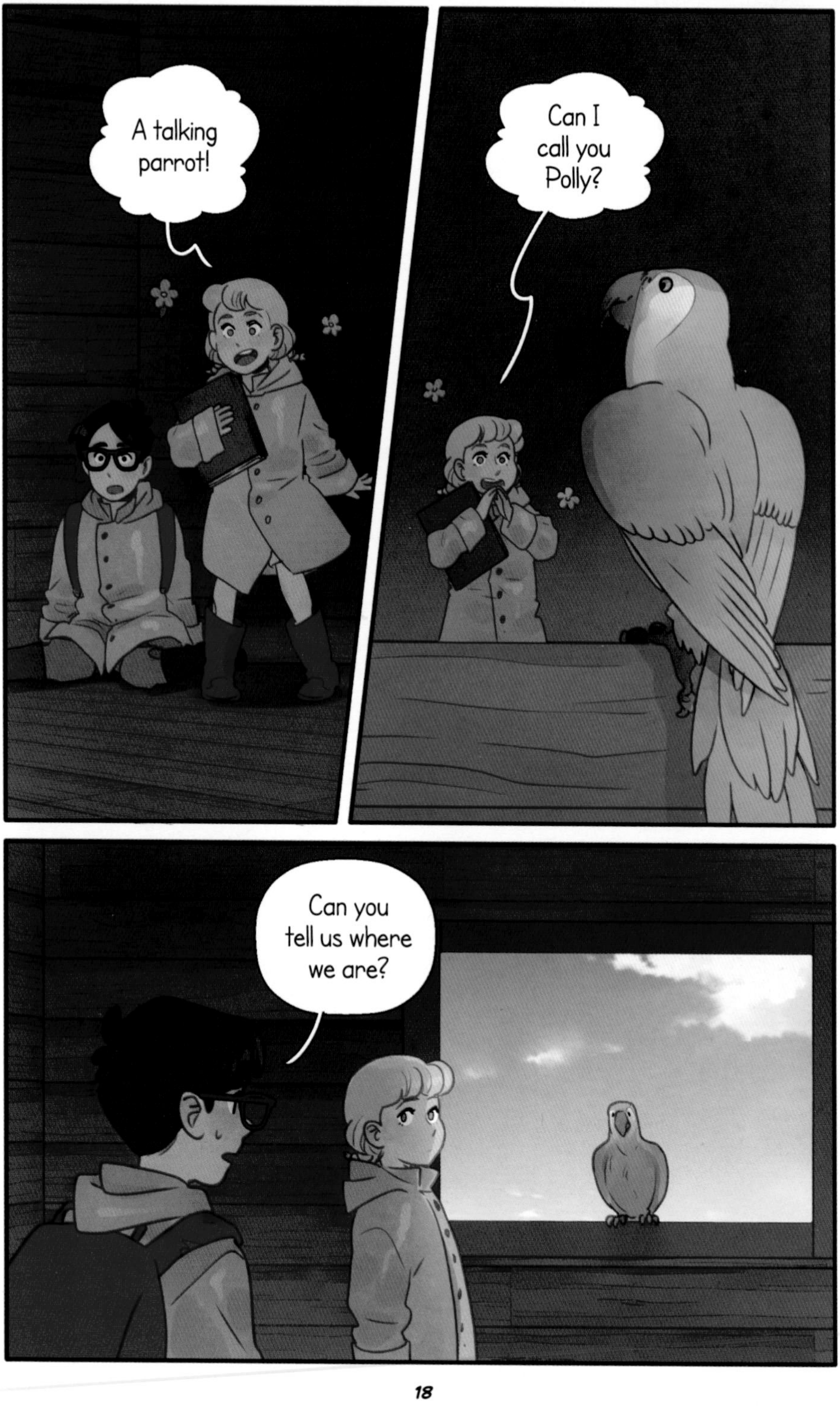
A talking parrot!
Can I call you Polly?
Can you tell us where we are?

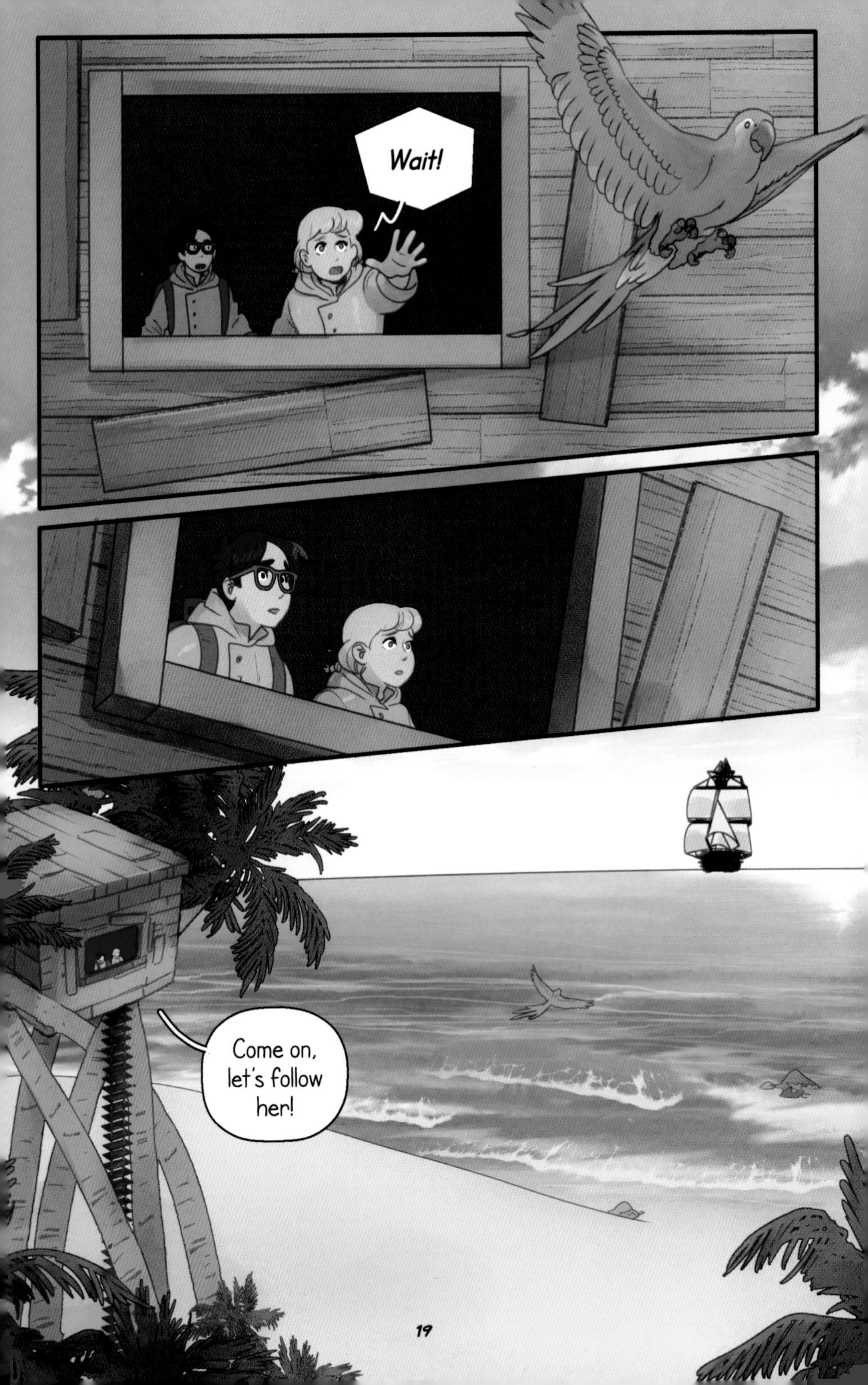
Wait!
Come on, let's follow her!

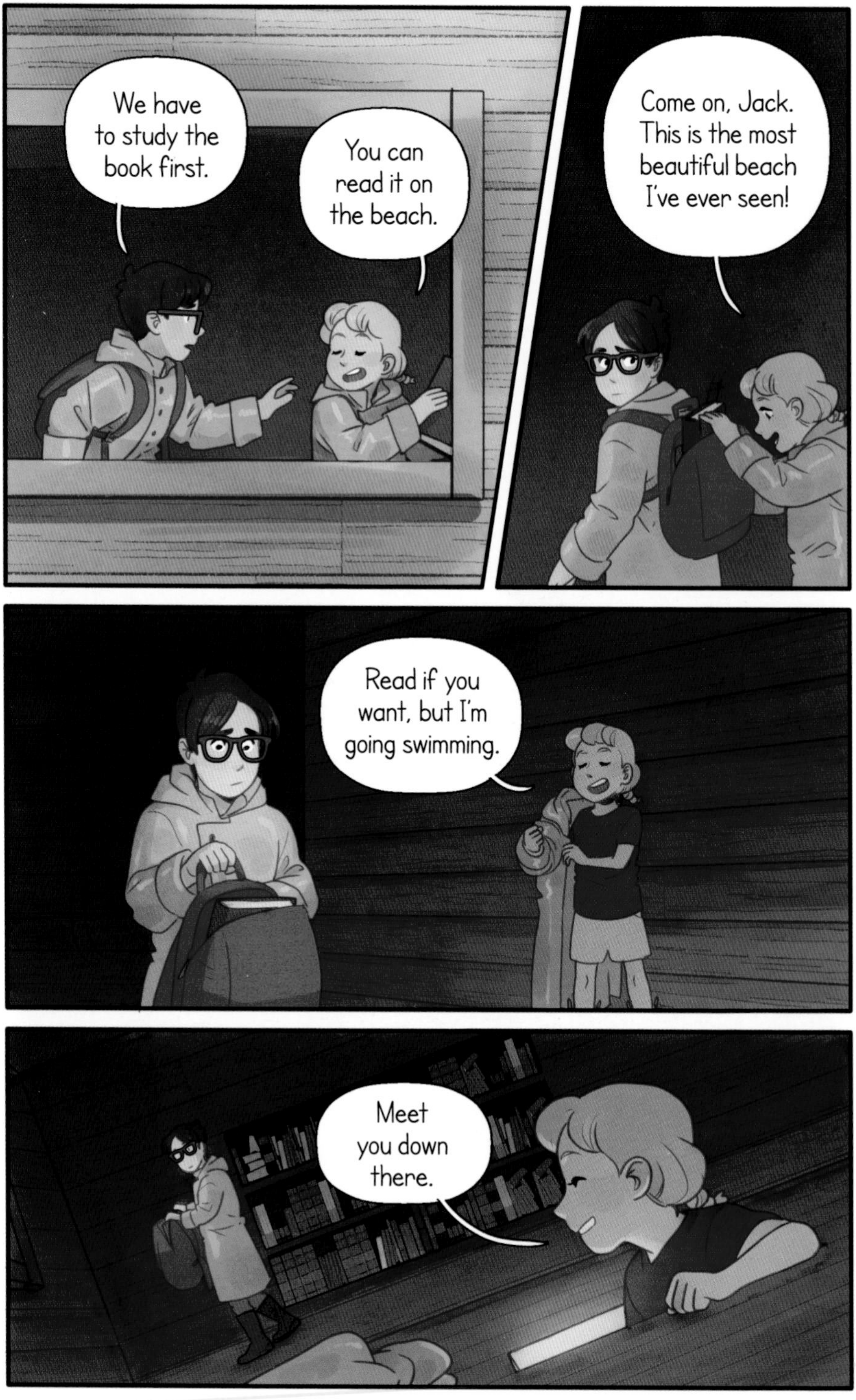
We have to study the book first.
You can read it on the beach.
Come on, Jack. This is the most beautiful beach I've ever seen!
Read if you want, but I'm going swimming.
Meet you down there.

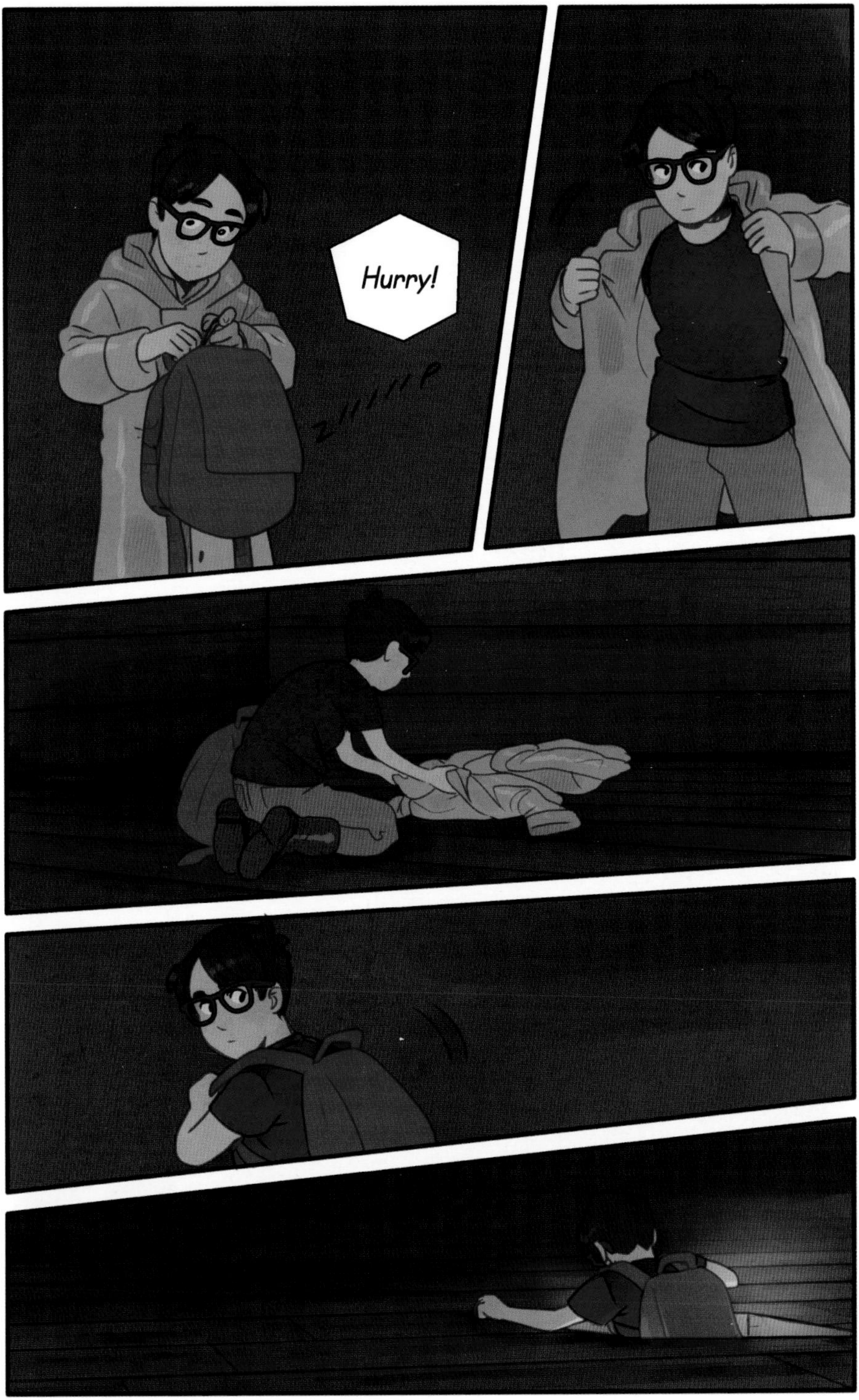
Hurry!

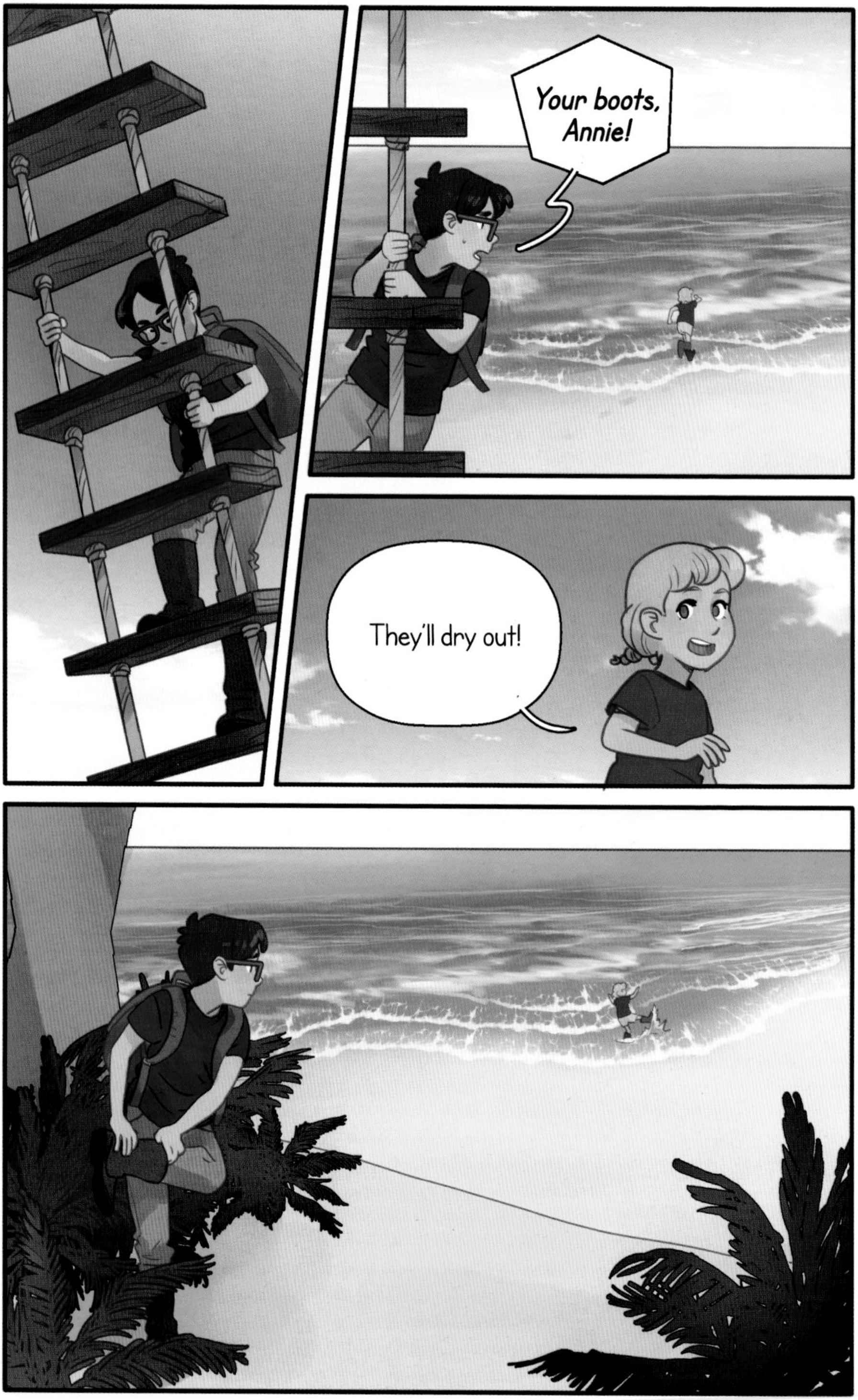
Your boots, Annie!
They'll dry out!

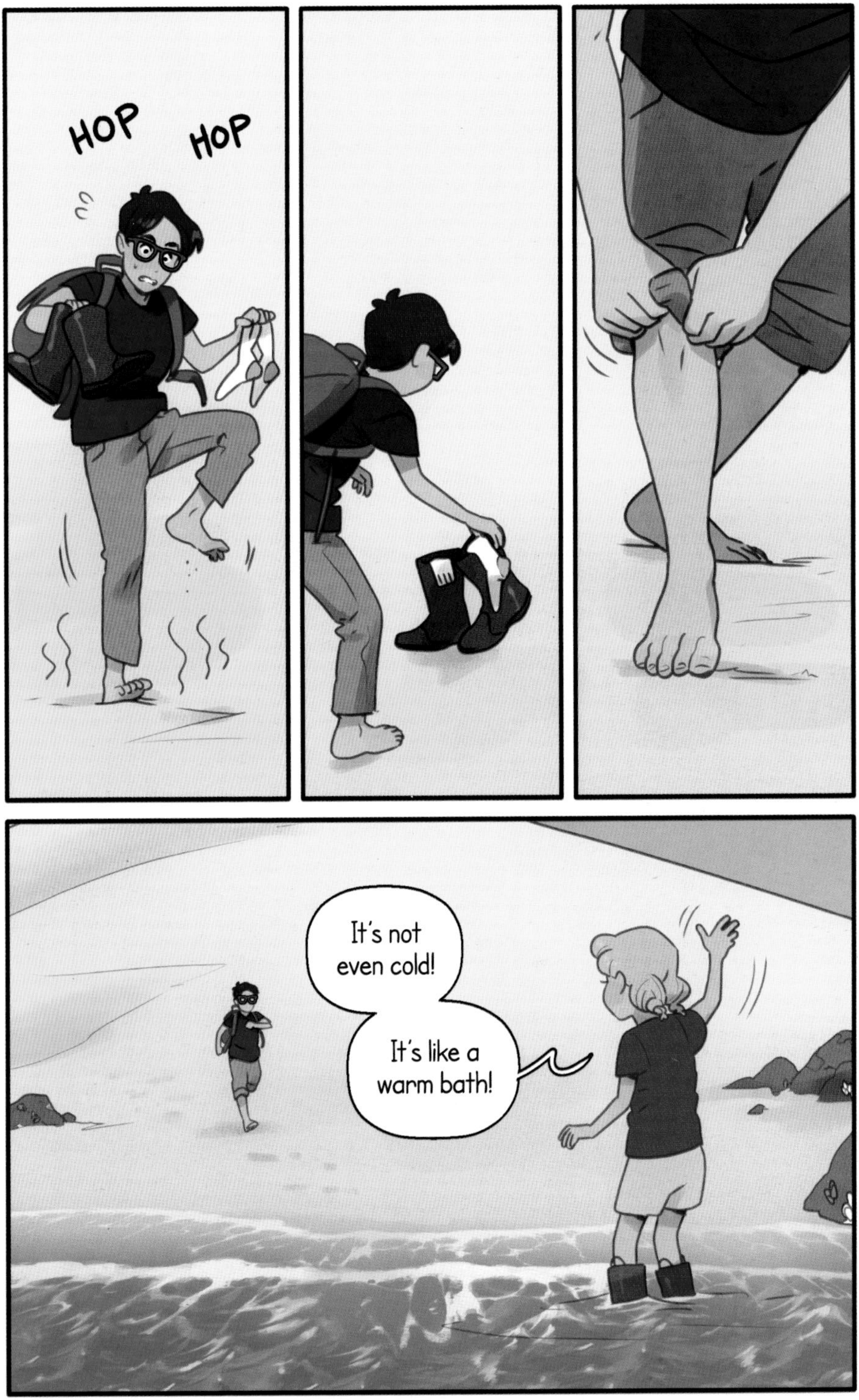
HOP HOP
It's not even cold!
It's like a warm bath!

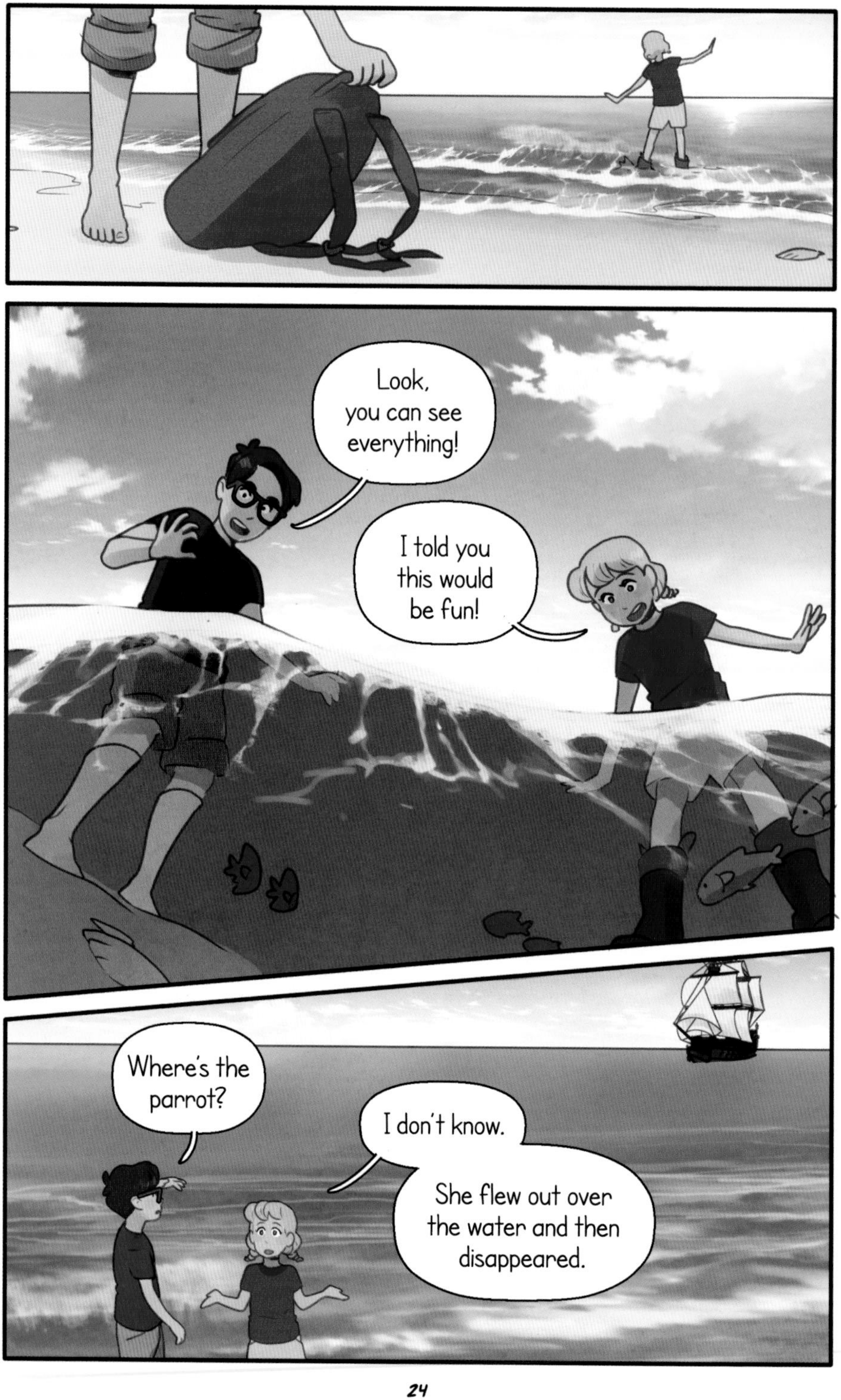
Look, you can see everything!
I told you this would be fun!
Where's the parrot?
I don't know.
She flew out over the water and then disappeared.

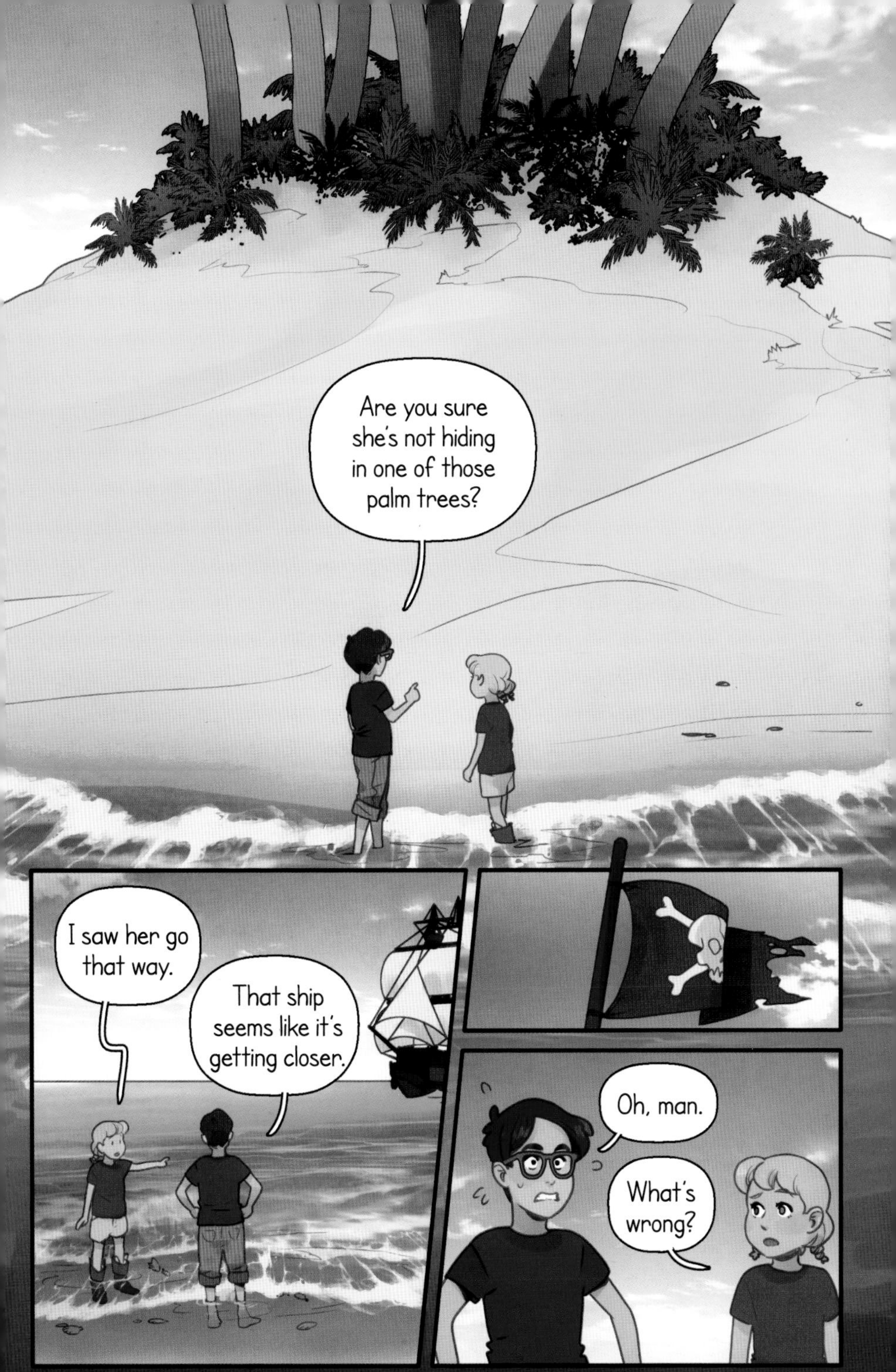
Are you sure she's not hiding in one of those palm trees?
I saw her go that way.
That ship seems like it's getting closer.
Oh, man.
What's wrong?

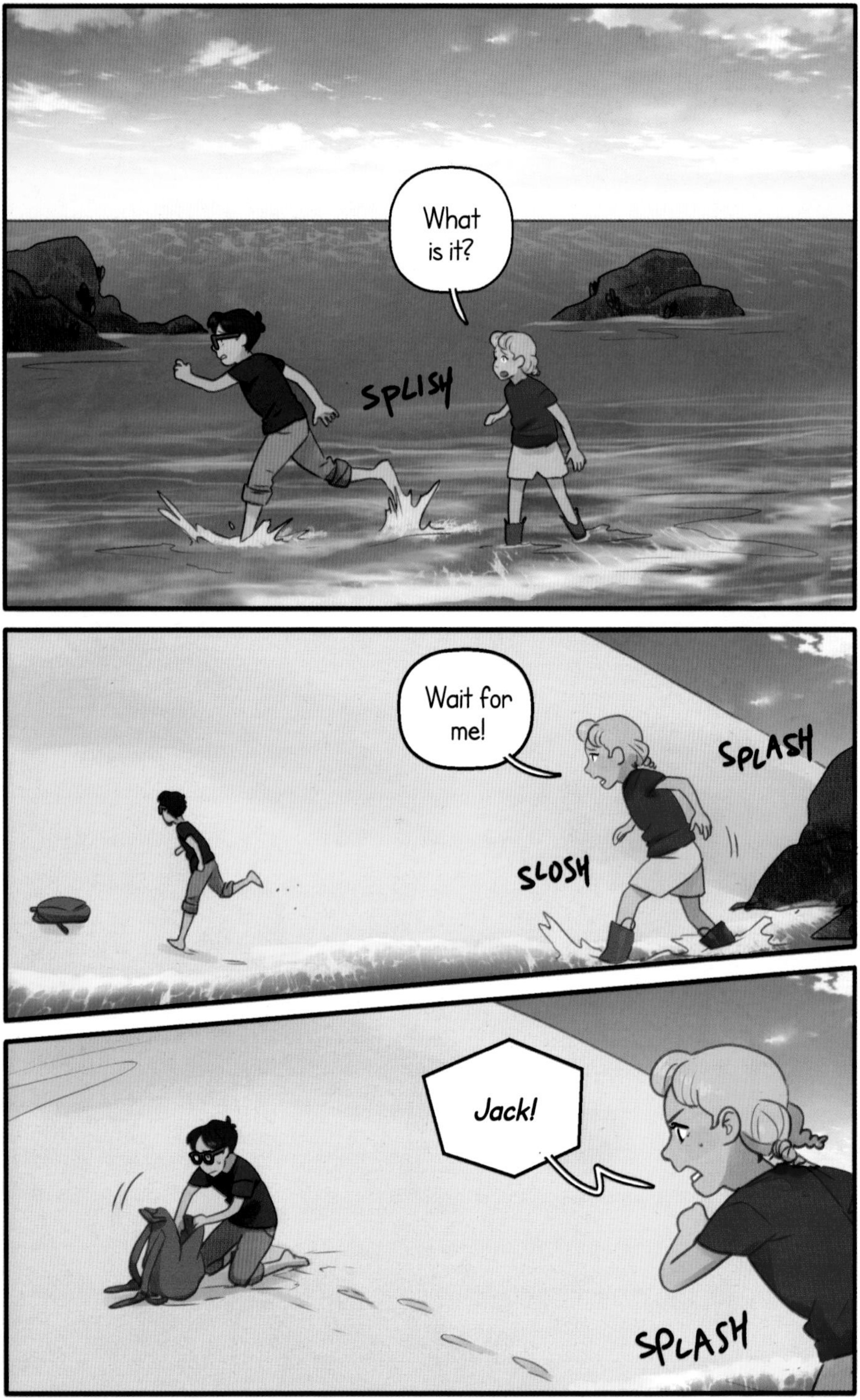
What is it?
SPLISH
Wait for me!
SPLASH
SLOSH
Jack!
SPLASH

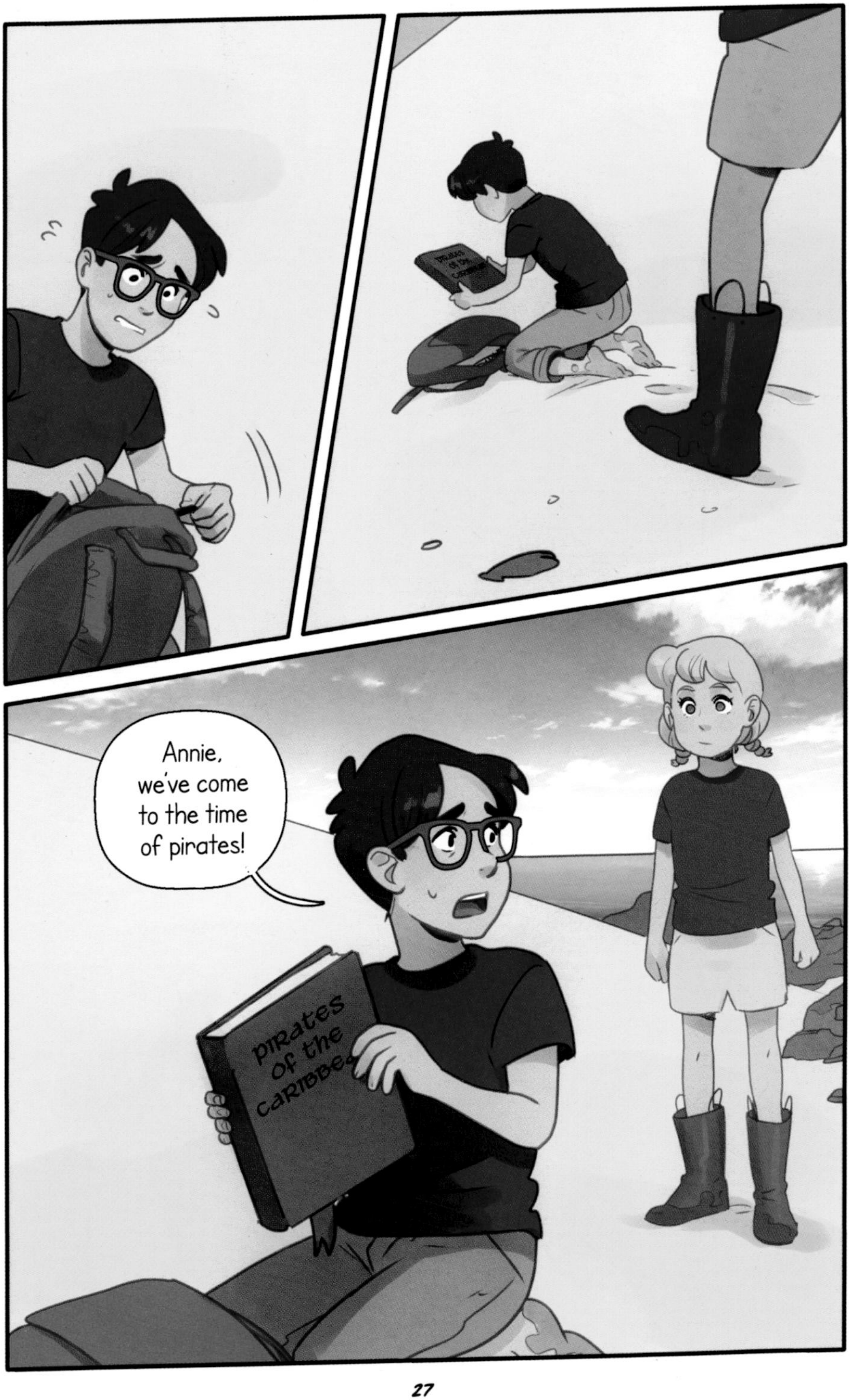
PIRATES OF THE CARIBBEAN
Annie, we've come to the time of pirates!
PIRATES of the CARIBBEA

CHAPTER THREE
Three Men in a Boat

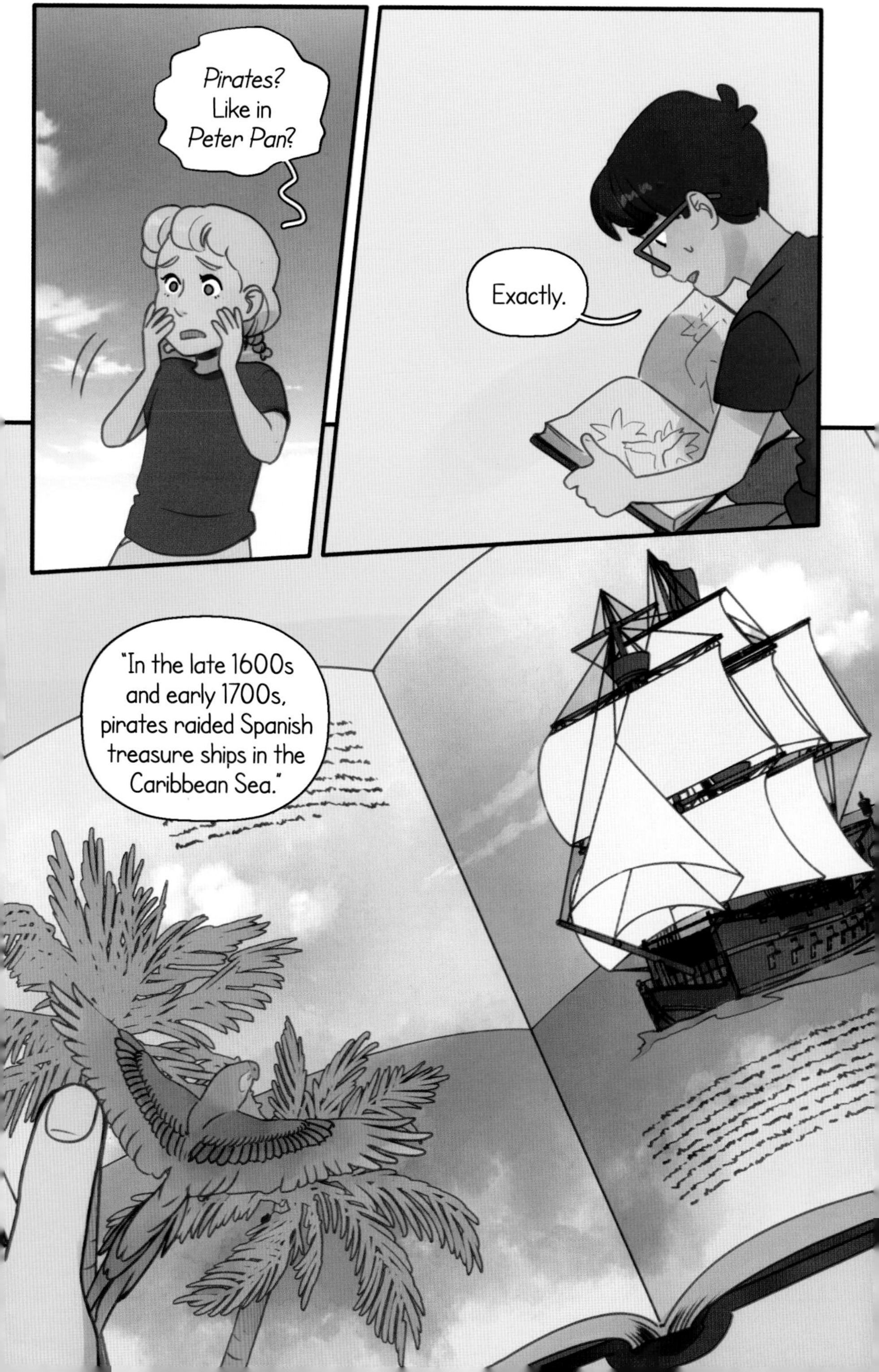
Pirates? Like in Peter Pan?
Exactly.
"In the late 1600s and early 1700s, pirates raided Spanish treasure ships in the Caribbean Sea."

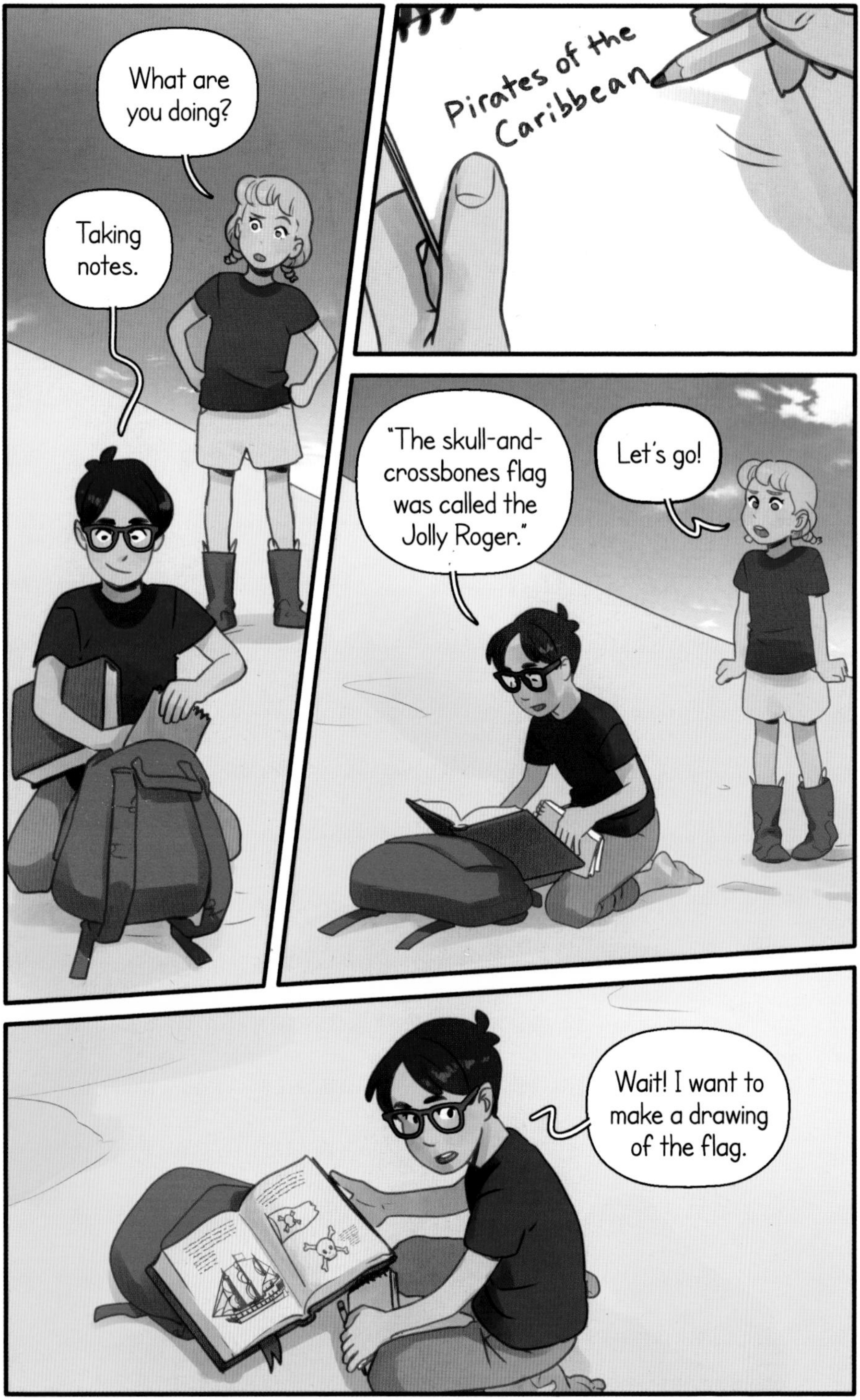
What are you doing?
Taking notes.
Pirates of the Caribbean
"The skull-and-crossbones flag was called the Jolly Roger."
Let's go!
Wait! I want to make a drawing of the flag.

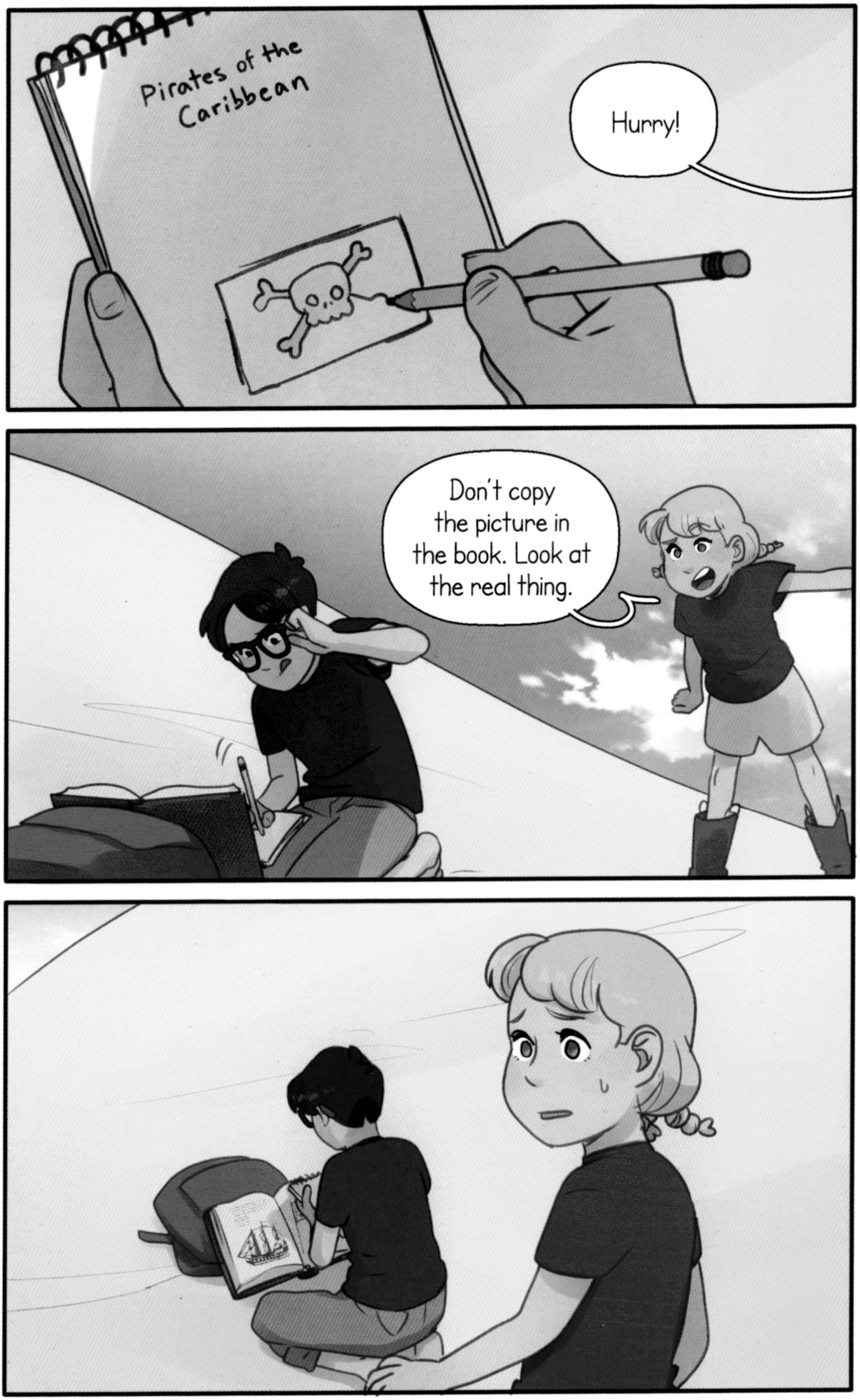
Pirates of the Caribbean
Hurry!
Don't copy the picture in the book. Look at the real thing.

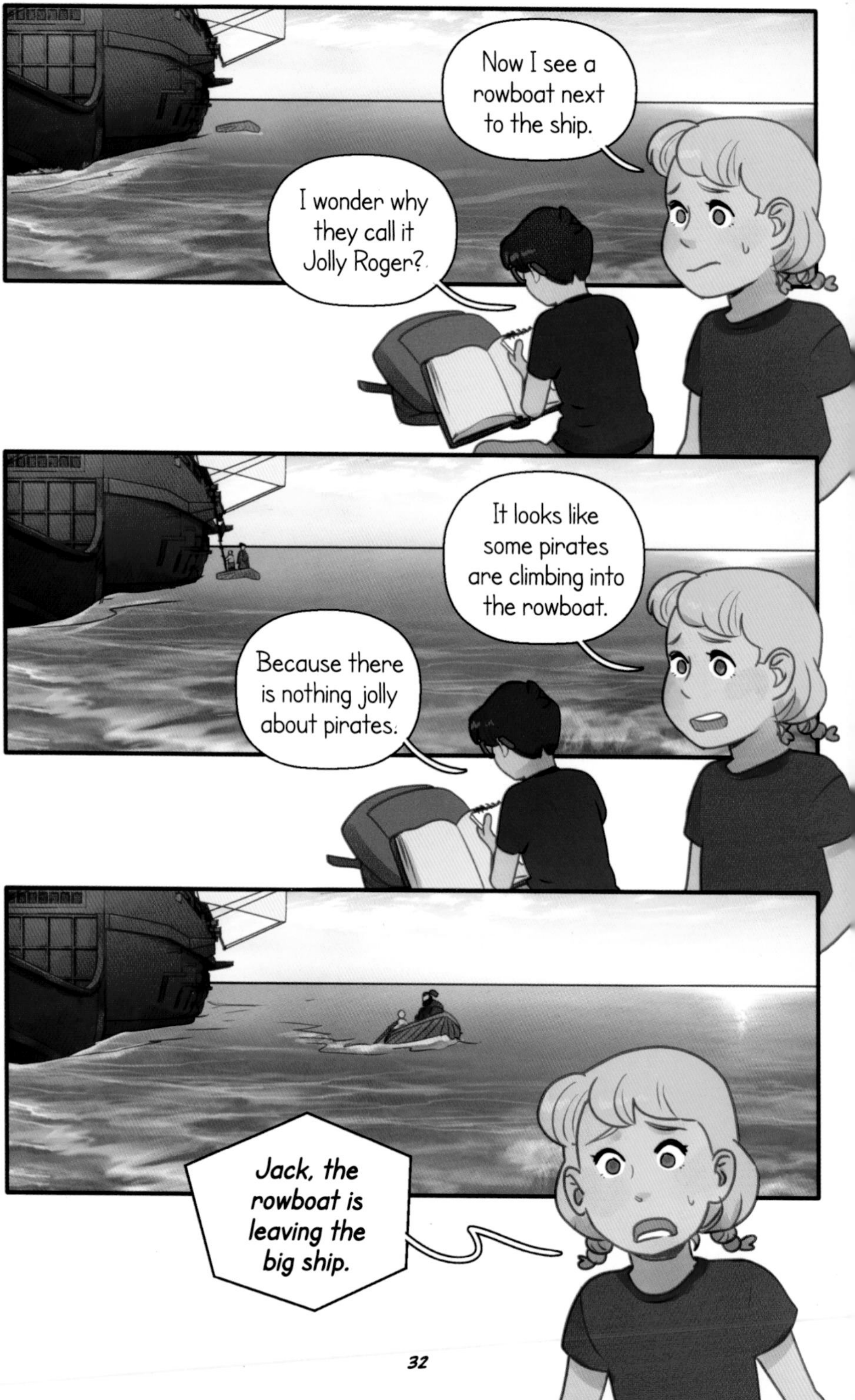
Now I see a rowboat next to the ship.
I wonder why they call it Jolly Roger?
It looks like some pirates are climbing into the rowboat.
Because there is nothing jolly about pirates.
Jack, the rowboat is leaving the big ship.

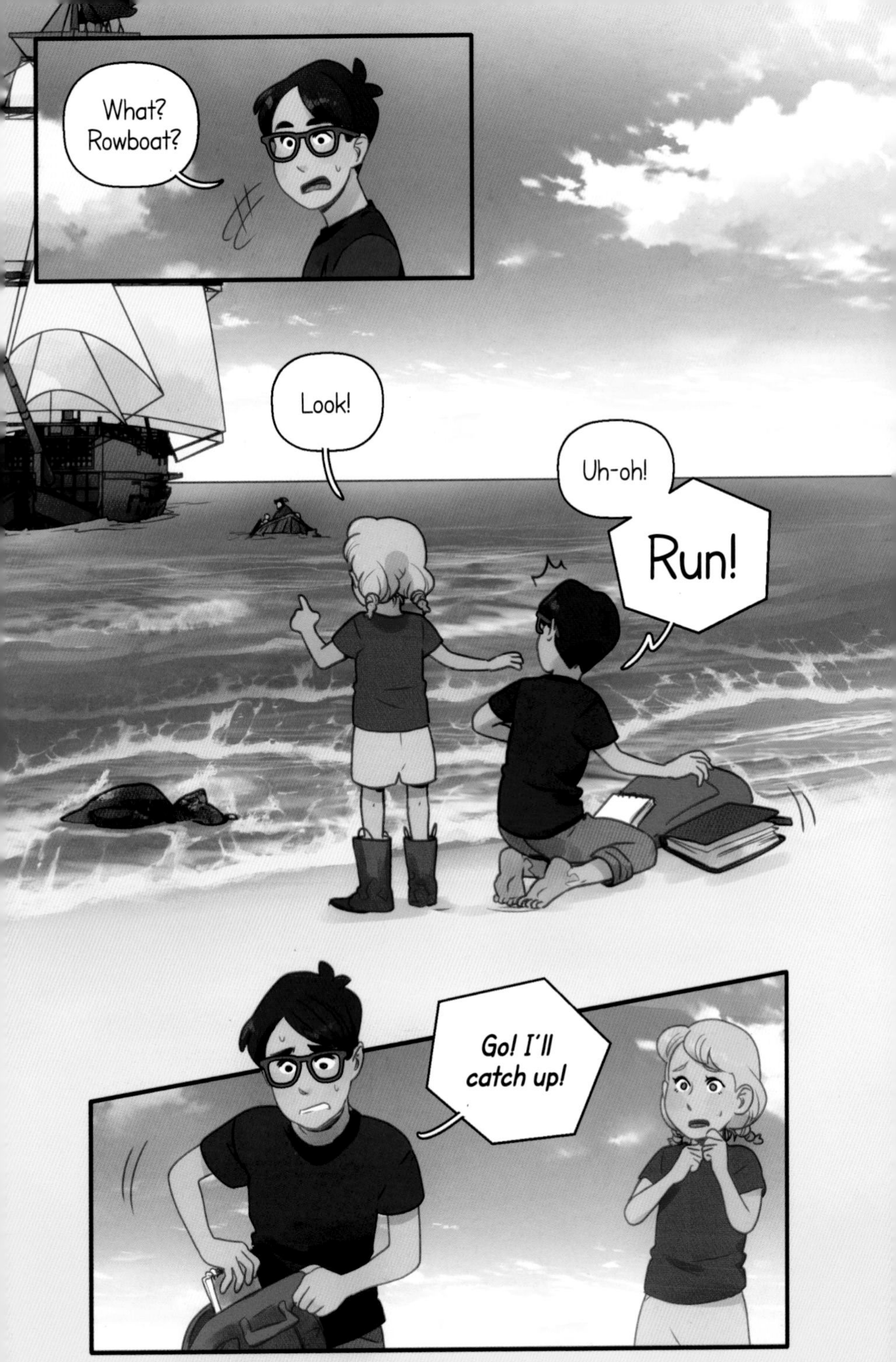
What? Rowboat?
Look!
Uh-oh!
Run!
Go! I'll catch up!

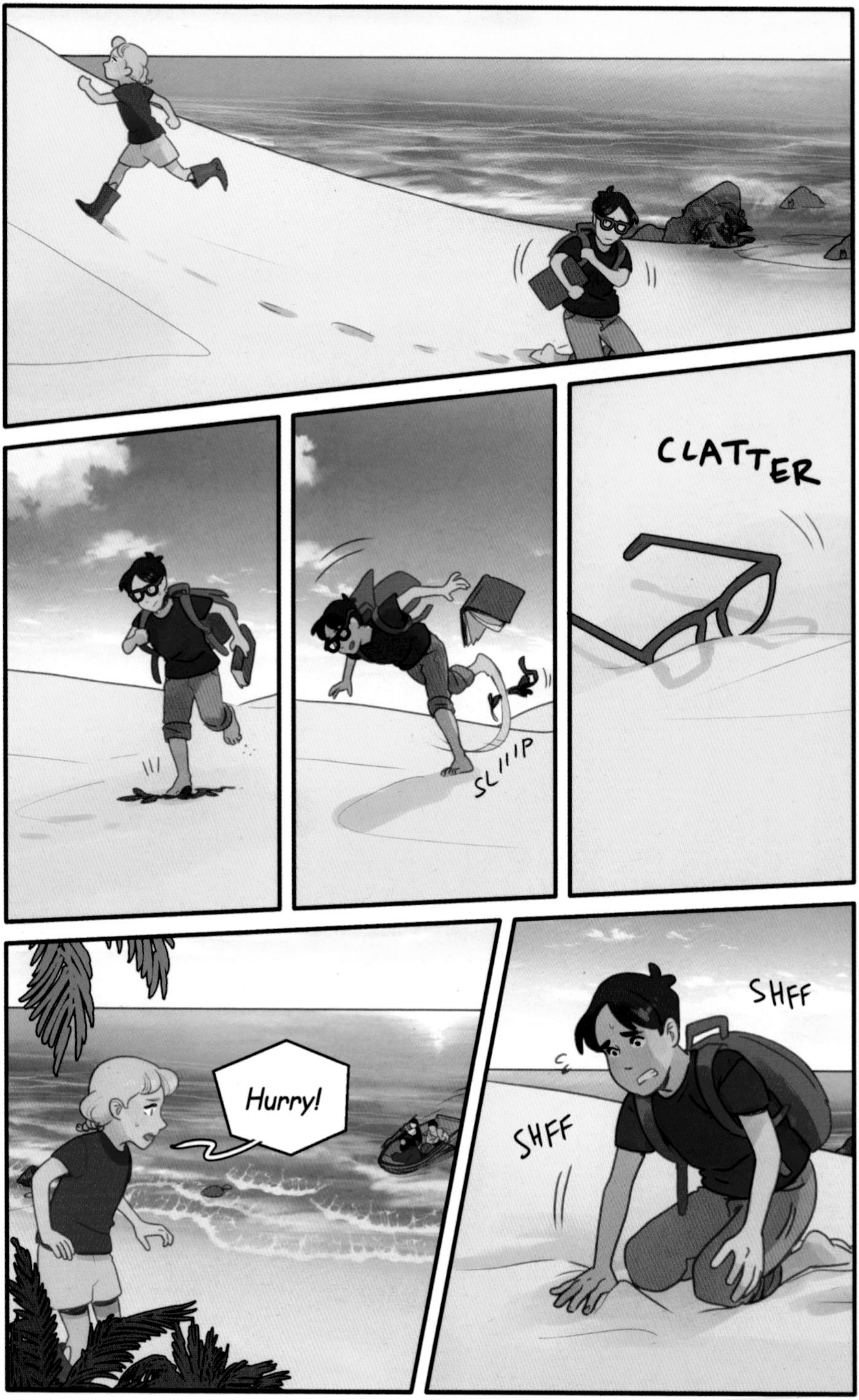
CLATTER
SLIIIP
Hurry!
SHFF
SHFF

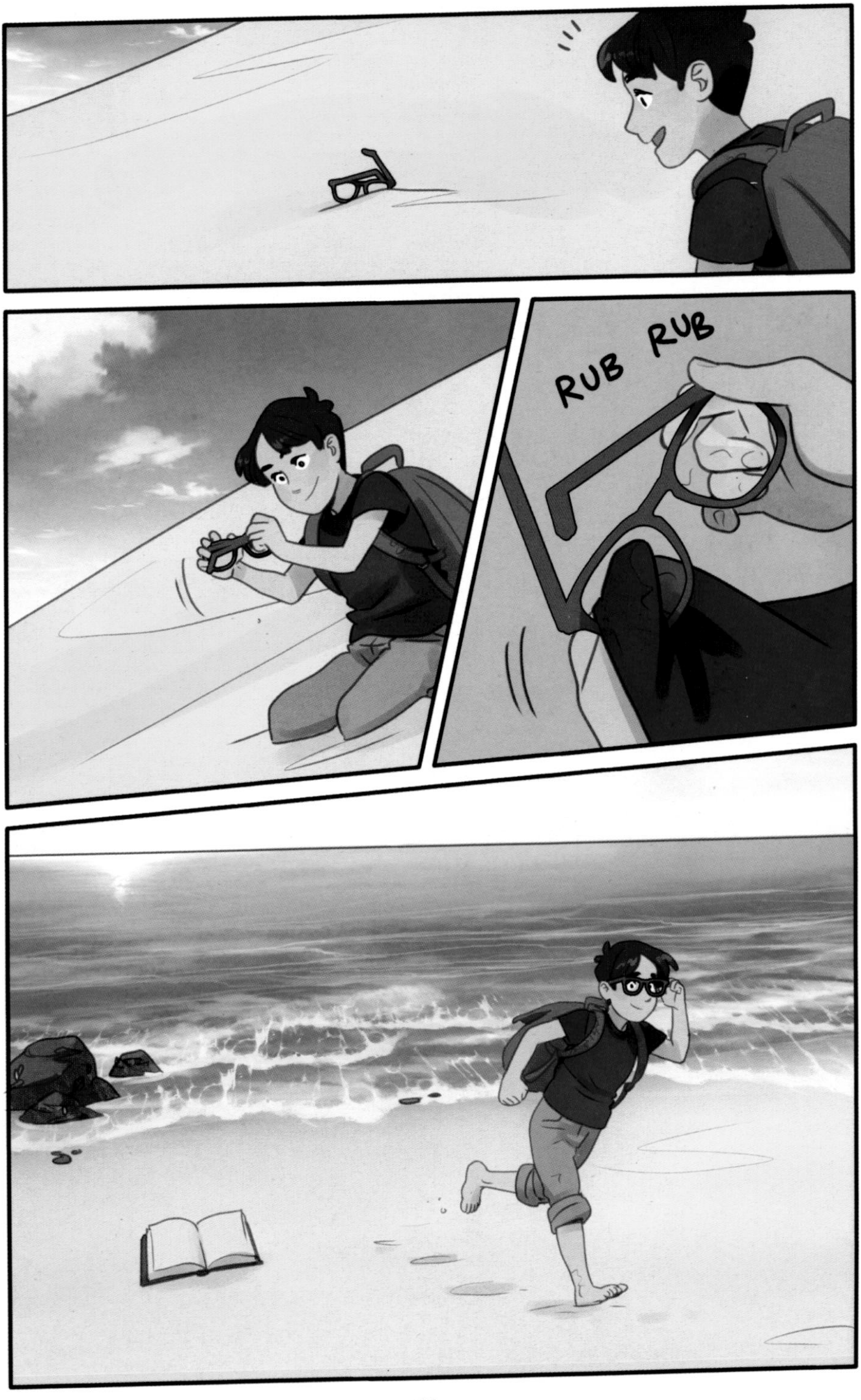
RUB RUB

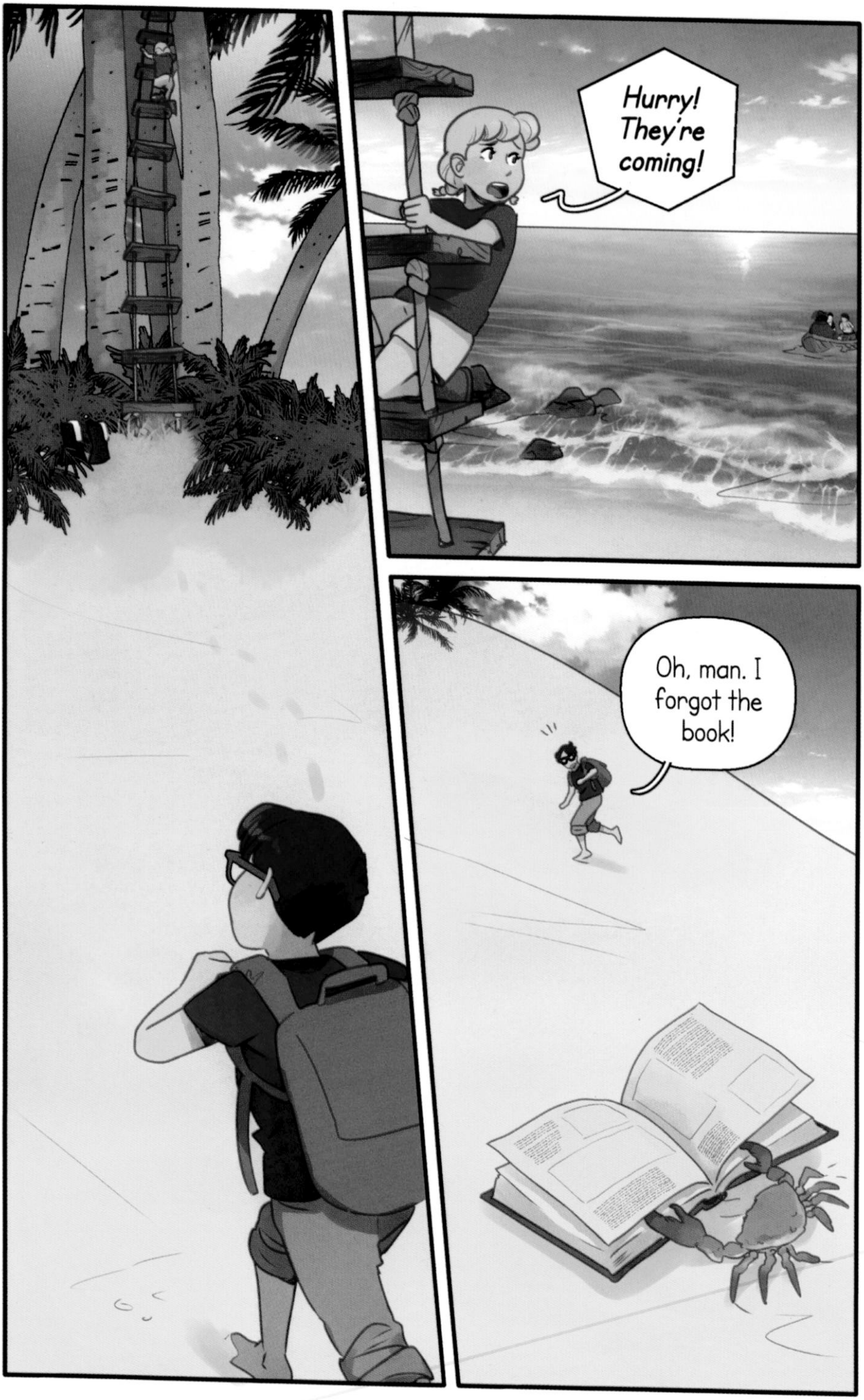
Hurry! They're coming!
Oh, man. I forgot the book!

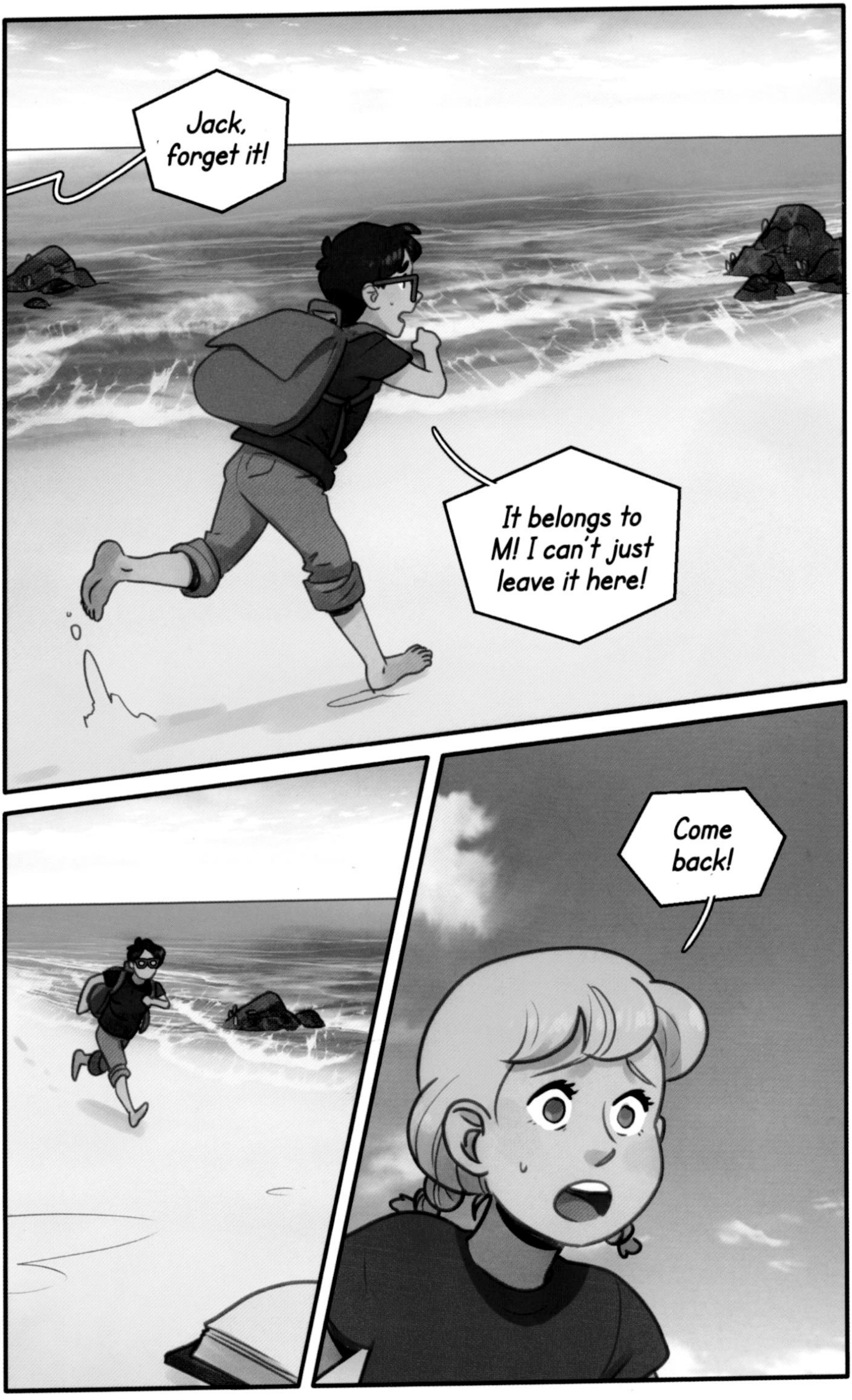
Jack,
forget it!
It belongs to
M! I can't just
leave it here!
Come
back!

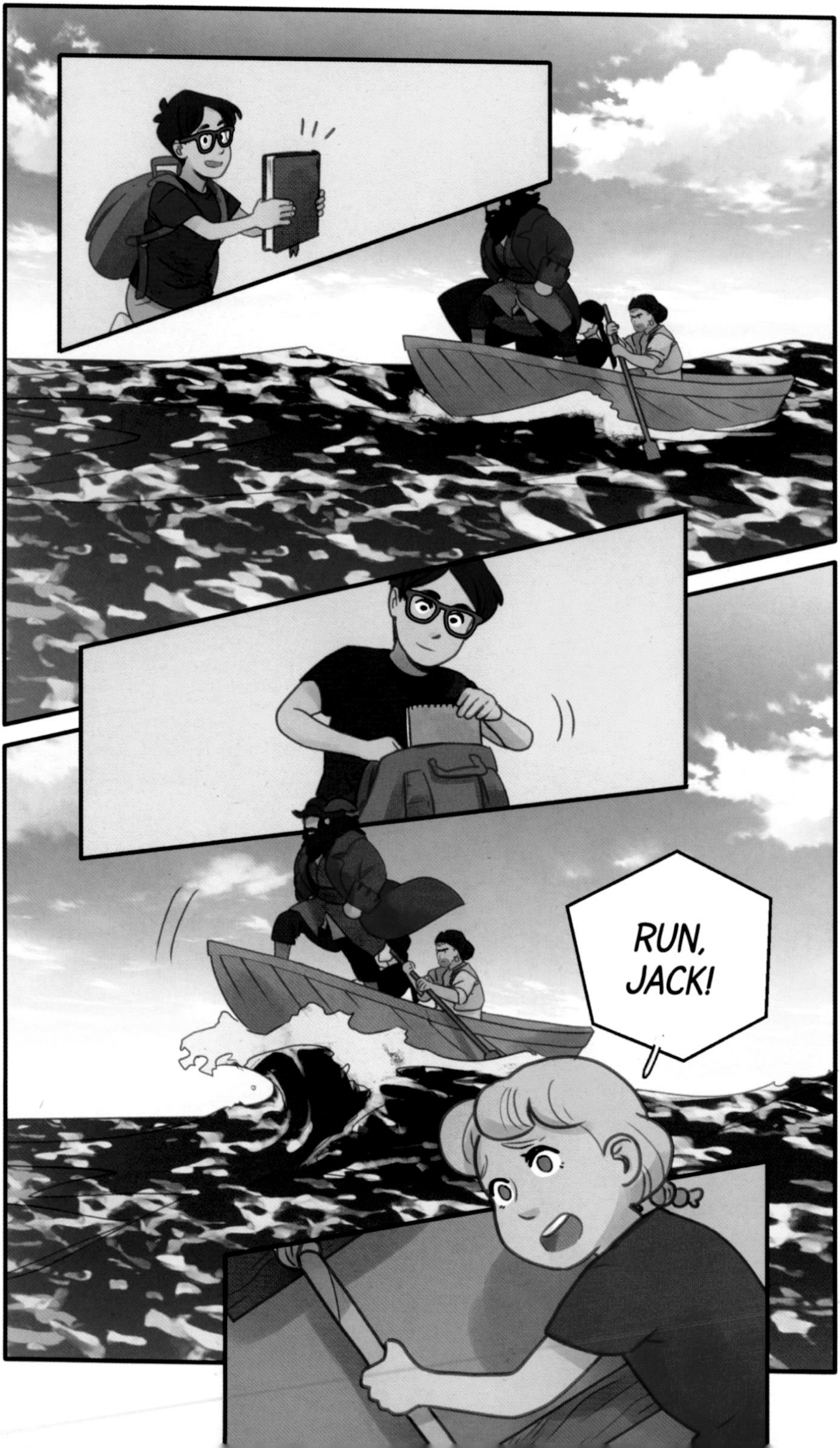
RUN, JACK!

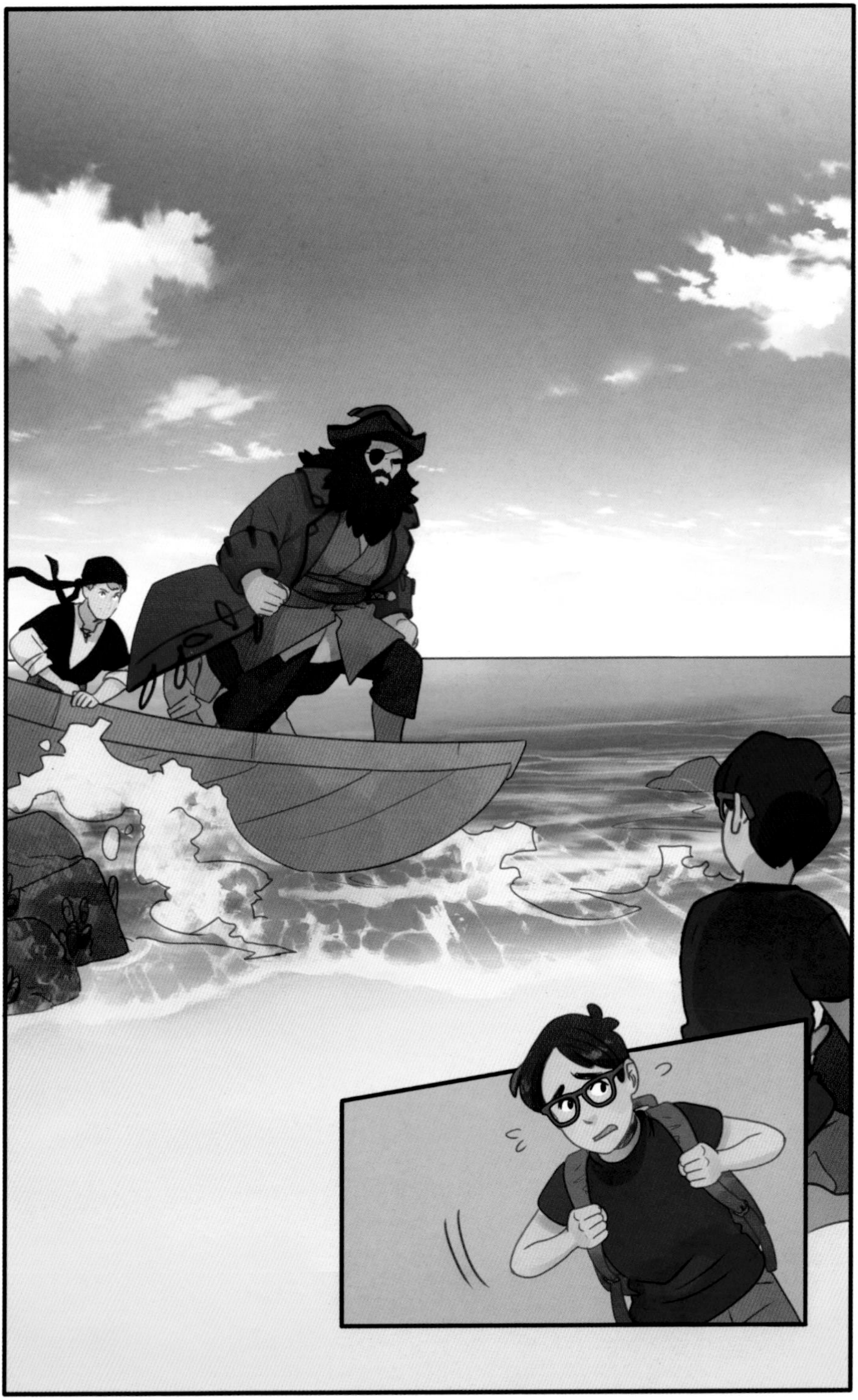

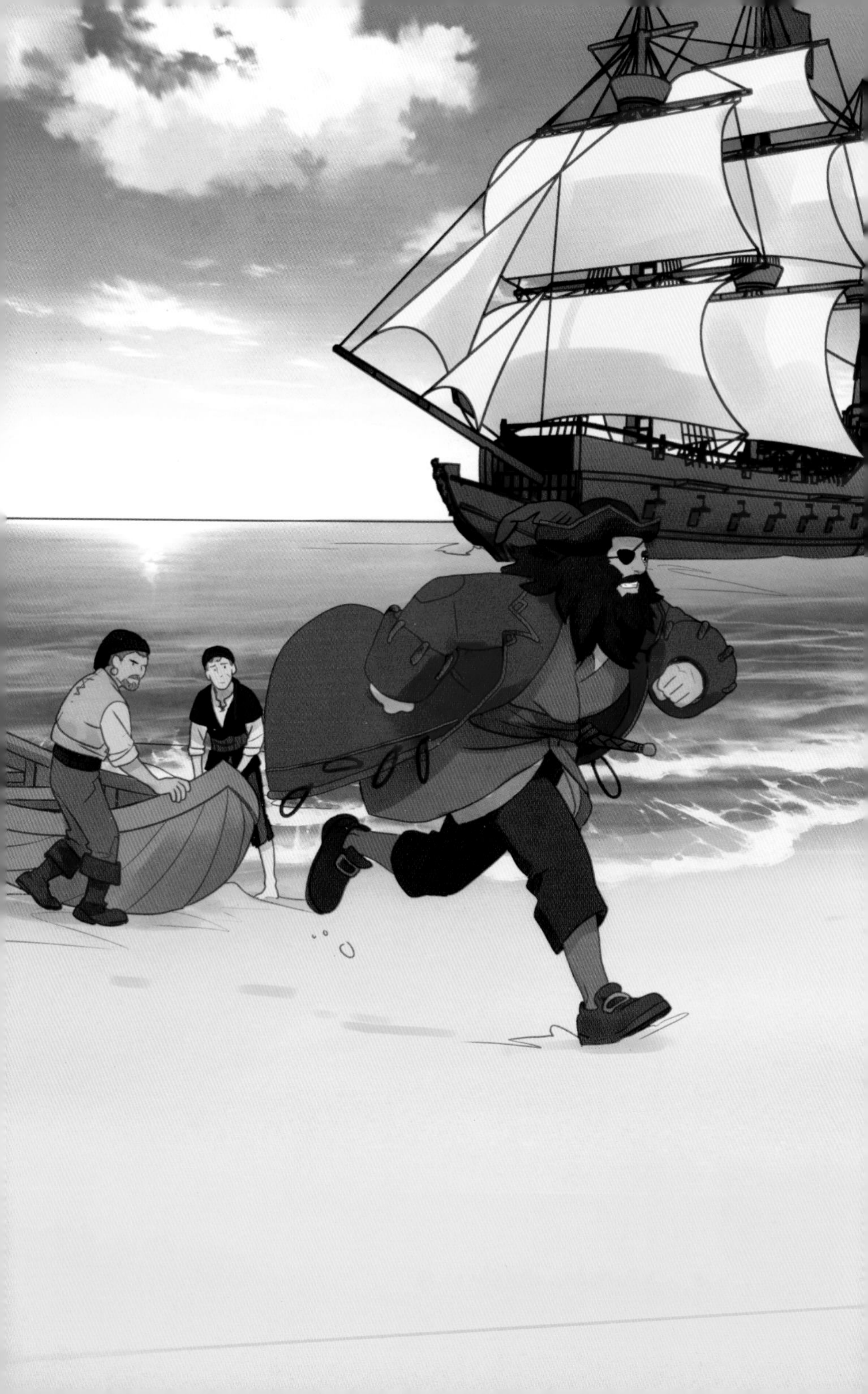

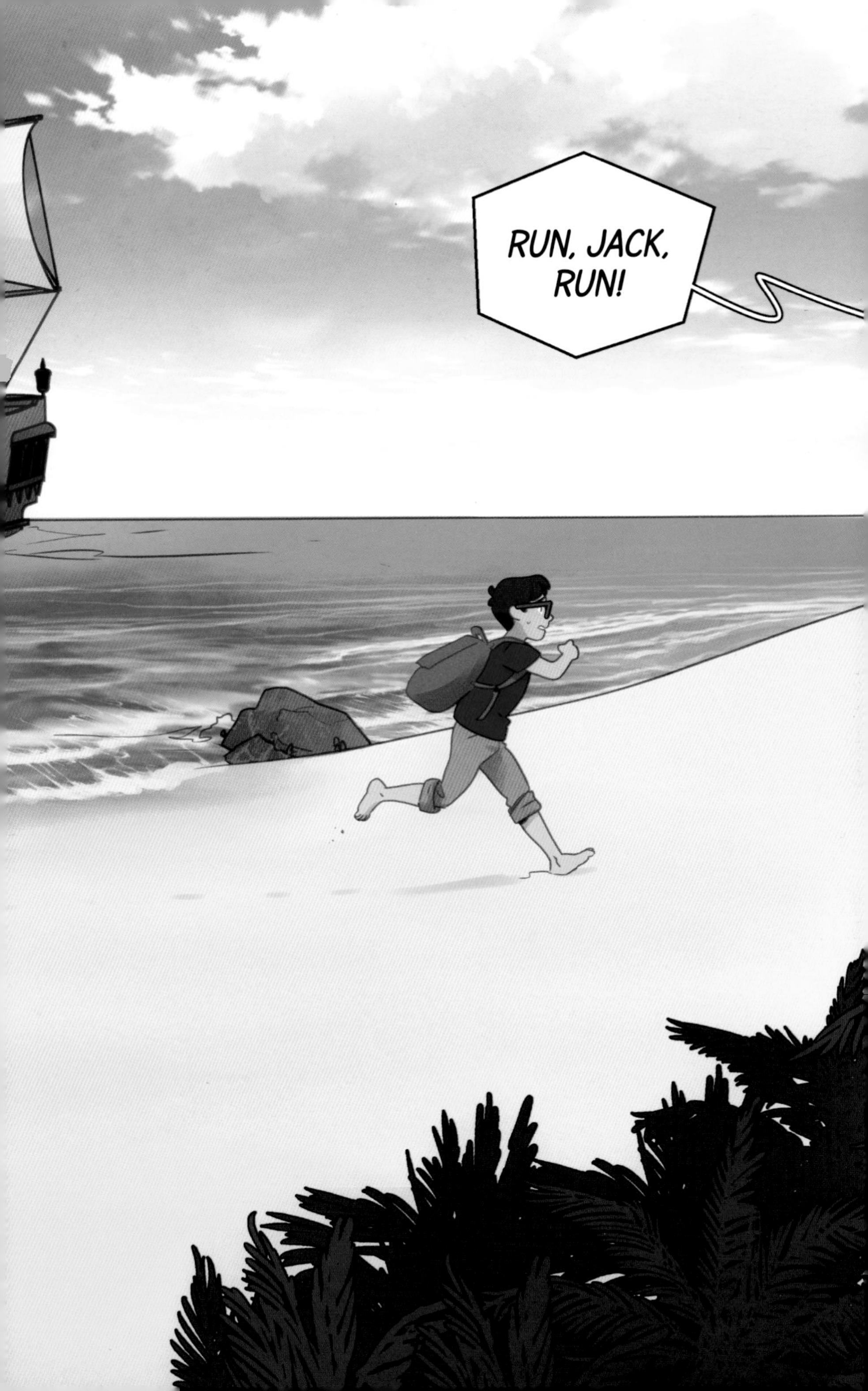
RUN, JACK, RUN!

CHAPTER FOUR
Vile Booty

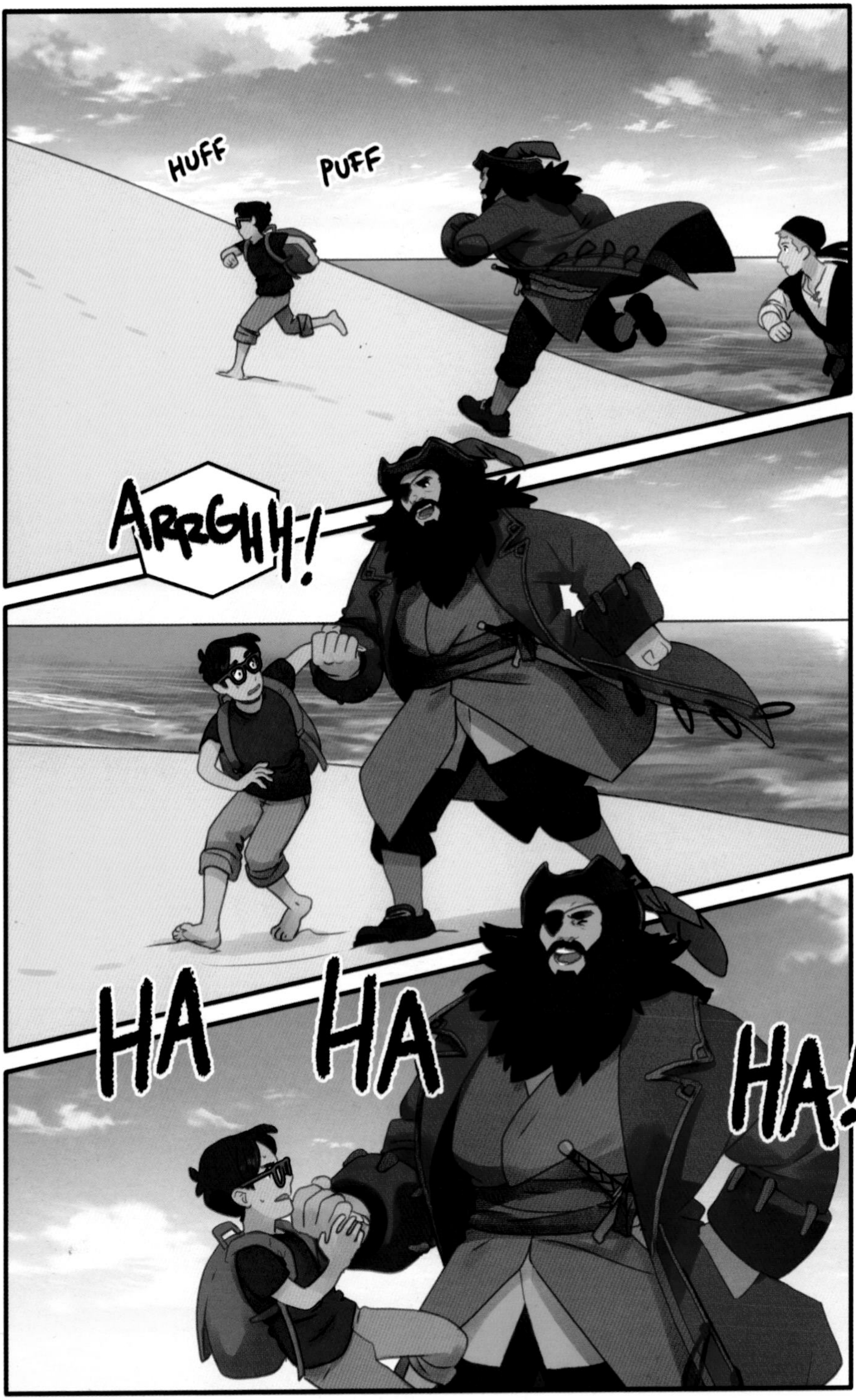
HUFF
PUFF
ARRGHH!
HA HA HA!

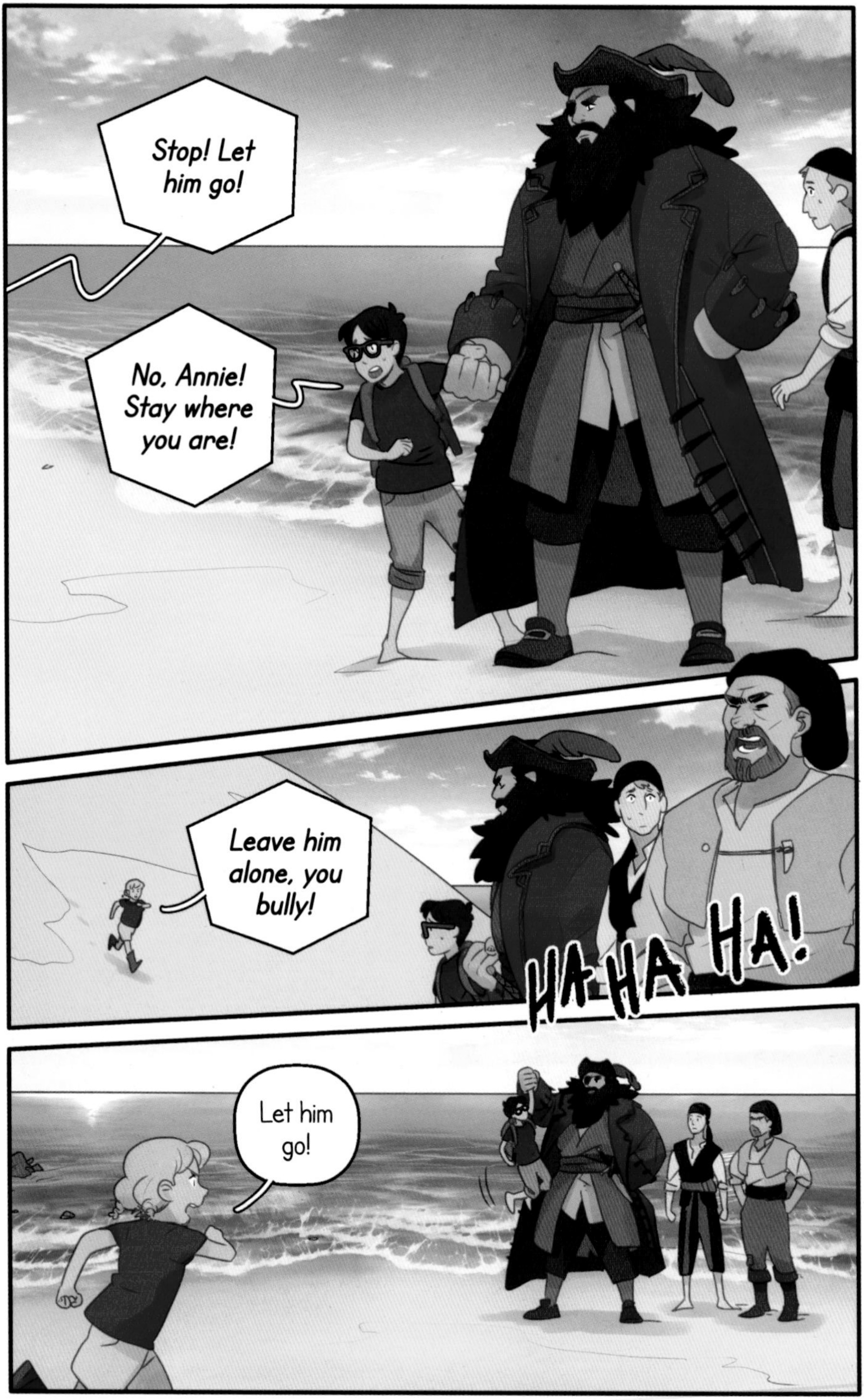
Stop! Let him go!
No, Annie! Stay where you are!
Leave him alone, you bully!
HA HA HA!
Let him go!

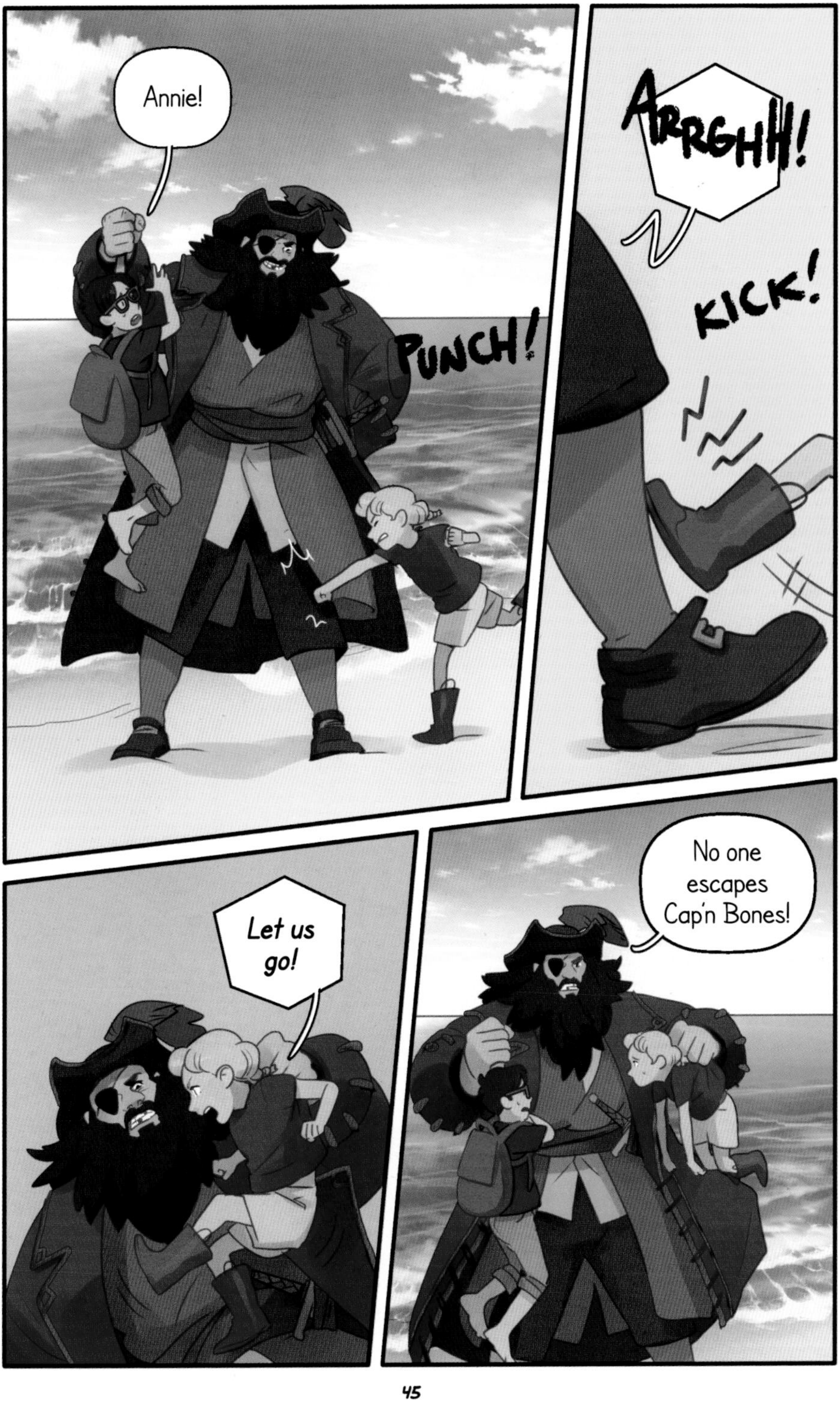
Annie!
PUNCH!
ARRGHH!
KICK!
Let us go!
No one escapes Cap'n Bones!

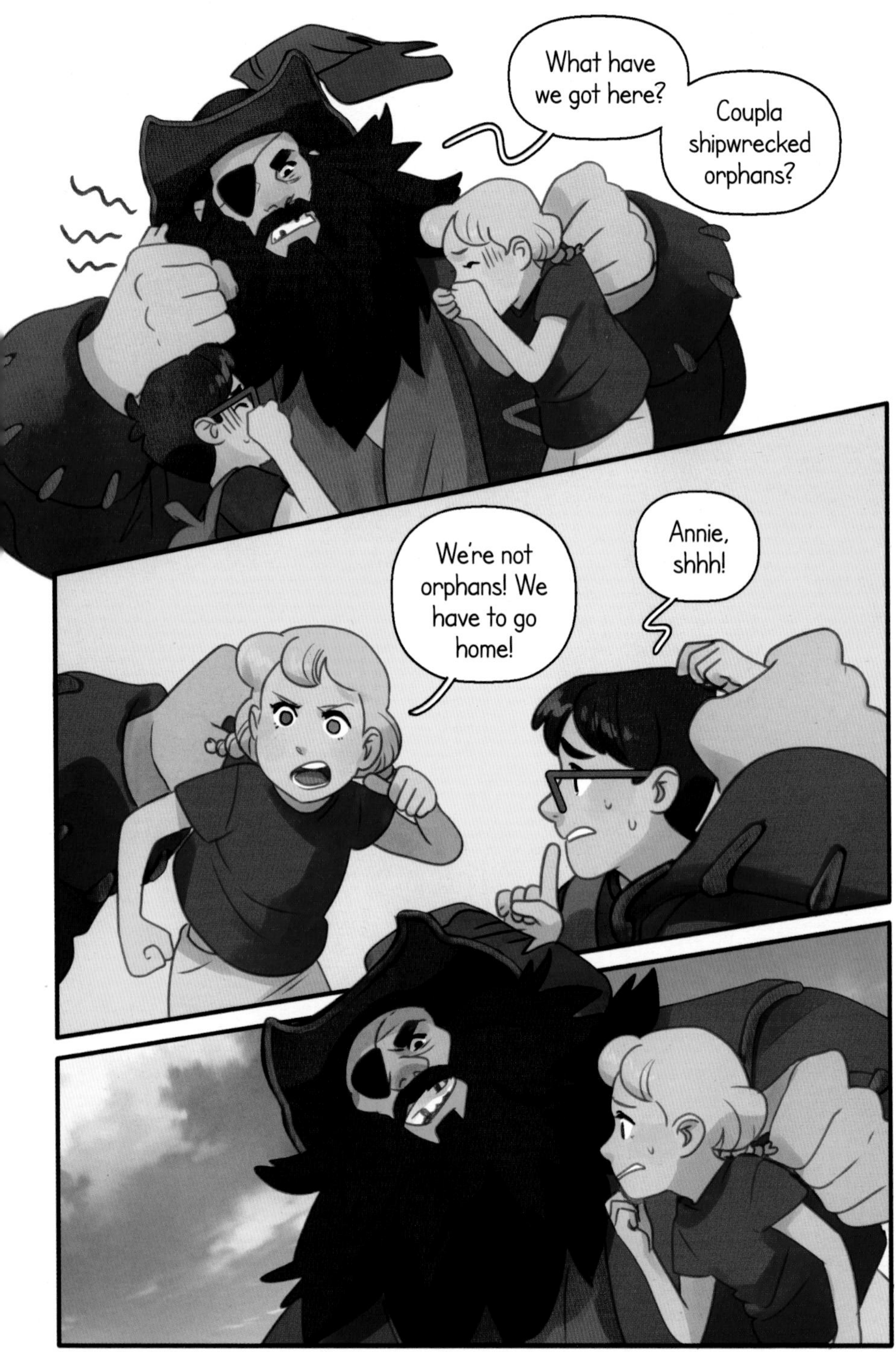
What have we got here?
Coupla shipwrecked orphans?
We're not orphans! We have to go home!
Annie, shhh!

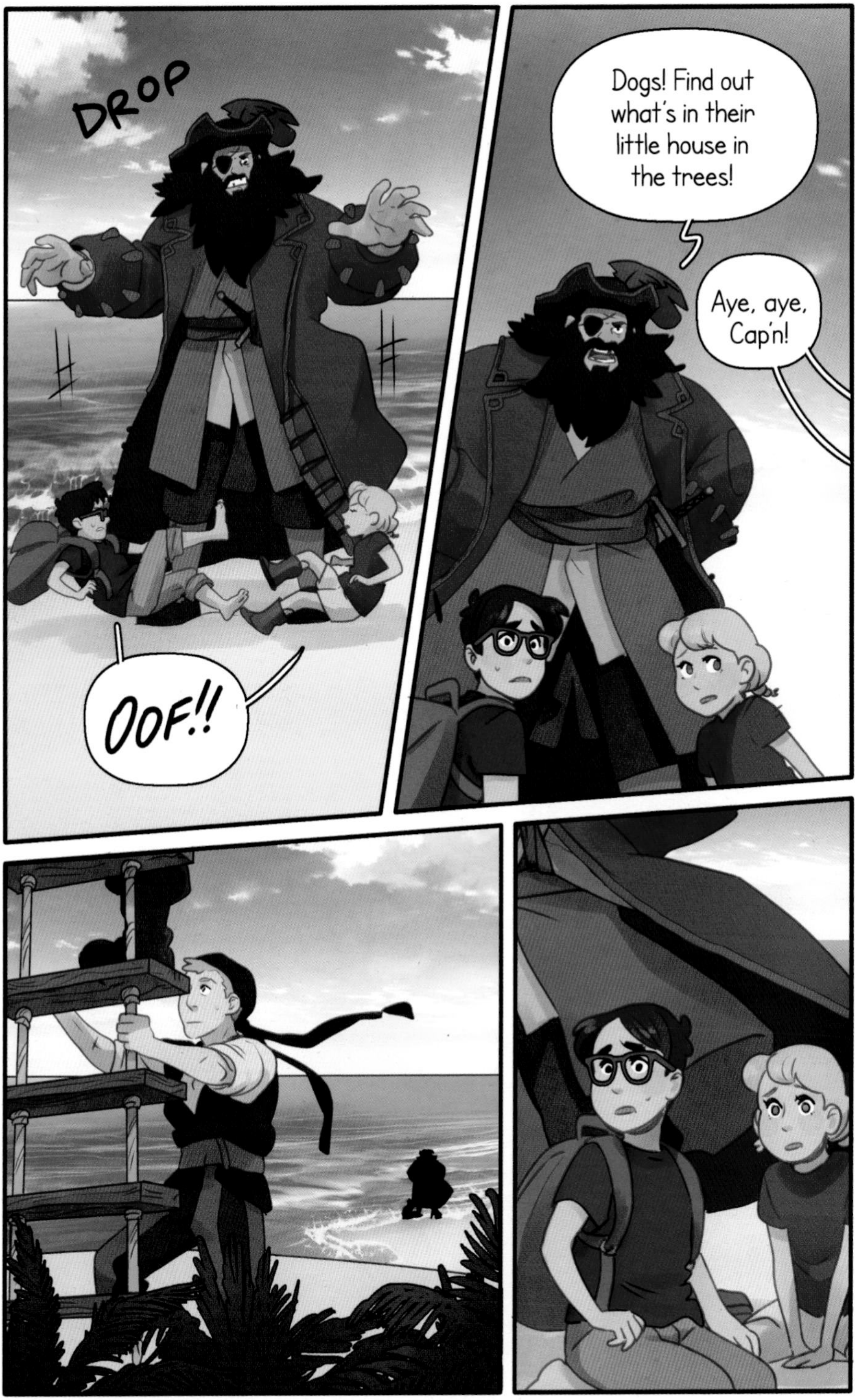
DROP
OOF!!
Dogs! Find out what's in their little house in the trees!
Aye, aye, Cap'n!

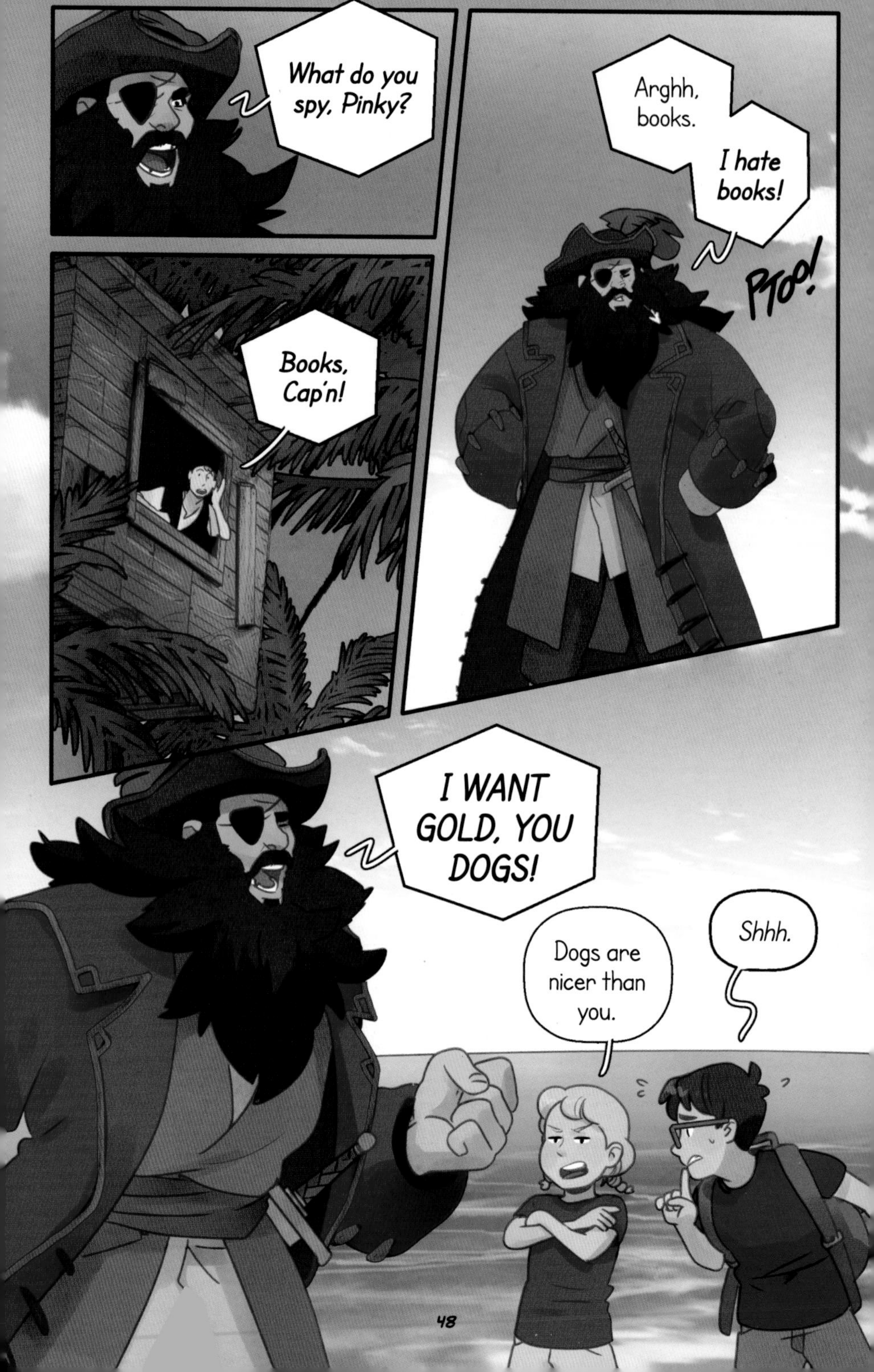
What do you spy, Pinky?
Arghh, books.
I hate books!
PTOO!
Books, Cap'n!
I WANT GOLD, YOU DOGS!
Dogs are nicer than you.
Shhh.

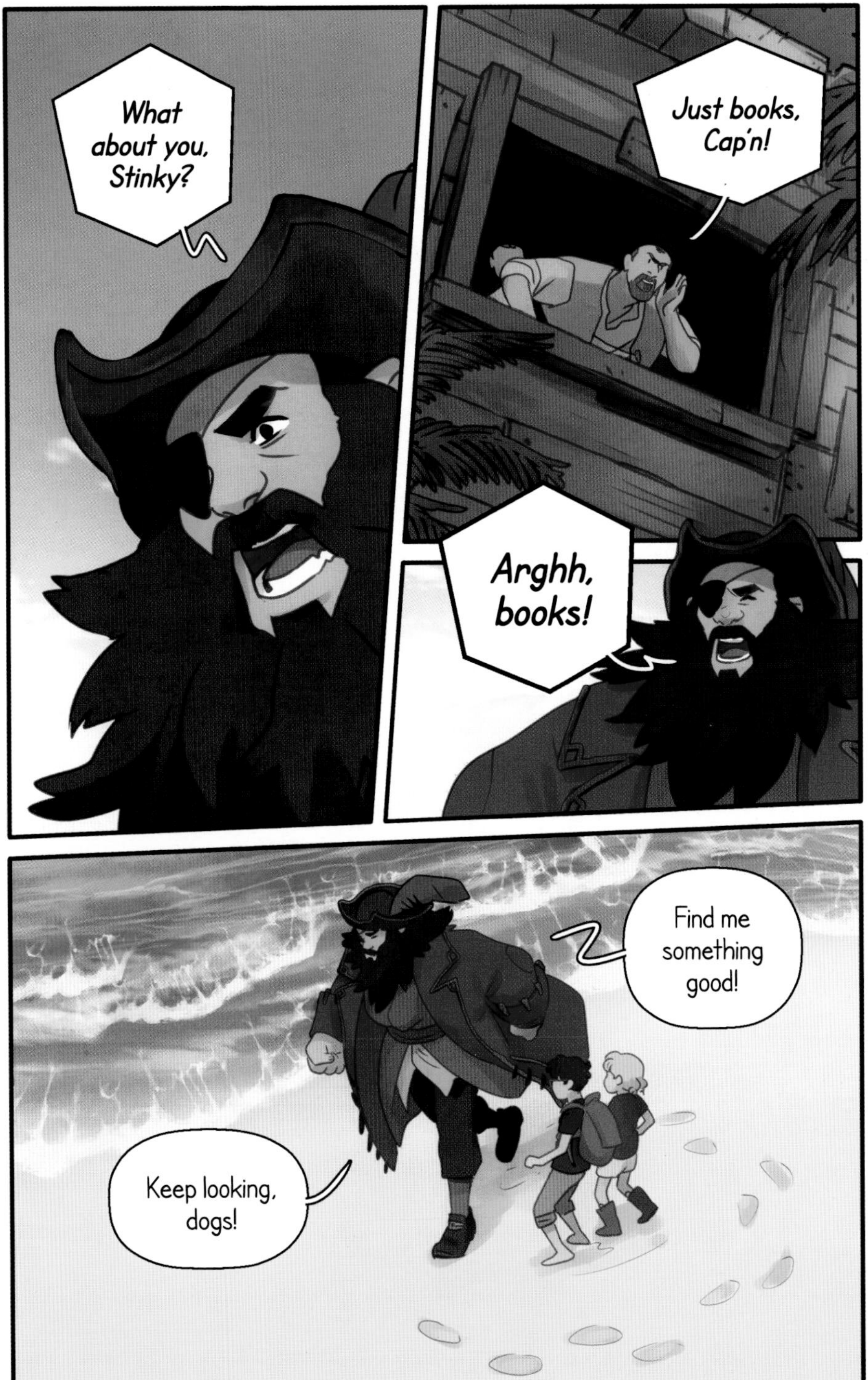
What about you, Stinky?
Just books, Cap'n!
Arghh, books!
Find me something good!
Keep looking, dogs!

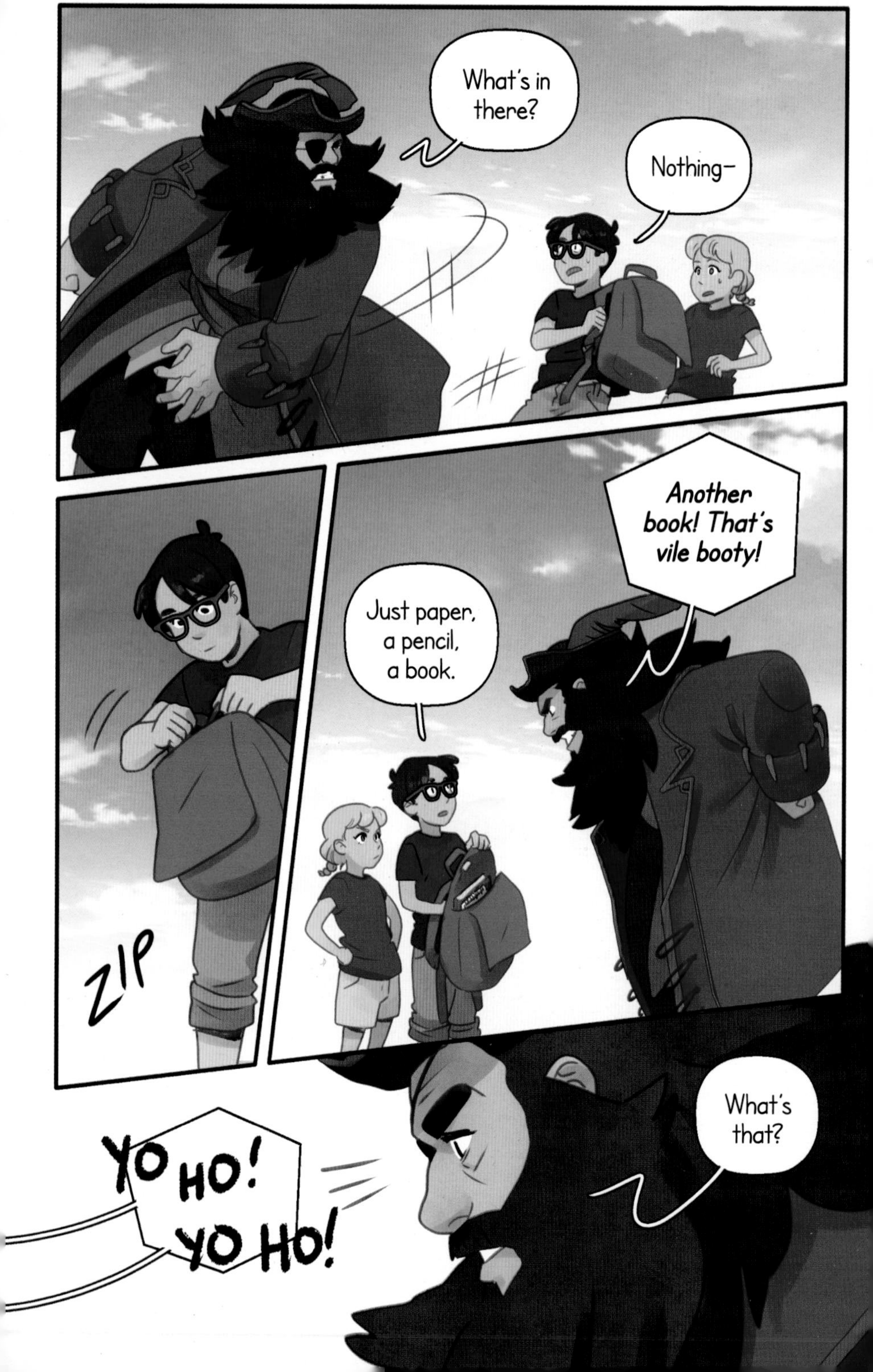
What's in there?
Nothing–
Just paper, a pencil, a book.
Another book! That's vile booty!
ZIP
YO HO! YO HO!
What's that?

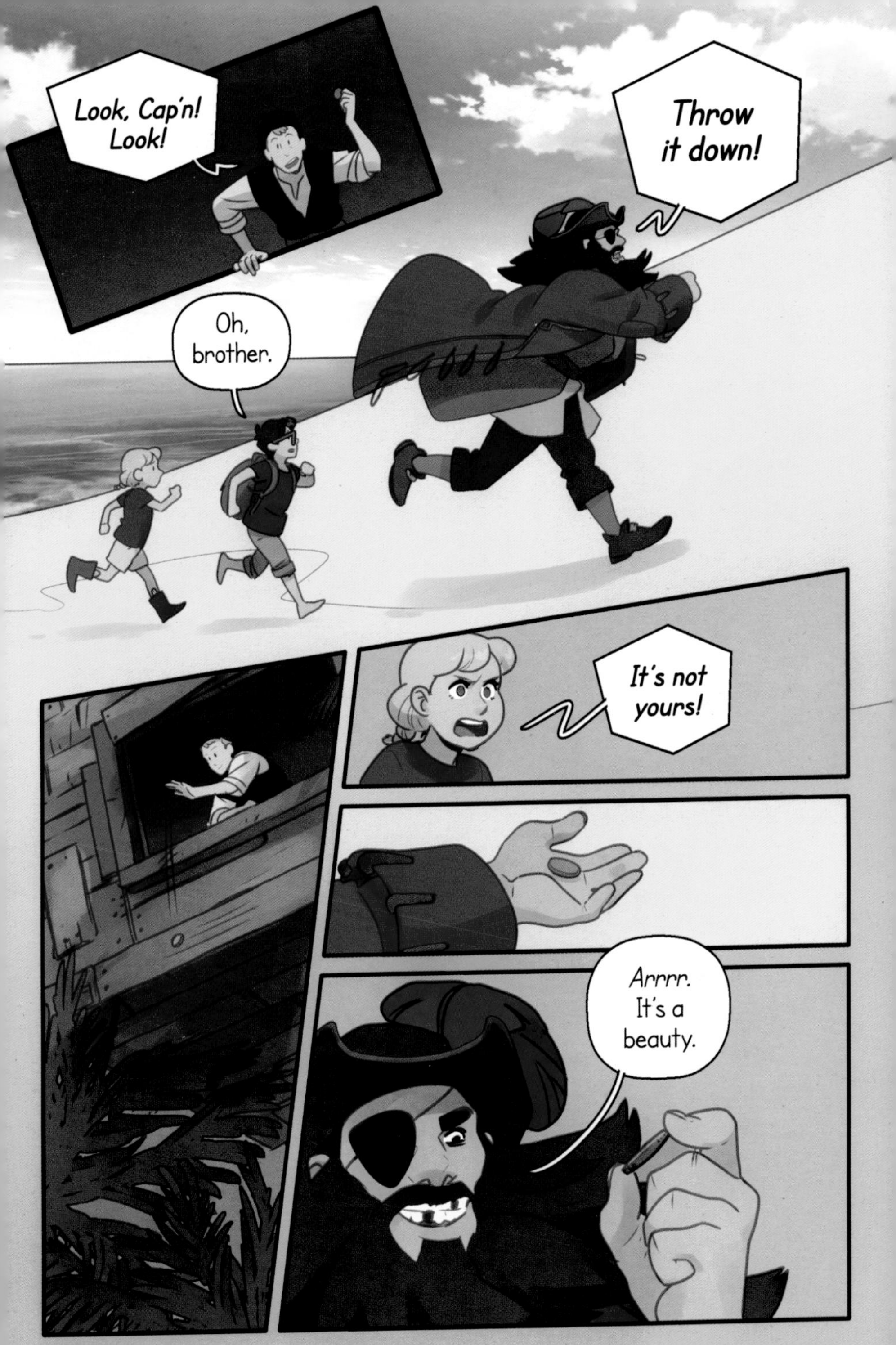

Look, Cap'n! Look!
Throw it down!
Oh, brother.
It's not yours!
Arrrr. It's a beauty.

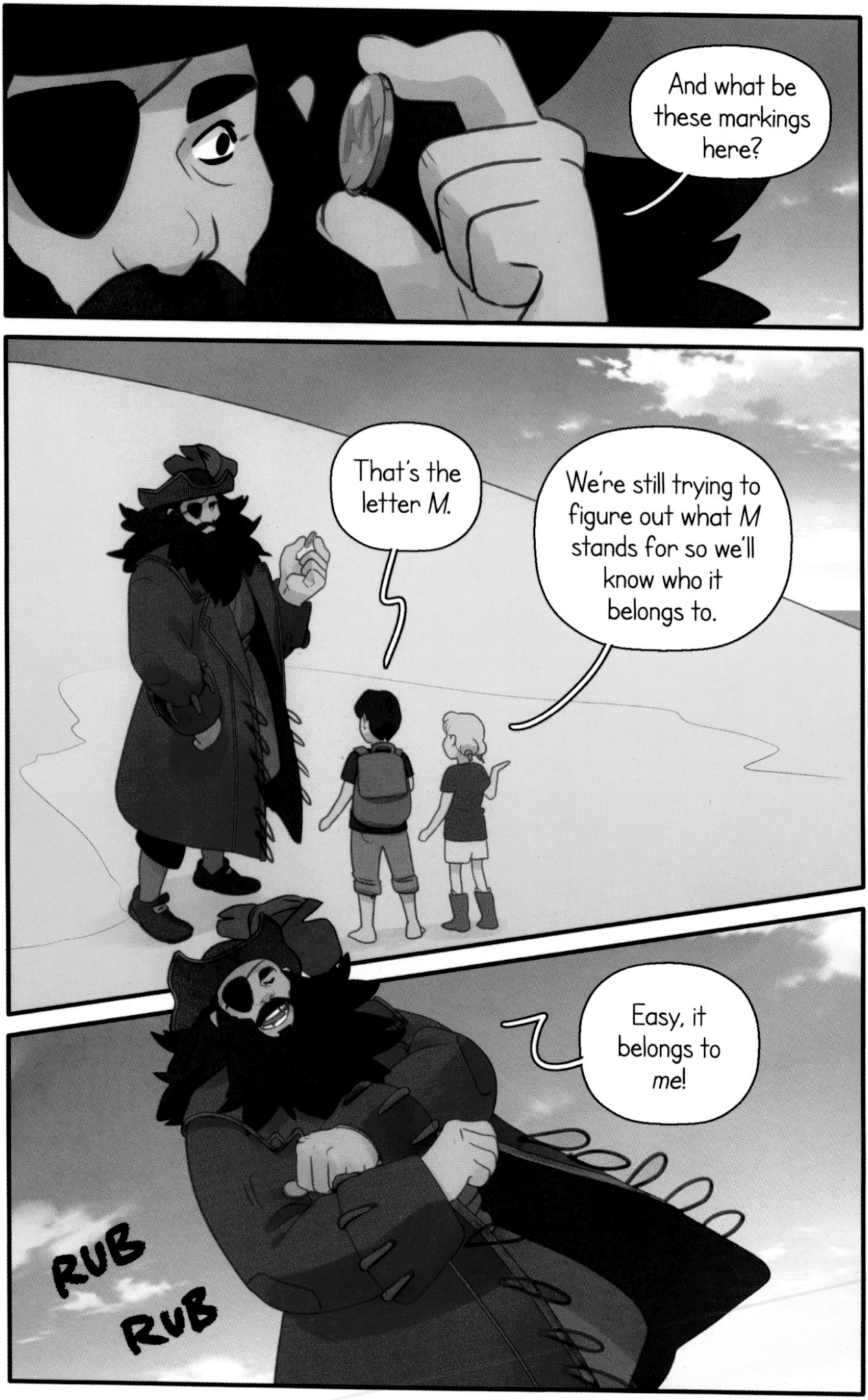
And what be these markings here?
That's the letter *M*.
We're still trying to figure out what *M* stands for so we'll know who it belongs to.
Easy, it belongs to *me*!
RUB
RUB

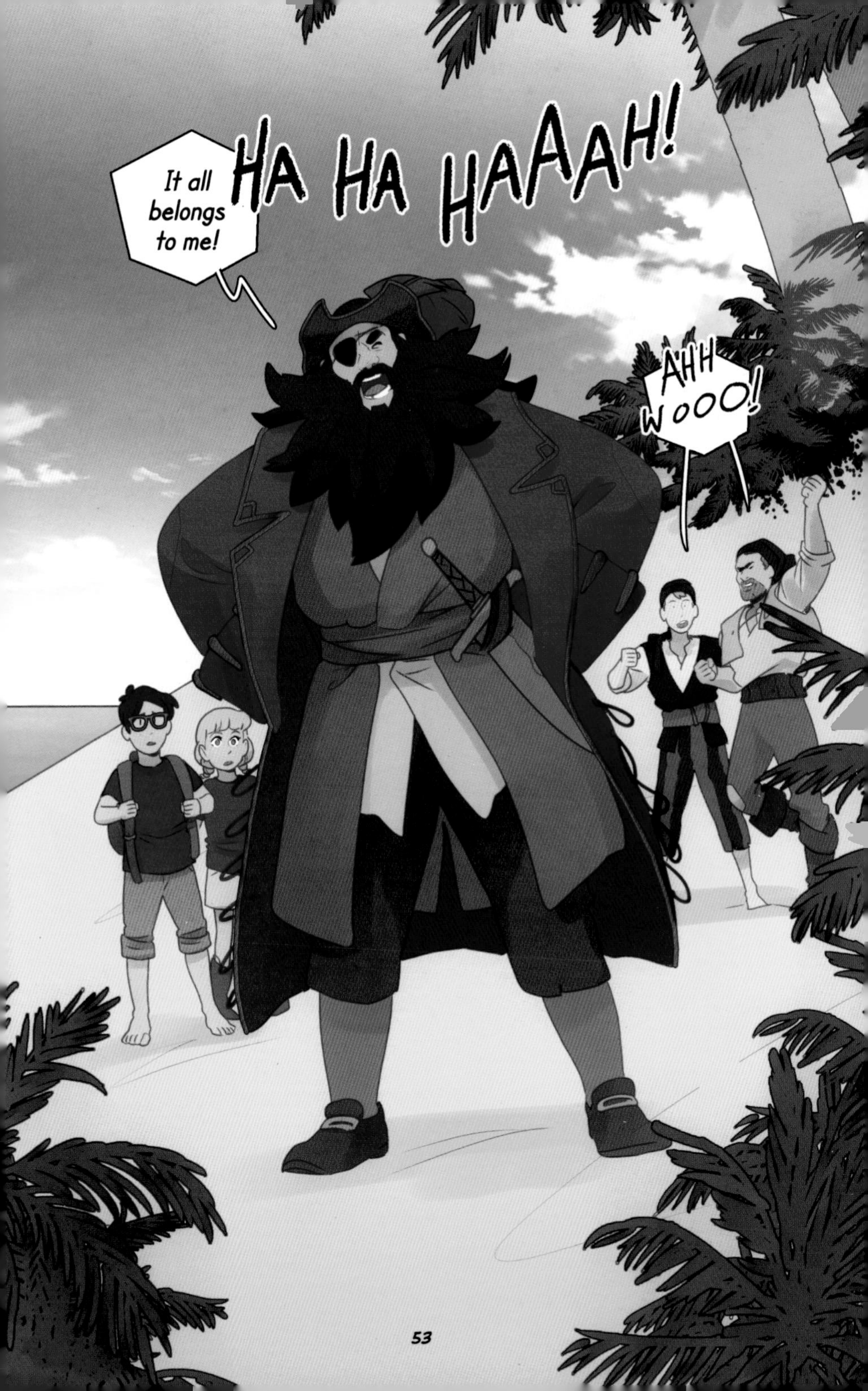
HA HA HAAAH!
It all belongs to me!
AHH WOOO!

CHAPTER FIVE
The Kid's Treasure

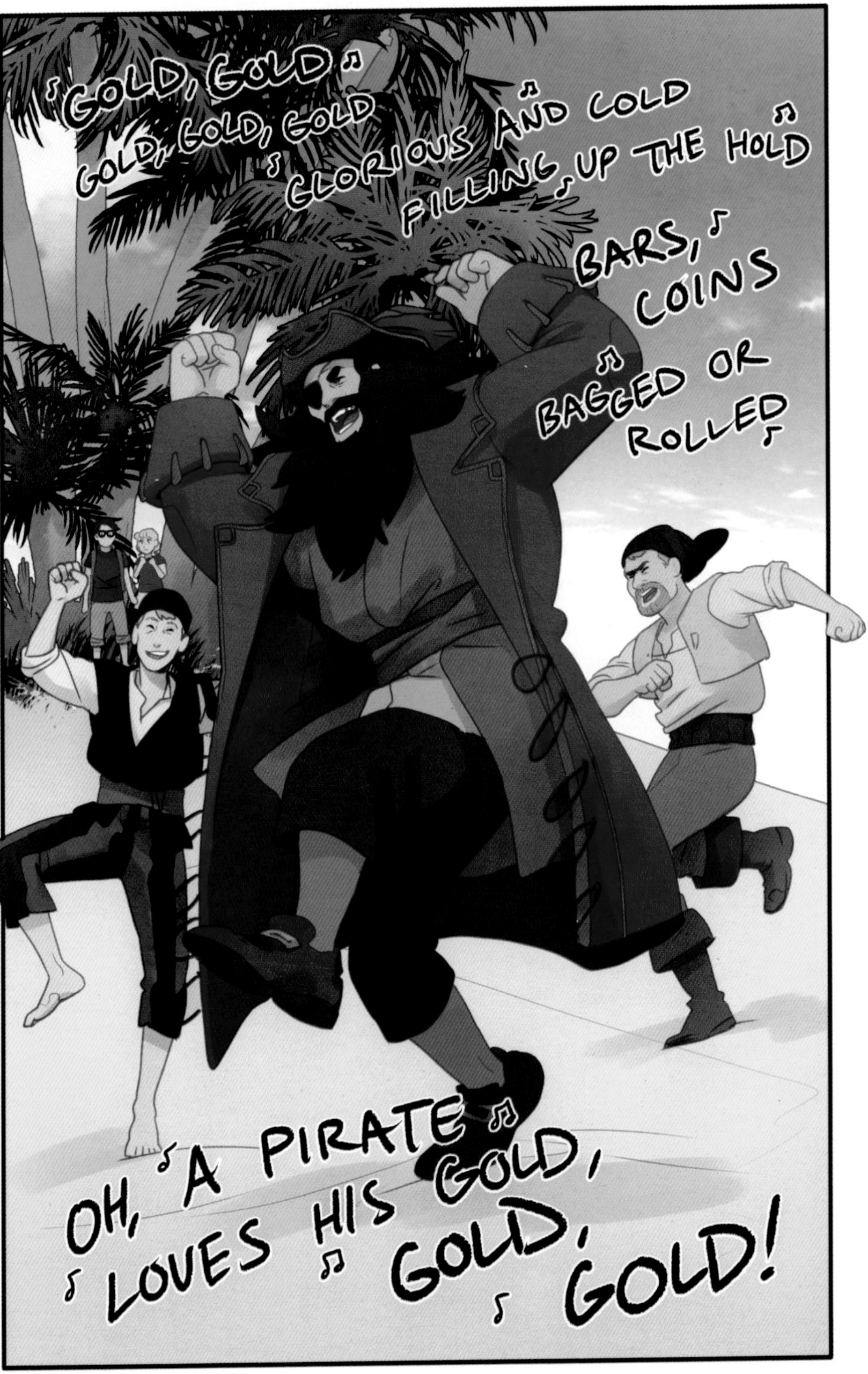
GOLD, GOLD
GOLD, GOLD, GOLD
GLORIOUS AND COLD
FILLING UP THE HOLD
BARS, COINS
BAGGED OR ROLLED
OH, A PIRATE LOVES HIS GOLD, GOLD, GOLD!

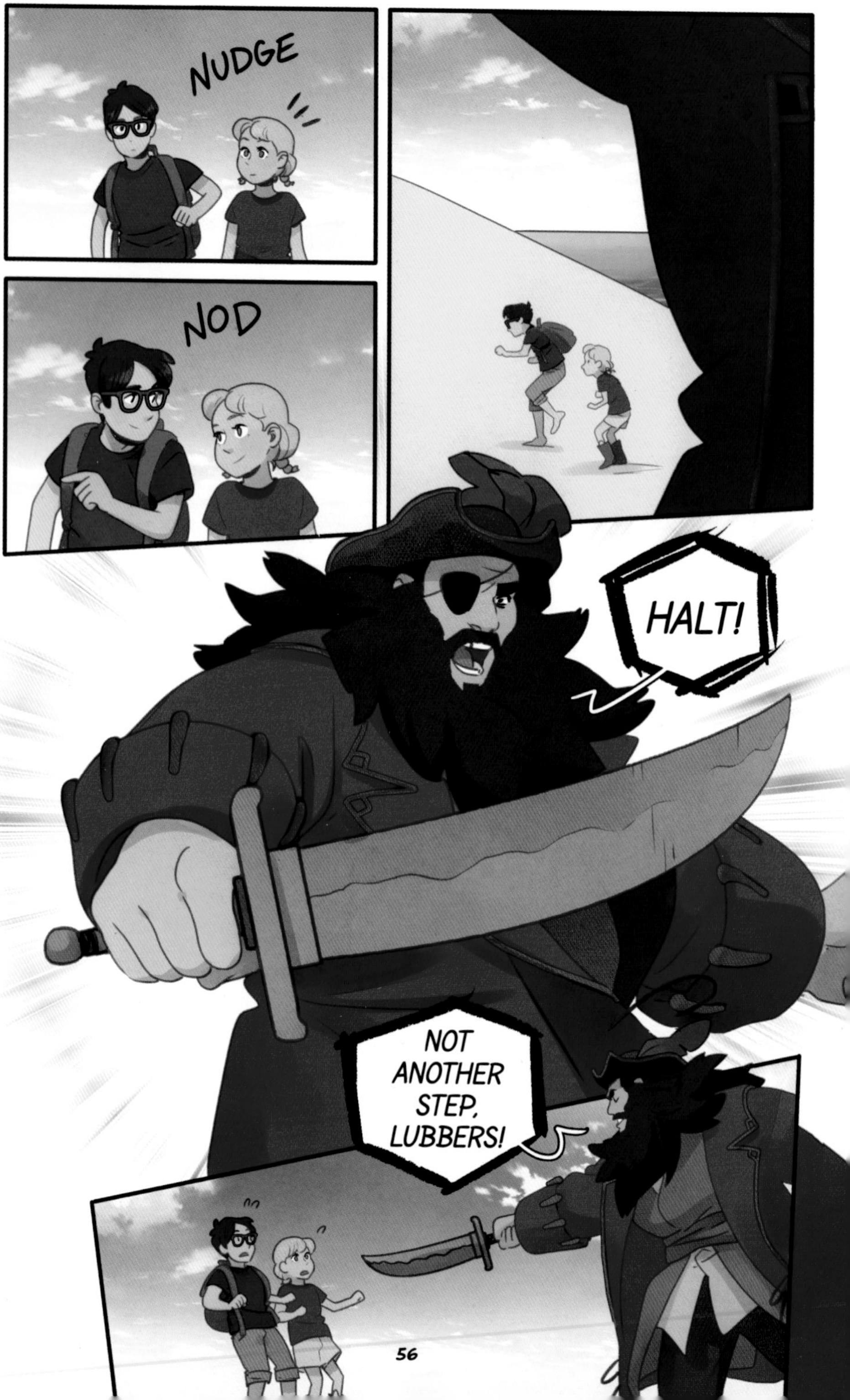
NUDGE
NOD
HALT!
NOT ANOTHER STEP, LUBBERS!

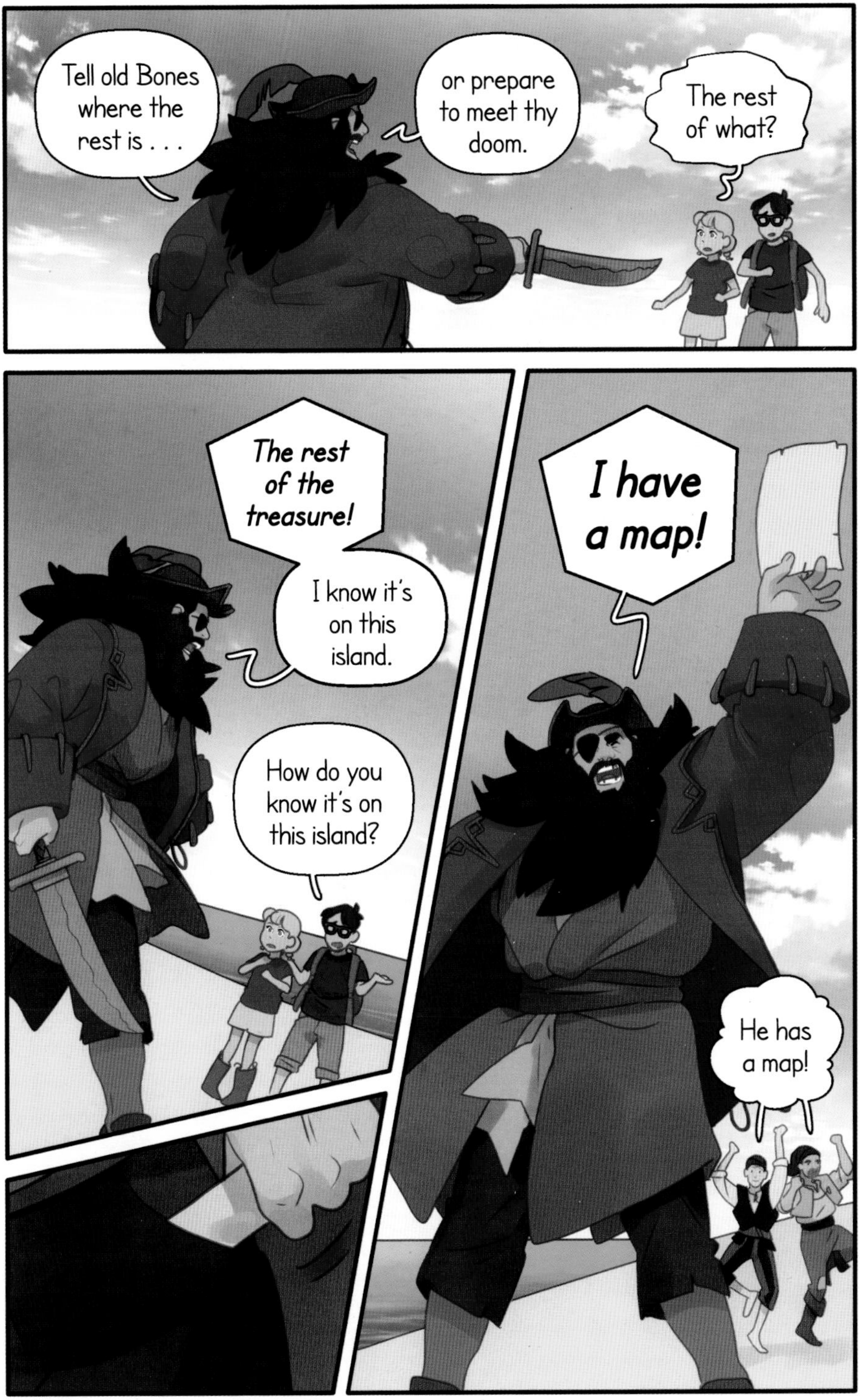
Tell old Bones where the rest is . . .
or prepare to meet thy doom.
The rest of what?
The rest of the treasure!
I know it's on this island.
How do you know it's on this island?
I have a map!
He has a map!

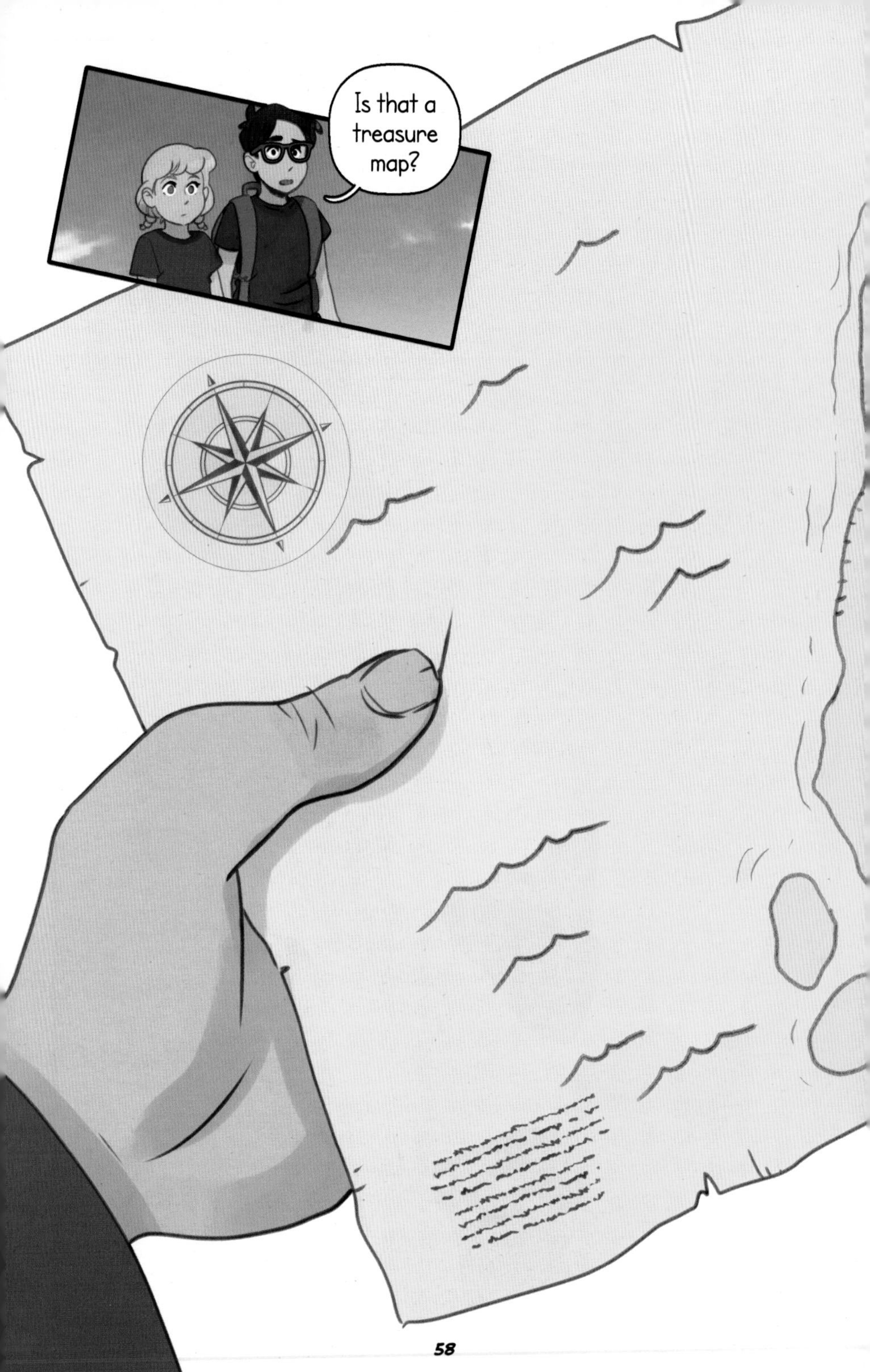
Is that a treasure map?

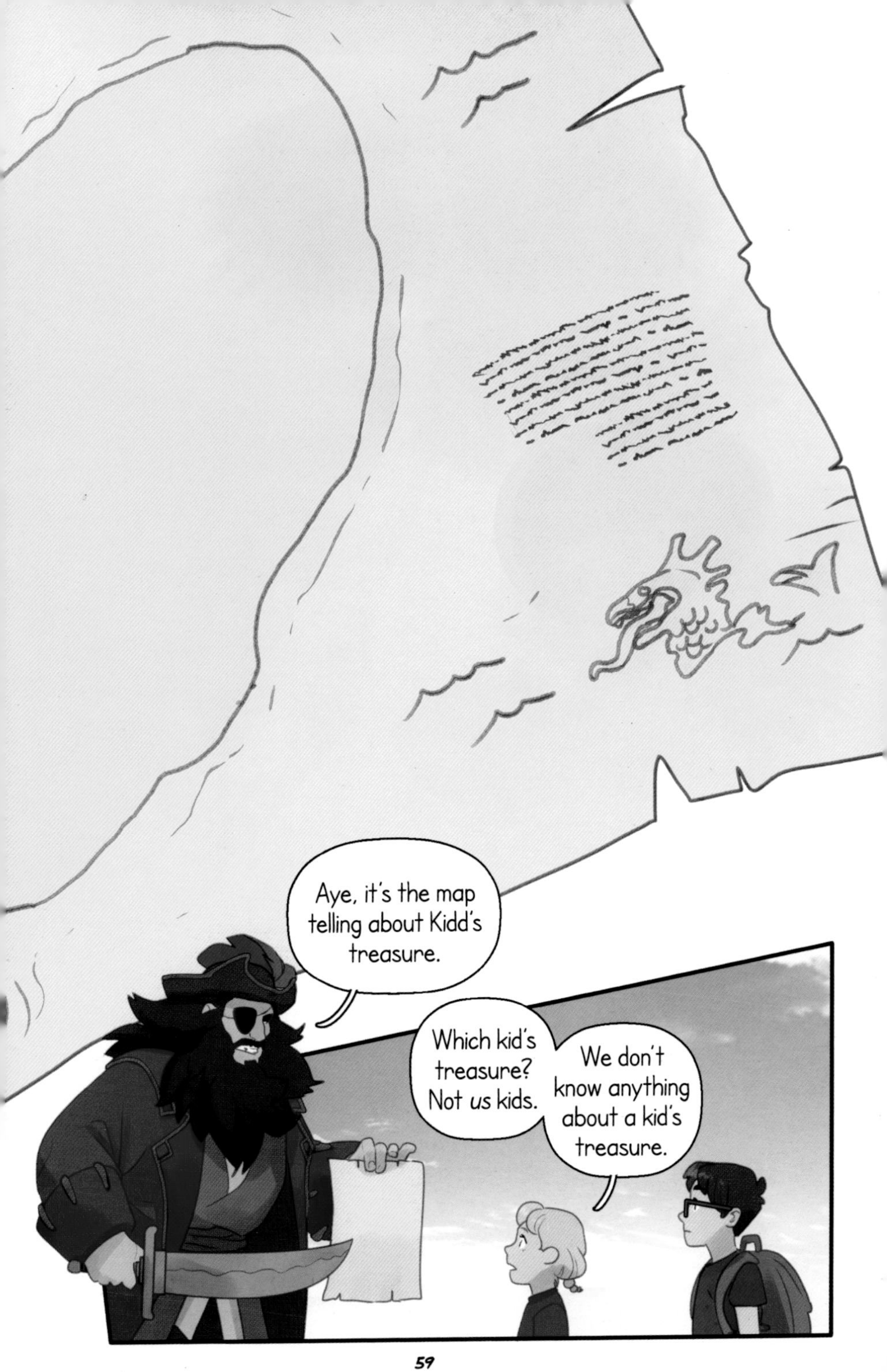
Aye, it's the map telling about Kidd's treasure.
Which kid's treasure? Not *us* kids.
We don't know anything about a kid's treasure.

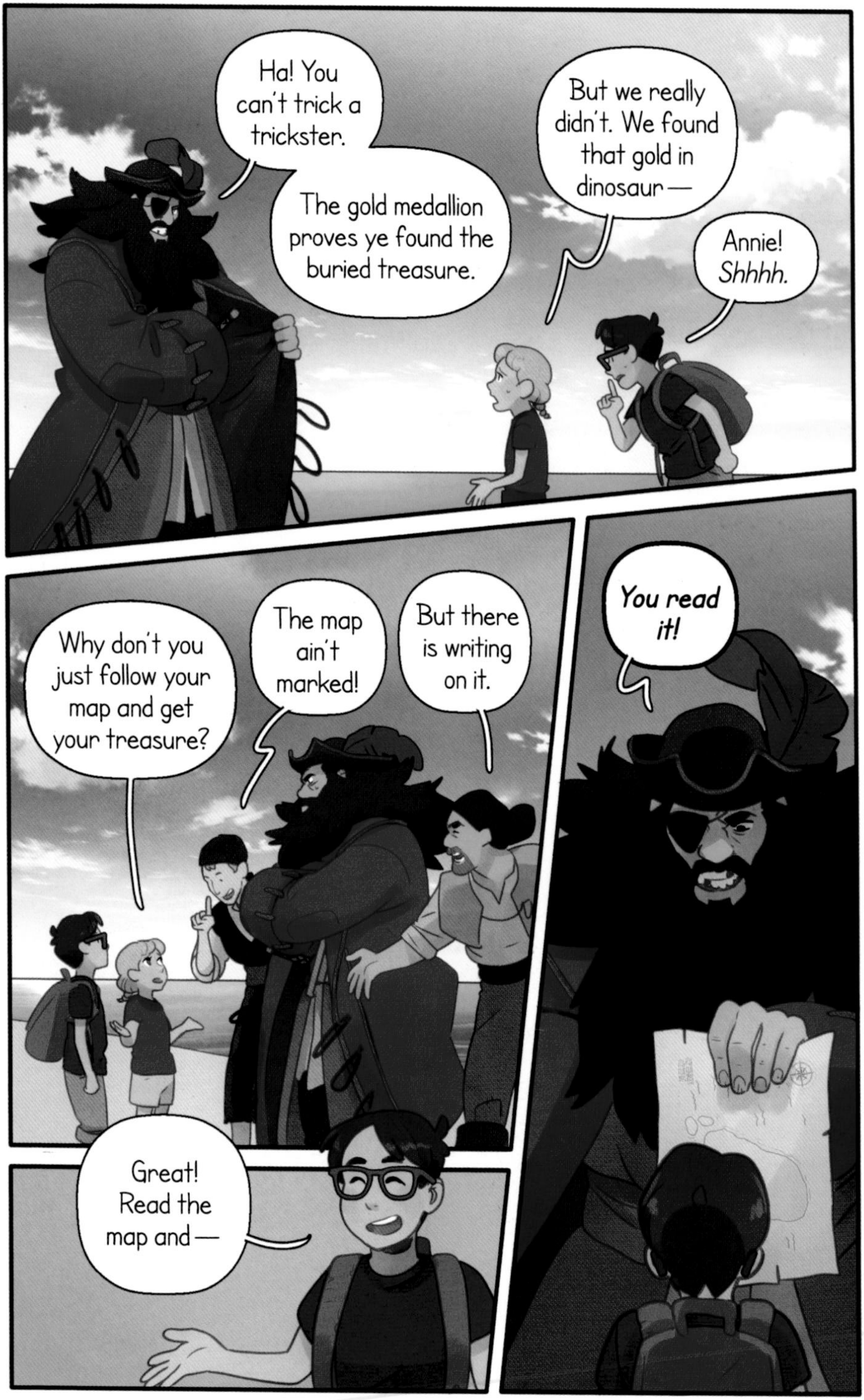
Ha! You can't trick a trickster.
The gold medallion proves ye found the buried treasure.
But we really didn't. We found that gold in dinosaur—
Annie! *Shhhh.*
Why don't you just follow your map and get your treasure?
The map ain't marked!
But there is writing on it.
Great! Read the map and—
You read it!

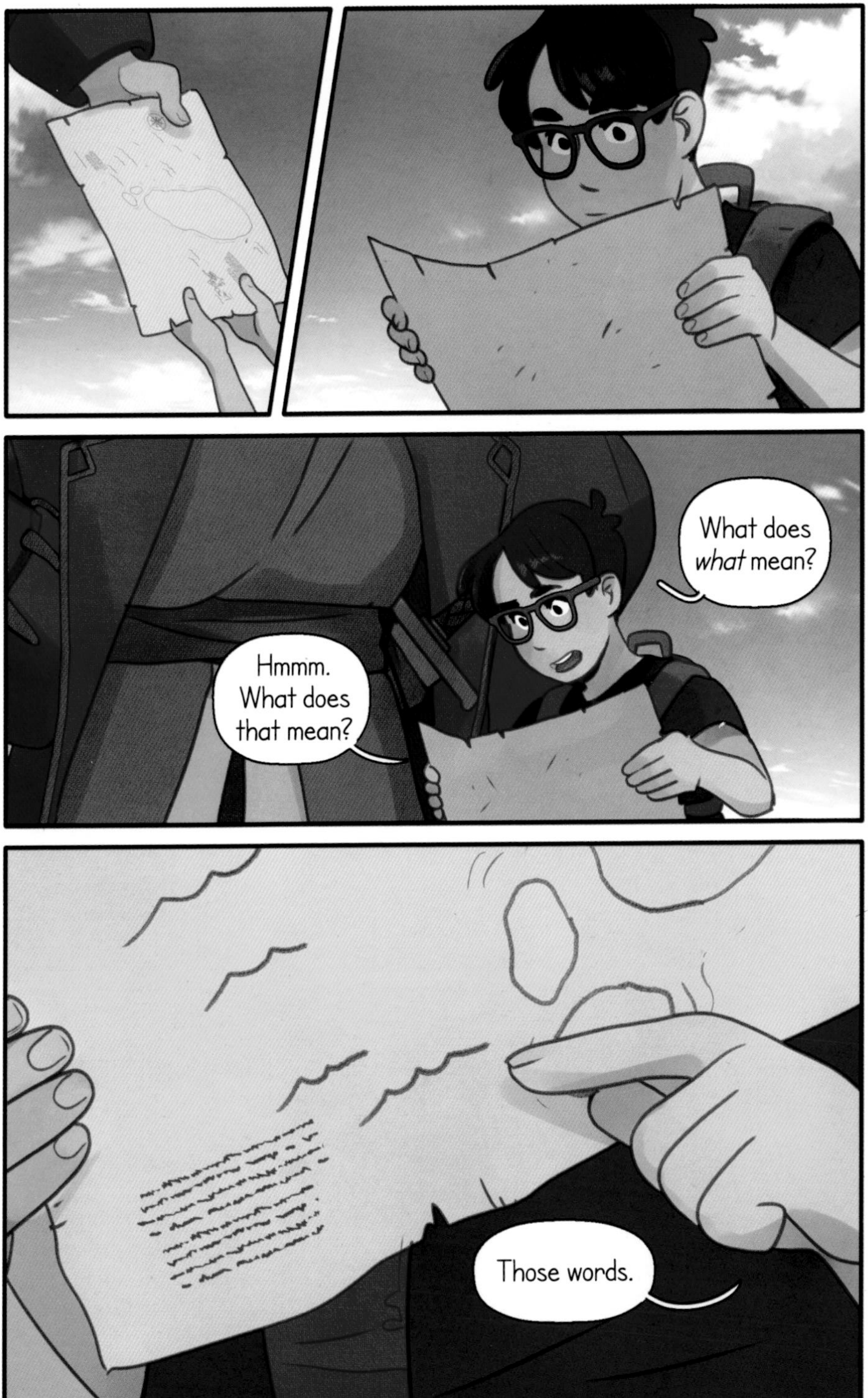
Hmmm.
What does
that mean?
What does
what mean?
Those words.

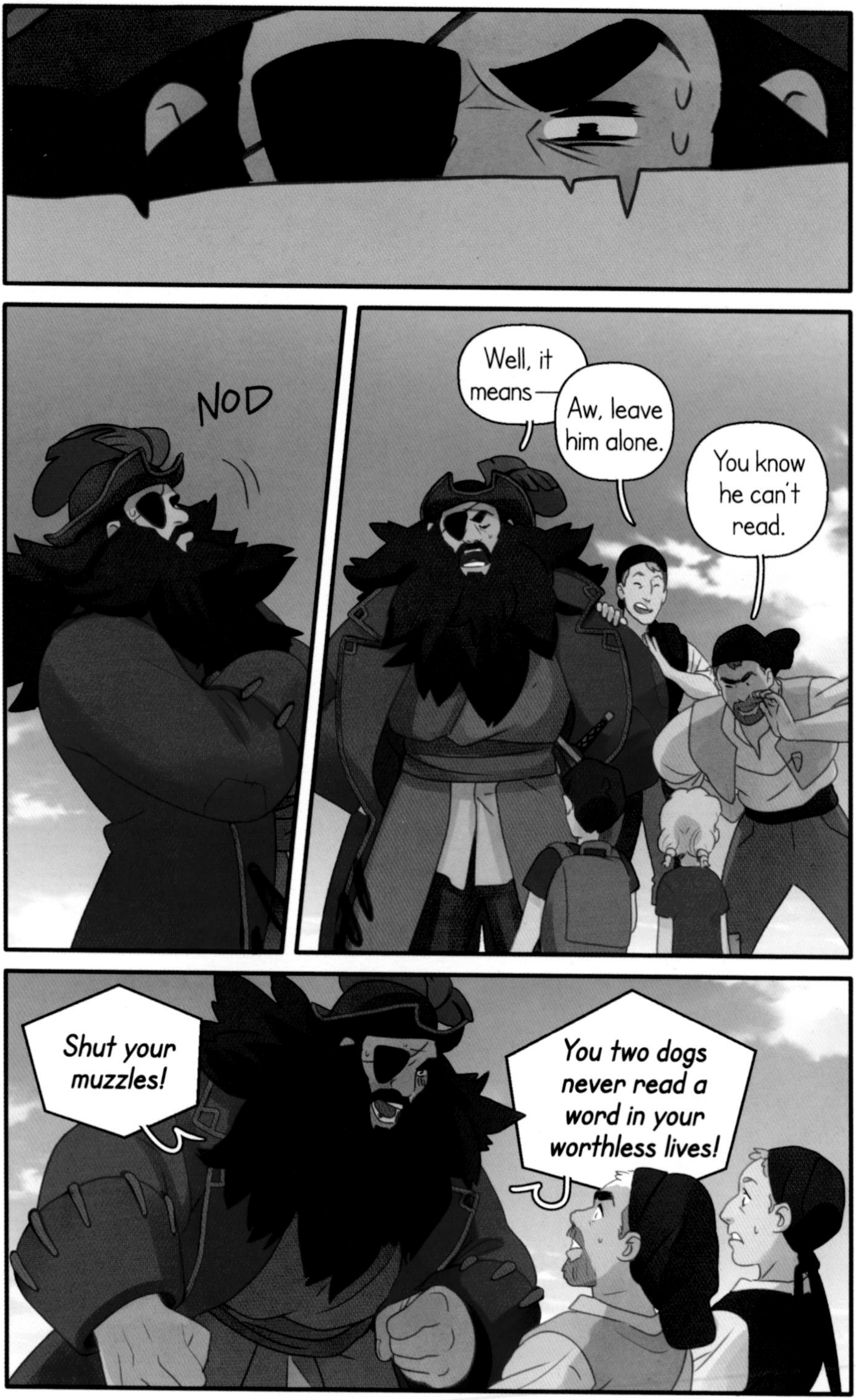
NOD
Well, it means—
Aw, leave him alone.
You know he can't read.
Shut your muzzles!
You two dogs never read a word in your worthless lives!

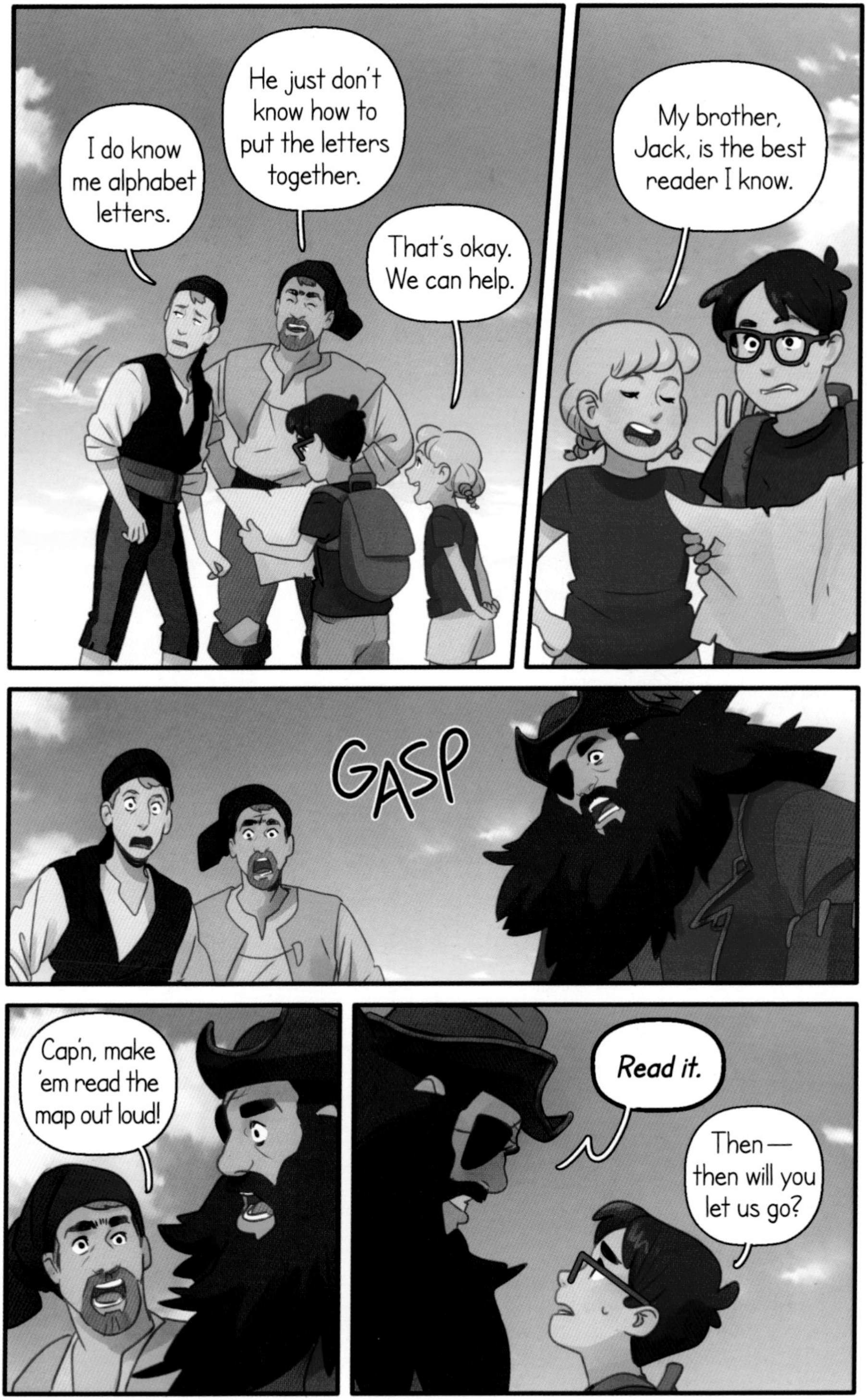
I do know me alphabet letters.
He just don't know how to put the letters together.
That's okay. We can help.
My brother, Jack, is the best reader I know.
GASP
Cap'n, make 'em read the map out loud!
Read it.
Then— then will you let us go?

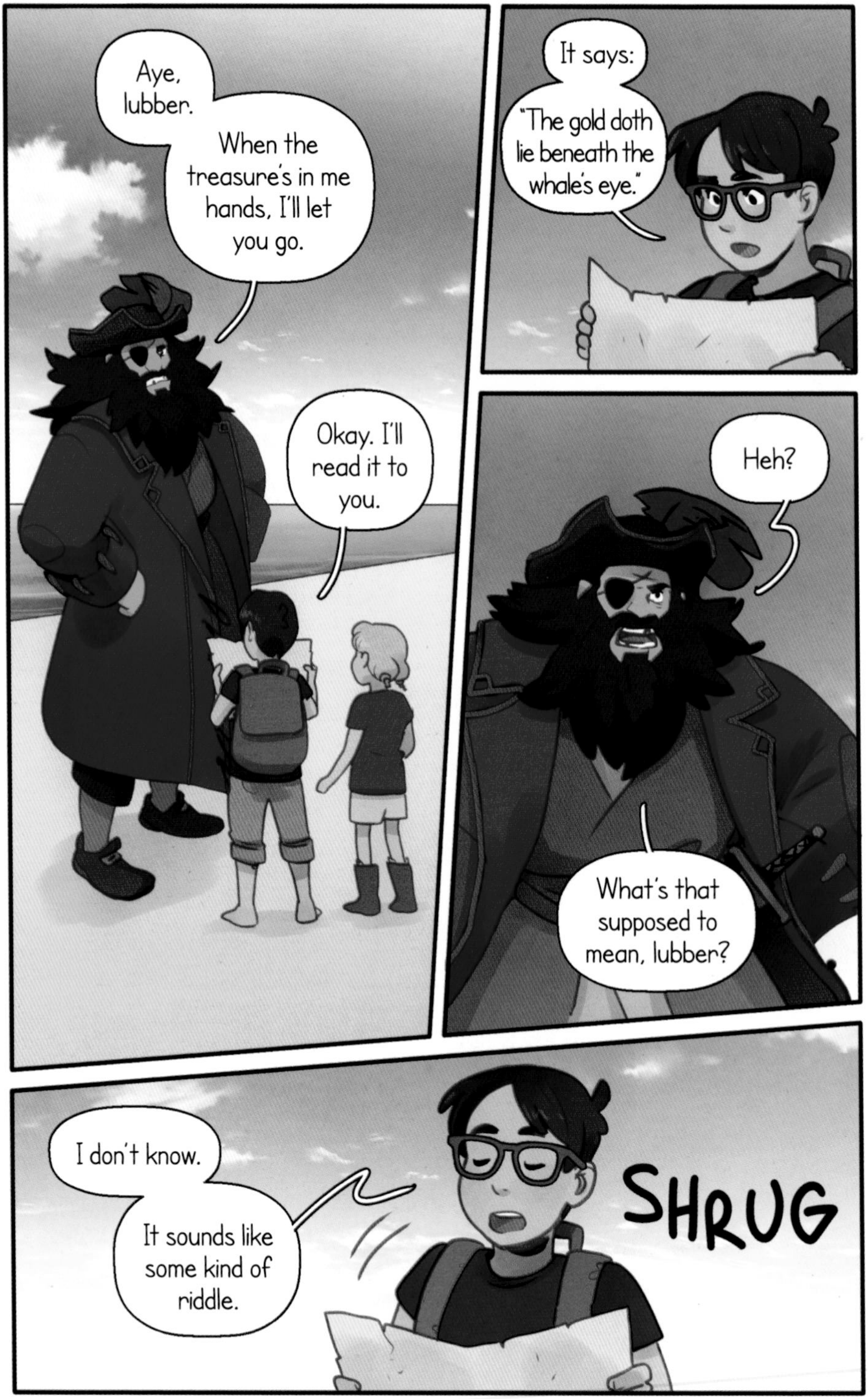
Aye, lubber.
When the treasure's in me hands, I'll let you go.
Okay. I'll read it to you.
It says:
"The gold doth lie beneath the whale's eye."
Heh?
What's that supposed to mean, lubber?
I don't know.
It sounds like some kind of riddle.
SHRUG

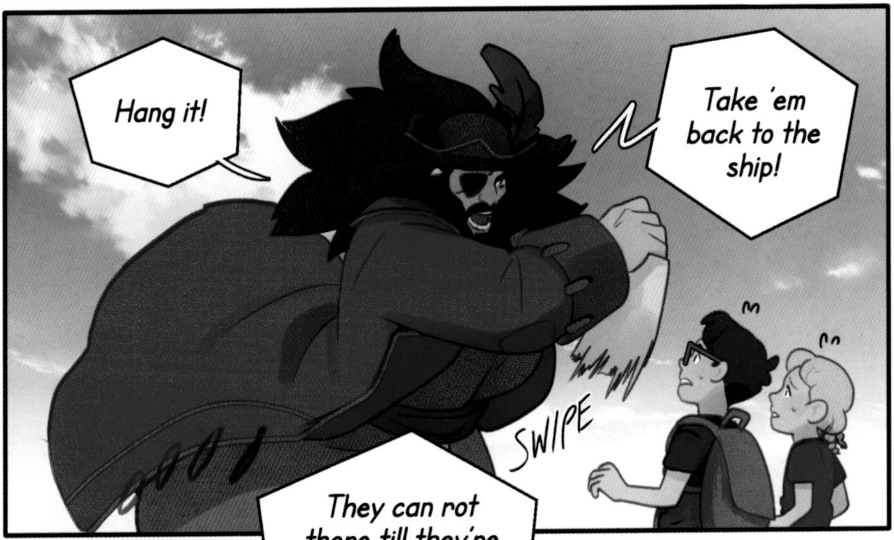
Hang it!
Take 'em back to the ship!
SWIPE

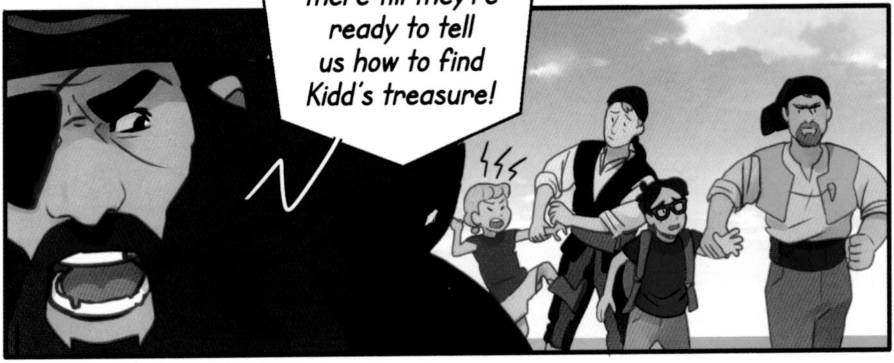
They can rot there till they're ready to tell us how to find Kidd's treasure!

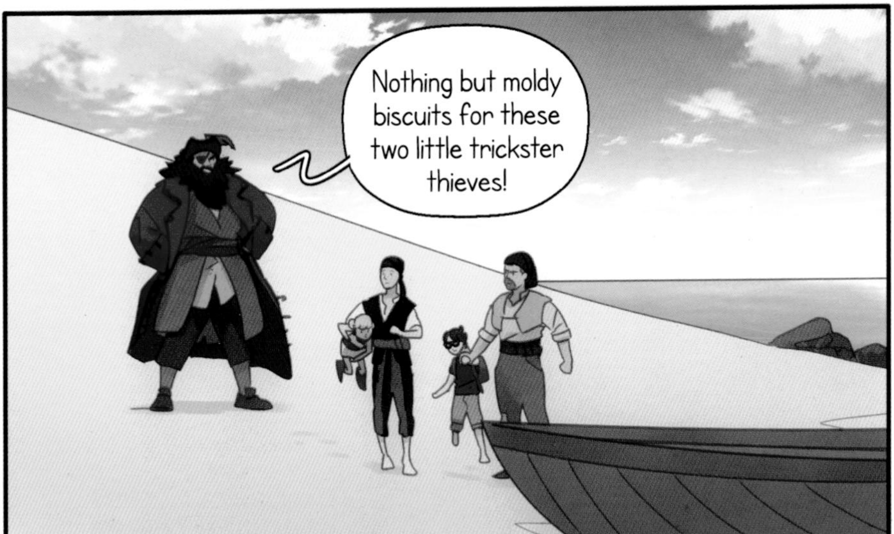
Nothing but moldy biscuits for these two little trickster thieves!

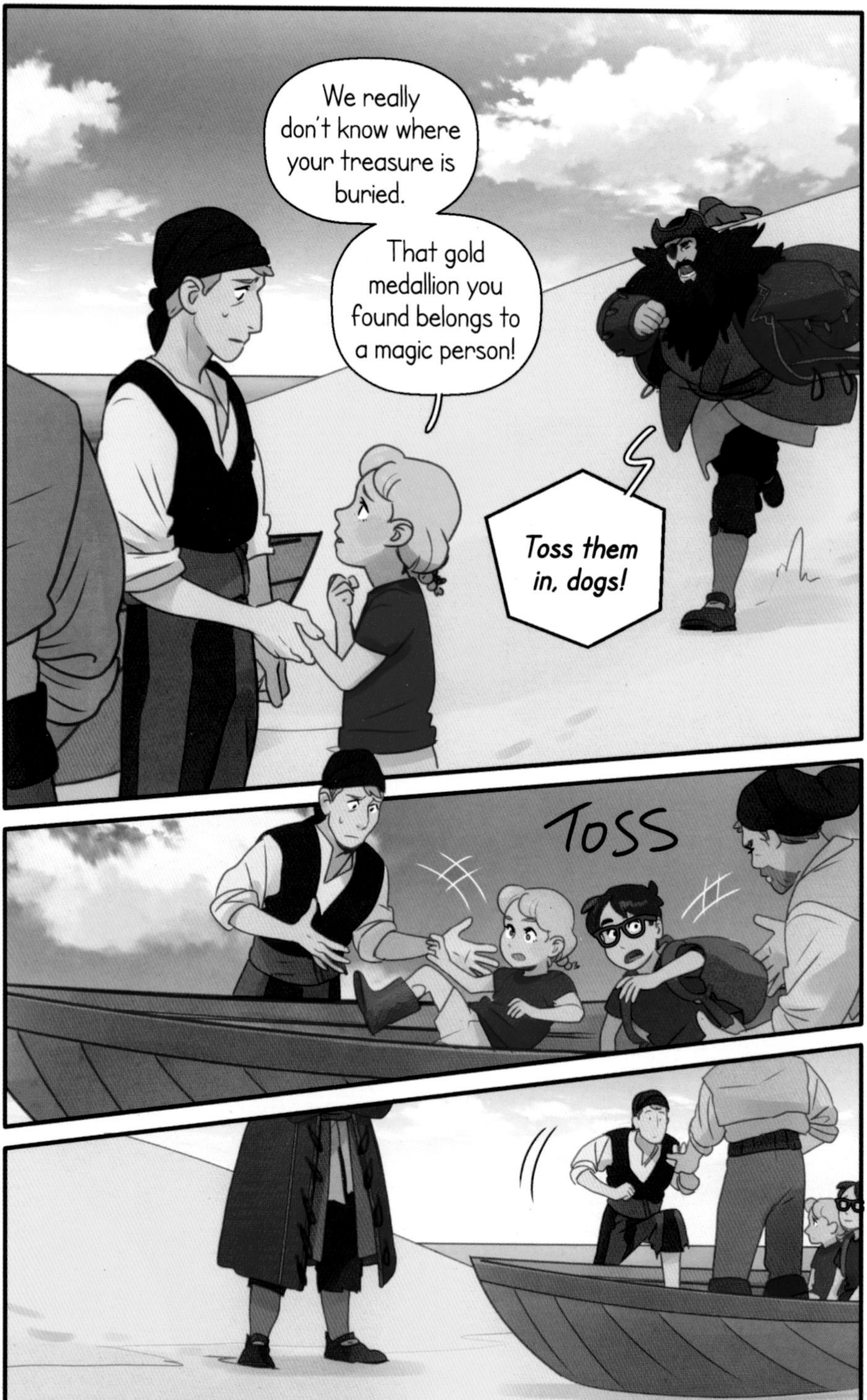
We really don't know where your treasure is buried.
That gold medallion you found belongs to a magic person!
Toss them in, dogs!
TOSS

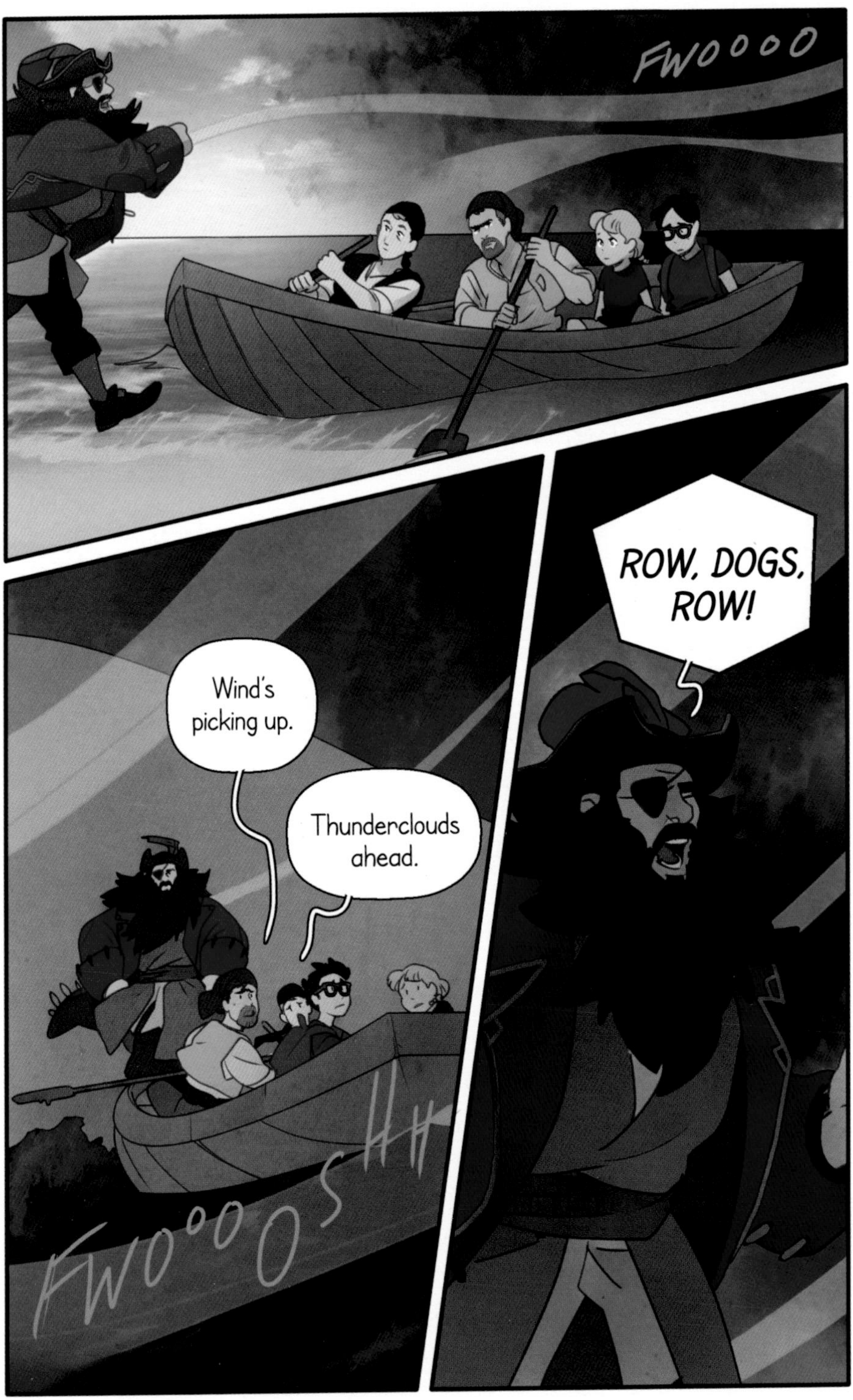
FWOOOO
Wind's picking up.
Thunderclouds ahead.
FWOOOOSHH
ROW, DOGS, ROW!

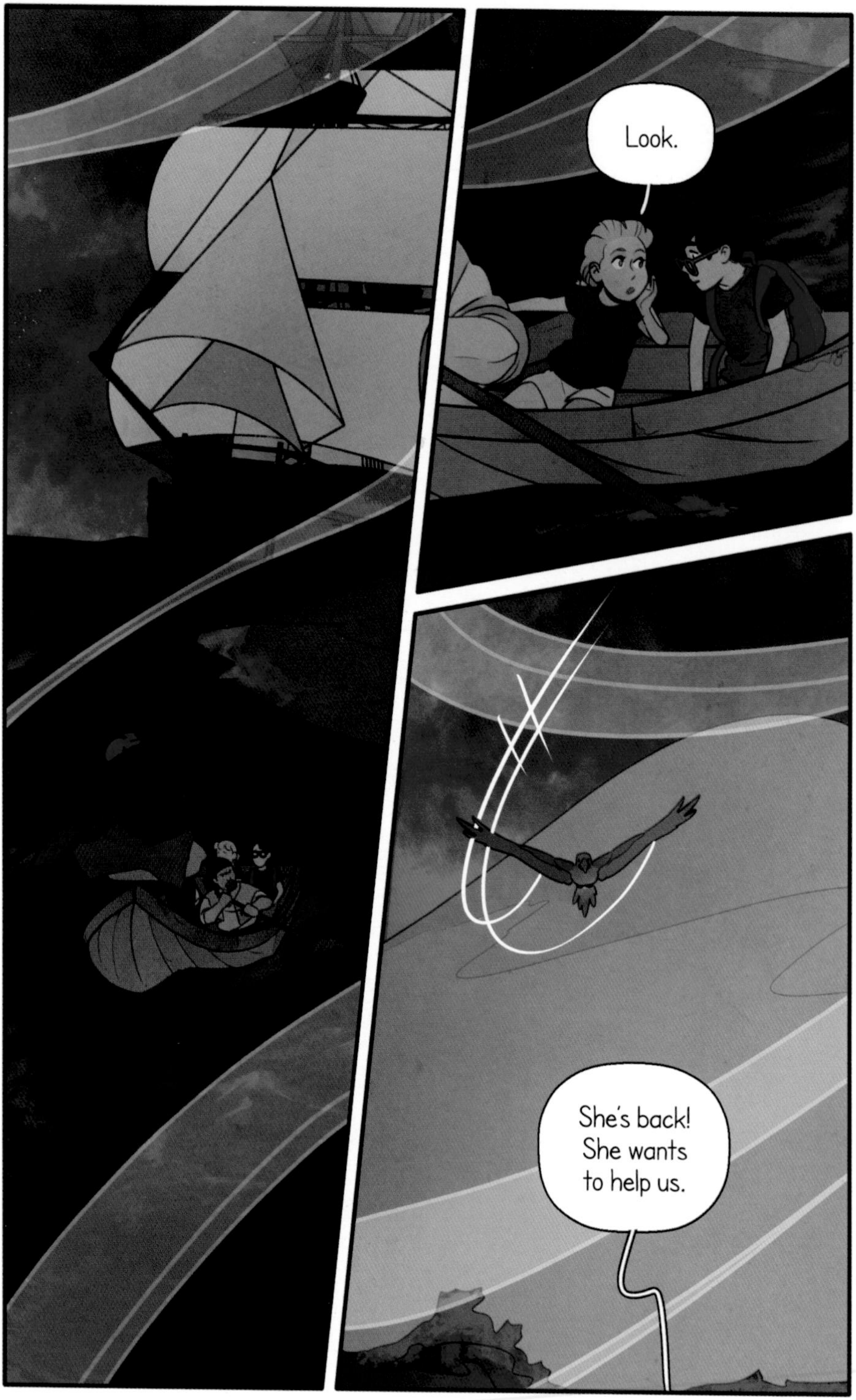
Look.
She's back! She wants to help us.

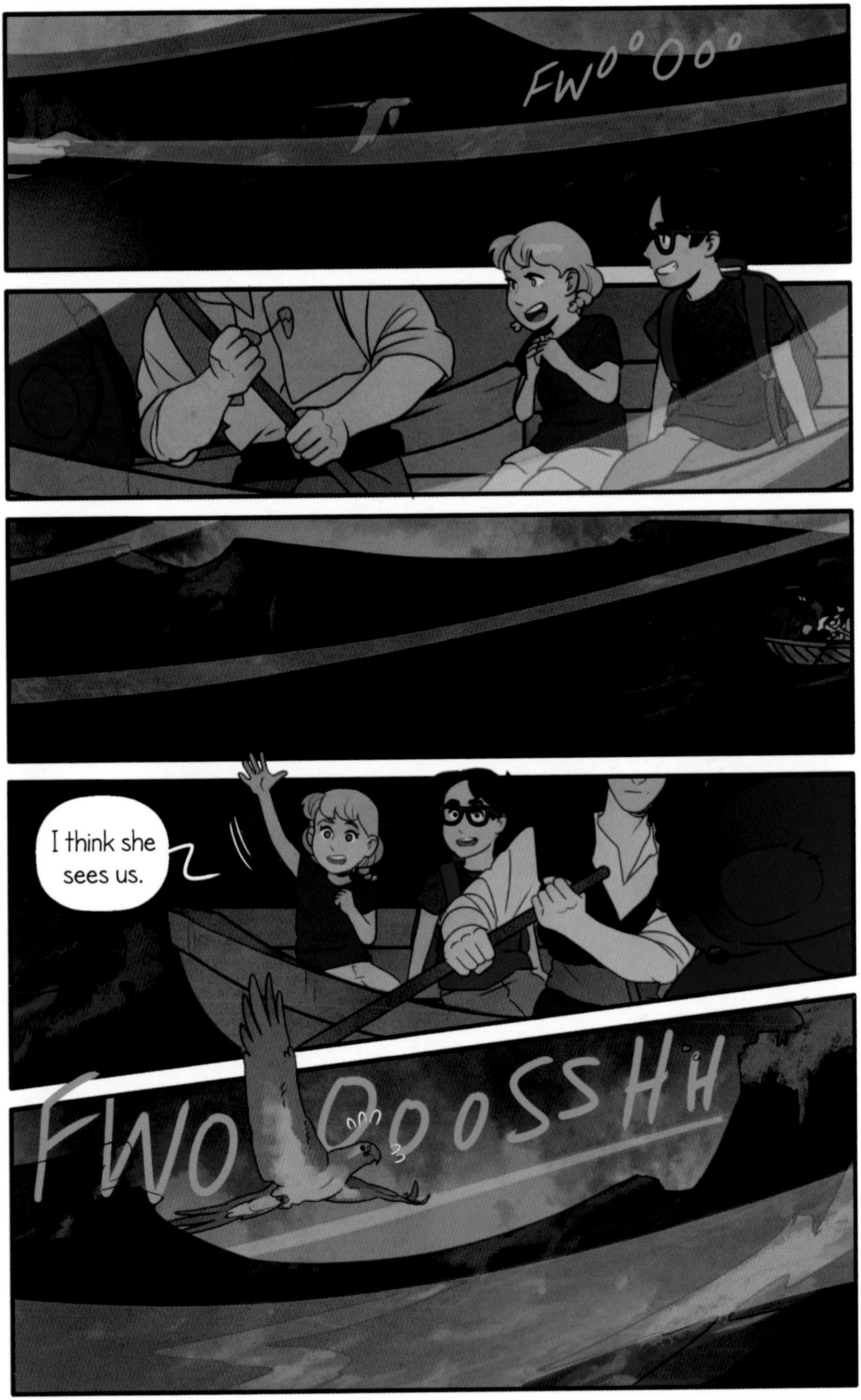
FWOOOOO
I think she sees us.
FWOOOOSSHH

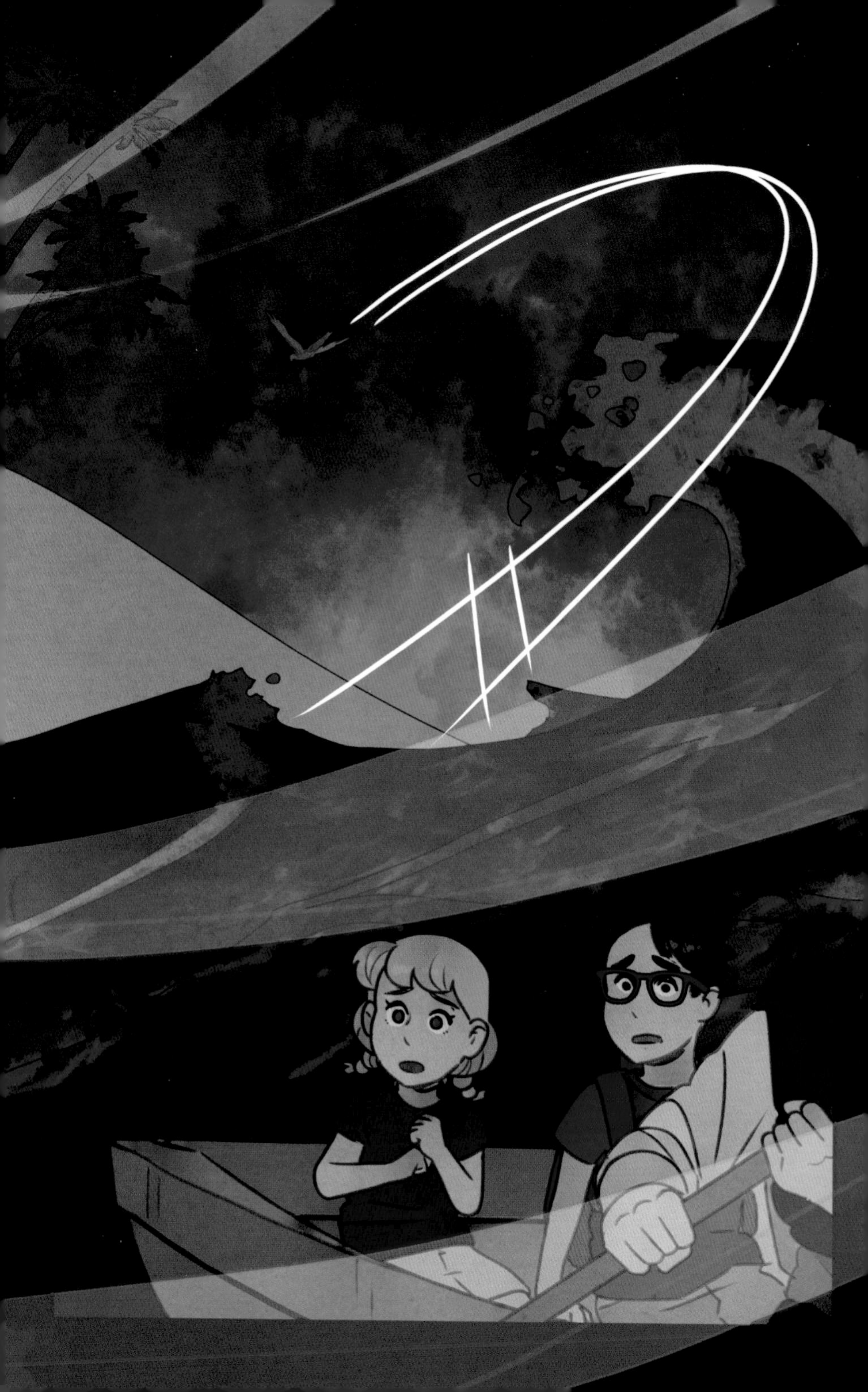

CHAPTER SIX
The Whale's Eye

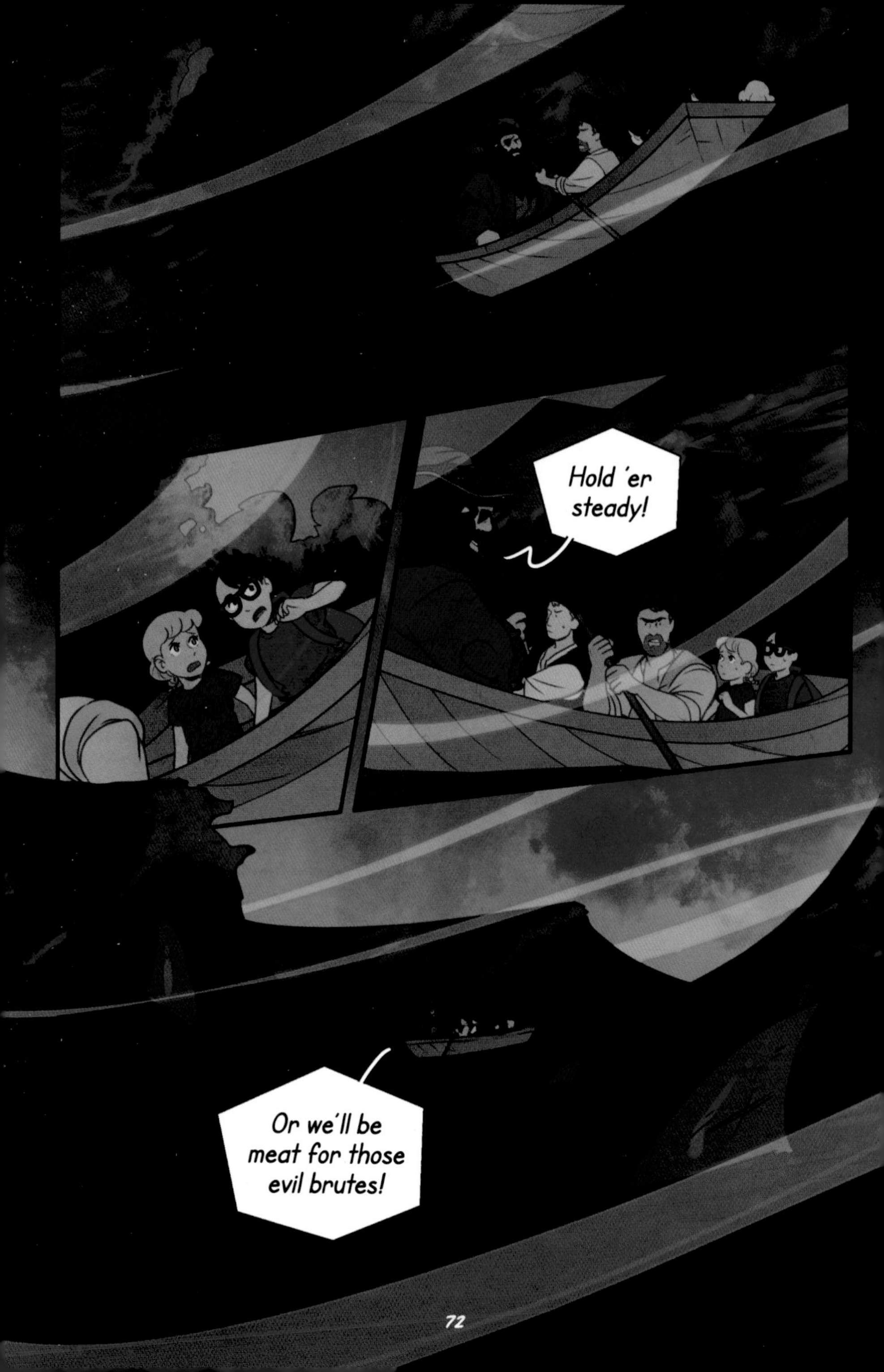
Hold 'er steady!
Or we'll be meat for those evil brutes!

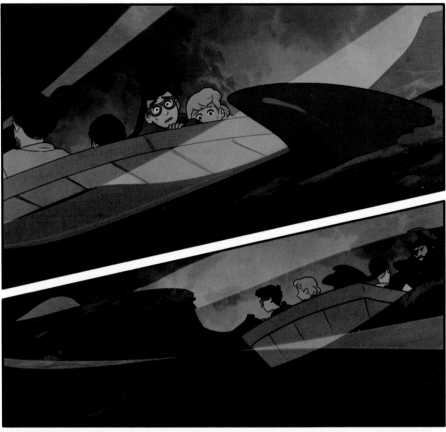

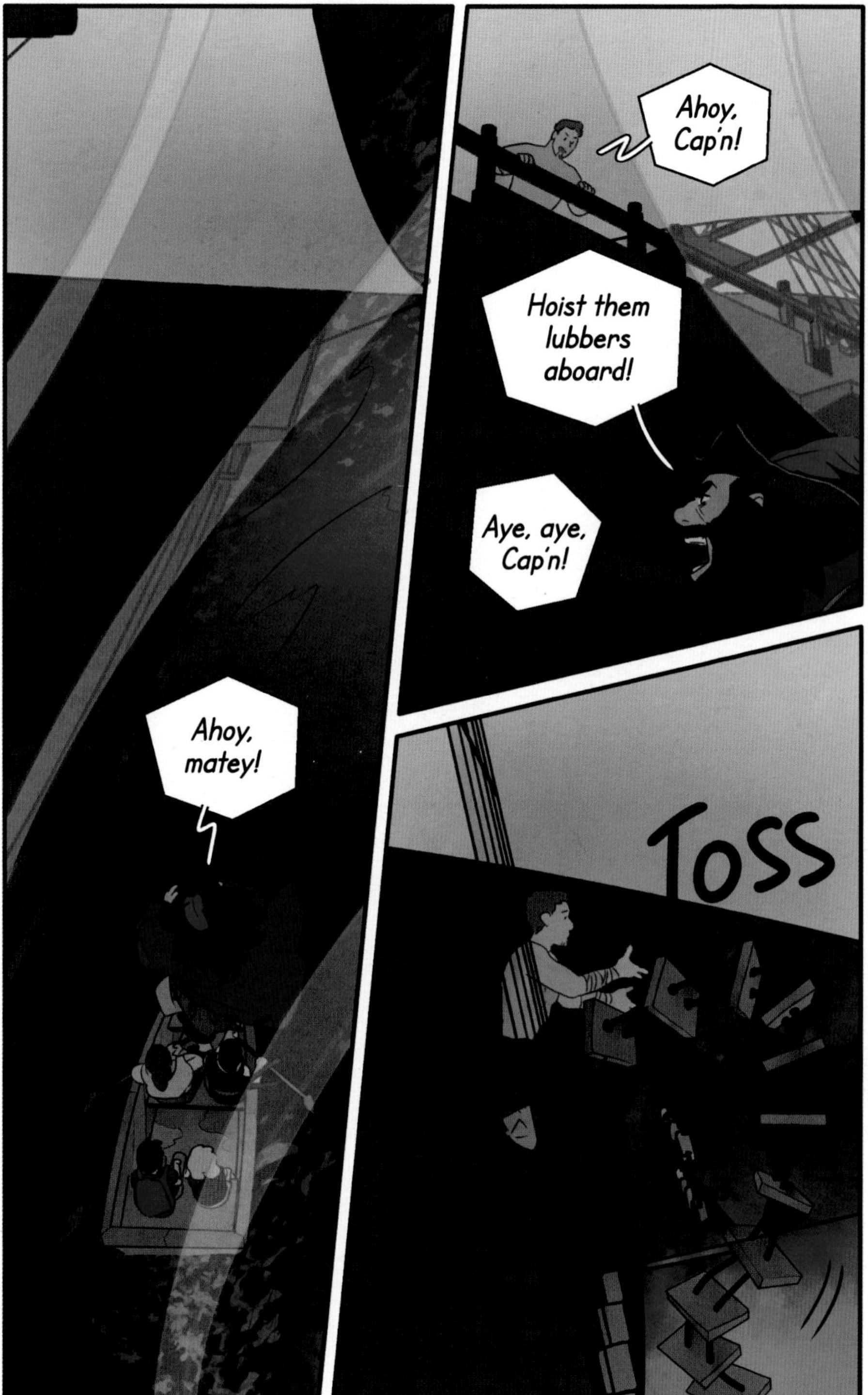
Ahoy, matey!
Ahoy, Cap'n!
Hoist them lubbers aboard!
Aye, aye, Cap'n!
TOSS

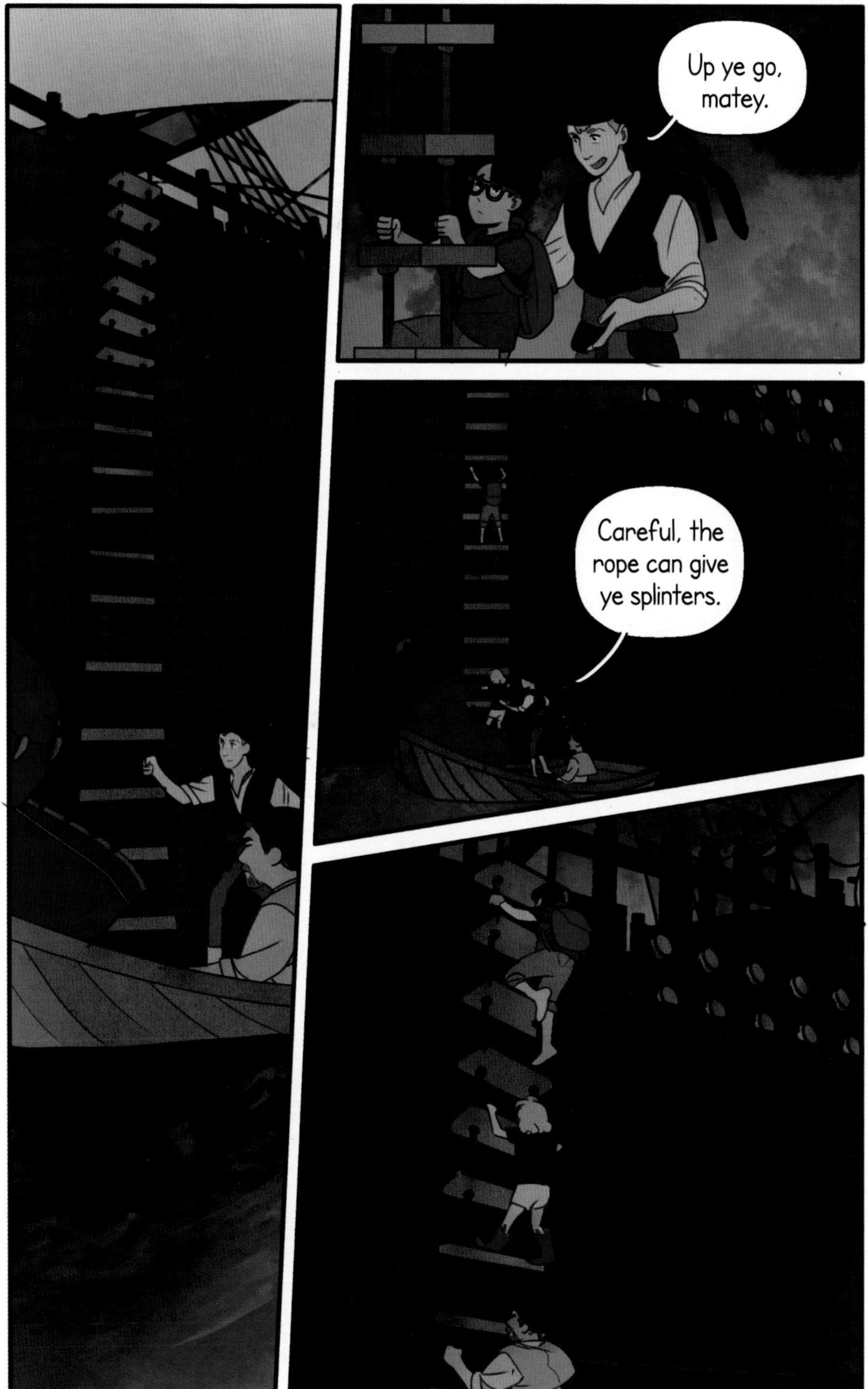
Up ye go, matey.
Careful, the rope can give ye splinters.

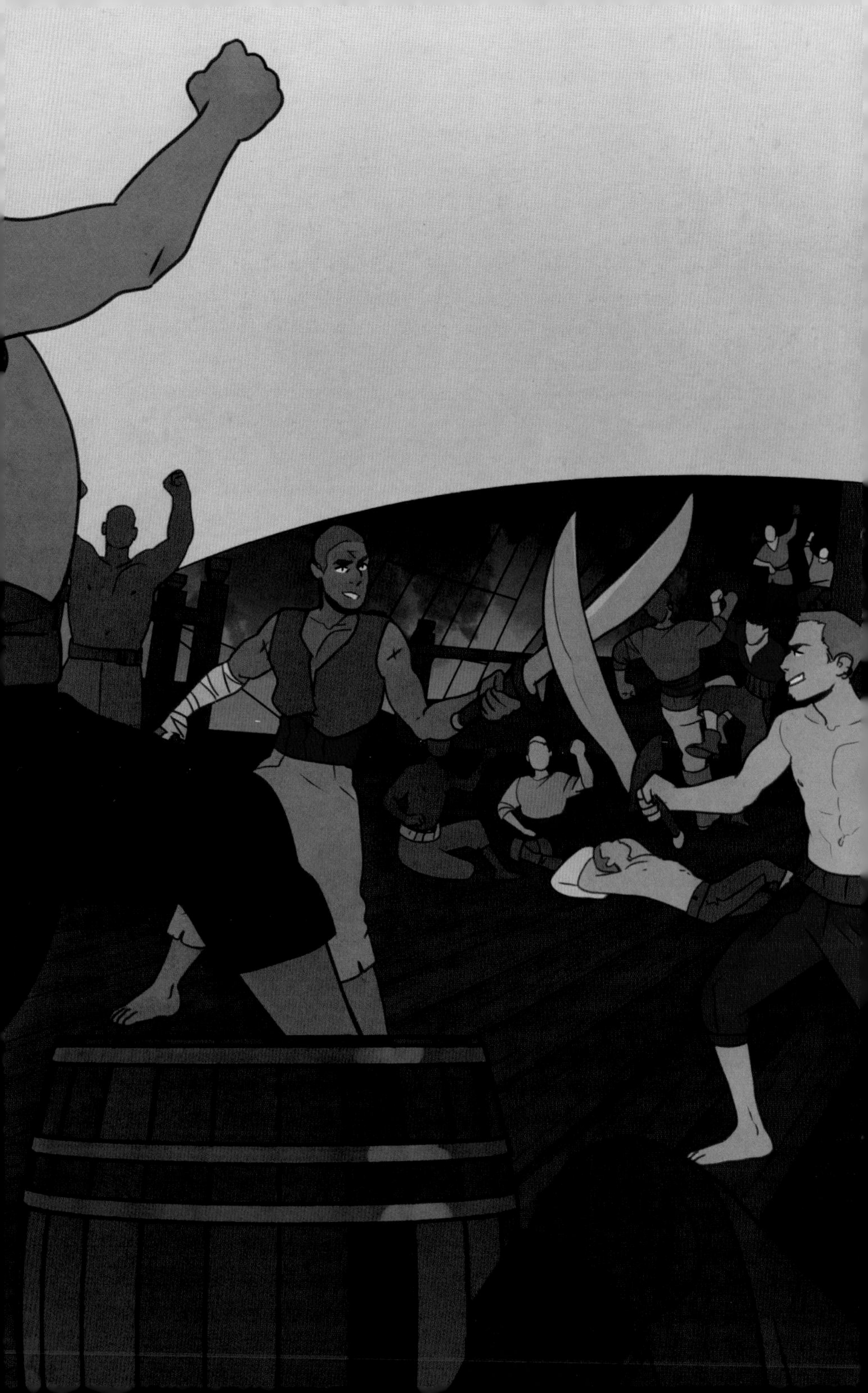

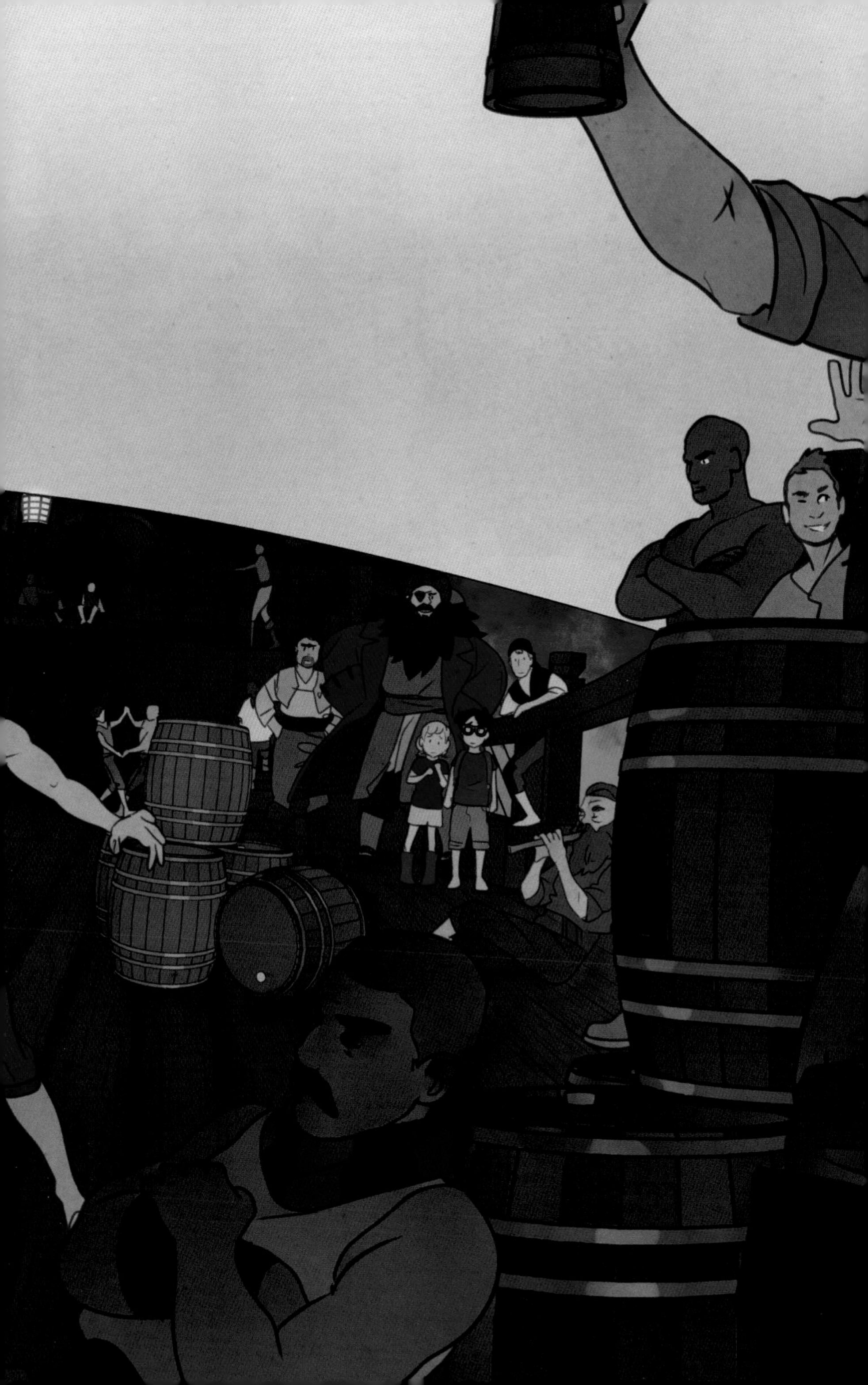

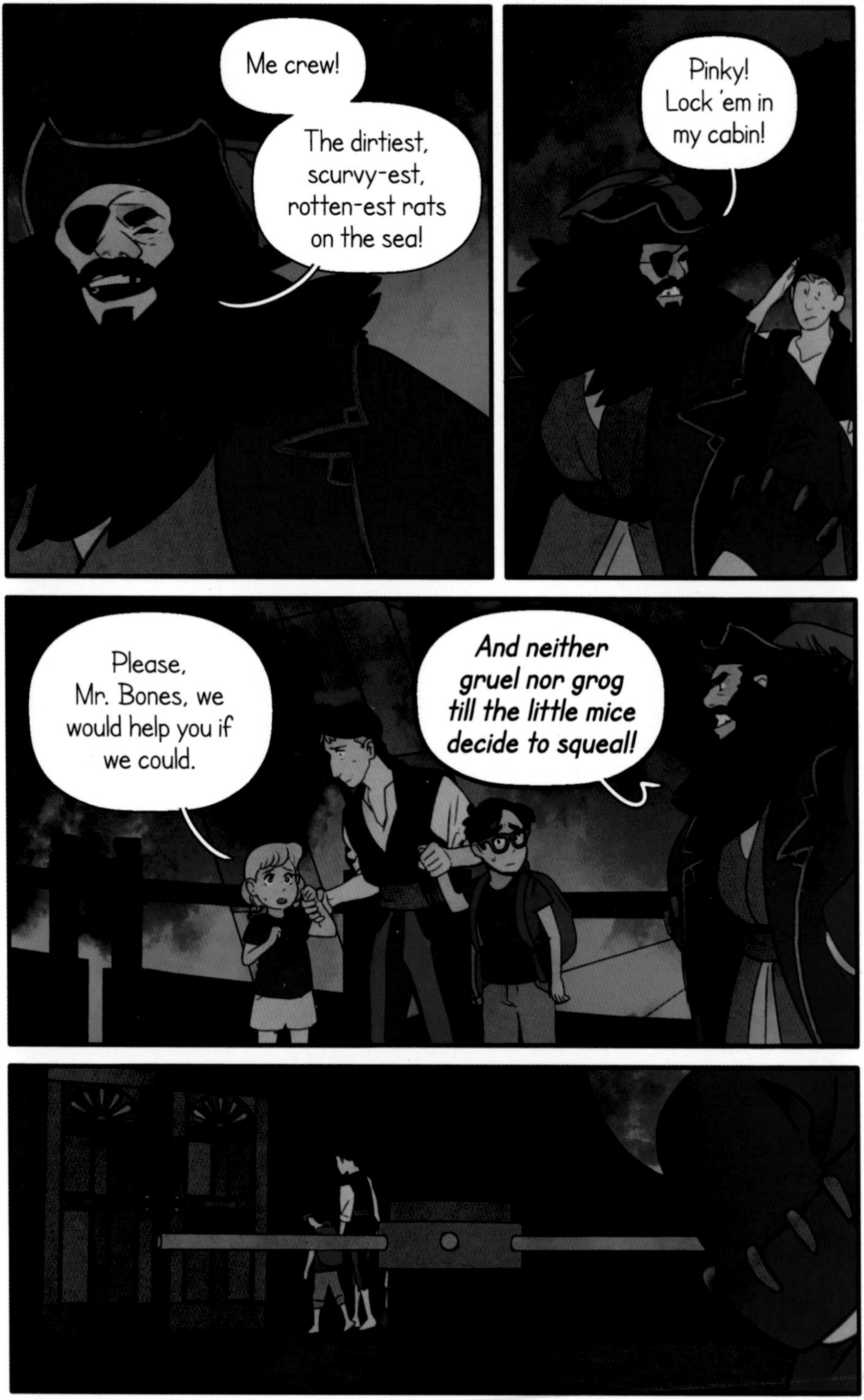
Me crew!
The dirtiest, scurvy-est, rotten-est rats on the sea!
Pinky! Lock 'em in my cabin!
Please, Mr. Bones, we would help you if we could.
And neither gruel nor grog till the little mice decide to squeal!

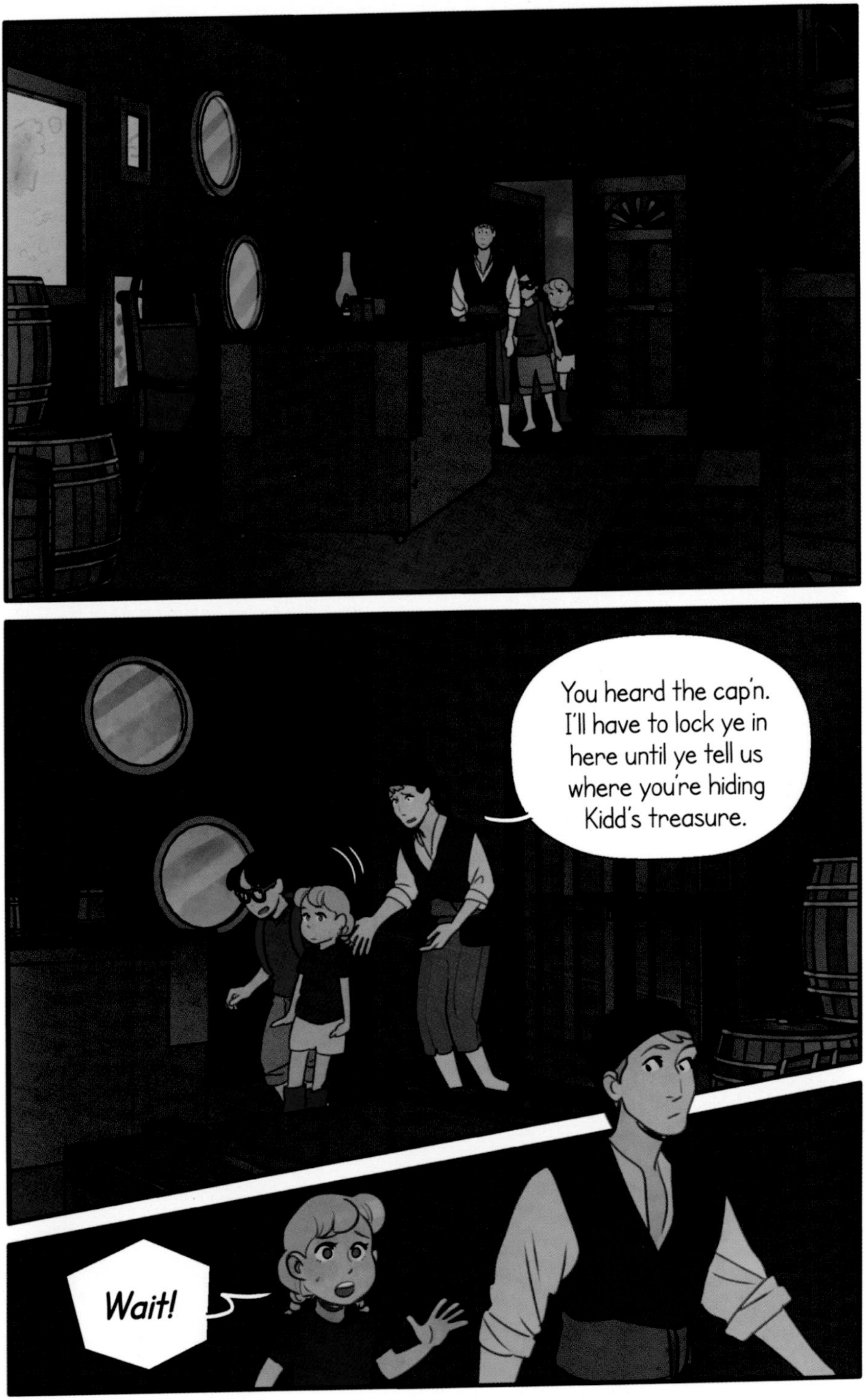
You heard the cap'n. I'll have to lock ye in here until ye tell us where you're hiding Kidd's treasure.
Wait!

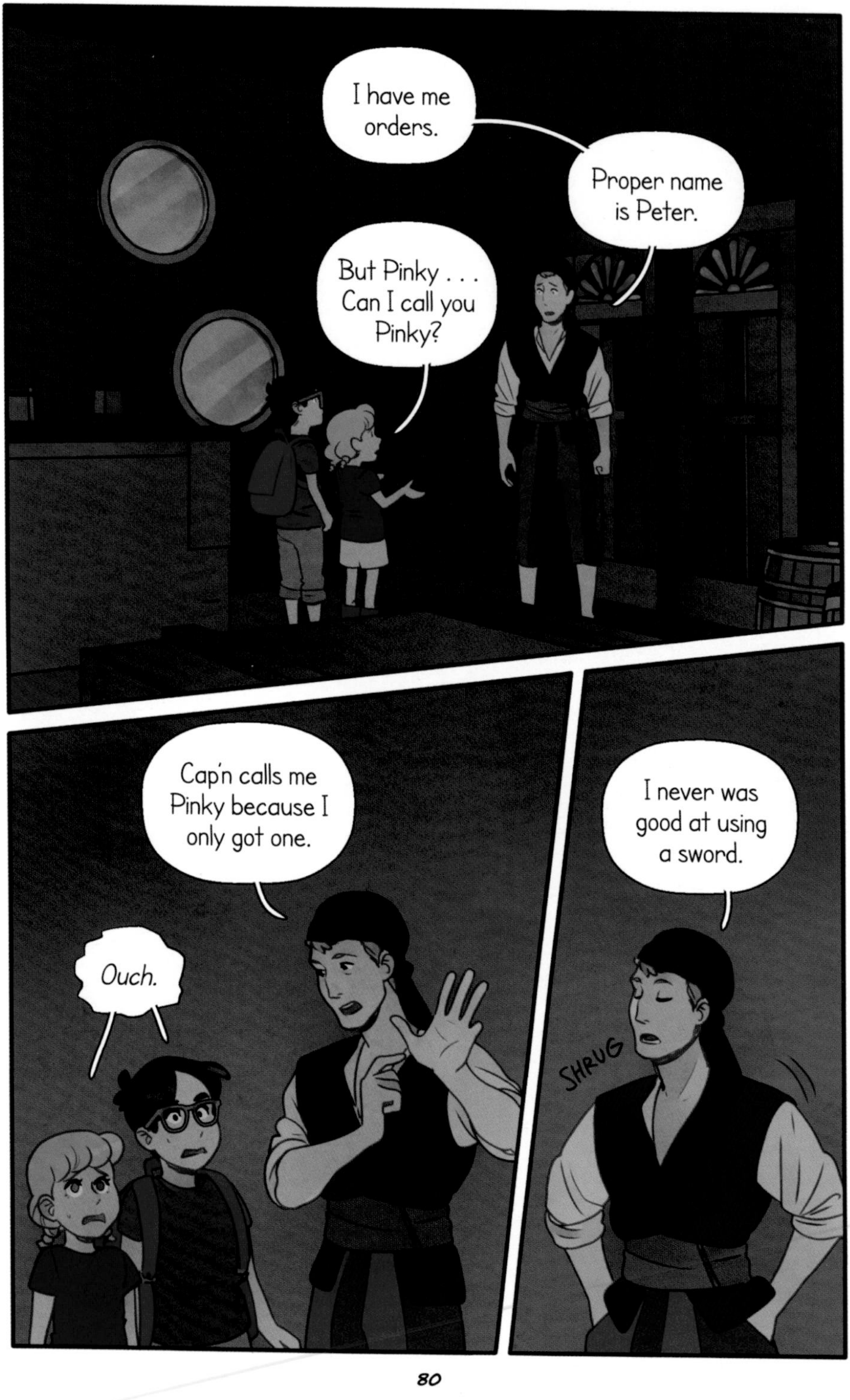
I have me orders.
Proper name is Peter.
But Pinky . . . Can I call you Pinky?
Cap'n calls me Pinky because I only got one.
Ouch.
I never was good at using a sword.
SHRUG

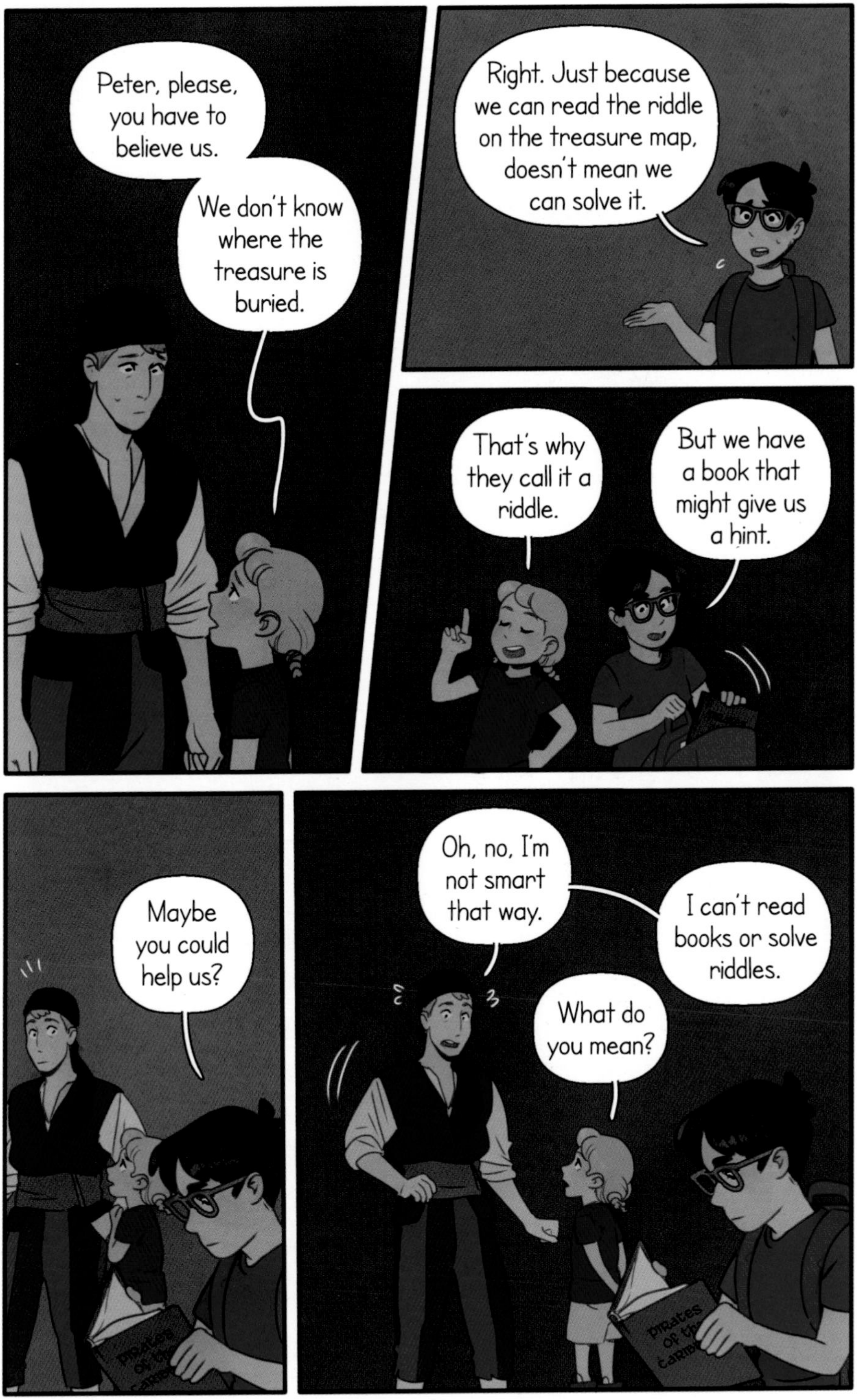
Peter, please, you have to believe us.
We don't know where the treasure is buried.
Right. Just because we can read the riddle on the treasure map, doesn't mean we can solve it.
That's why they call it a riddle.
But we have a book that might give us a hint.
Maybe you could help us?
Oh, no, I'm not smart that way.
I can't read books or solve riddles.
What do you mean?
PIRATES OF THE CARIBBEAN

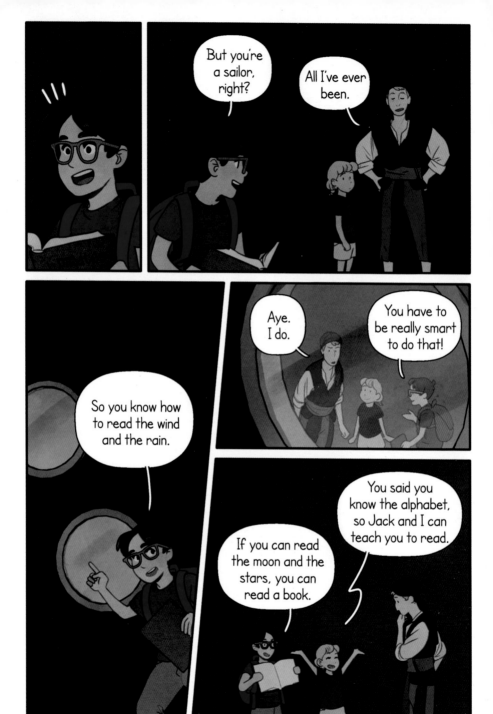

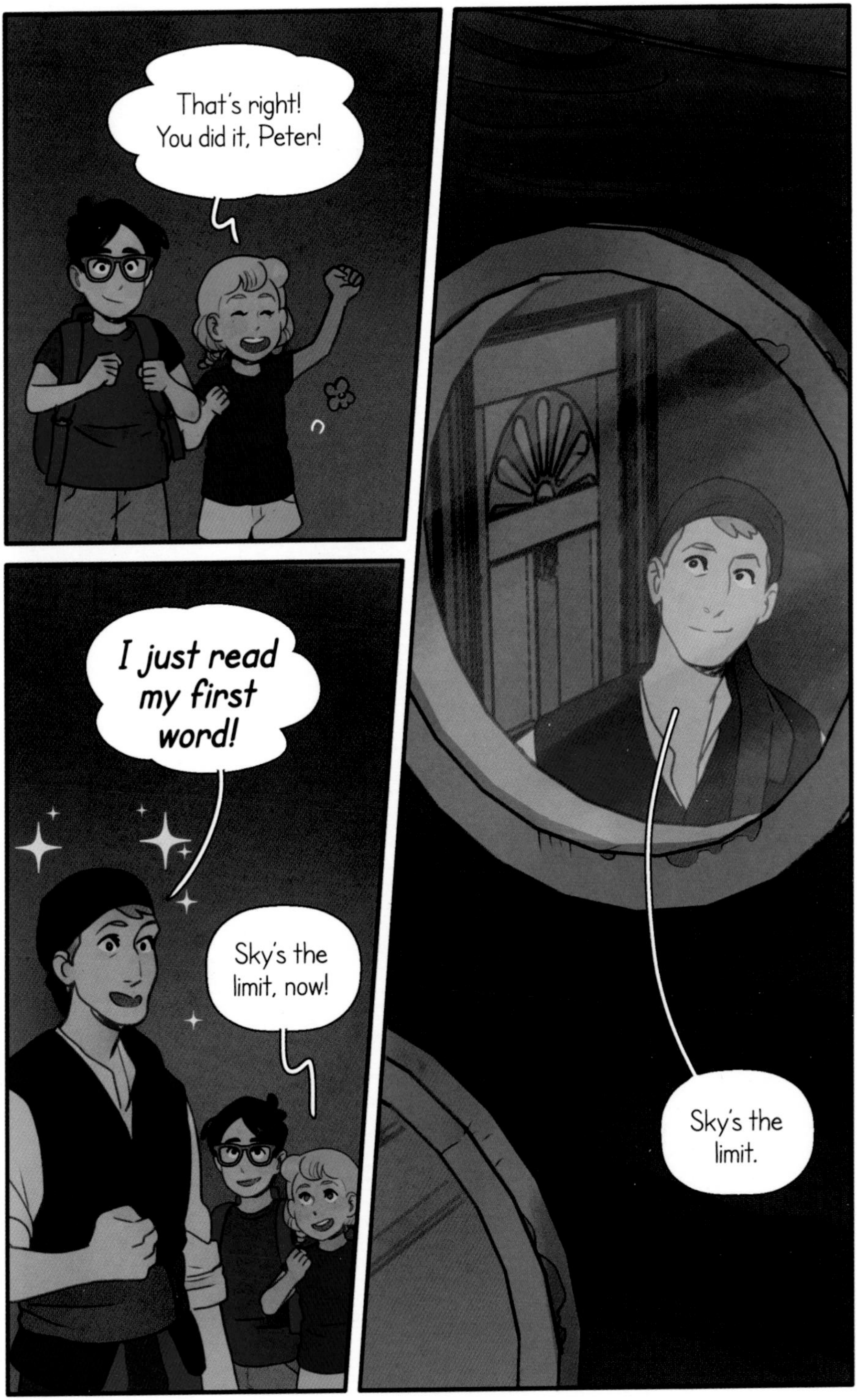
That's right! You did it, Peter!
I just read my first word!
Sky's the limit, now!
Sky's the limit.

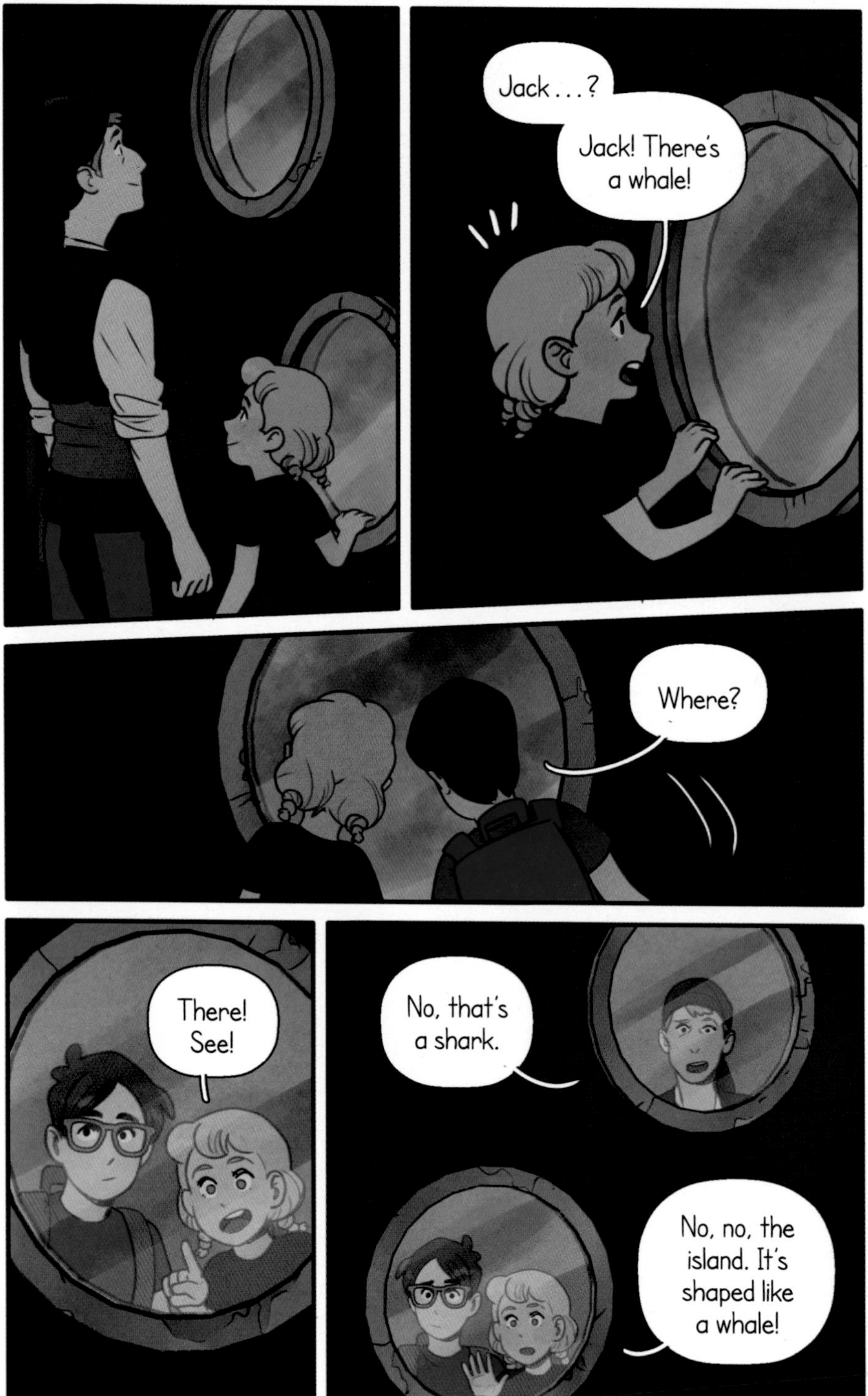
Jack...?
Jack! There's a whale!
Where?
There! See!
No, that's a shark.
No, no, the island. It's shaped like a whale!

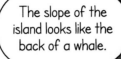

CHAPTER SEVEN
Gale's a-Blowin'

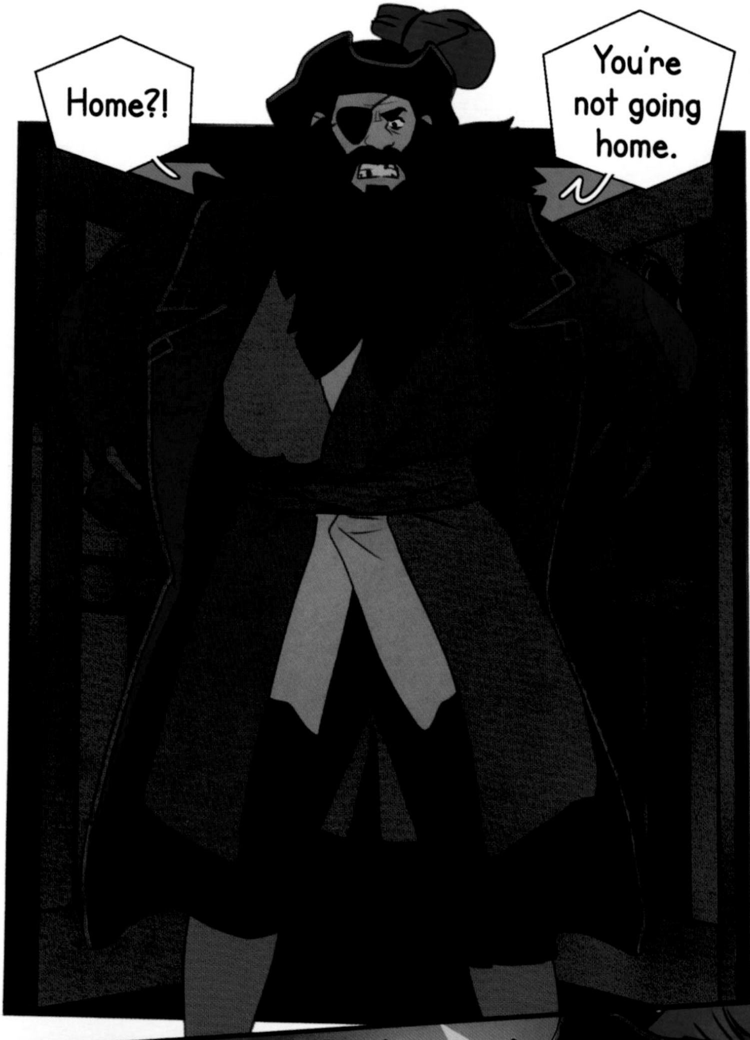
Home?!
You're not going home.

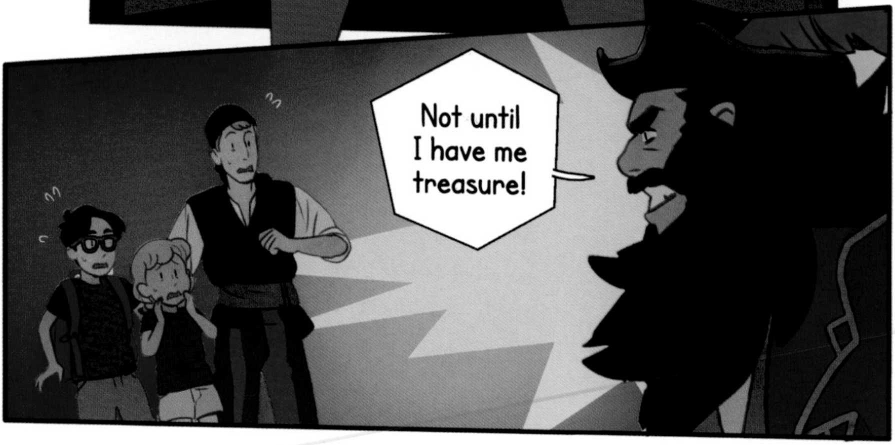
Not until I have me treasure!

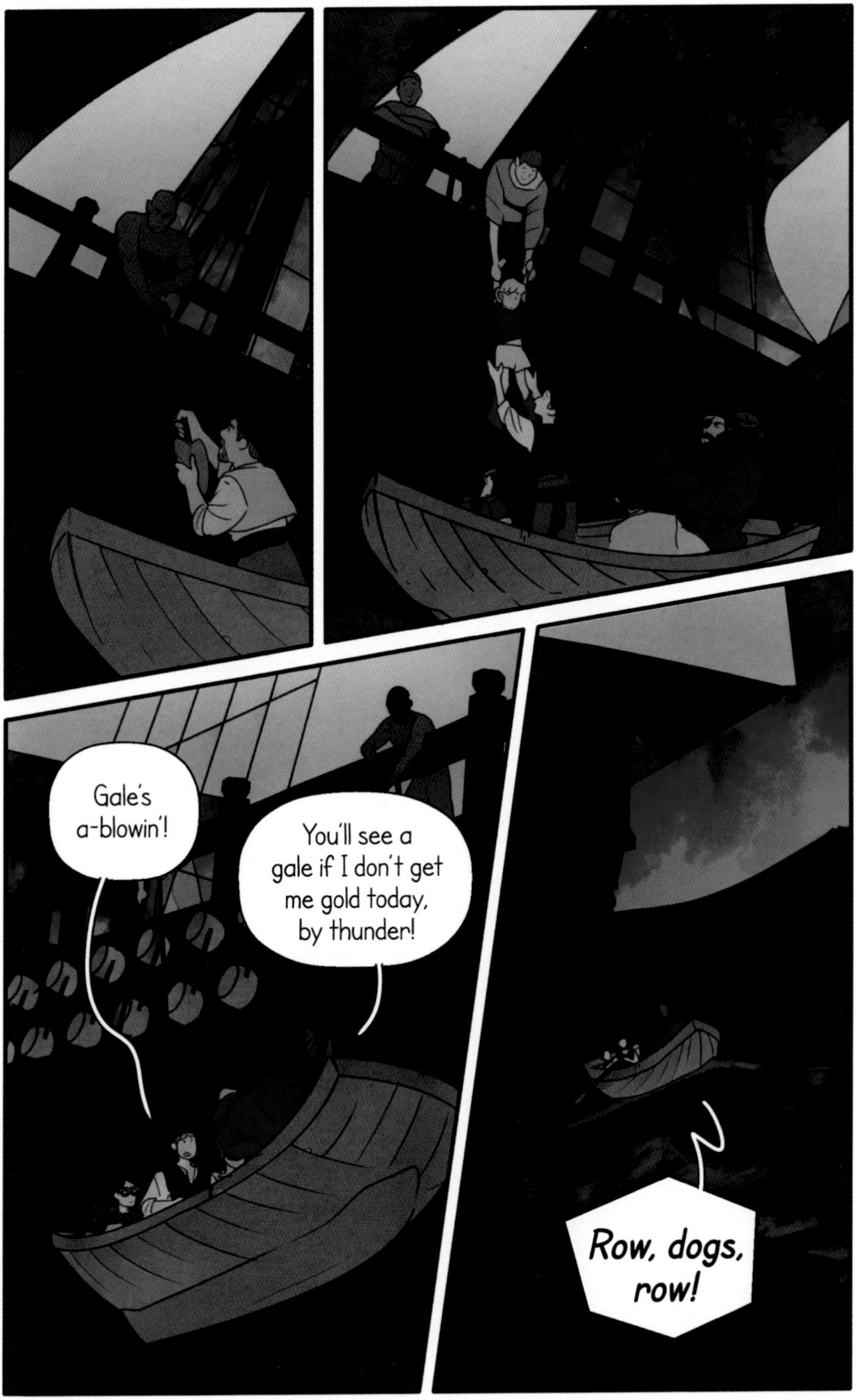
Gale's a-blowin'!
You'll see a gale if I don't get me gold today, by thunder!
Row, dogs, row!

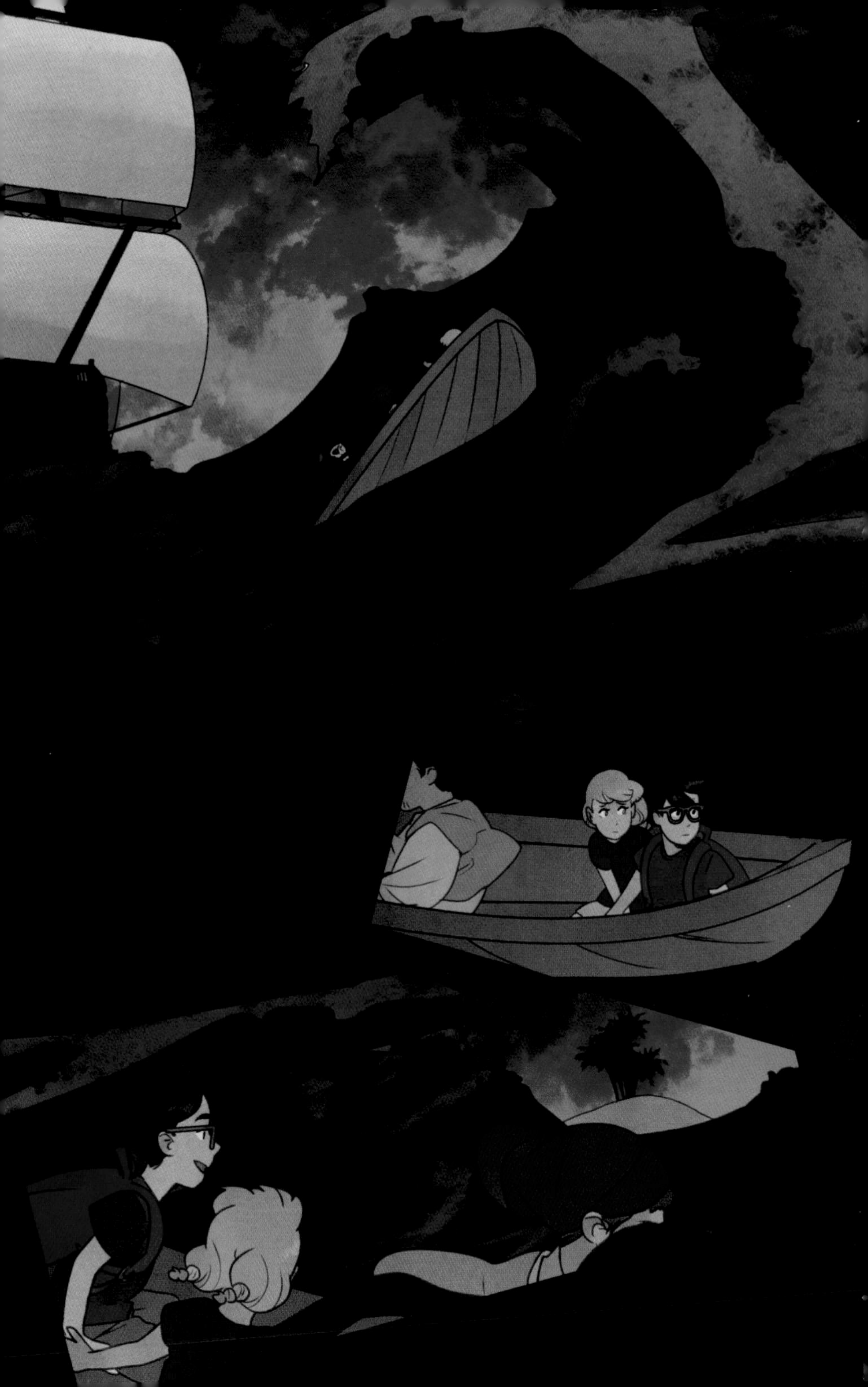

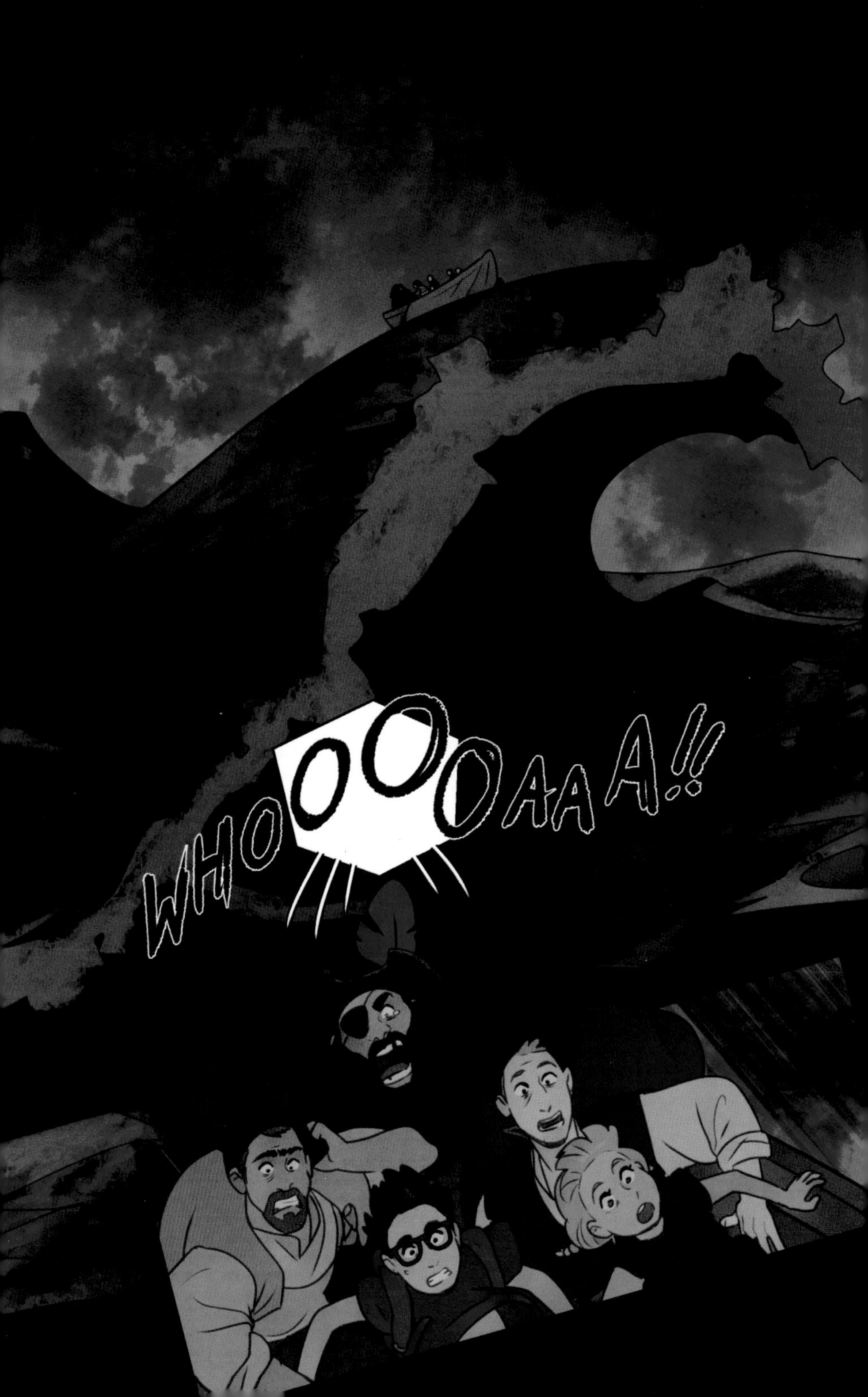
WHOOOOAAAA!!

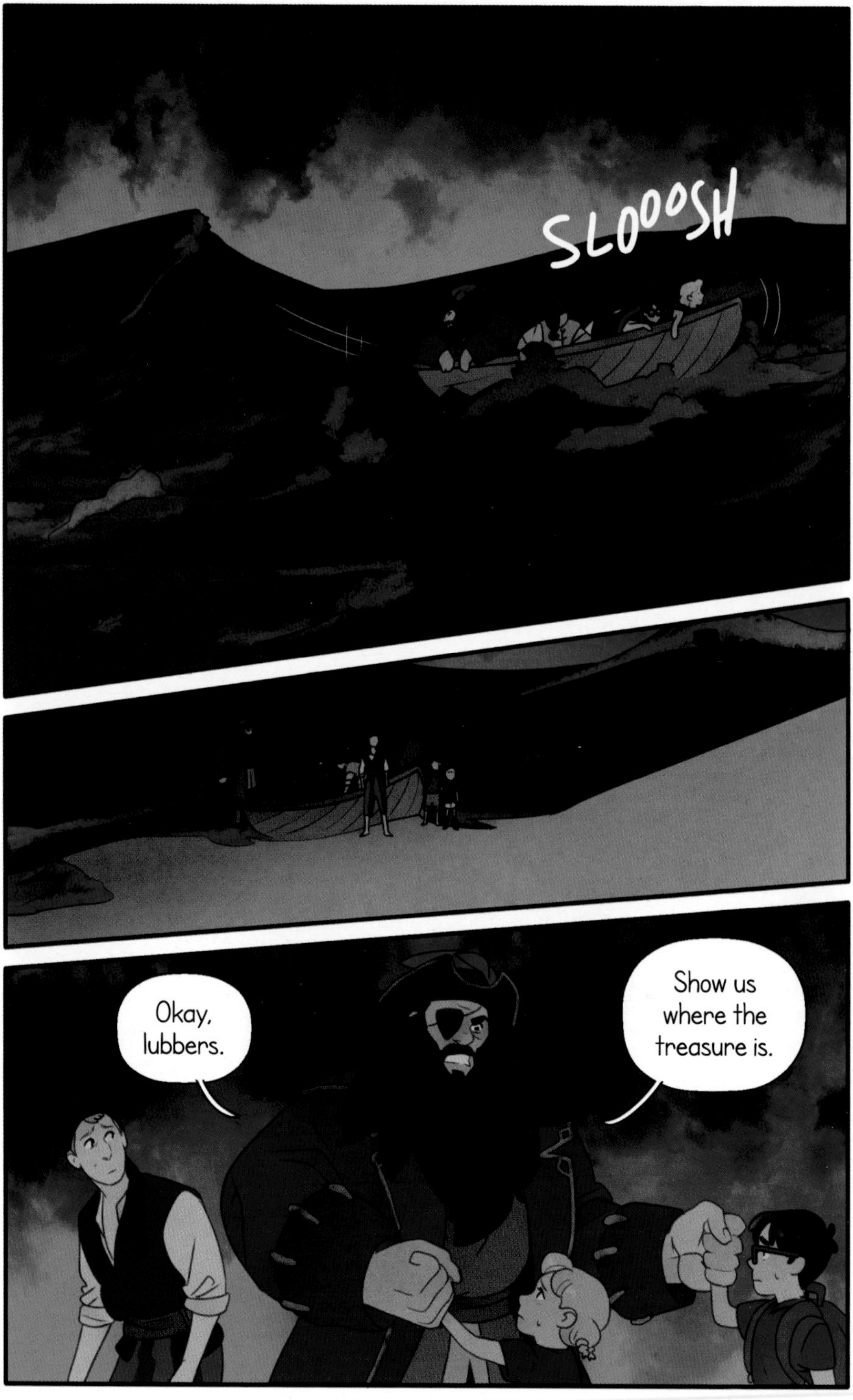
SLOOOSH
Okay, lubbers.
Show us where the treasure is.

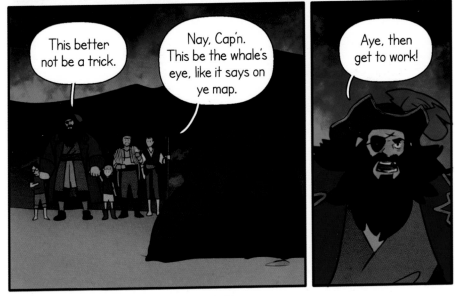

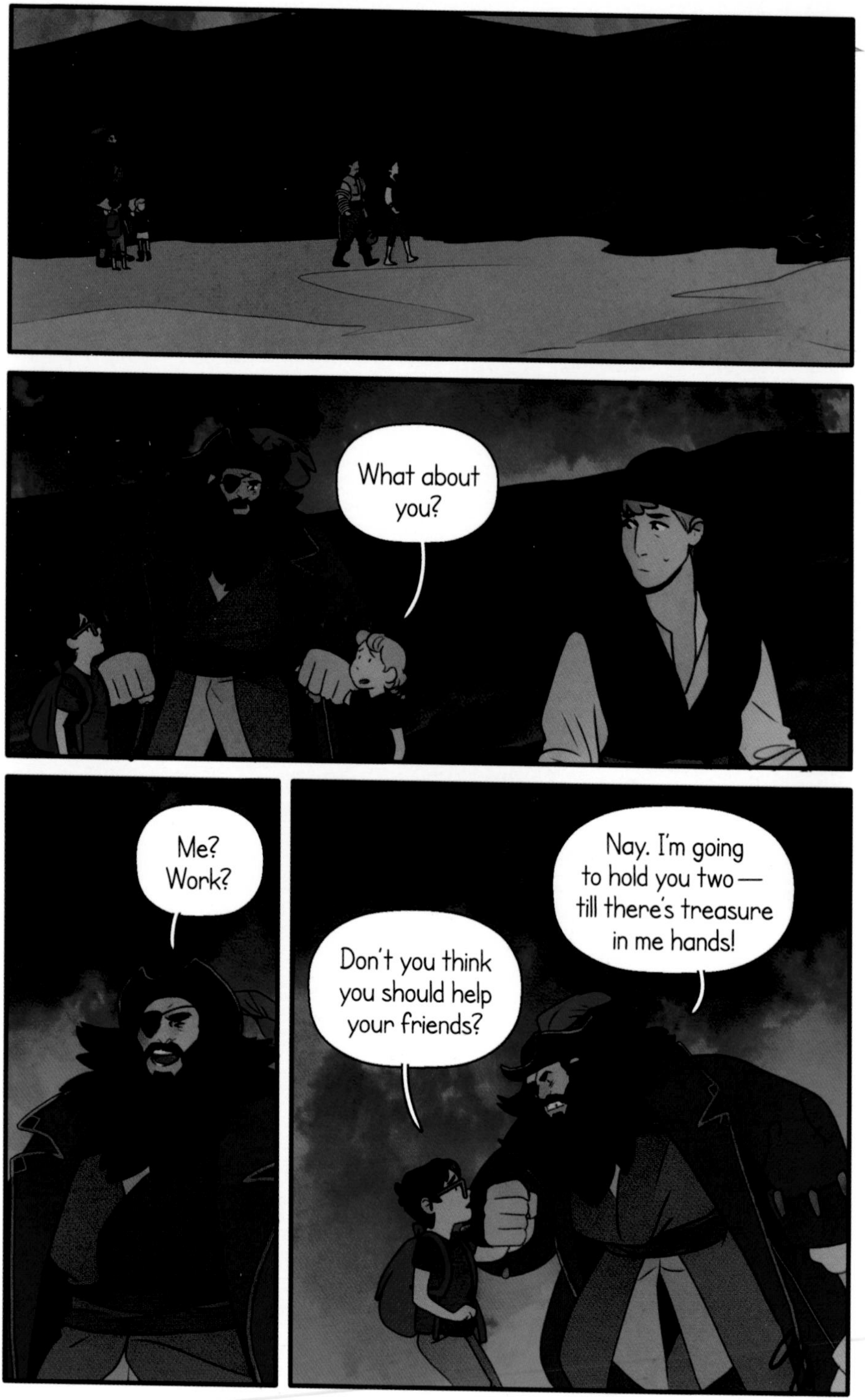
What about you?
Me? Work?
Don't you think you should help your friends?
Nay. I'm going to hold you two— till there's treasure in me hands!

CHAPTER EIGHT
Dig, Dogs, Dig

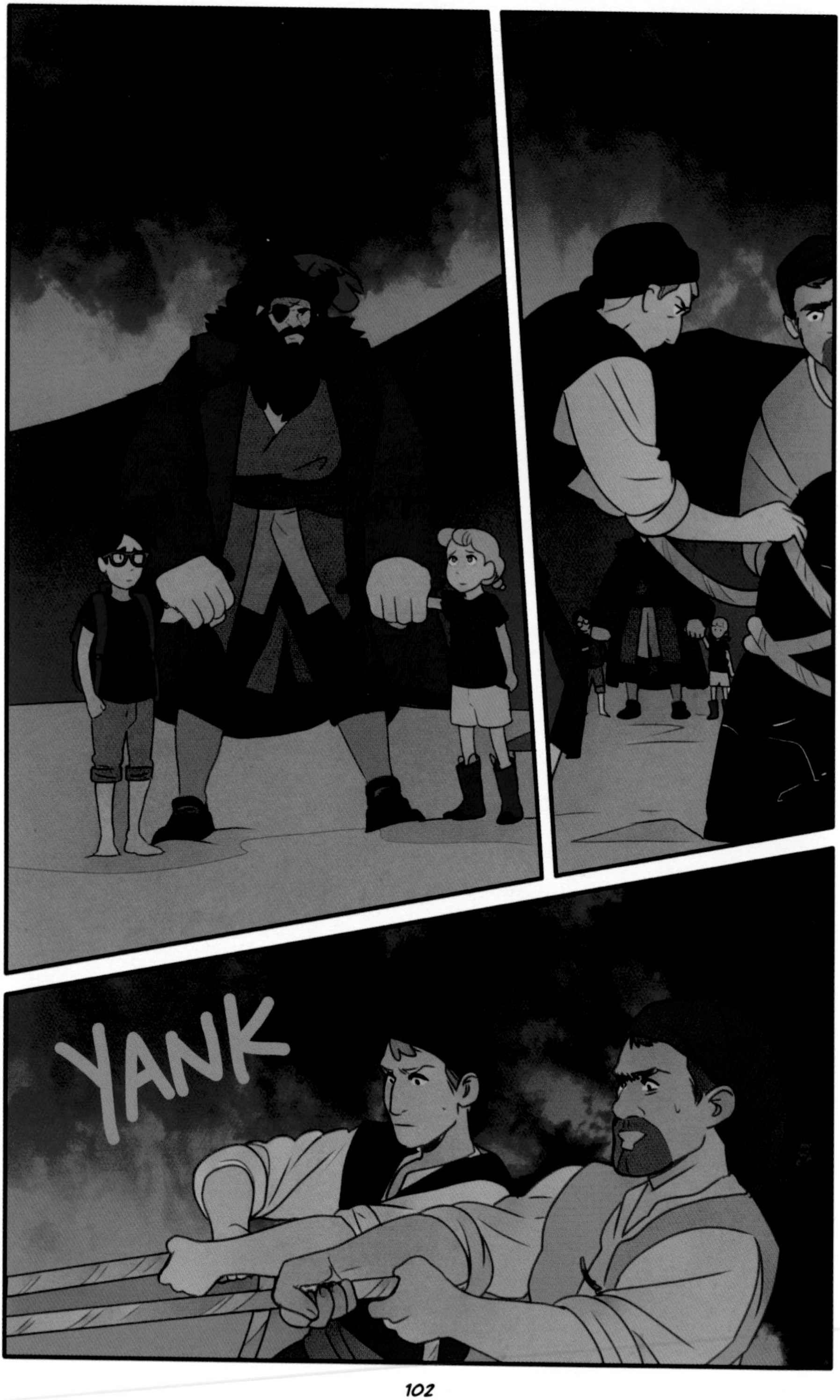
YANK

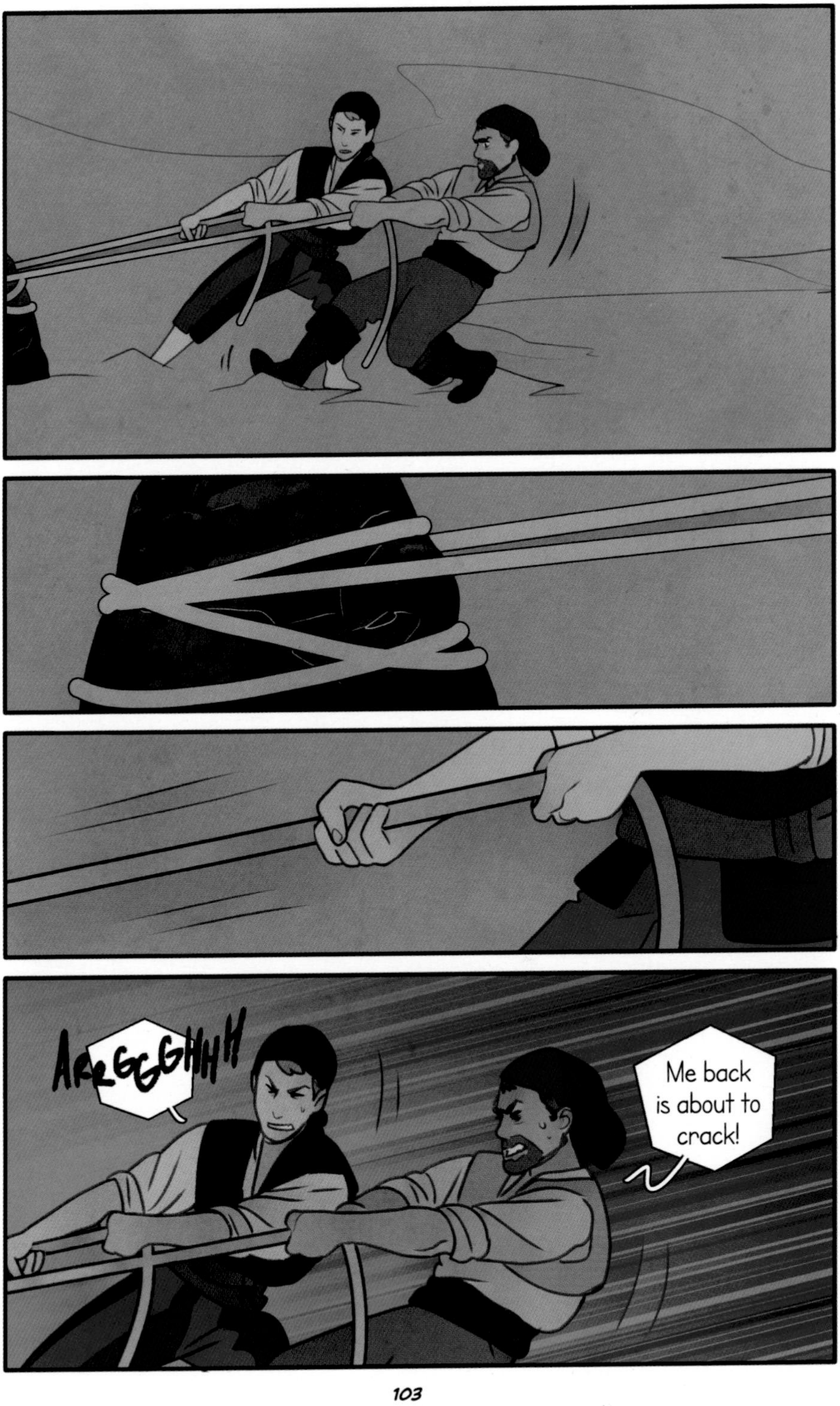
ARRGGGHHH!
Me back is about to crack!

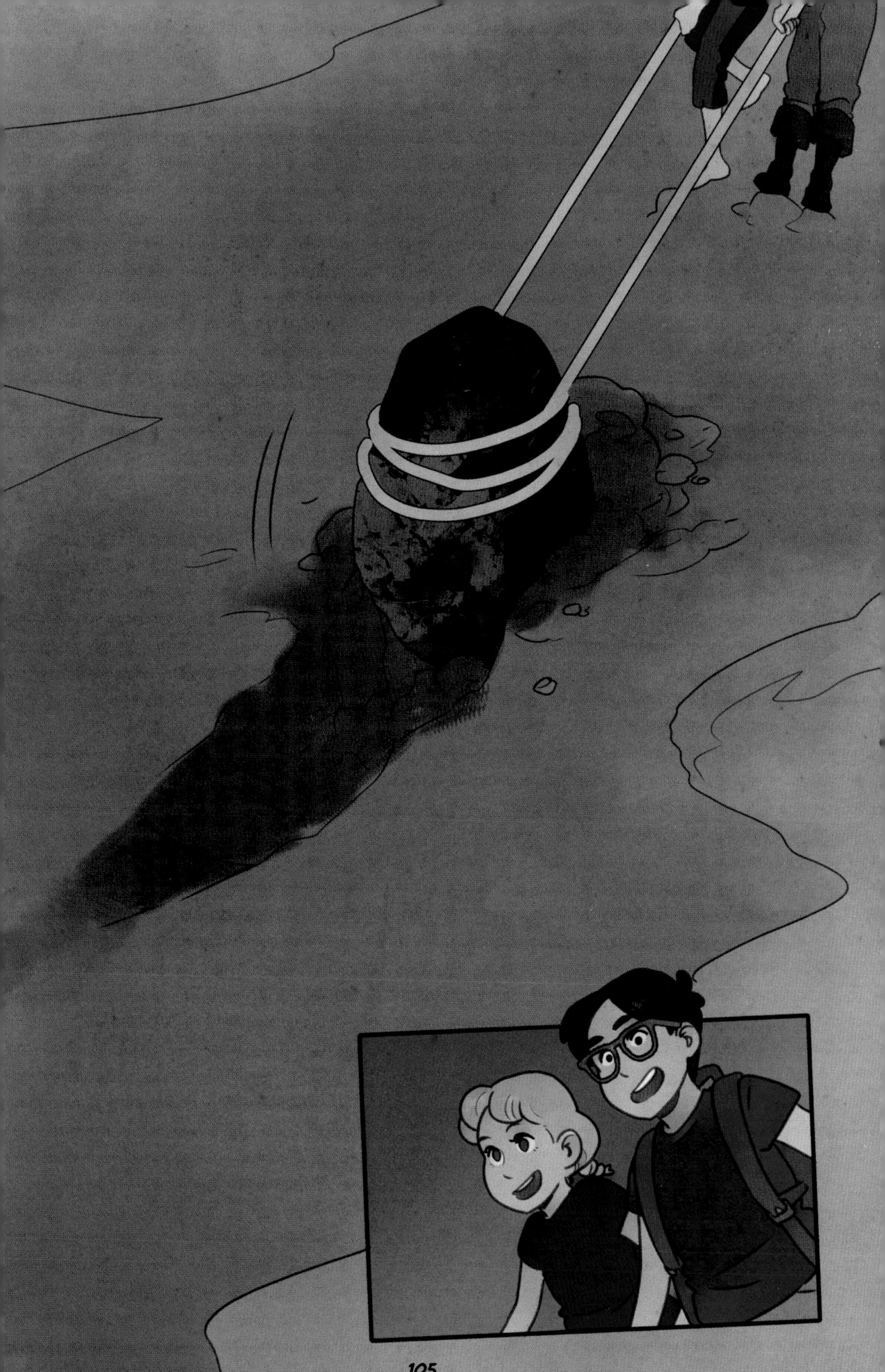

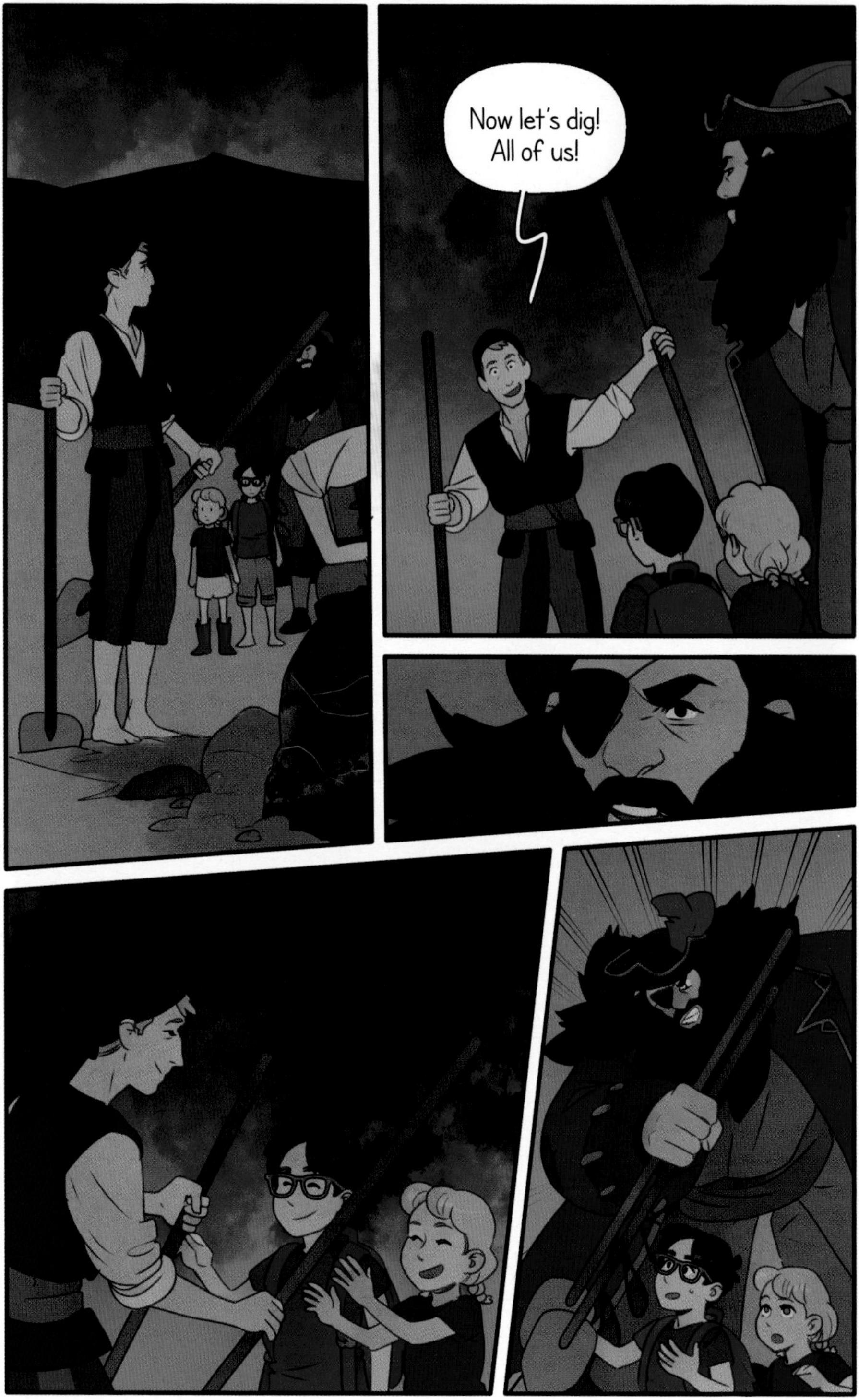
Now let's dig! All of us!

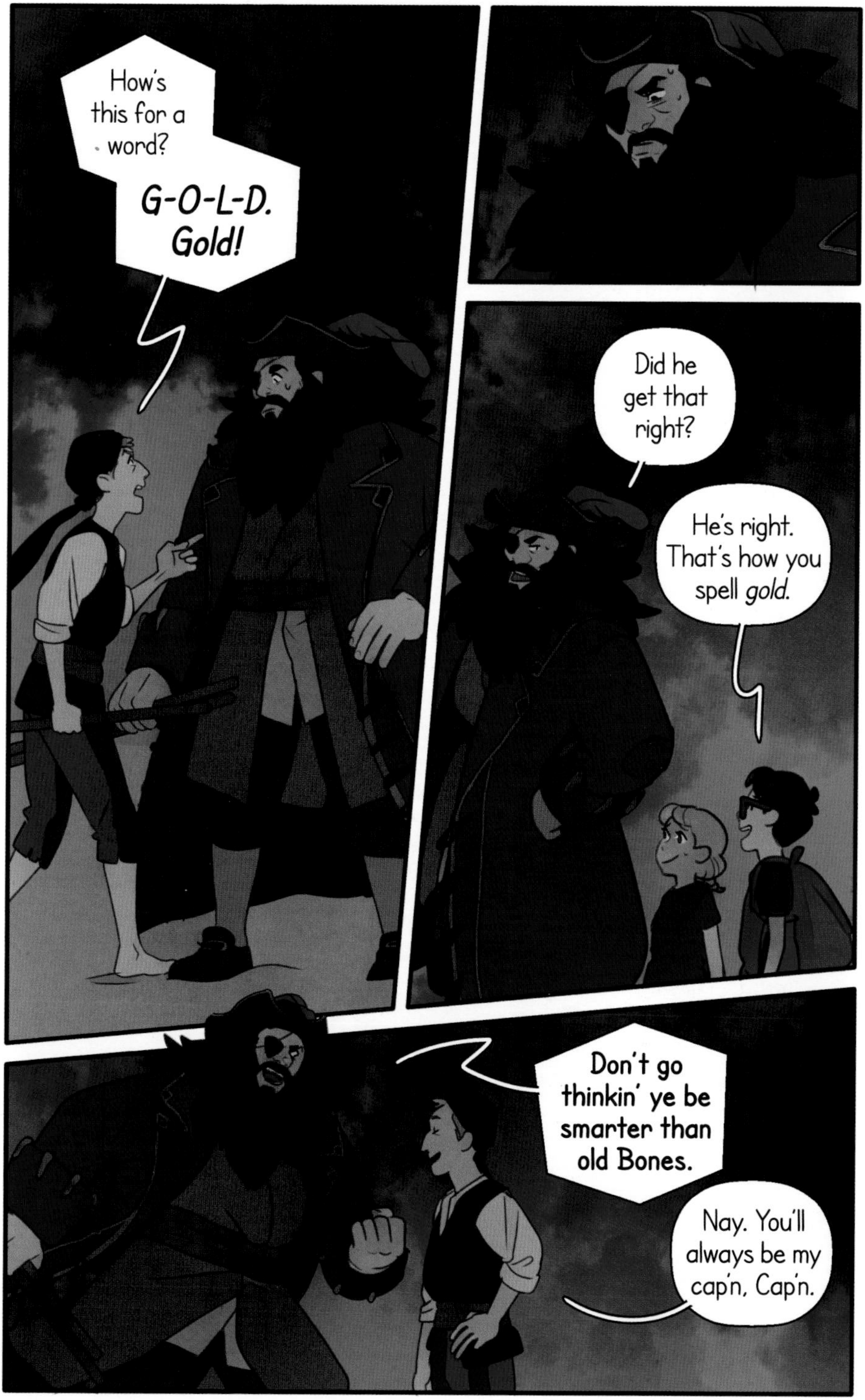
How's this for a word?
G-O-L-D. Gold!
Did he get that right?
He's right. That's how you spell *gold*.
Don't go thinkin' ye be smarter than old Bones.
Nay. You'll always be my cap'n, Cap'n.

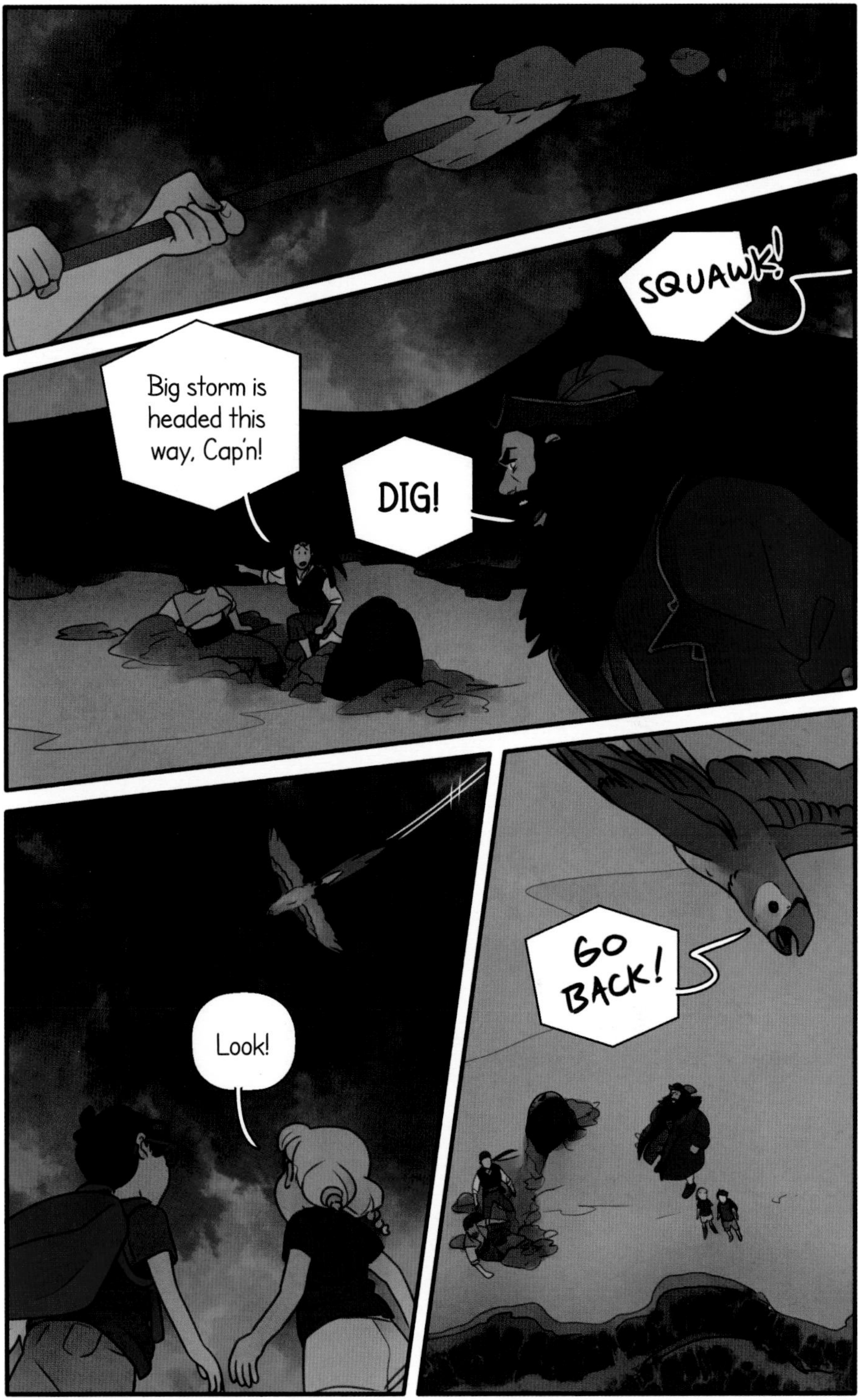
SQUAWK!
Big storm is headed this way, Cap'n!
DIG!
GO BACK!
Look!

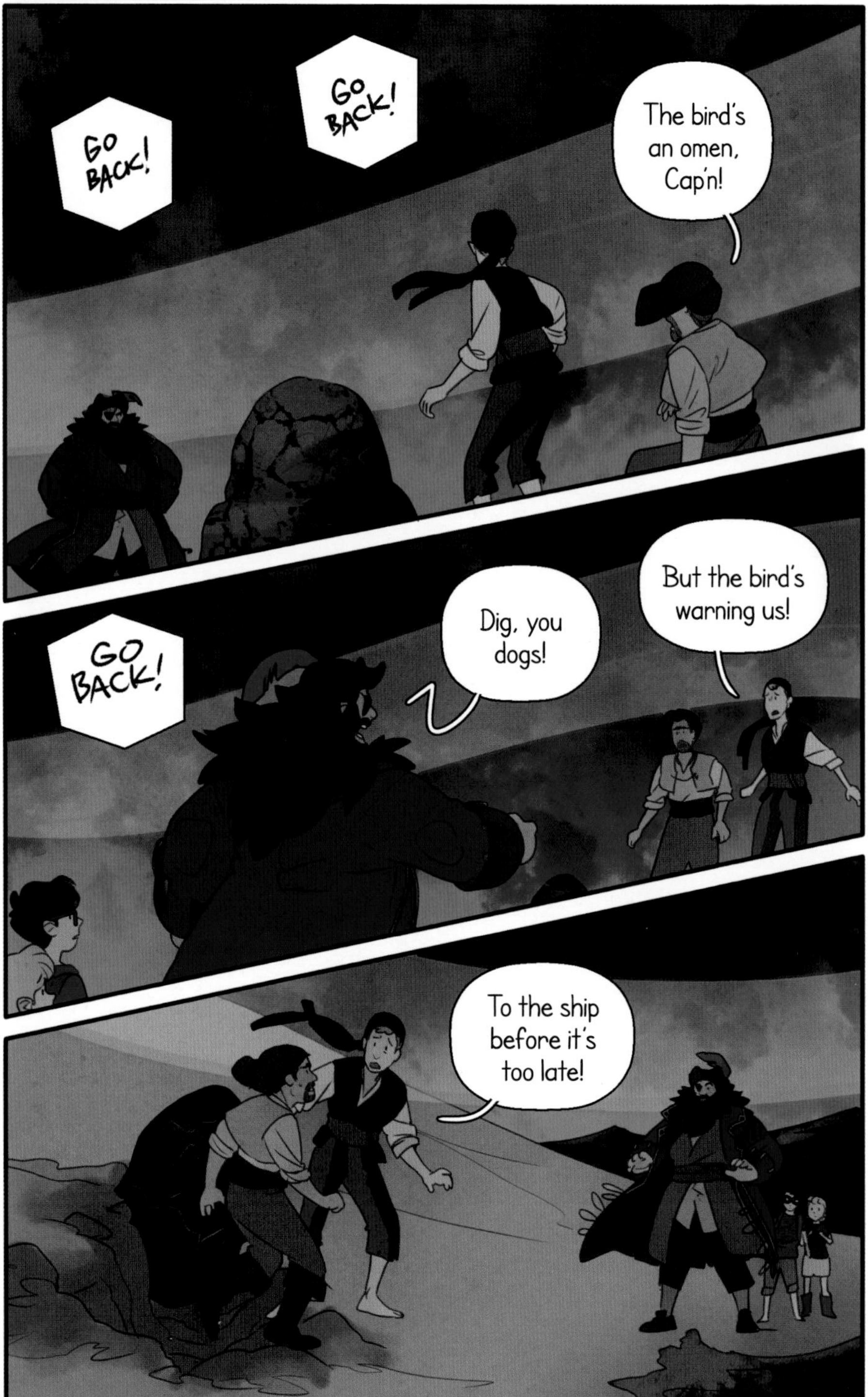
GO BACK!
GO BACK!
The bird's an omen, Cap'n!
GO BACK!
Dig, you dogs!
But the bird's warning us!
To the ship before it's too late!

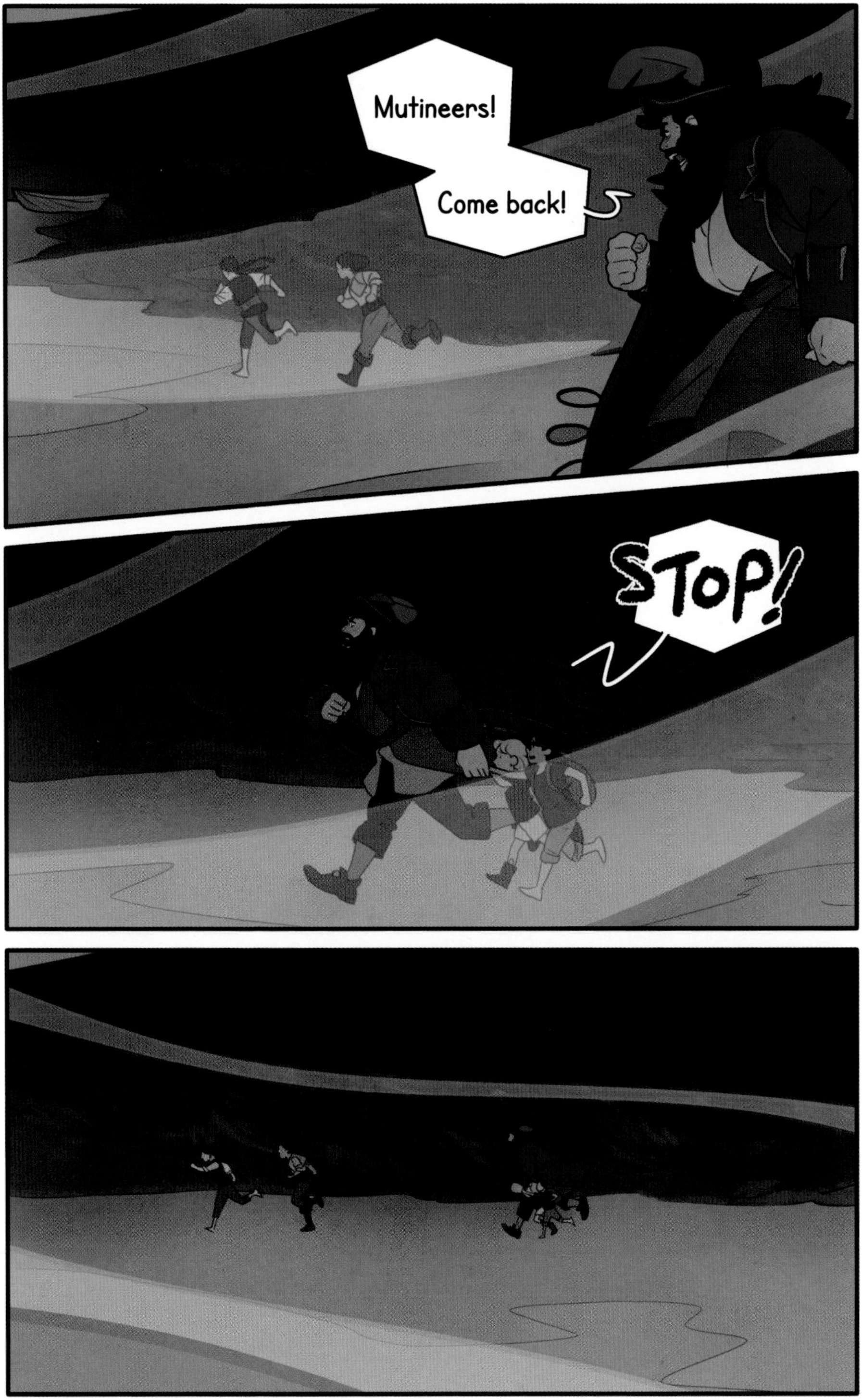
Mutineers!
Come back!
STOP!

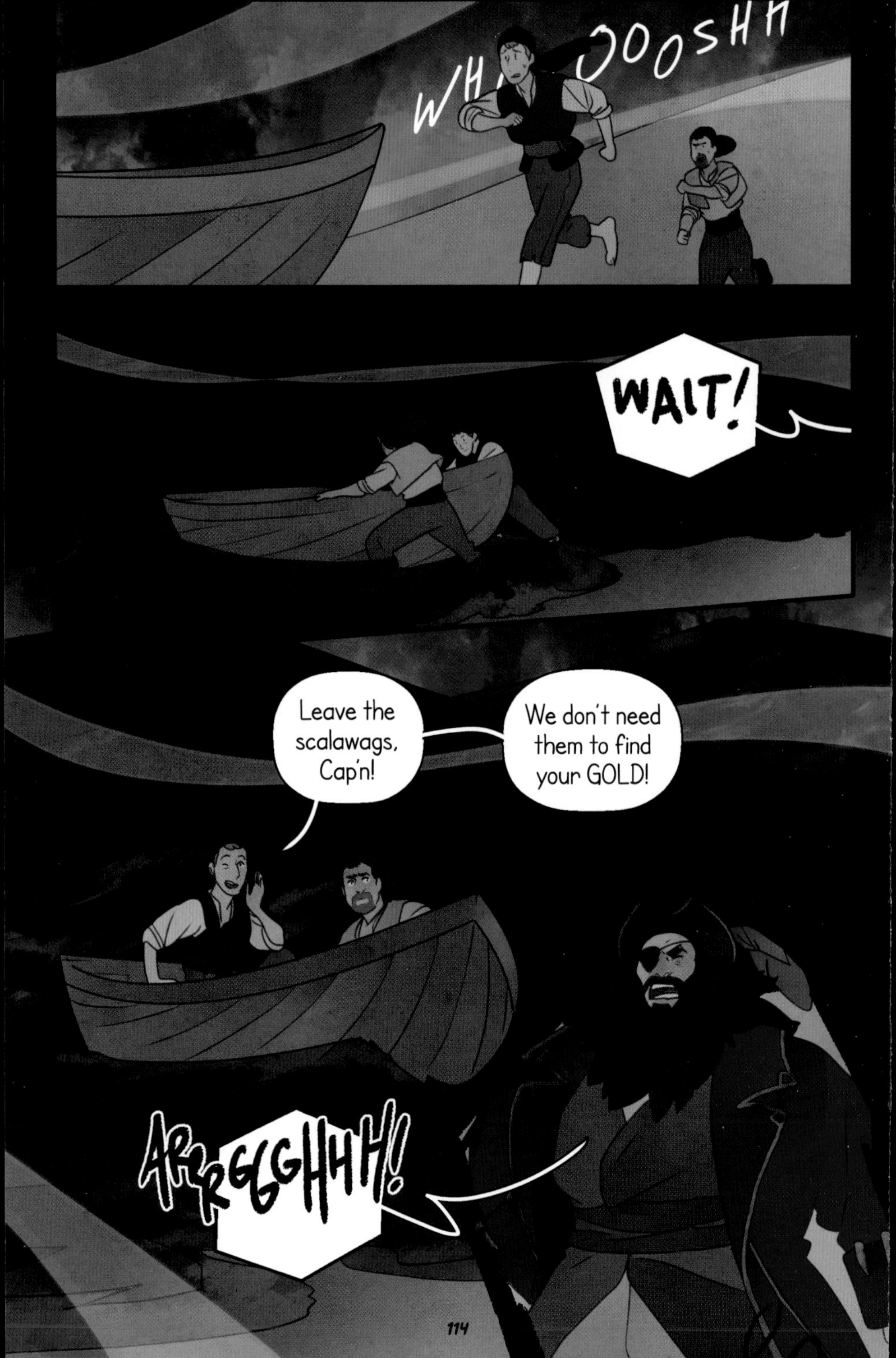
WH...OOOSHH
WAIT!
Leave the scalawags, Cap'n!
We don't need them to find your GOLD!
ARRRGGHHH!

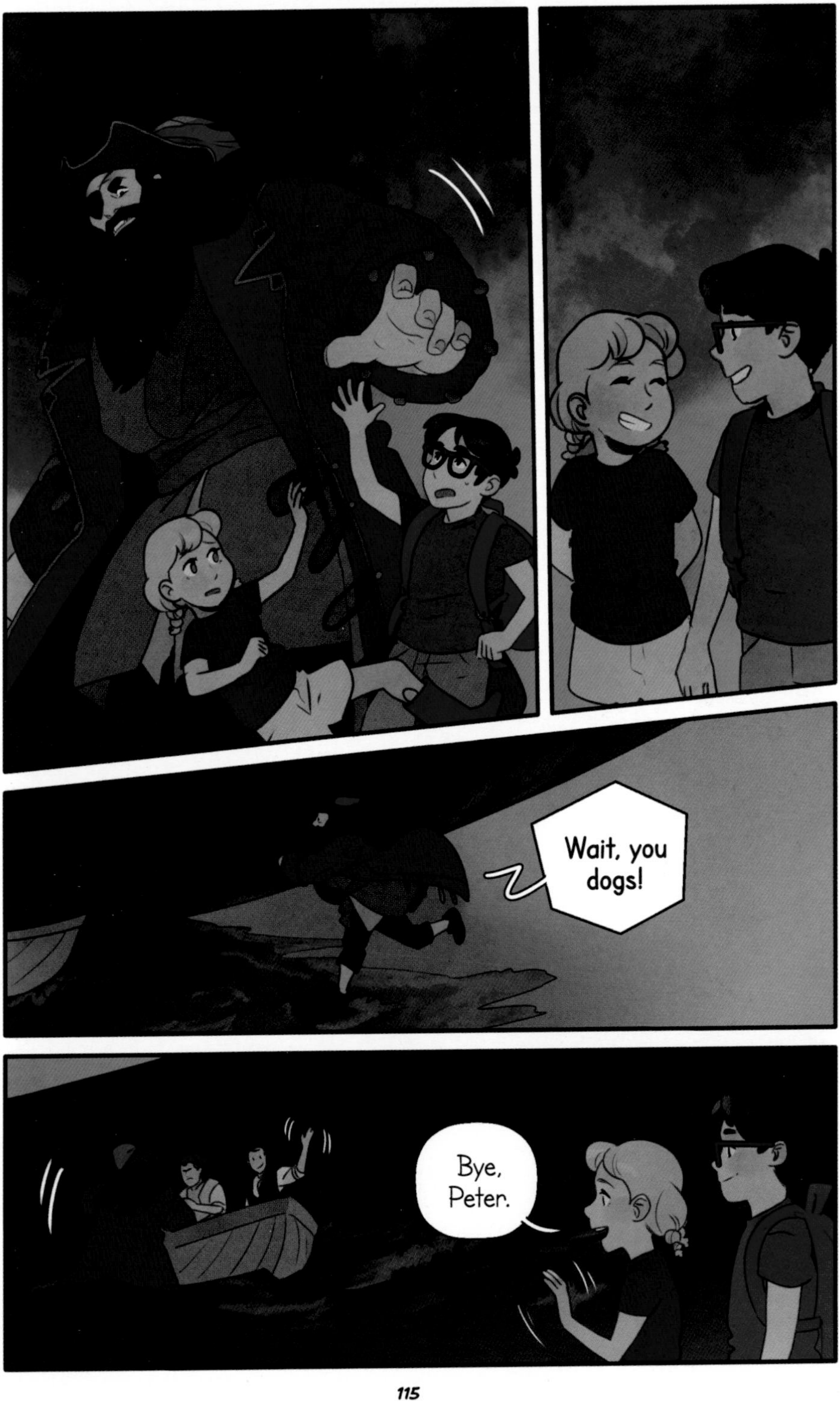
Wait, you dogs!
Bye, Peter.

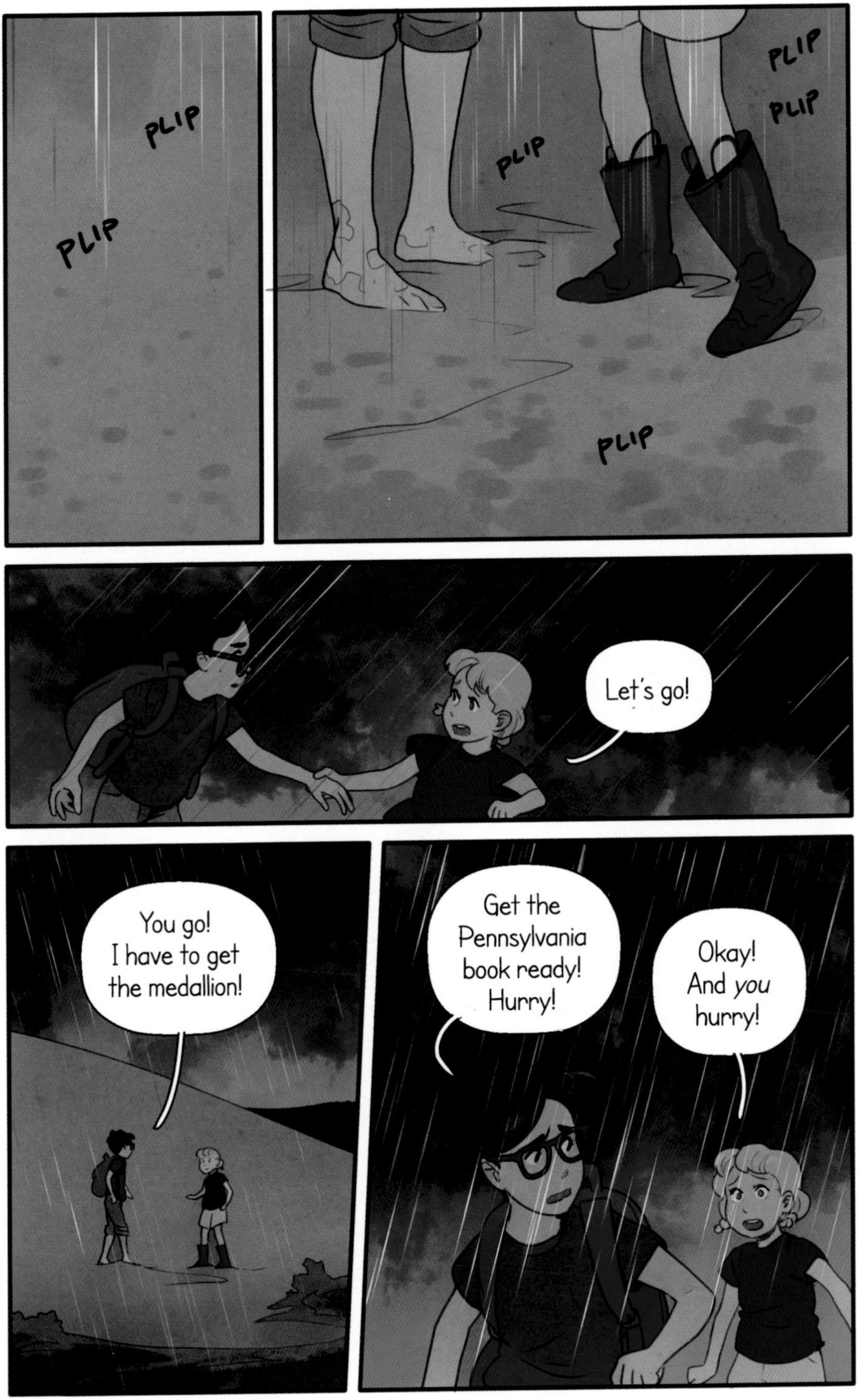
PLIP
PLIP
PLIP
PLIP
PLIP
PLIP
Let's go!
You go!
I have to get the medallion!
Get the Pennsylvania book ready! Hurry!
Okay! And *you* hurry!

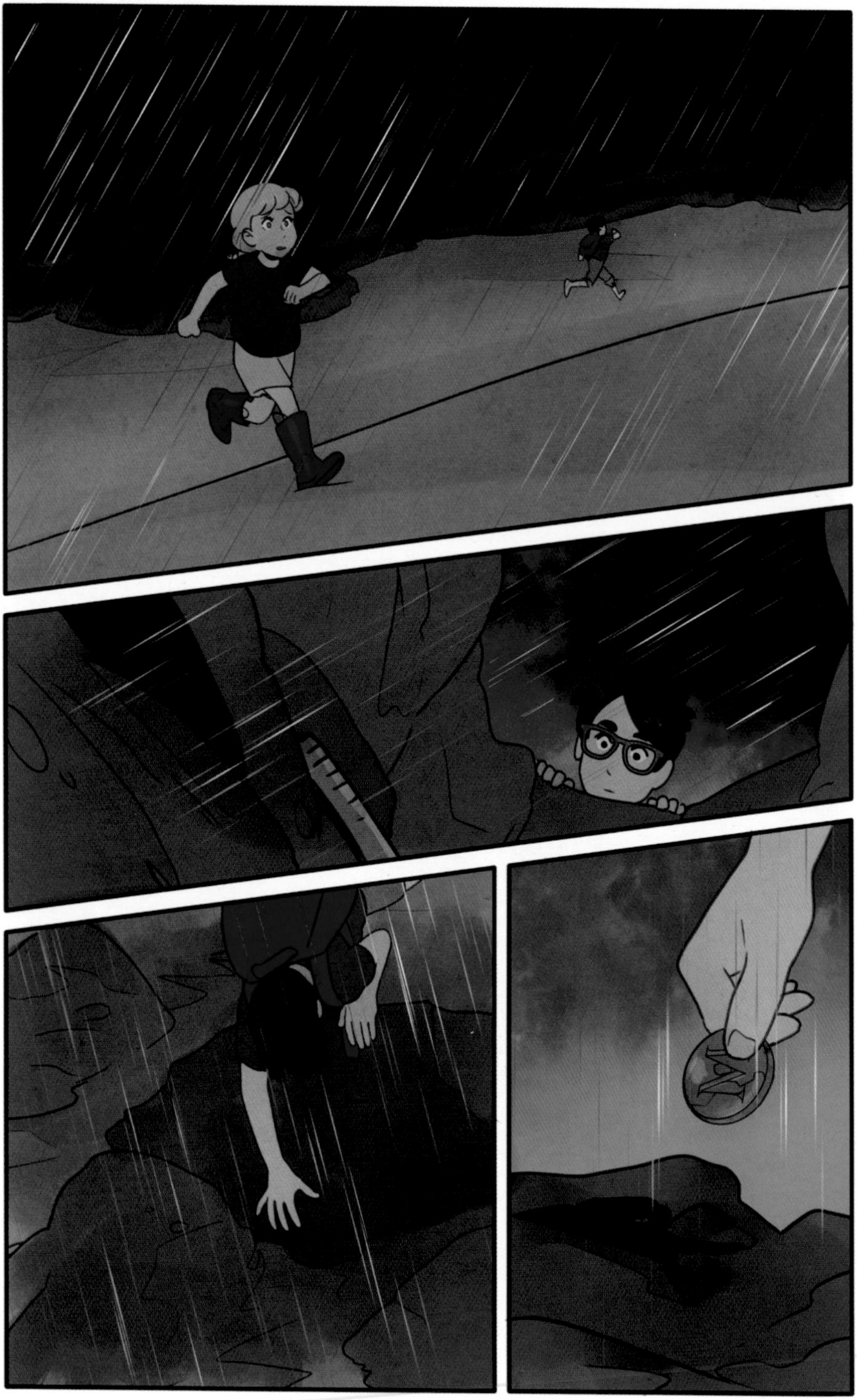

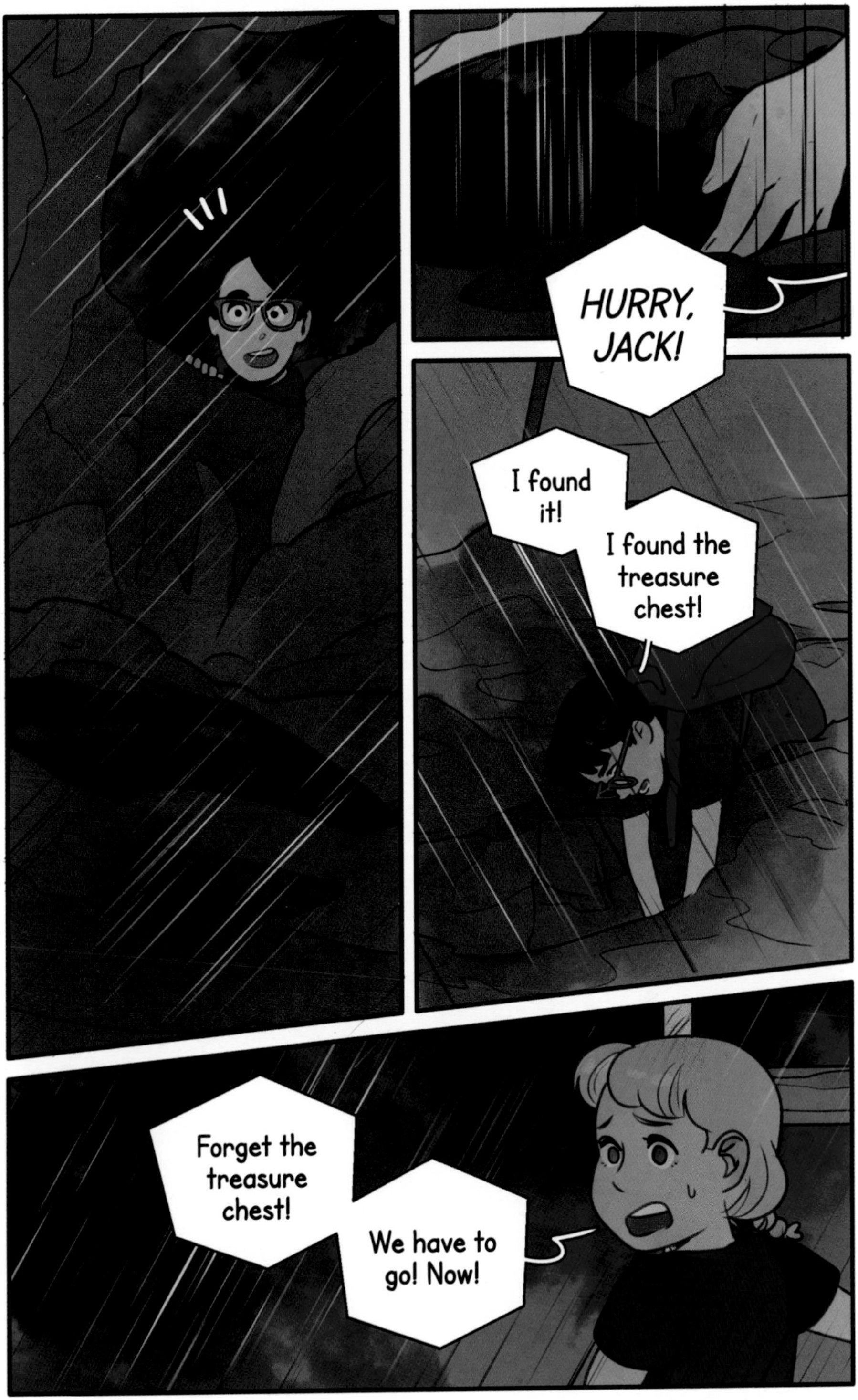
HURRY, JACK!
I found it!
I found the treasure chest!
Forget the treasure chest!
We have to go! Now!

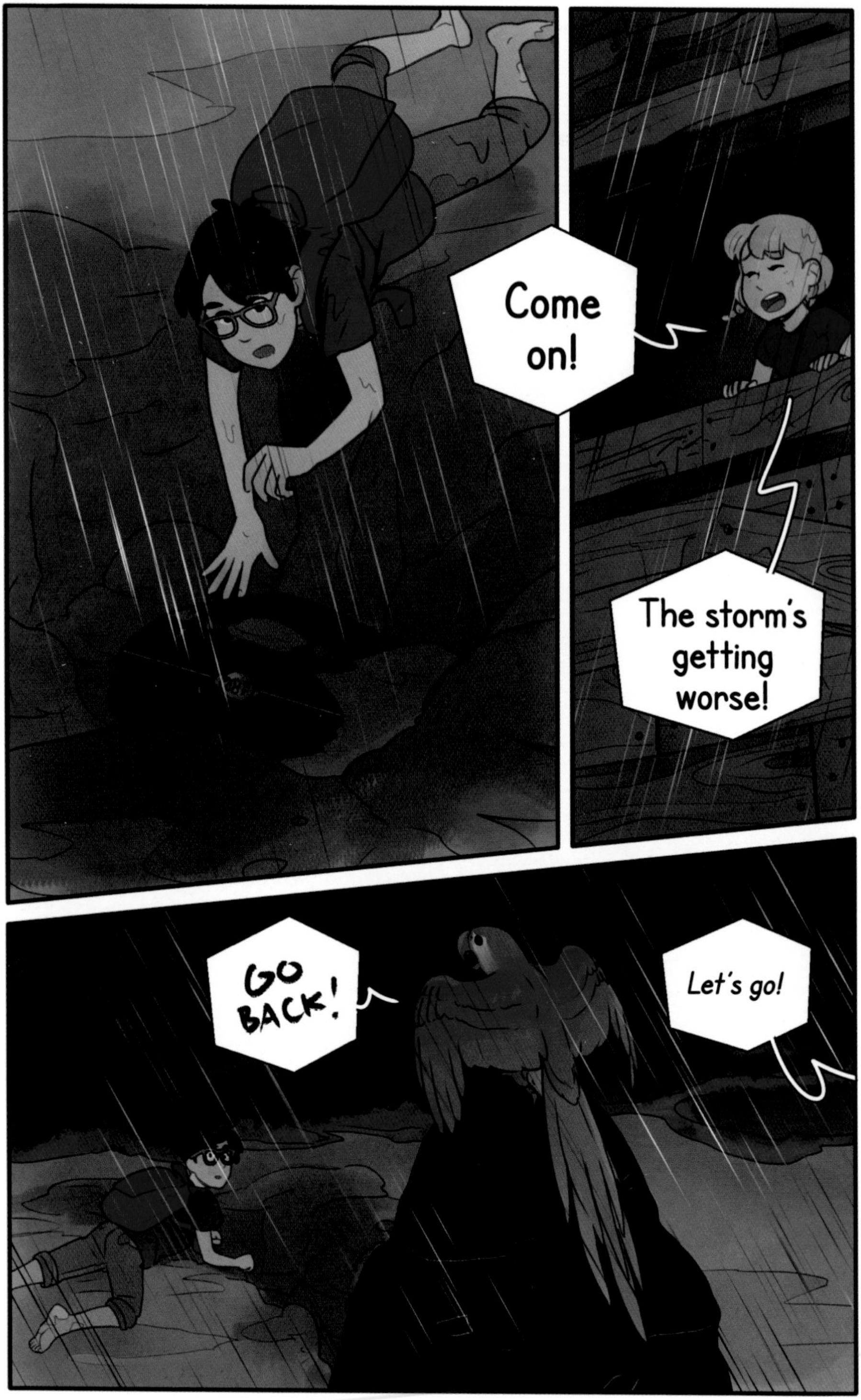
Come on!
The storm's getting worse!
GO BACK!
Let's go!

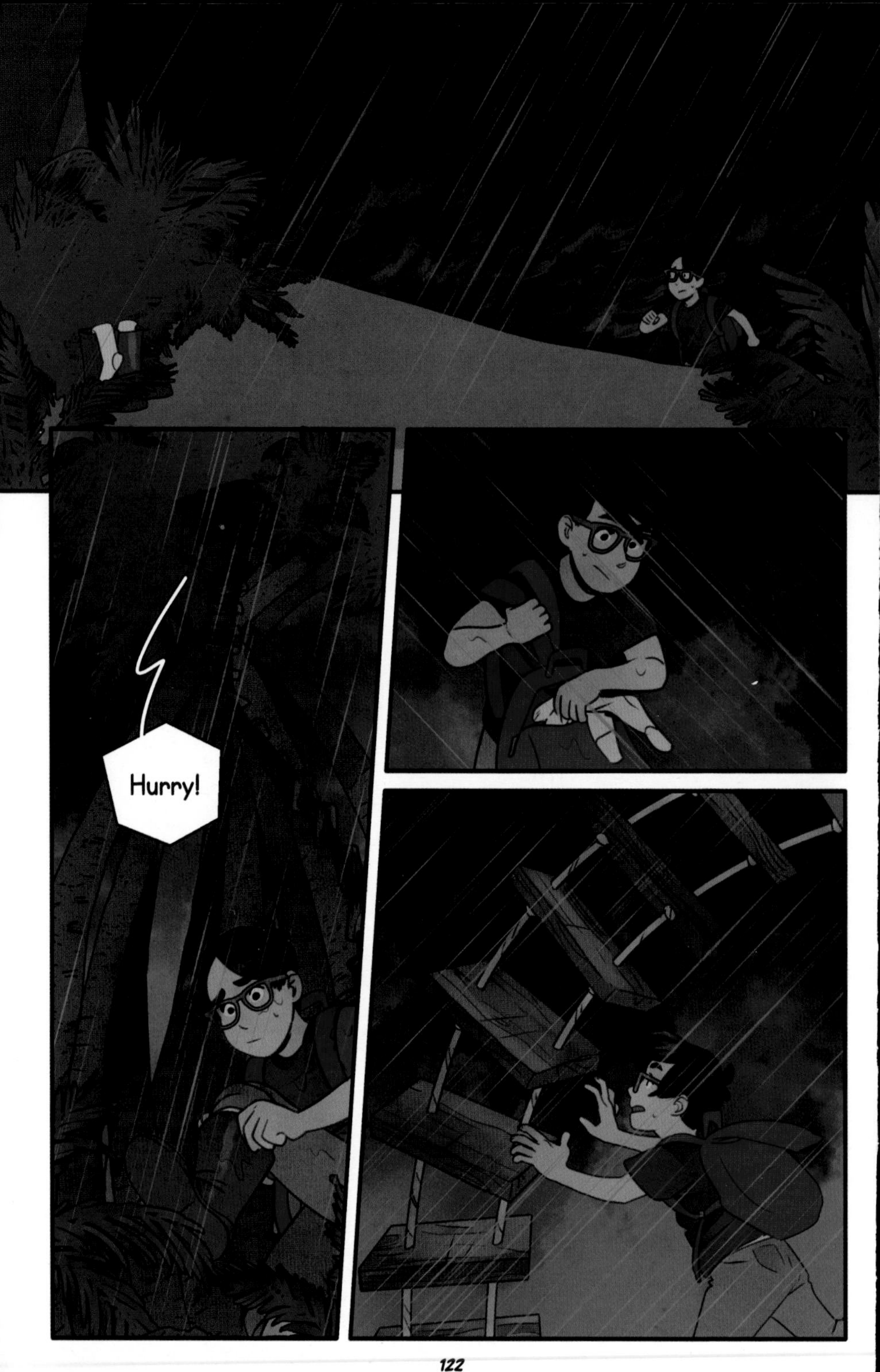
Hurry!

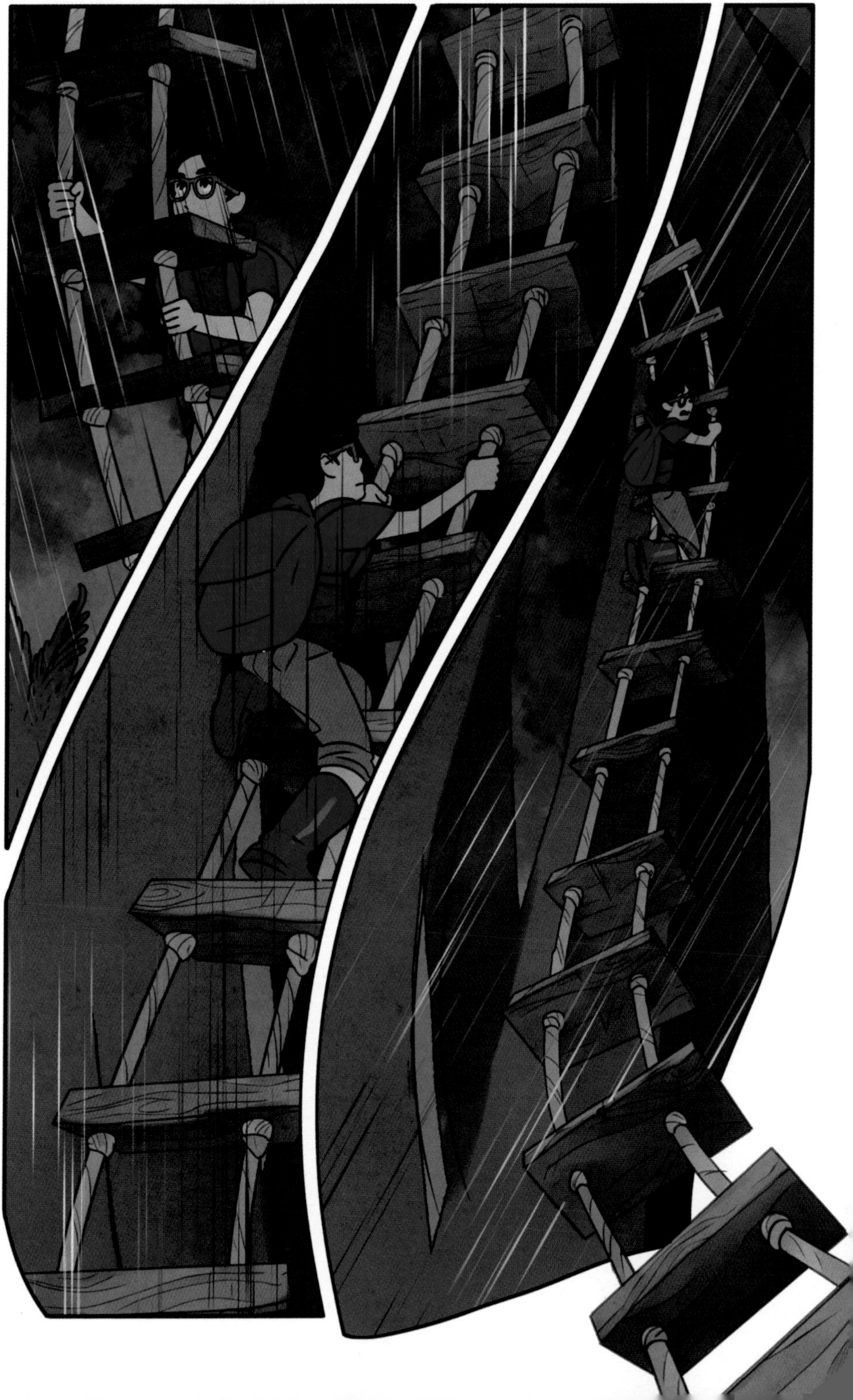

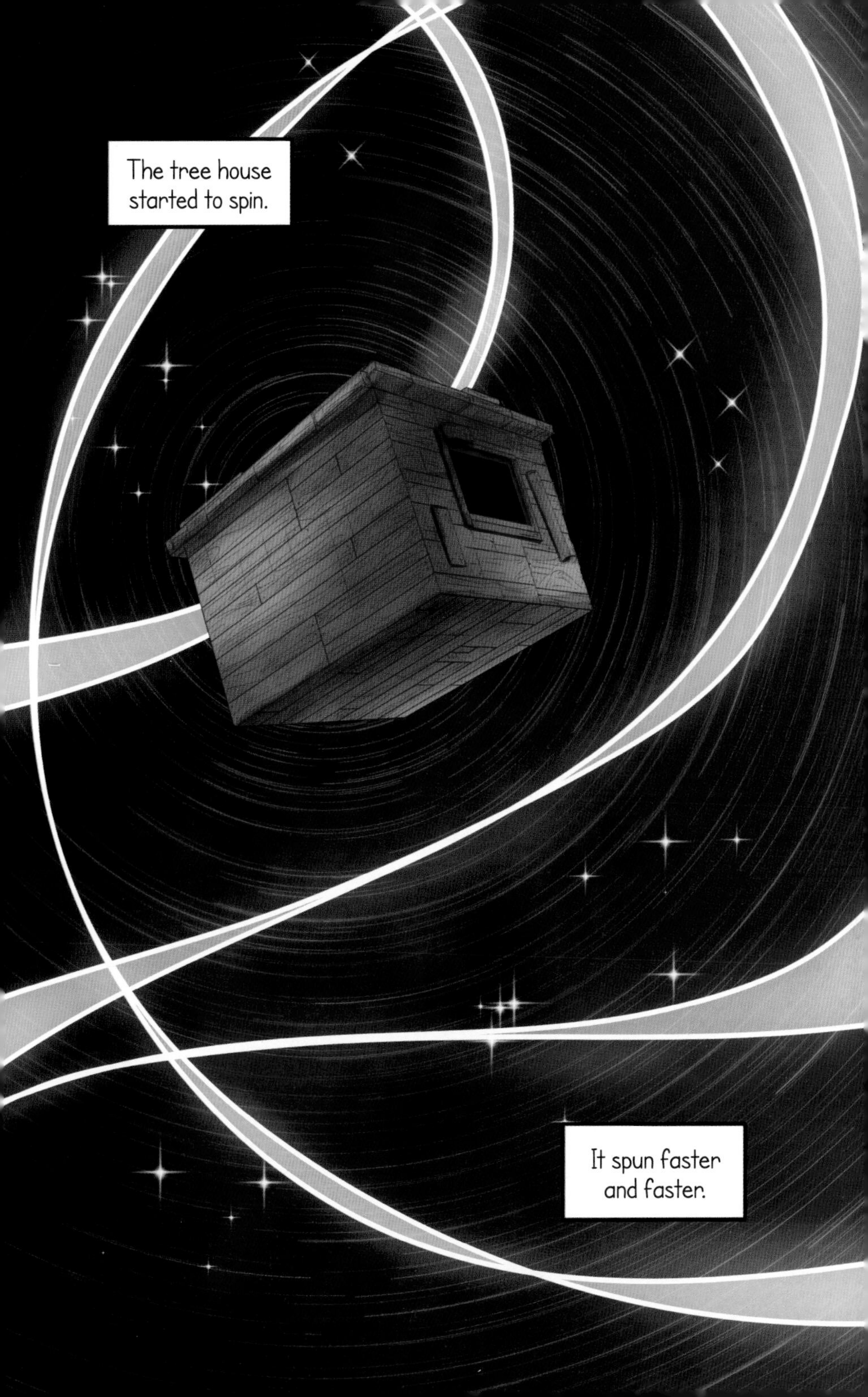
The tree house started to spin.
It spun faster and faster.

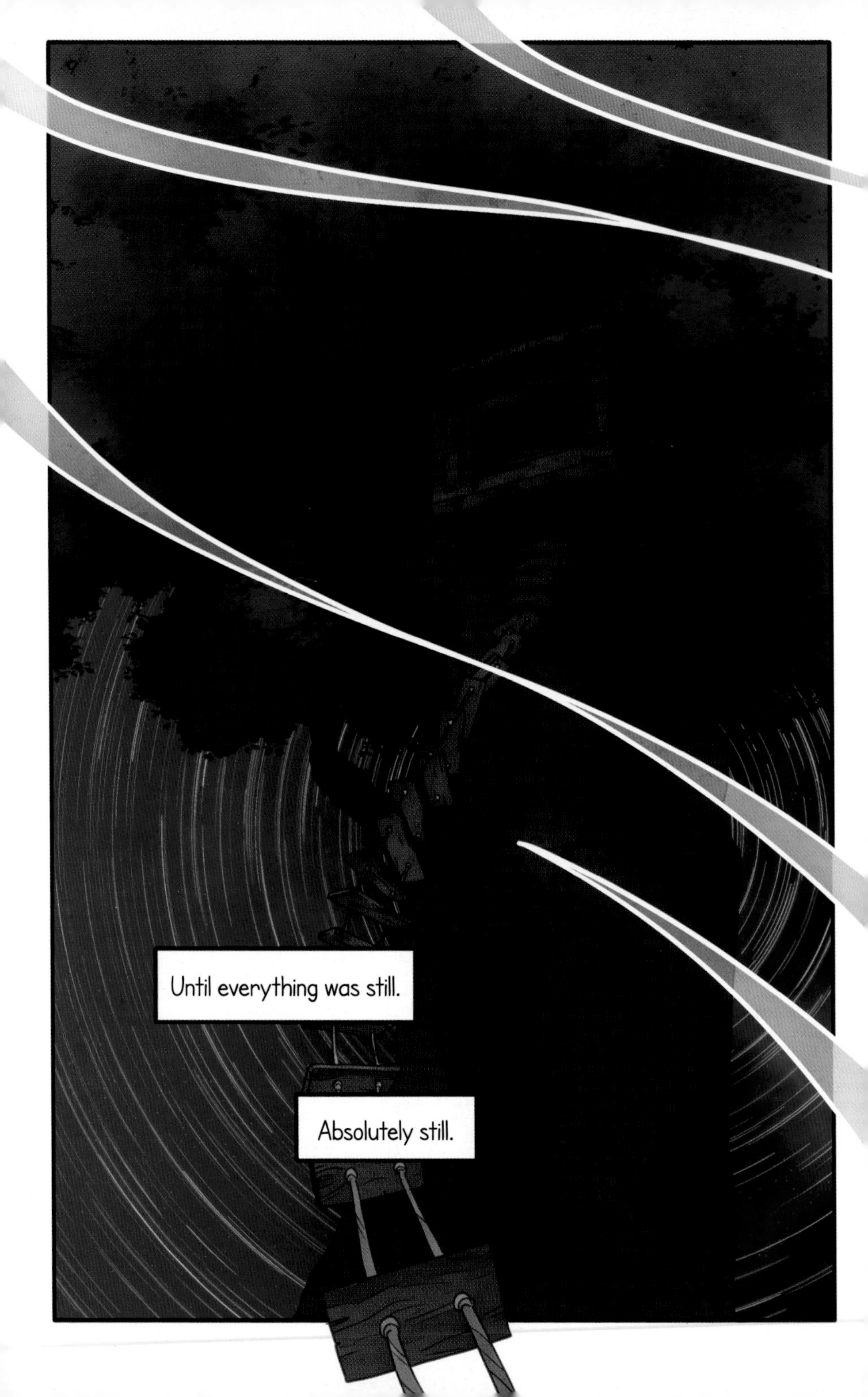
Until everything was still.
Absolutely still.

CHAPTER NINE
The Mysterious M

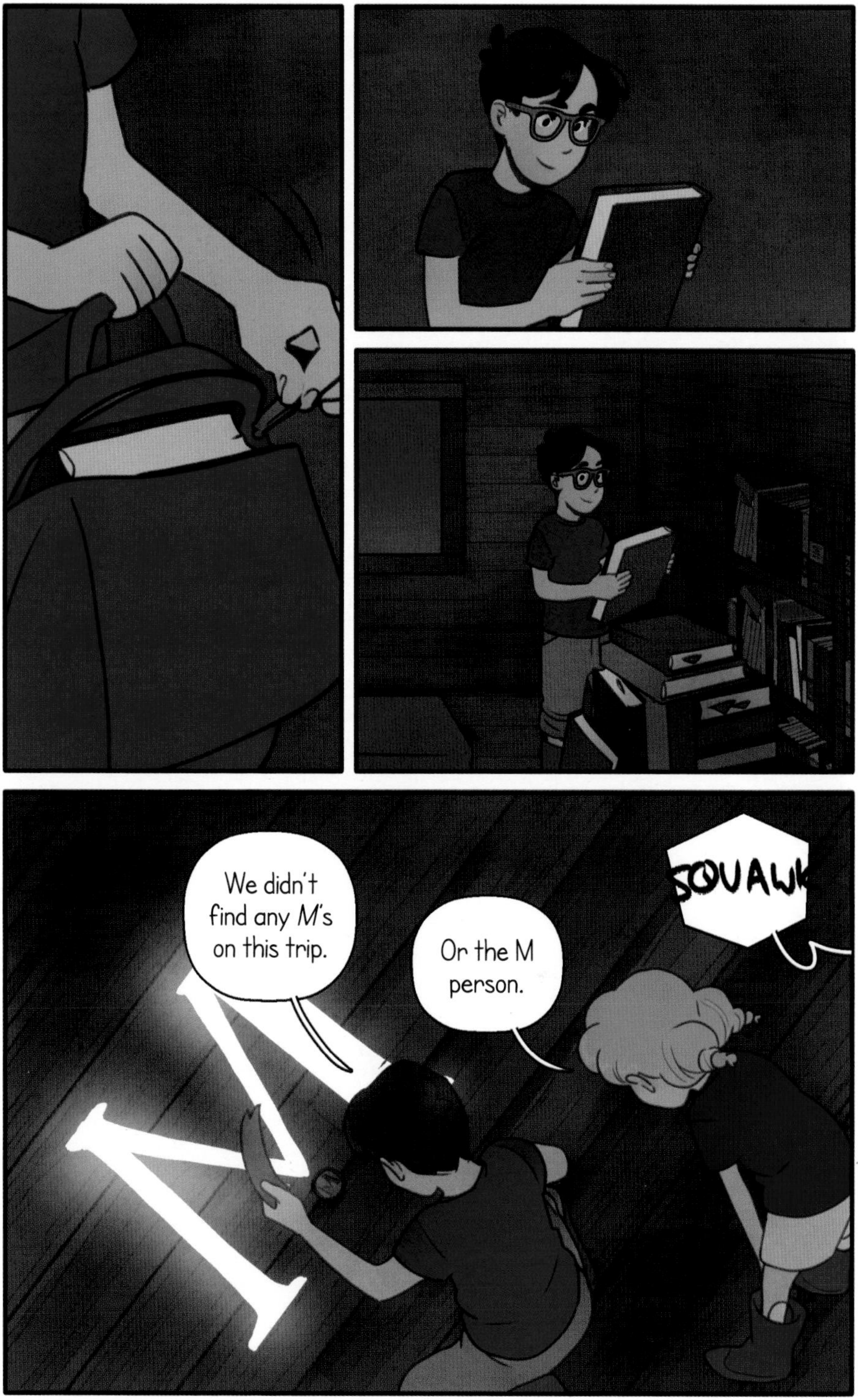
We didn't find any M's on this trip.
Or the M person.
SQUAWK

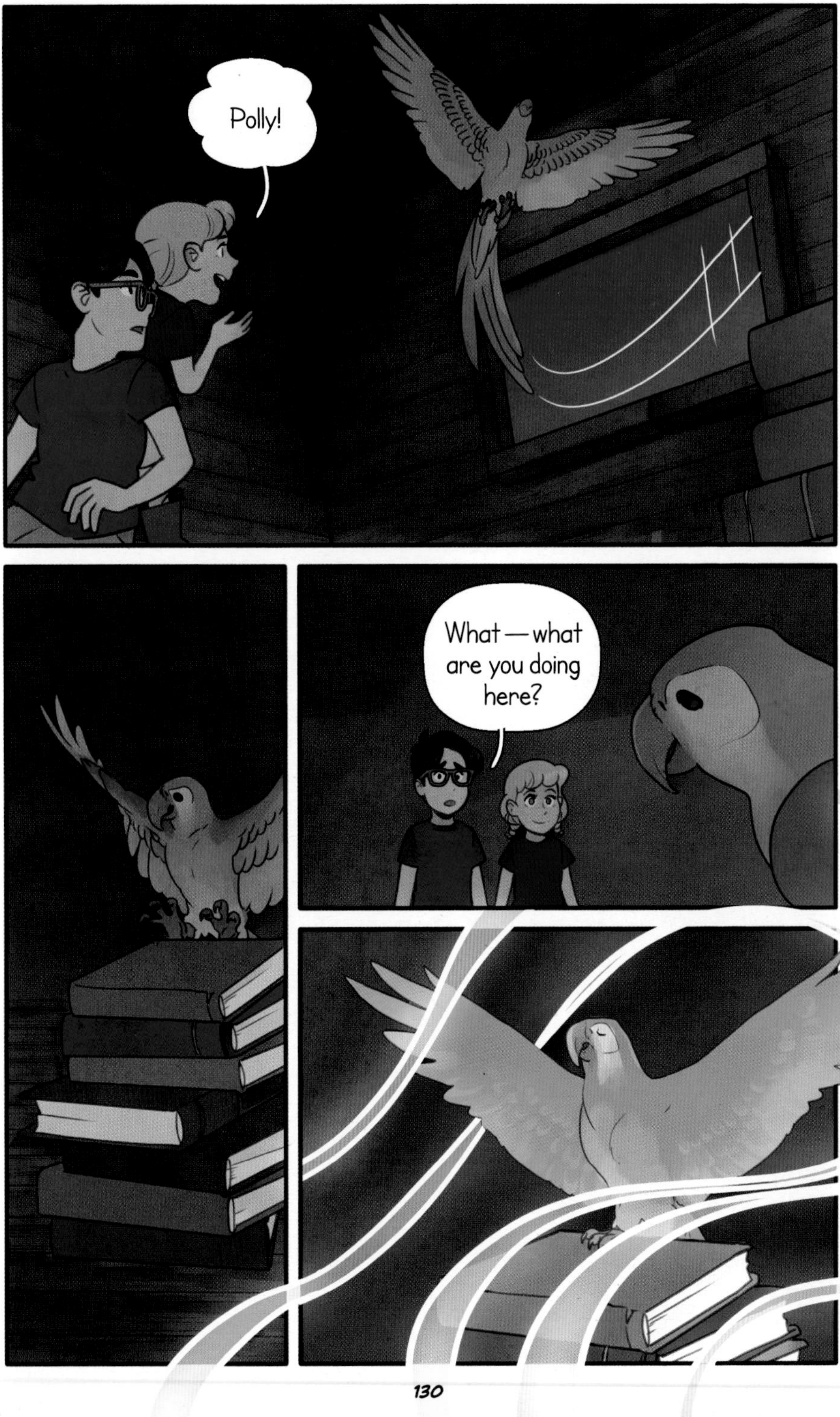
Polly!
What—what are you doing here?

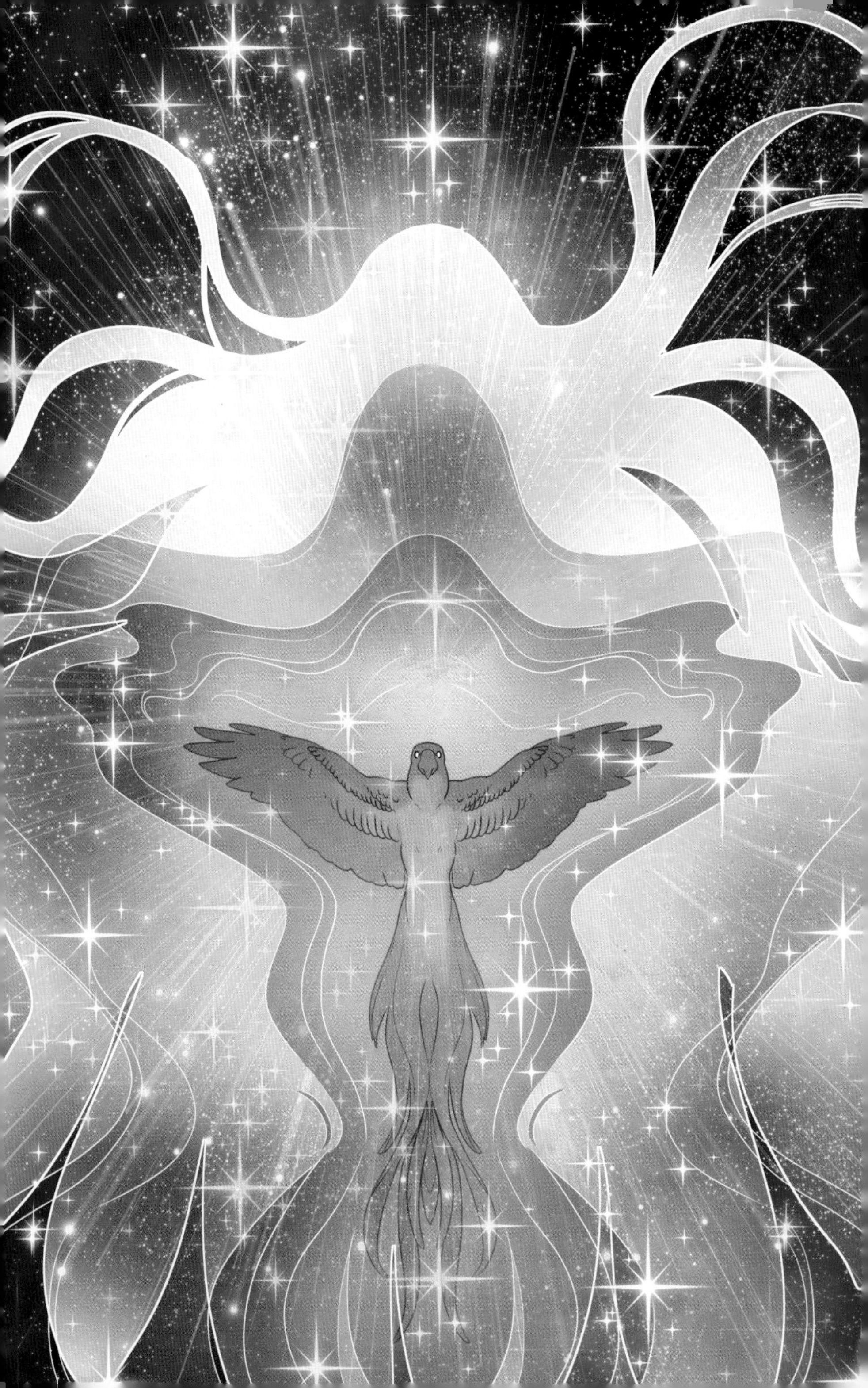

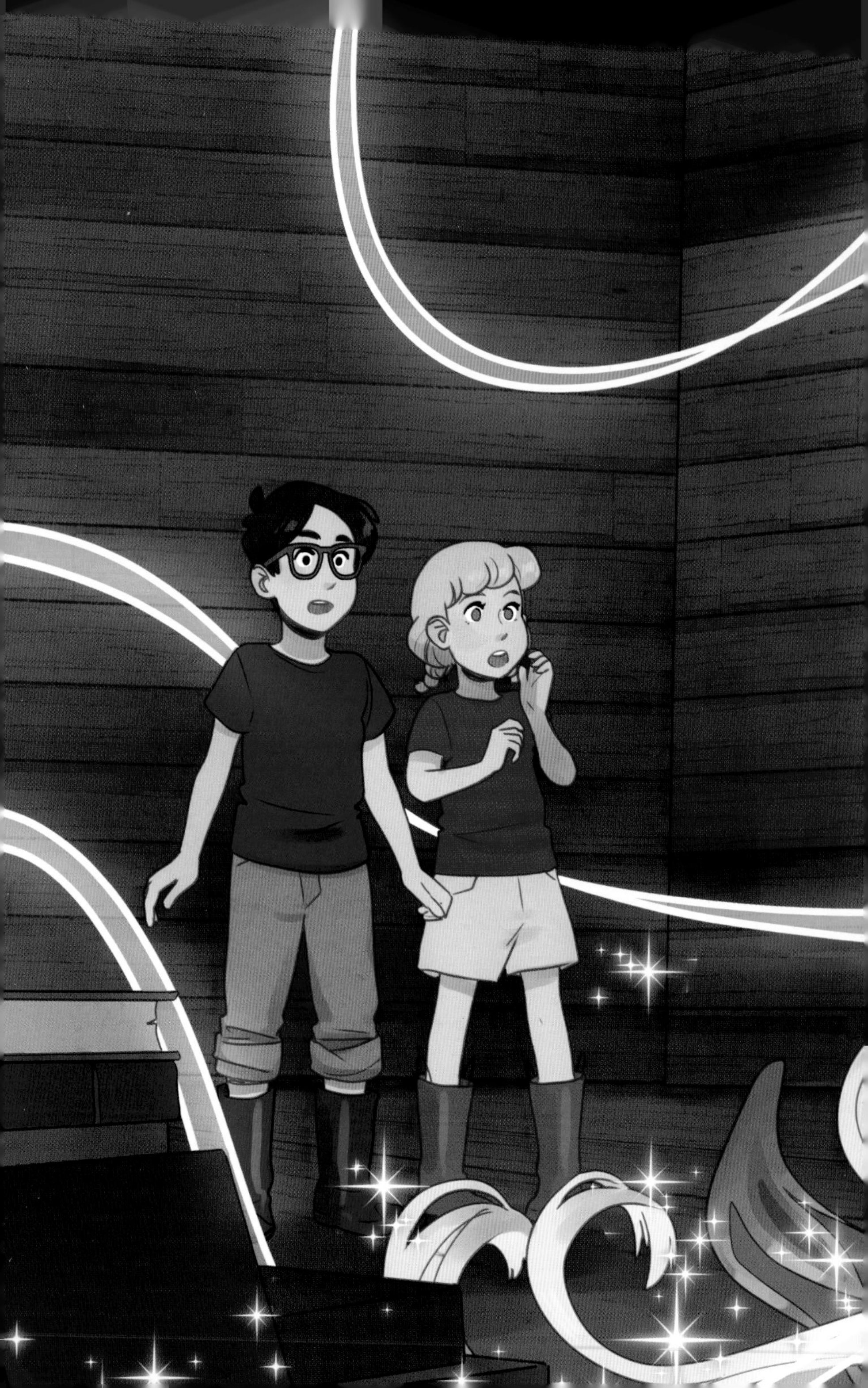

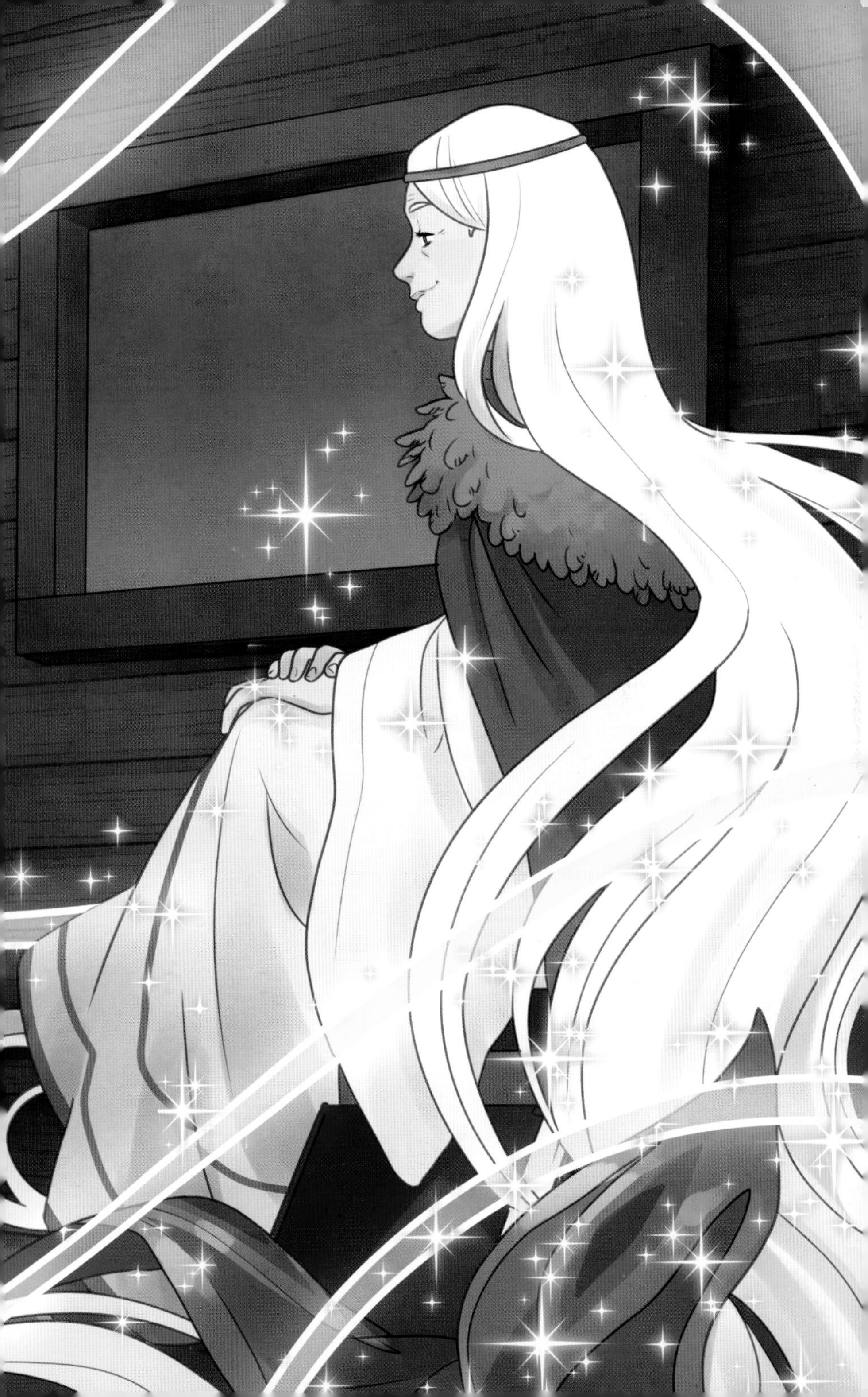

CHAPTER TEN
Treasure Again

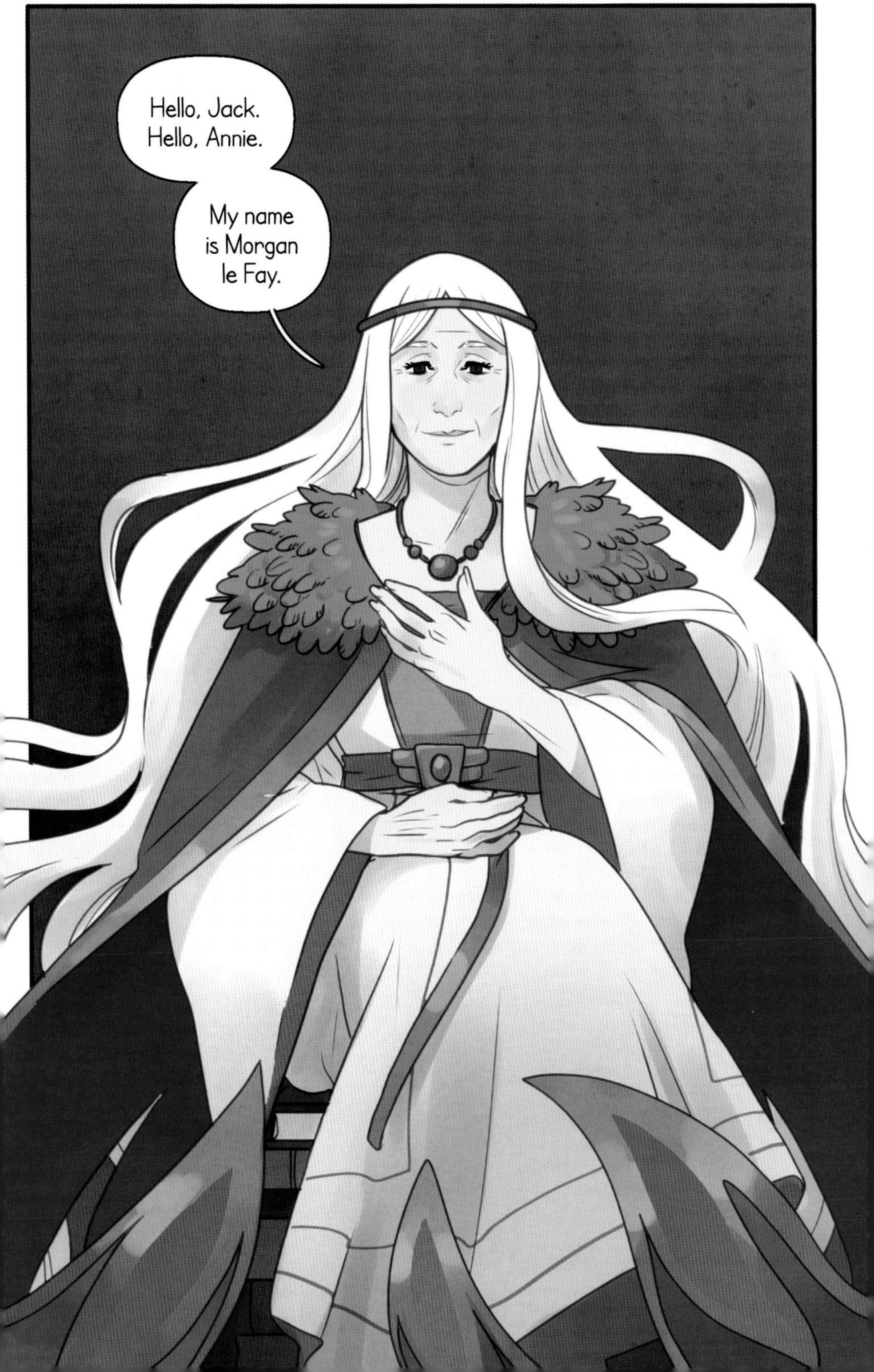
Hello, Jack. Hello, Annie.
My name is Morgan le Fay.

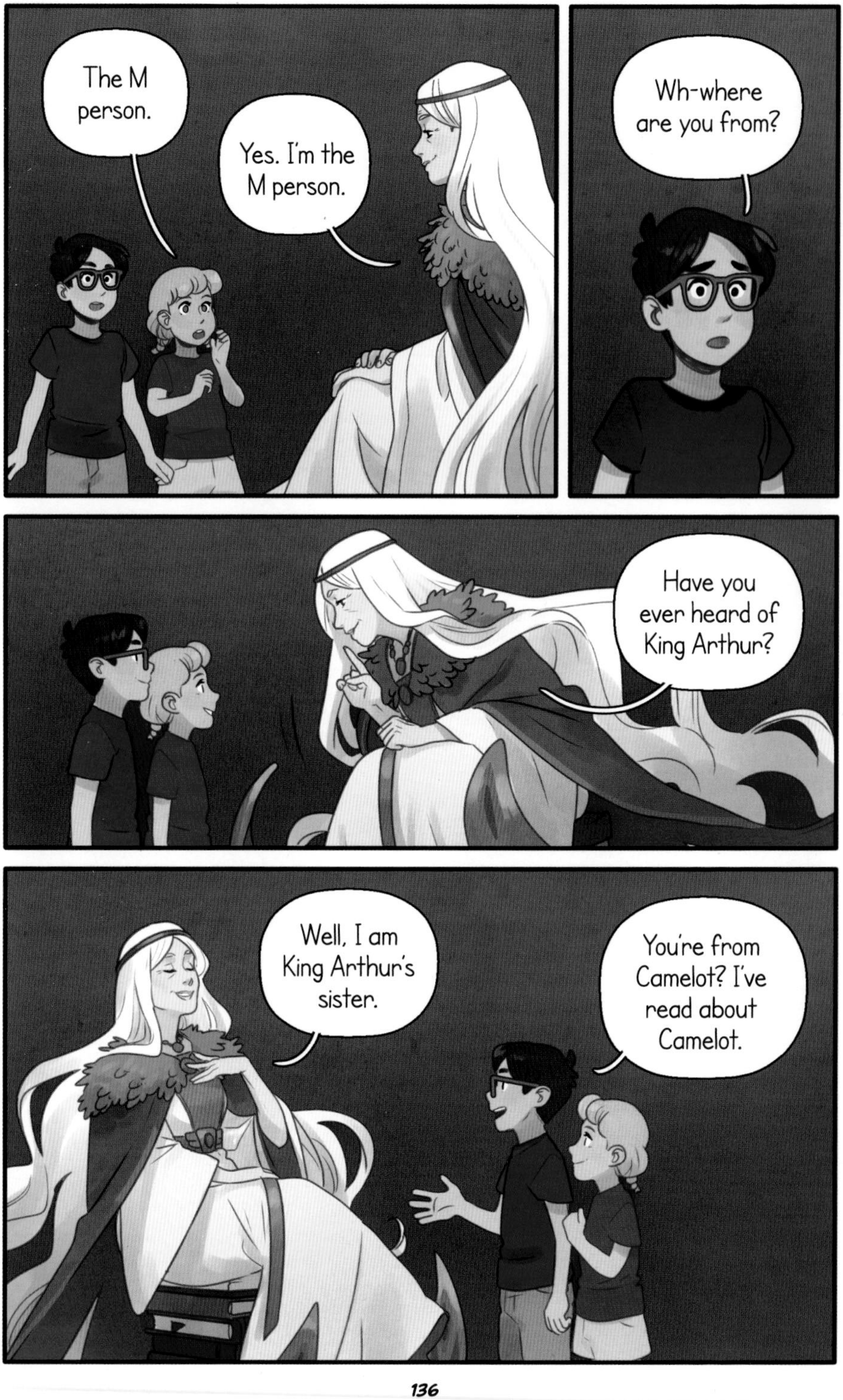
The M person.
Yes. I'm the M person.
Wh-where are you from?
Have you ever heard of King Arthur?
Well, I am King Arthur's sister.
You're from Camelot? I've read about Camelot.

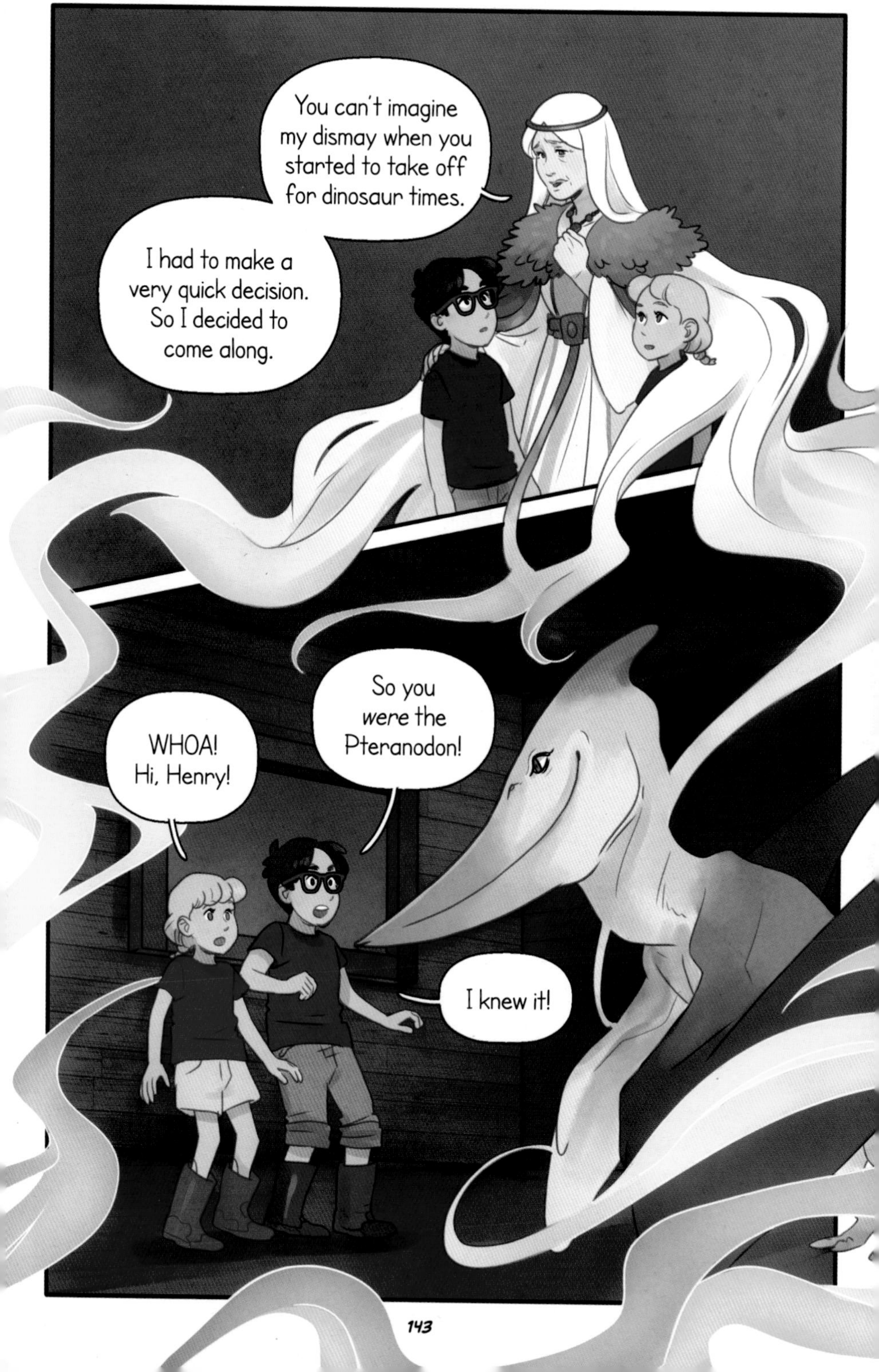
You can't imagine my dismay when you started to take off for dinosaur times.
I had to make a very quick decision. So I decided to come along.
WHOA! Hi, Henry!
So you *were* the Pteranodon!
I knew it!

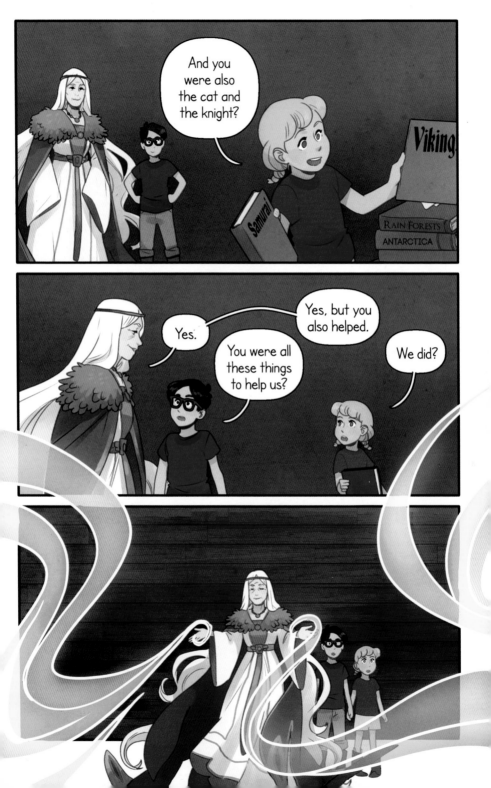

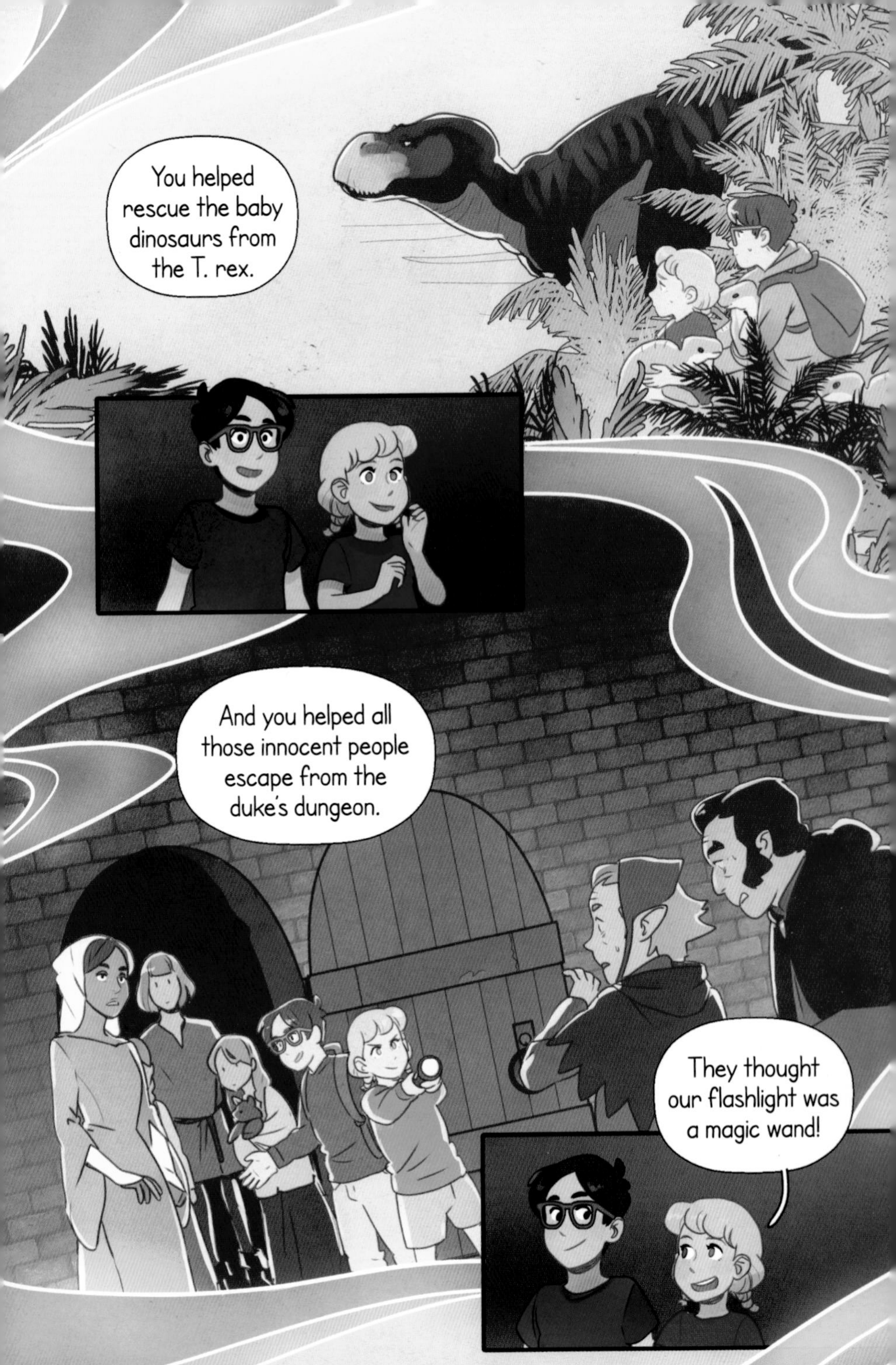
You helped rescue the baby dinosaurs from the T. rex.
And you helped all those innocent people escape from the duke's dungeon.
They thought our flashlight was a magic wand!

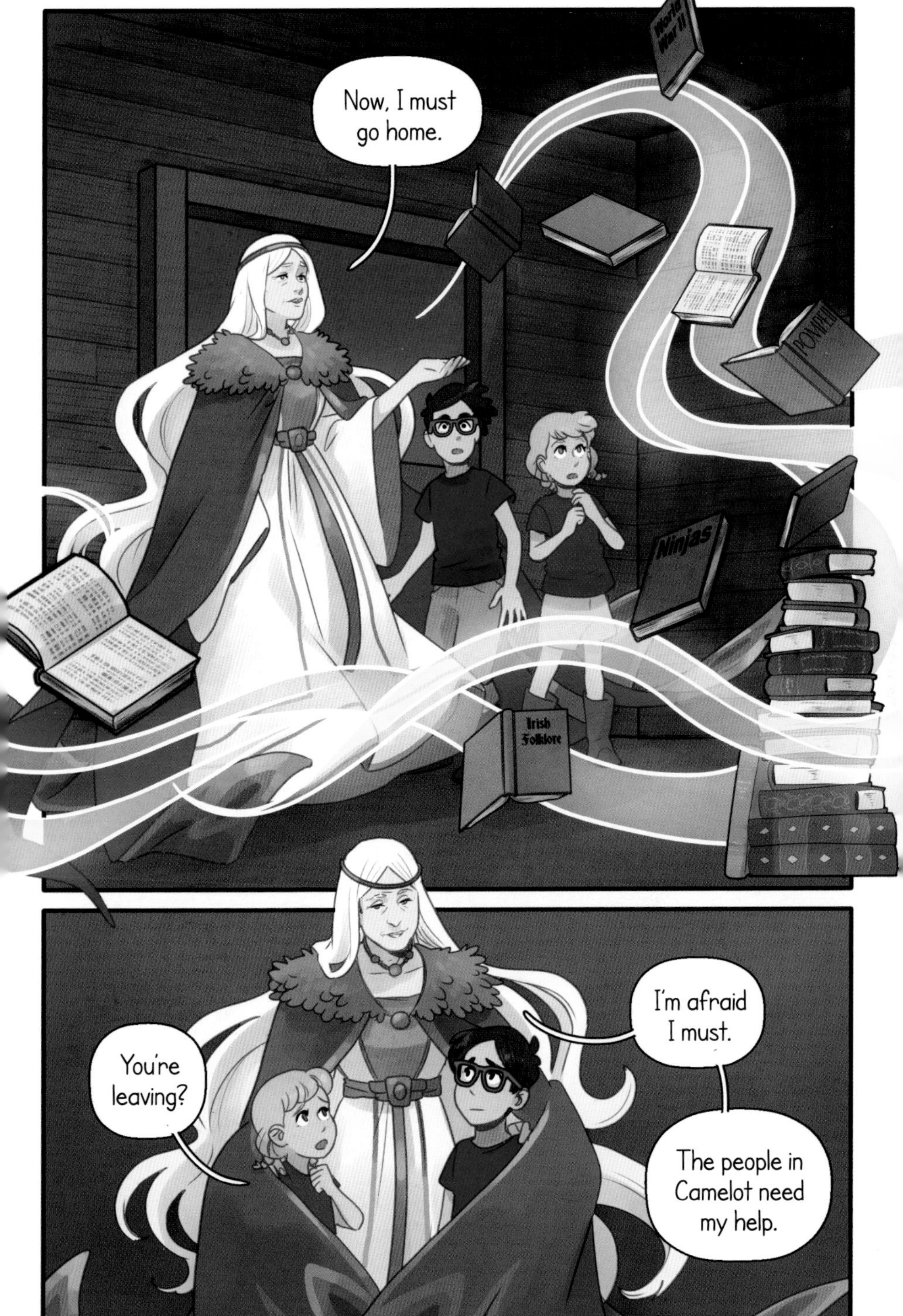
Now, I must go home.
World War II
POMPEII
Ninjas
Irish Folklore
You're leaving?
I'm afraid I must.
The people in Camelot need my help.

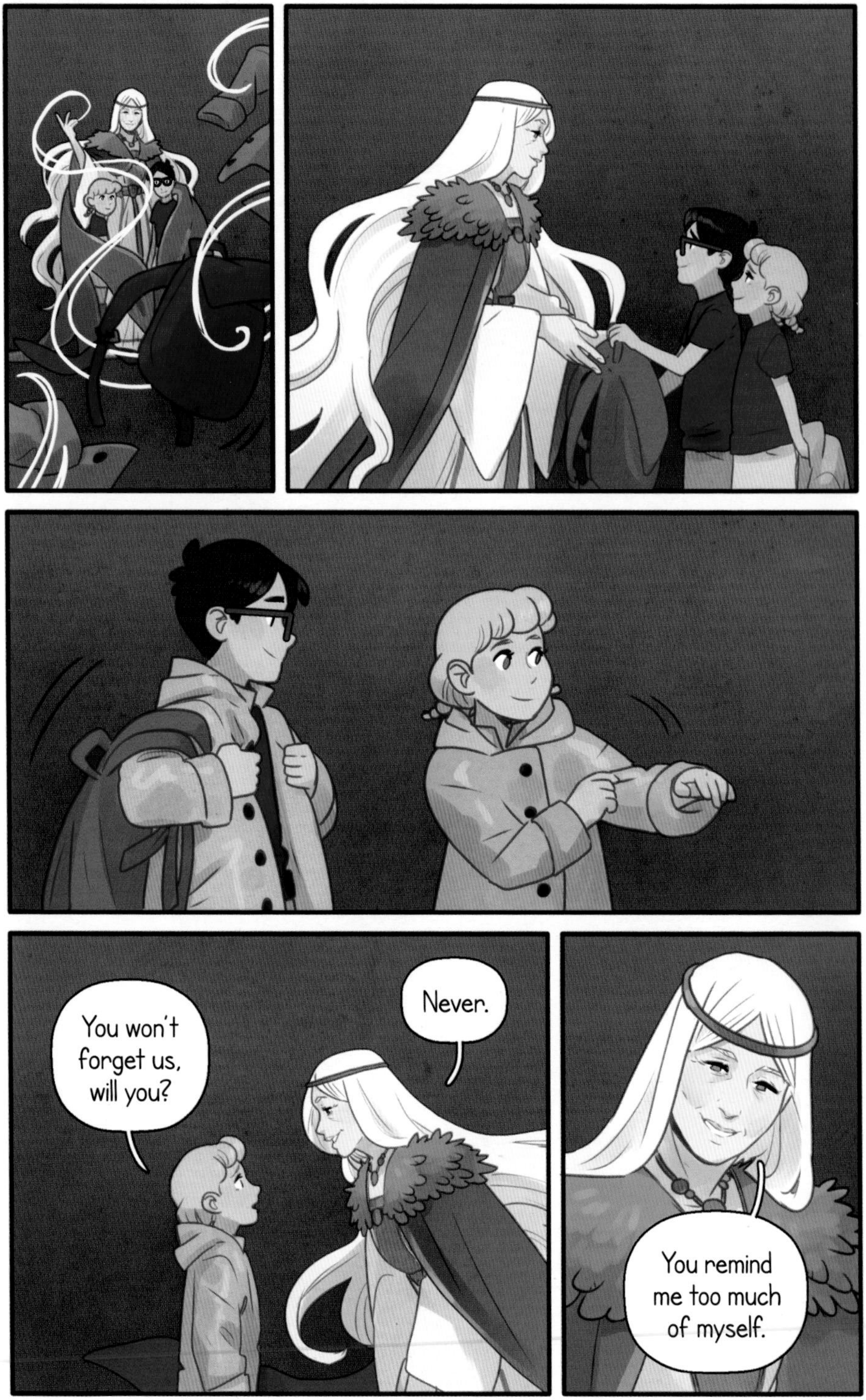
You won't forget us, will you?
Never.
You remind me too much of myself.

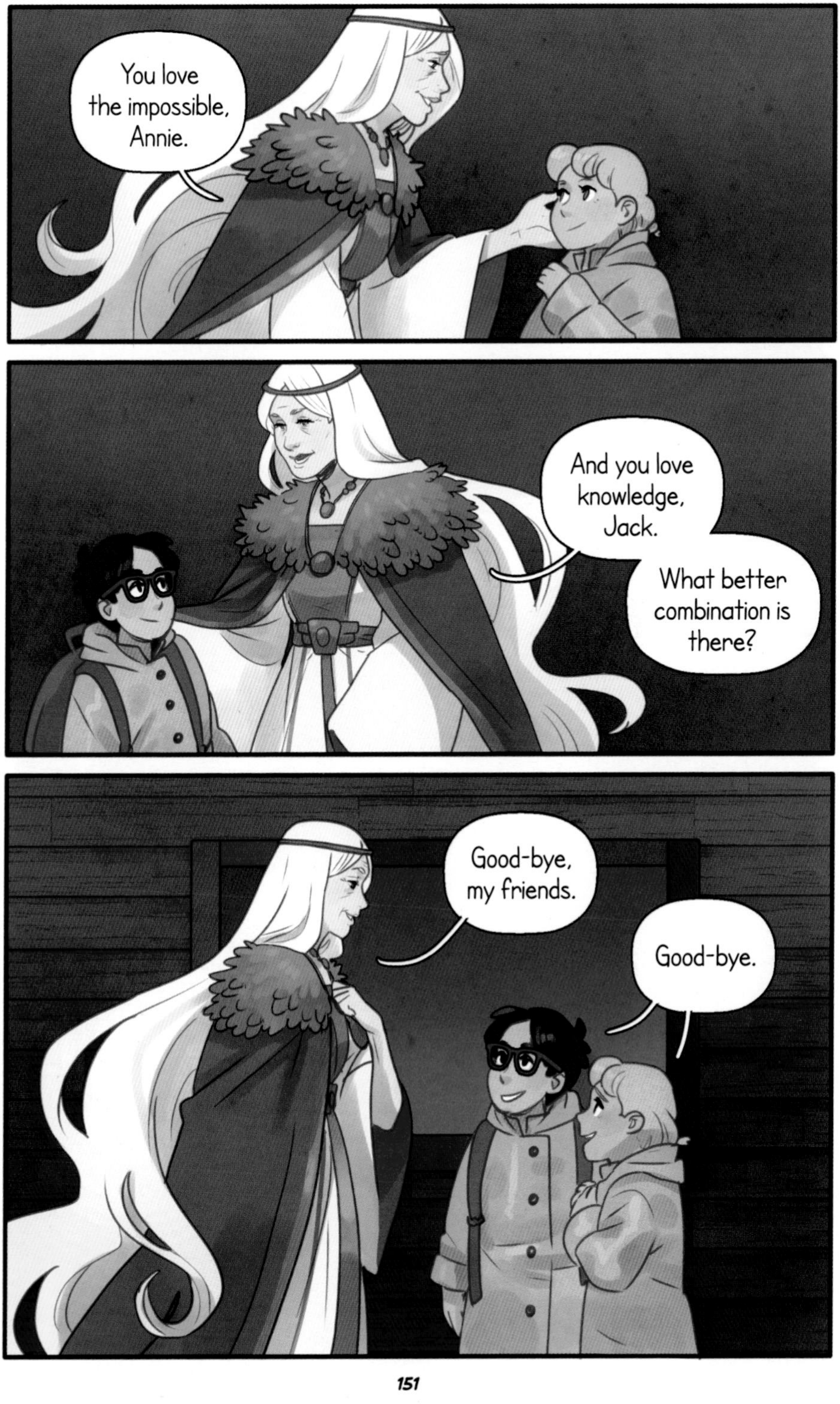
You love the impossible, Annie.
And you love knowledge, Jack.
What better combination is there?
Good-bye, my friends.
Good-bye.

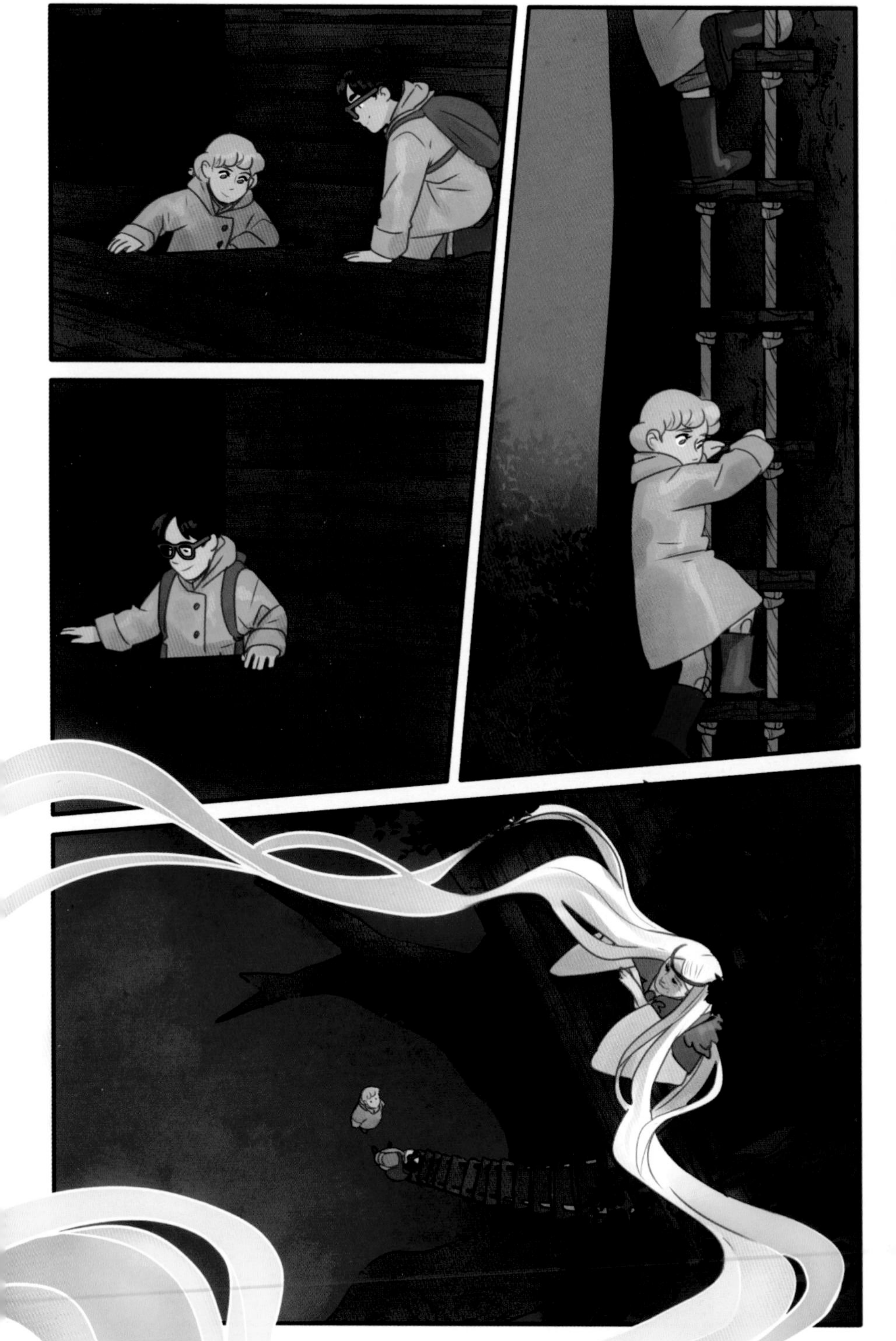

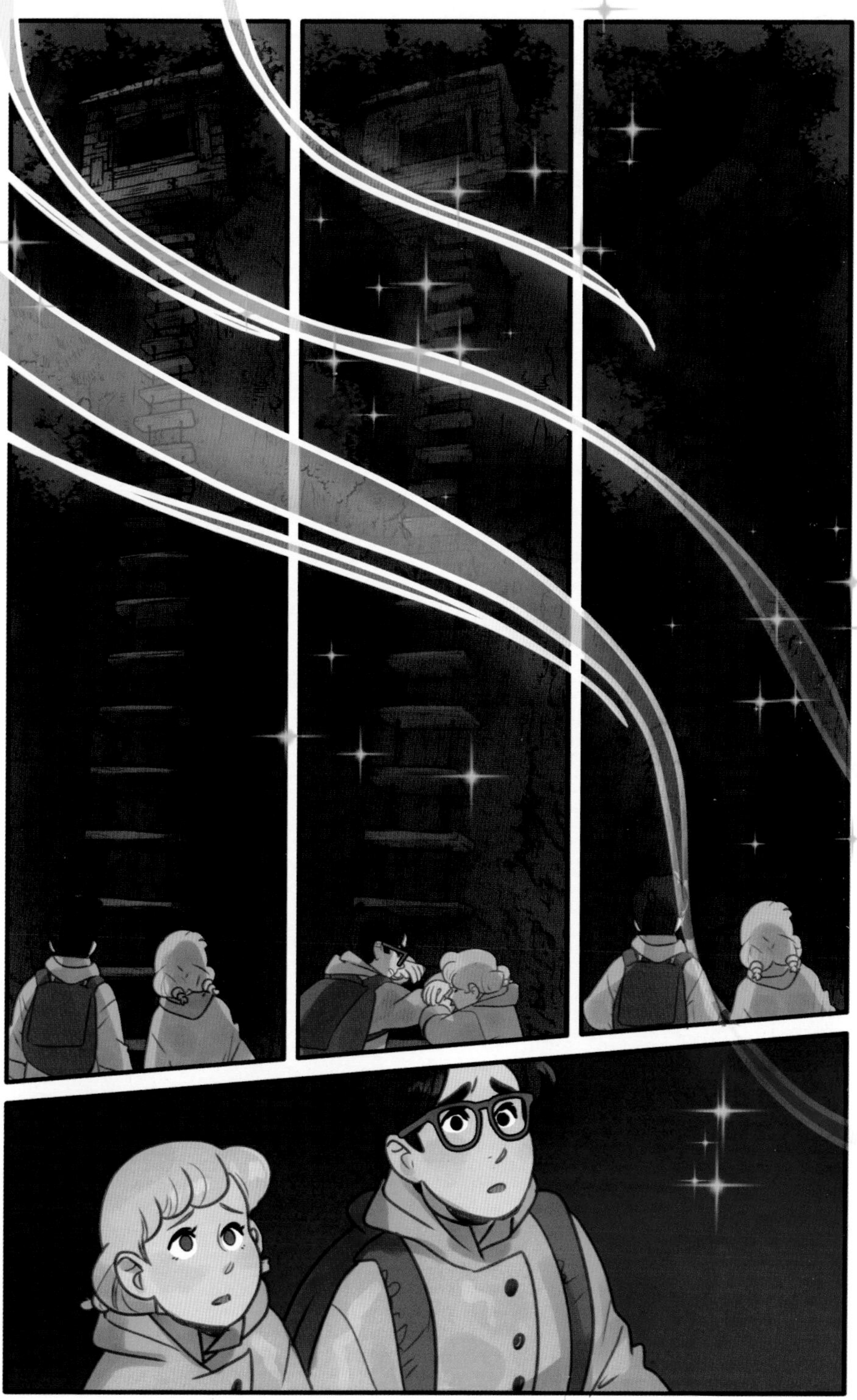

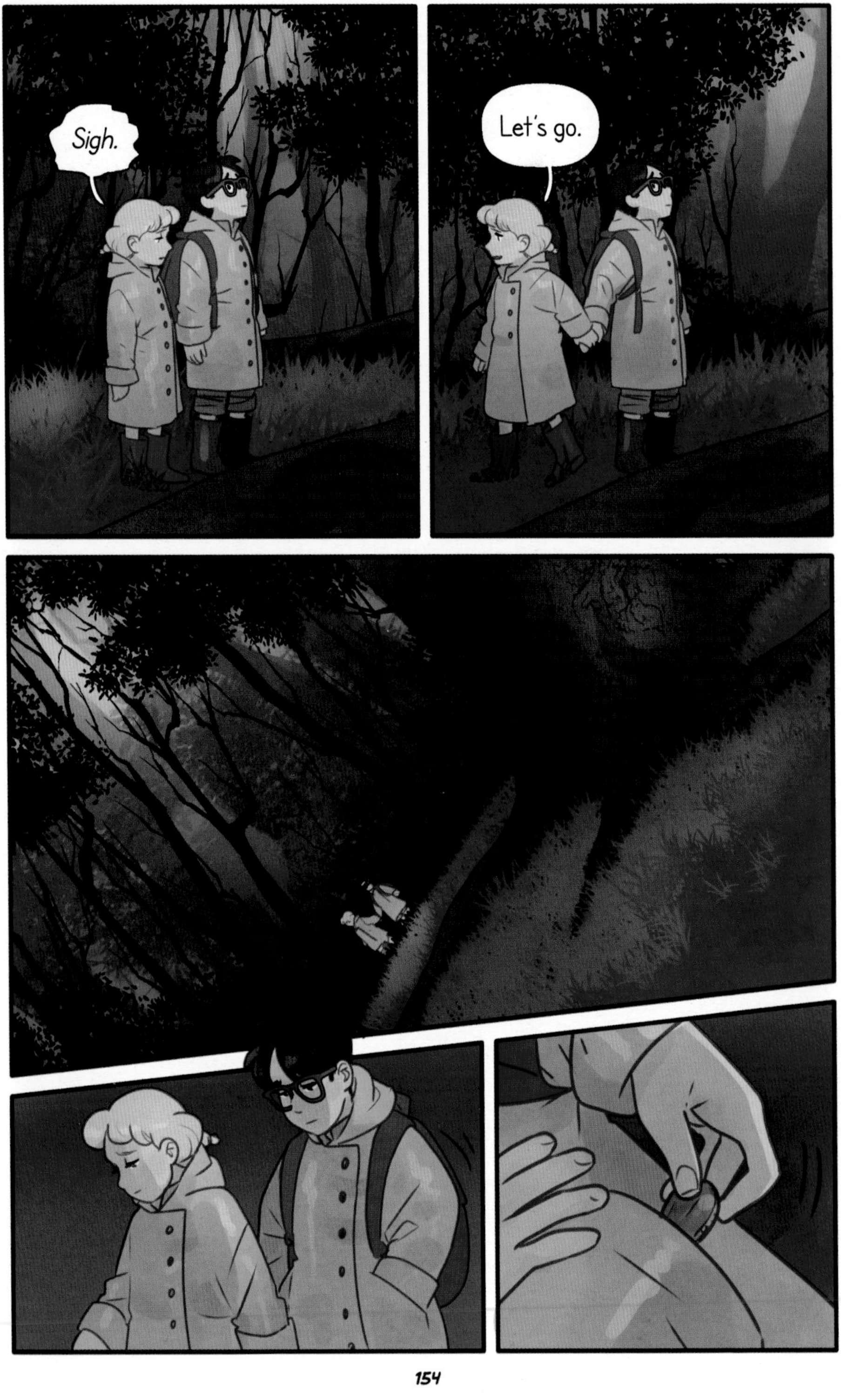
Sigh.
Let's go.

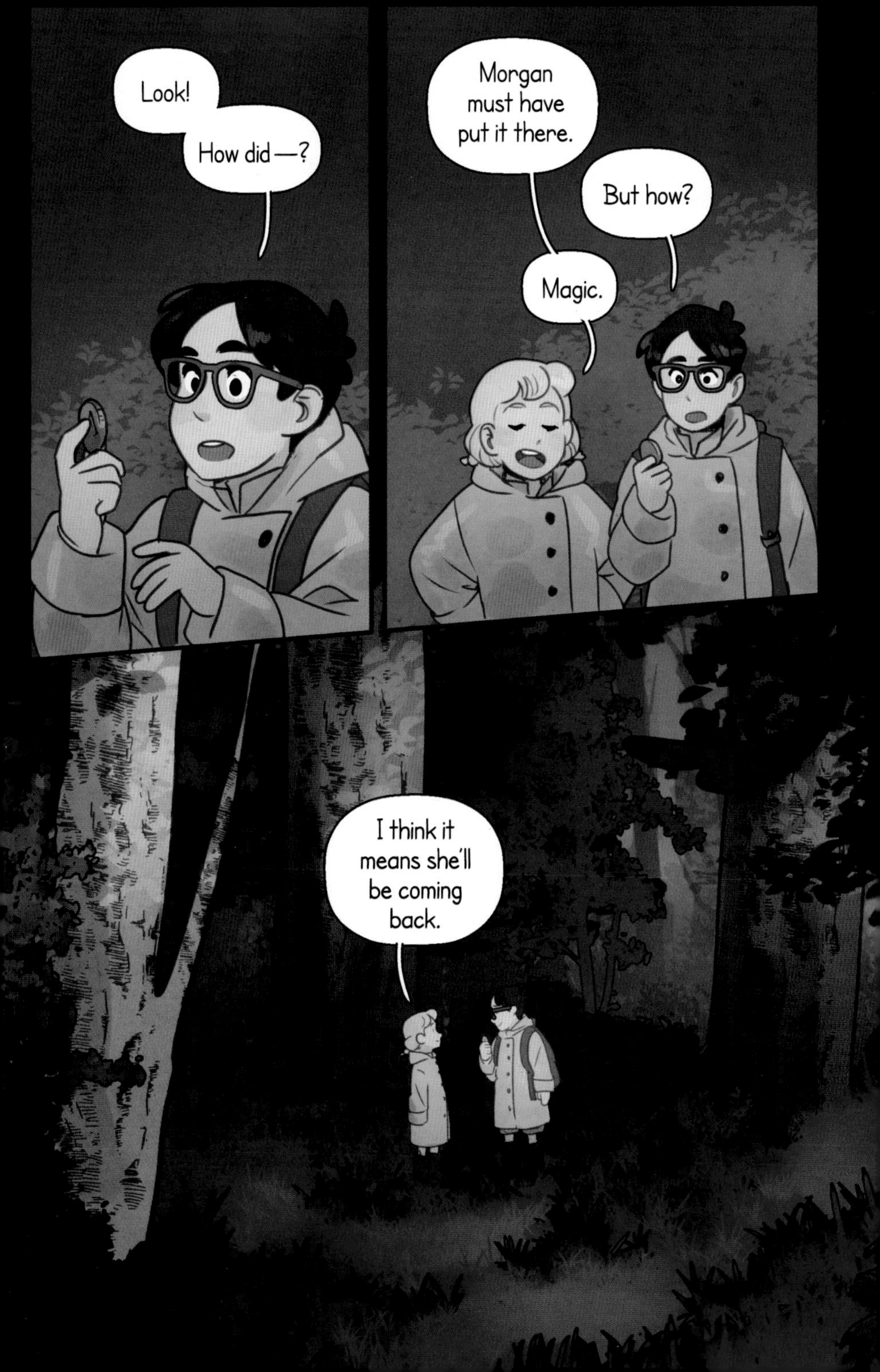
Look!
How did—?
Morgan must have put it there.
But how?
Magic.
I think it means she'll be coming back.

Don't miss another adventure in the Magic Tree House
where Jack and Annie get whisked away to ancient Egypt!

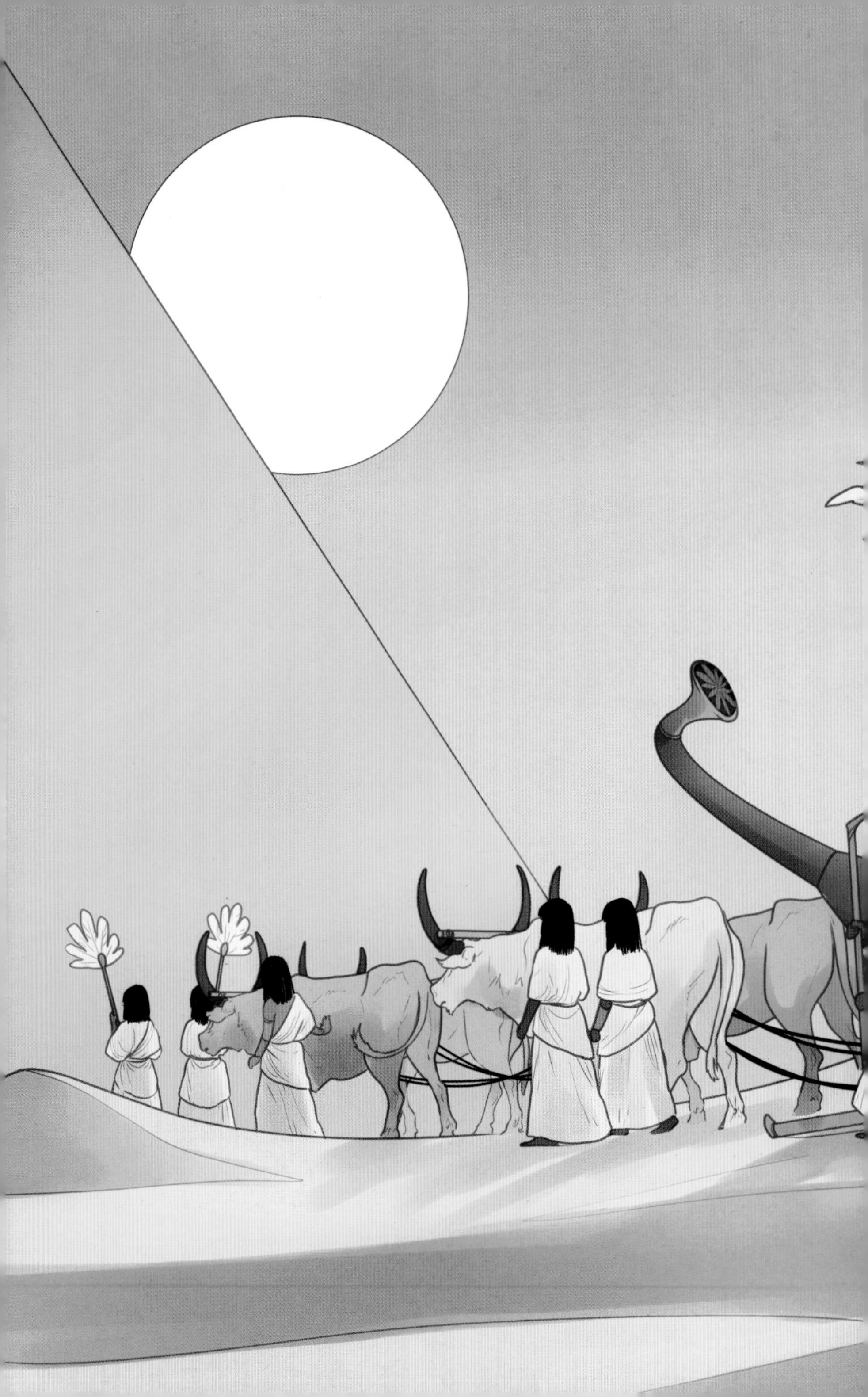

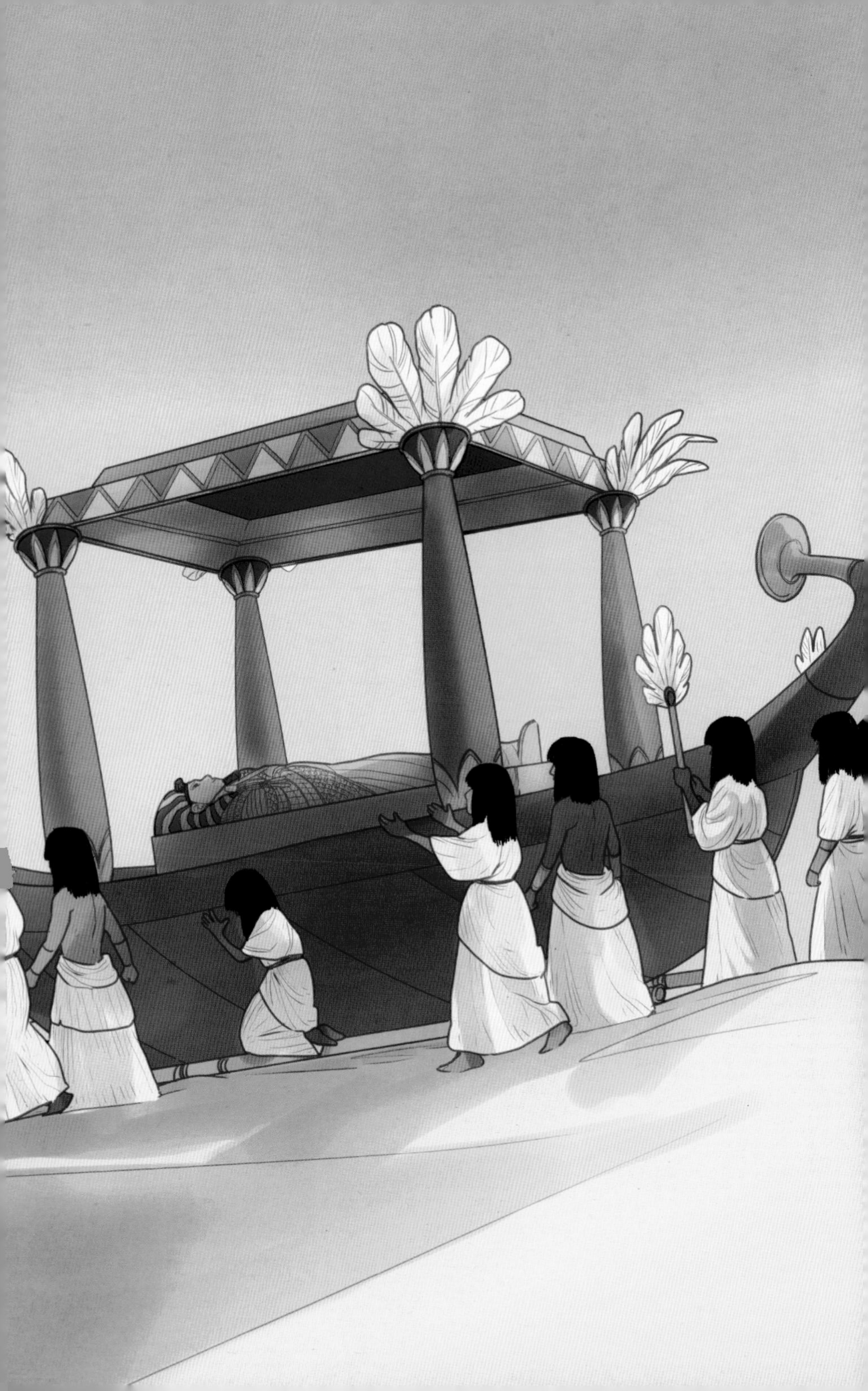

LET THE
MAGIC TREE HOUSE®
WHISK YOU AWAY!

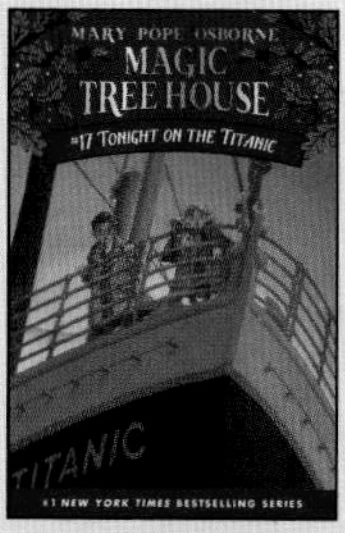
MARY POPE OSBORNE
MAGIC TREE HOUSE
#17 Tonight on the Titanic
TITANIC
#1 NEW YORK TIMES BESTSELLING SERIES

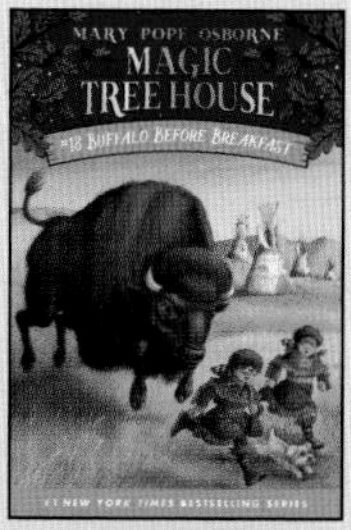
MARY POPE OSBORNE
MAGIC TREE HOUSE
#18 Buffalo Before Breakfast
#1 NEW YORK TIMES BESTSELLING SERIES

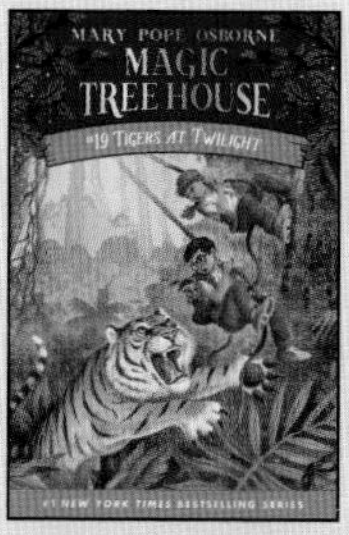
MARY POPE OSBORNE
MAGIC TREE HOUSE
#19 Tigers at Twilight
#1 NEW YORK TIMES BESTSELLING SERIES

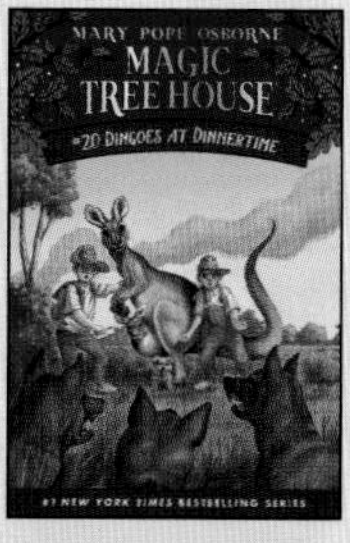
MARY POPE OSBORNE
MAGIC TREE HOUSE
#20 Dingoes at Dinnertime
#1 NEW YORK TIMES BESTSELLING SERIES

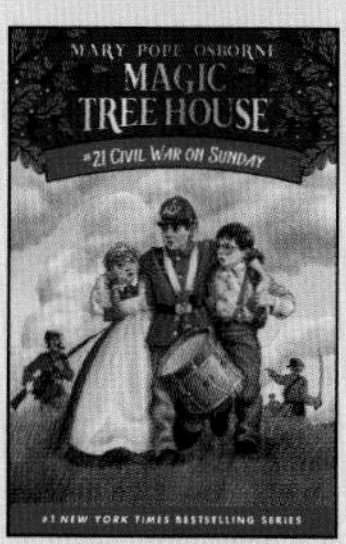
MARY POPE OSBORNE
MAGIC TREE HOUSE
#21 Civil War on Sunday
#1 NEW YORK TIMES BESTSELLING SERIES

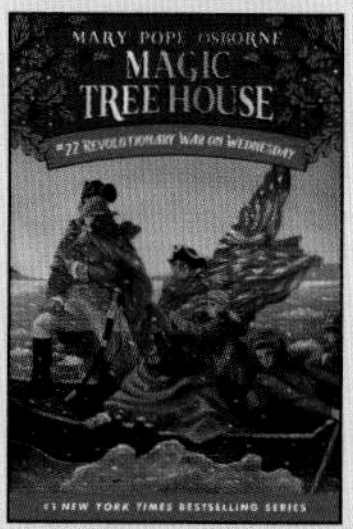
MARY POPE OSBORNE
MAGIC TREE HOUSE
#22 Revolutionary War on Wednesday
#1 NEW YORK TIMES BESTSELLING SERIES

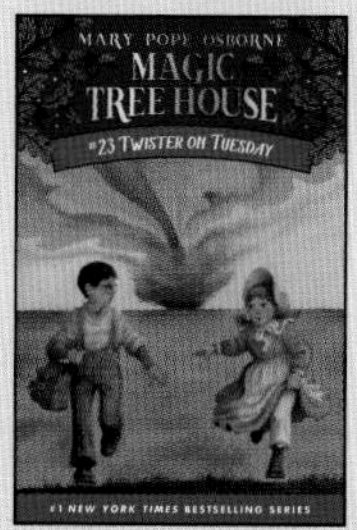
MARY POPE OSBORNE
MAGIC TREE HOUSE
#23 Twister on Tuesday
#1 NEW YORK TIMES BESTSELLING SERIES

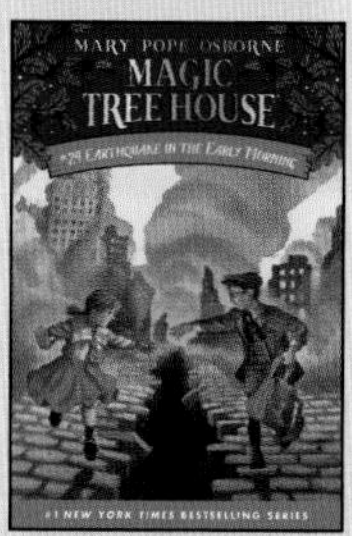
MARY POPE OSBORNE
MAGIC TREE HOUSE
#24 Earthquake in the Early Morning
#1 NEW YORK TIMES BESTSELLING SERIES

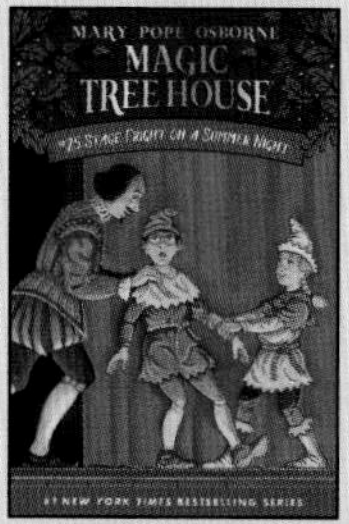
MARY POPE OSBORNE
MAGIC TREE HOUSE
#25 Stage Fright on a Summer Night
#1 NEW YORK TIMES BESTSELLING SERIES

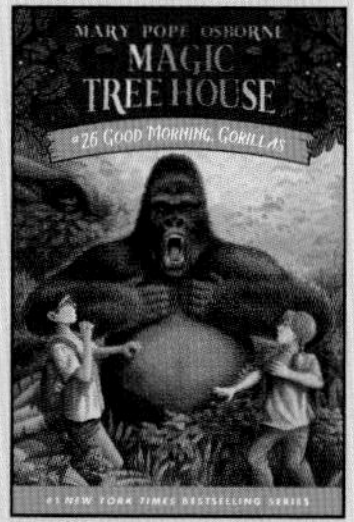
MARY POPE OSBORNE
MAGIC TREE HOUSE
#26 Good Morning, Gorillas
#1 NEW YORK TIMES BESTSELLING SERIES

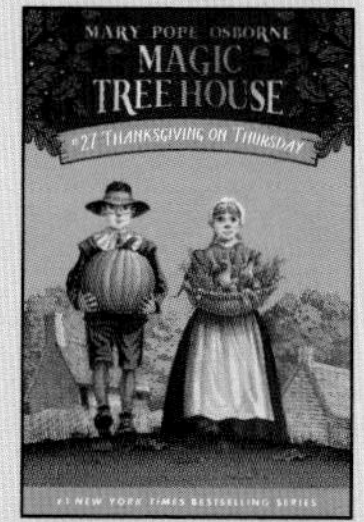
MARY POPE OSBORNE
MAGIC TREE HOUSE
#27 Thanksgiving on Thursday
#1 NEW YORK TIMES BESTSELLING SERIES

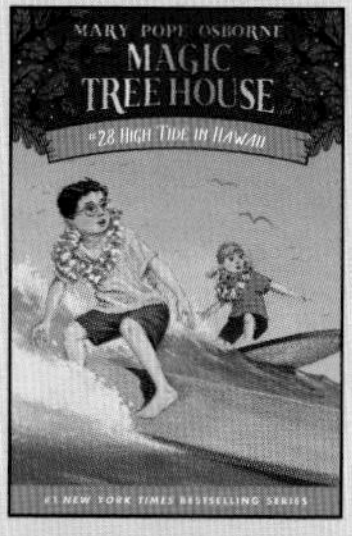
MARY POPE OSBORNE
MAGIC TREE HOUSE
#28 High Tide in Hawaii
#1 NEW YORK TIMES BESTSELLING SERIES

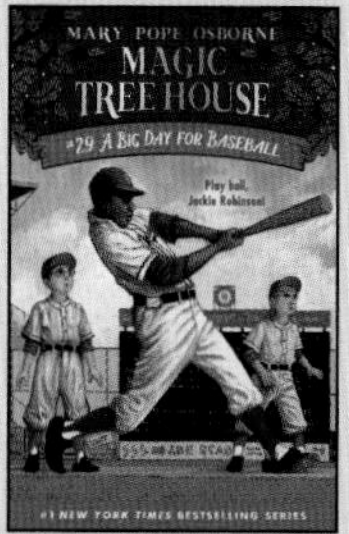
MARY POPE OSBORNE
MAGIC TREE HOUSE
#29 A Big Day for Baseball
Play ball, Jackie Robinson!
#1 NEW YORK TIMES BESTSELLING SERIES

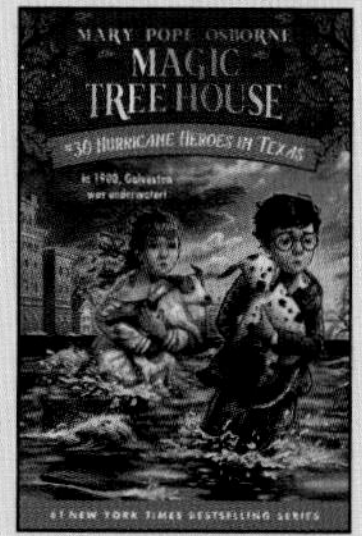
MARY POPE OSBORNE
MAGIC TREE HOUSE
#30 Hurricane Heroes in Texas
In 1900, Galveston was underwater!
#1 NEW YORK TIMES BESTSELLING SERIES

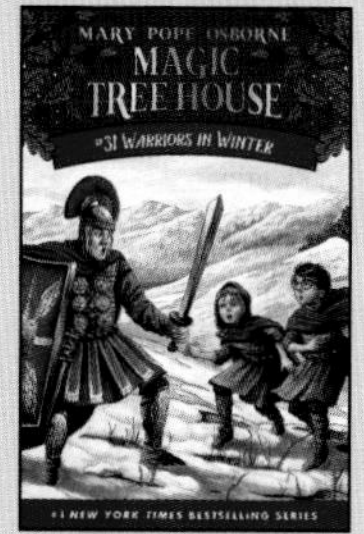
MARY POPE OSBORNE
MAGIC TREE HOUSE
#31 Warriors in Winter
#1 NEW YORK TIMES BESTSELLING SERIES

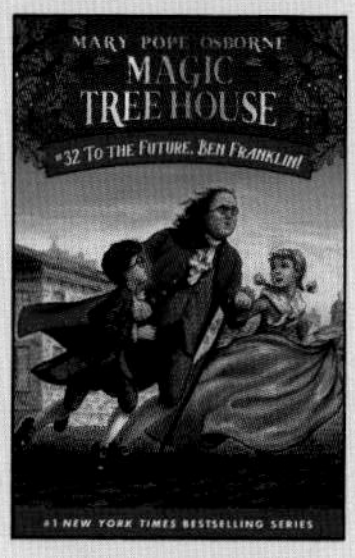
MARY POPE OSBORNE
MAGIC TREE HOUSE
#32 To the Future, Ben Franklin!
#1 NEW YORK TIMES BESTSELLING SERIES

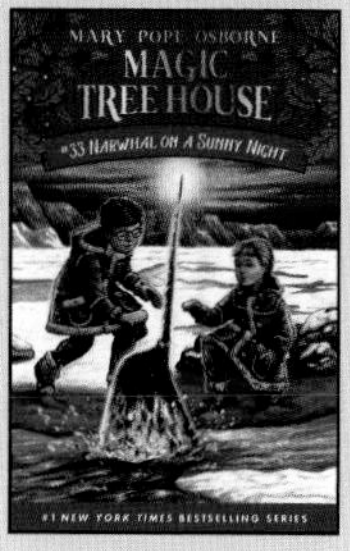
MARY POPE OSBORNE
MAGIC TREE HOUSE
#33 Narwhal on a Sunny Night
#1 NEW YORK TIMES BESTSELLING SERIES

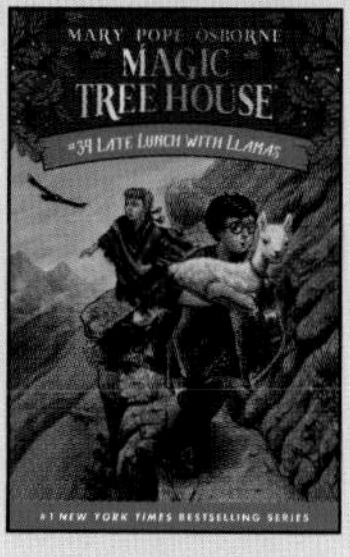
MARY POPE OSBORNE
MAGIC TREE HOUSE
#34 Late Lunch with Llamas
#1 NEW YORK TIMES BESTSELLING SERIES

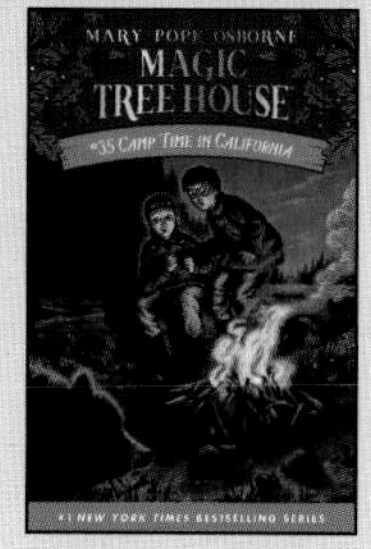
MARY POPE OSBORNE
MAGIC TREE HOUSE
#35 Camp Time in California
#1 NEW YORK TIMES BESTSELLING SERIES

Read all the novels in the #1 bestselling chapter book series of all time!

TRACK THE FACTS WITH JACK & ANNIE!

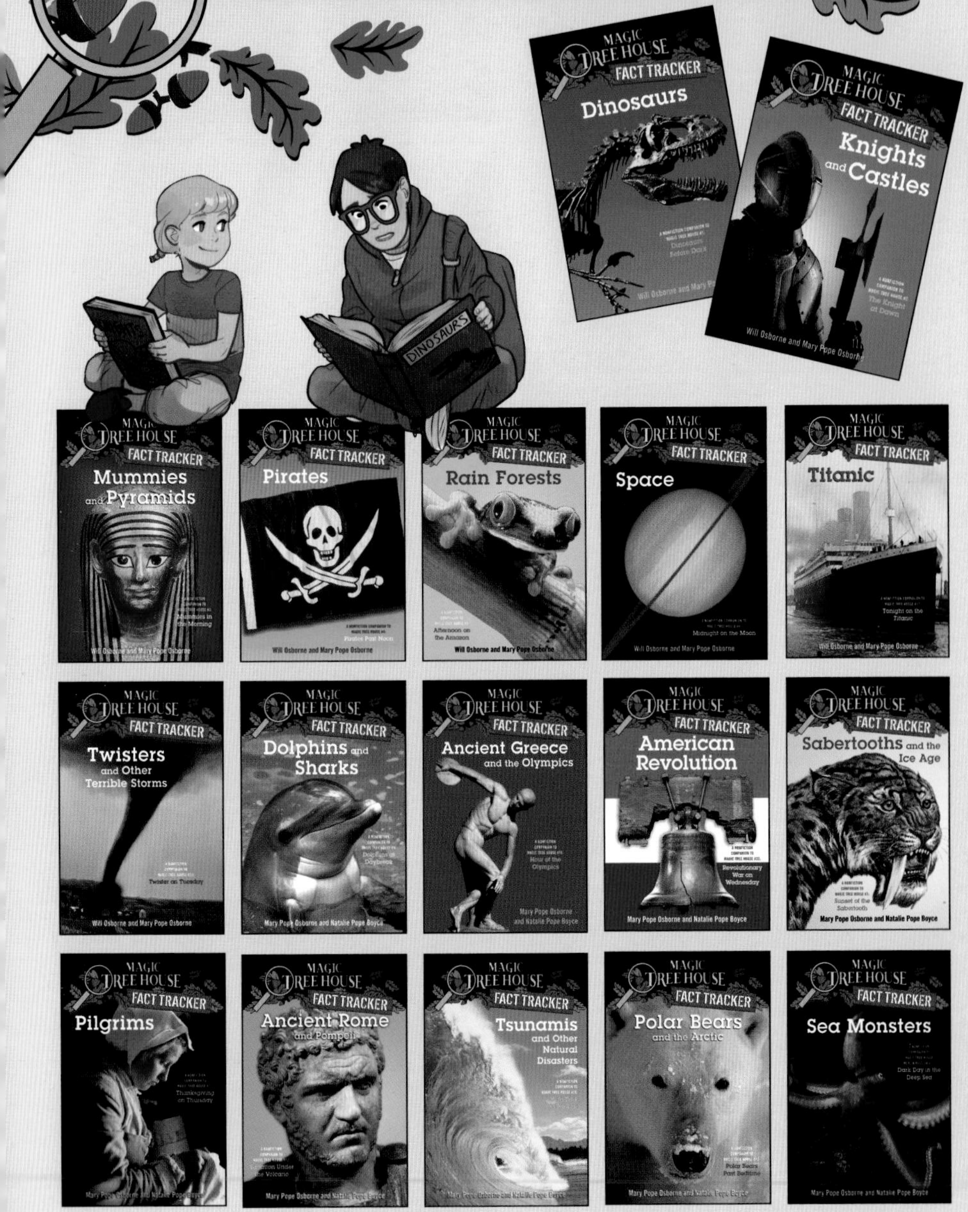
MAGIC TREE HOUSE FACT TRACKER
Dinosaurs
Knights and Castles
DINOSAURS
Mummies and Pyramids
Pirates
Rain Forests
Space
Titanic
Twisters and Other Terrible Storms
Dolphins and Sharks
Ancient Greece and the Olympics
American Revolution
Sabertooths and the Ice Age
Pilgrims
Ancient Rome and Pompeii
Tsunamis and Other Natural Disasters
Polar Bears and the Arctic
Sea Monsters
Will Osborne and Mary Pope Osborne
Mary Pope Osborne and Natalie Pope Boyce

MARY POPE OSBORNE is the author of many novels, picture books, story collections, and nonfiction books. Her #1 *New York Times* bestselling Magic Tree House® series has been translated into numerous languages around the world. Highly recommended by parents and educators everywhere, the series introduces young readers to different cultures and times, as well as to the world's legacy of ancient myth and storytelling.

JENNY LAIRD is an award-winning playwright. She collaborates with Will Osborne and Randy Courts on creating musical theater adaptations of the Magic Tree House® series for both national and international audiences. Their work also includes shows for young performers, available through Music Theatre International's Broadway Junior® Collection. Currently the team is working on a Magic Tree House® animated television series.

KELLY & NICHOLE MATTHEWS are twin sisters and a comic-art team. They get to do their dream job every day, drawing comics for a living. They've worked with Boom Studios!, Archaia, the Jim Henson Company, Hiveworks, and now Random House!